New Wun Ching Developmental Publishing Co., Ltd.

New Age · New Choice · The Best Selected Educational Publications — NEW WCDP

TOUR MANAGER &
TOUR GUIDE ENGLISH

免費下載
朗讀 MP3

領隊導遊
英文

王清煌、張誠仁
林溢祥、劉明德 編著

本書特色 ｜ FEATURES OF THE BOOK

　　《領隊導遊英文》是一本精心規劃，並敦聘國內知名大專院校優良教師及中華民國觀光導遊協會優良講師集結而成之大作，是市面上第一本以「帶團實務知識、溝通式語言教學」編排的書籍。其專有特色如下：

1. 本書以「溝通式語言教學法」為基礎，也是「英國劍橋大學英語教師認證」(CELTA) 所奉行的教學法。讀者可同時學習 Reading、Speaking、Listening、Writing「聽說讀寫」四種技能。

2. 本書分為〈準備篇〉、〈領隊篇〉、〈導遊篇〉三大部分，深入淺出，不但囊括不同情境對話與相關狀況應對方式，更有臺灣特有景點及節慶的精闢介紹。

3. 〈領隊篇〉READING（閱讀）及 LISTENING（聽力）使用方法：
   (1) 練習之前，讀者必須先看「GIST 大意類型」問題，了解此次閱讀或聆聽的目的，迅速抓到重點。
   (2) 快速閱讀 GIST 問題之後，再以「Skim & Scan」（略讀與掃讀）技巧閱讀或聆聽全文。
   (3) 閱讀或聆聽全文後再回答細節問題，
   (4) 以上教學方式不但能讓讀者留意「細節」，更能引導讀者思考更全面的「大意」。

　　一切語言教學都是為了「溝通」，不是為了考試而考試、為了考試而學英文，期望讀者能快樂學英文、讓英文生活化，這才是本書最終的目的。

編輯部　謹識

序言 | PREFACE

　　《領隊導遊英文》可以引領我們跟著旅行團或是選擇自助旅行的方式，一起環遊世界與臺灣環島旅行。全書面面是重點，包含多變用字及句型、實用句與聽力訓練等廣泛內容，最重要的是「環境營造開口說」。本書適用於文化觀光或休閒事業管理、餐飲管理或旅遊經營相關科系等專業課程教學必修，以及應用外語教學指定選修用書，是旅遊專業人員進修和準備「英語領隊及導遊」證照的首選考試用書，甚至可以成為愛好旅遊人士的休閒指南，同時增加旅行專業知識。

　　《領隊導遊英文》深入淺出，精闢又經典，囊括國內外旅遊景點與不同情境對話，書中〈領隊篇〉的 READING（閱讀）及 LISTENING（聽力）部分與〈導遊篇〉特請專業外師錄音，並以 QR Code 的方式呈現，讓讀者在練習的同時，還可以精進本身的發音。另外，為期望讀者「英語導遊筆試及格」，本書還收錄了近十年領隊導遊人員歷屆考試試題與解答供讀者參考練習，並準備了應考口試的自我介紹及各章節豐富內容的通關祕訣重點提示。

　　《領隊導遊英文》一書能夠順利完成出版，首先要感謝國立虎尾科技大學應用外語系王清煌教授（前系主任）與張誠仁講師，撰寫〈領隊篇〉與部分附錄等，而最主要的編修，則是有賴於張誠仁

講師大力協助，初稿經由他的細心與用心，逐章整合完成；以及難得的是，邀請到中華民國觀光導遊協會林溢祥講師撰寫〈導遊篇〉；而我有幸也參與開門見山的旅遊「領隊導遊帶團技巧」必知又實用的〈準備篇〉。另外加上資深導遊、也是導遊協會理事賴秀美老師提供寶貴經歷之危機處置要點，以及相關活用在出入境準備可帶出國之必要用品的一部分附錄，其中會見到機場公共空間告示指標常用語的中英文對照等，一目瞭然。本書得力於以上優秀師資，非常感謝！

每個人生命中都會有自己的興趣或樂在其中要學習的領域課程，我始終感謝並慶幸有機會得到教學之經歷，感恩有出版過《觀光英語》教學用書的經驗，同時具有英語領隊及華語導遊（英語導遊筆試及格）的身分，可以與王清煌教授、張誠仁及林溢祥講師共同參與策劃《領隊導遊英文》大專教學用書的撰寫。最後要感謝新文京出版股份有限公司的推薦和邀請，給予我們每位參與作者，投入《領隊導遊英文》共同編著的機緣。

國立聯合大學&弘光科技大學通識教育中心

劉明德 講師　謹識

編者簡介 | ABOUT THE AUTHORS

王清煌

學歷
1. 美國印地安那大學語言教育博士
2. 美國印地安那大學教育心理碩士
3. 國立臺灣大學外國語文學士

現職
國立虎尾科技大學應外系教授

經歷
1. 國立虎尾科技大學語言中心主任
2. 國立虎尾科技大學應外系系主任

張誠仁

學歷

國立雲林科技大學應用外語碩士

現職

1. 大學講師（雲林科技大學、虎尾科技大學、南華大學）

2. 英語領隊

經歷

1. 寶力淂國際有限公司國際貿易業務及客服經理

2. 誠品聯合會計師事務所資深專員及網路工程師

3. 國際村及 Aplus 語言中心英語講師

4. 彰化縣警察局課員

證照

1. CELTA（英國劍橋大學英語教師認證）

2. 外語領隊執業證（英語、華語）

3. 考試院英語導遊及格證書

林溢祥

學歷

美國華府喬治華盛頓大學 (The George Washington University) 企管碩士 (MBA)，國際關係碩士 (MA)

現職

1. 中華民國觀光導遊協會理事
2. 英語導遊及領隊

經歷

1. 中華民國觀光導遊協會常務監事
2. 中華民國觀光導遊協會職前訓練及在職訓練講師
3. 中華民國觀光導遊協會導遊考照班講師
4. 曾出版導遊領隊國家考試歷屆試題解析等六本書

劉明德

學歷

1. 國立臺灣大學流行病學與預防醫學研究所升等研究

2. 國立臺灣大學微生物學研究所碩士（榜首）

3. 國立臺灣大學公共衛生學系學士

現職

1. 國立聯合大學通識教育中心傳染病與微生物、健康與生活、環保與生活講師

2. 弘光科技大學通識學院微生物與人類文明、健康與生活及環境教育講師

3. 中華民國觀光旅遊英語領隊／華語導遊（英語導遊筆試及格）

4. 中華民國觀光導遊協會會員代表

學術演講

1. 輔英科技大學應用外語系演講「跨領域醫護英文教學」

2. 國立臺灣大學健康政策與管理研究所演講「婚姻與生活品質」

經歷

1. 弘光科技大學健康事業管理系、醫學英文及術語、解剖生理學講師、護理系微生物免疫學及在職專班生物學、物理治療系生物學講師

2. 中臺科技大學護理系醫護英文及通識教育中心環保教育、醫療暨健康管理系、醫管英文及醫院專用術語、護理系健康心理學、情緒管理講師

3. 臺灣首府大學觀光休閒系觀光英文講師、通識教育中心生物技術、健康科學講師

4. 聖母醫護管理專校護理科病理學、醫護英文、醫護術語、（微）生物學實驗講師

5. 育達科技大學通識教育中心健康科學與生活、生物醫學、環保與生活、綠建築與永續城市講師、行銷與流通管理系健康管理講師

6. 仁德醫護管理專校護理科解剖生理學講師、視光科解剖生理學、微生物學講師、復健科及健康美容觀光科生物學講師、通識教育中心微生物科技與生活、健康與生活講師

7. 行政院前衛生署全國公共衛生研修中心專員

8. 國立陽明大學醫學系碩士級研究助理

9. 臺北榮民總醫院內科部碩士級研究助理

10. 臺中市華府旅行社所屬翰翔旅行社特約導遊

目錄　CONTENTS

PART **04**　附錄　**215**

免費下載歷屆試題
https://reurl.cc/9Z37q8

準 備 篇

01 領隊及導遊帶團技巧入門
Basic skills for being a tour guide

　　身為領隊及導遊，能與團員分享不同的文化並散播歡樂，以禮待人，尊重他人，也樂於助人。

　　As a tour guide, you are someone that can share different cultures with and spread joy to the tourists. You must be polite, respectful, and helpful.

出發前必備 ✈

Before the tour

➡ 行前說明會
Orientation

與旅行社行政人員確認行程及預備方案

Check with the operator about the schedule and precautions.

➡ 搜尋帶團資料
Collect information

A. 查詢旅遊資訊

Search for tourist information.

B. 諮詢經驗豐富的領隊與導遊

Consult experienced tour managers/leaders and tour guides.

C. 利用網路下載資料

Download the information on the internet.

D. 搜尋目的地的旅遊地圖與旅遊專書資訊

Find the information from the tourist maps and tourist books of the destination.

➡ 加強帶團技巧
Enhance your skills for guiding tours

A. 自我介紹

Self-introduction.

B. 掌握旅客背景與特性

Learn about the background and characteristics of the tourists.

C. 學習如何與環境互動

Learn how to interact with the surroundings.

D. 巧妙比喻，激發聯想

Use clever similes and trigger their thoughts.

➡ 新手領隊機場通關步驟
Steps to going through customs for new tour guides

A. 教導旅客登機程序

Instruct the tour group members about the boarding procedure.

B. 告知團員飛航安檢及行李托運注意事項

Tell the tour group members the procedure for security check and baggage check-in.

C. 分發登機證並說明

Distribute boarding passes and explain.

D. 做好旅客未現身的應變措施

Be prepared for no-show passengers.

➡ 帶團必須做到的事
Things you must do

A. 與餐廳確認用餐時間

Check with restaurants about the time to eat.

B. 與飯店確認住宿事宜

Check with hotels about the accommodations.

C. 選擇交通運輸方式

Choose the modes for transportation.

D. 向旅客說明旅遊景點及自費行程的規劃

Show the tour group members the options for tourist spots and self-paid travel plan.

E. 建議旅客可以攜帶之物品

Make suggestions about the things to bring.

➡ 服務與價格
Services and prices

A. 強調在地特色，營造景點差異化

Distinguish the destination by emphasizing its local features.

B. 根據不同主題產品來設計活動

Design activities based on different themed products.

C. 留下對旅遊資訊有興趣的旅客聯絡方式，將來也許有助於活動推廣

Keep the contact information of interested tour group members, who might help with the promoting activity in the future.

D. 價格機制對於旅遊市場非常重要

Price mechanism is important in tourism.

宣導教育 ✈

Remind the tour group members of the following precautions

➡ **參觀風景區時，旅客應遵守相關法規**

Tour group members should follow the rules and laws when visiting scenic areas

A. 了解當地風俗習慣、文化和宗教信仰

Tour group members should know about the local customs, culture, and religious belief.

B. 不大聲喧譁，不互相推擠

Tour group members should not be too loud nor push others in the crowd.

C. 不亂扔垃圾，不破壞花草樹木

Tour group members should not litter nor cut plants.

D. 不留下任何痕跡

Tour group members should not leave marks of any kind.

E. 小心謹慎，不違法

Tour group members should be careful and not break laws.

➡ **出國旅行，旅客應確保已購買旅行意外險，並仔細檢查與旅行社的合約**

For their departure and travel, tour group members should make sure that they have travel accident insurance and double check their contract with the travel agency

A. 旅客應了解可能發生的風險和突發疾病的海外急難救助

Tour group members should be aware of the possible risks and the emergency relief aids for unexpected illness overseas.

B. 旅客應確認旅行社是否投保商業責任保險和履約保證金保險（可上網查詢）

Tour group members should make sure if the travel agency has business liability insurance and performance bond insurance (they can look it up on the internet).

C. 旅客應該知道旅遊糾紛申訴管道（如觀光局、海基會、中華民國旅行業品質保障協會等）

Tour group members should know how to appeal for disputes (Tourism Bureau, Straits Exchange Foundation, Travel Quality Assurance Association, and the like).

➡ **出入境注意事項**

Guidelines for departure and arrival

A. 請勿攜帶瓦斯噴霧器、伸縮警棍、電擊棒等違禁品

Dangerous goods, such as compressed gases, expandable batons, and stun guns are not allowed.

B. 預防 A 型流感

To avoid Influenza A.

■ 五要

Five things you must do

I. 要熟食

Eat only well-cooked food.

II. 要勤洗手

Wash your hands.

III. 要打流感疫苗

Get vaccinated.

IV. 有類流感症狀要就醫

Go see a doctor when you have influenza-like symptoms.

V. 要做好防護措施

Take precautions.

■ 六不

Six things you must not do

I. 不餵食或直接接觸禽類

Do not feed or have direct contact with poultry.

II. 不買走私及來源不明的禽鳥肉

Do not buy poultry from smuggling or questionable sources.

III. 不吃生蛋

Do not eat raw eggs.

IV. 不去養禽場

Do not go to poultry farms.

V. 不野放禽鳥

Do not release poultry into the wild.

準備篇

VI. 不與禽類共處，以免被感染

Do not stay with poultry or you might be infected.

解決問題的技巧 ✈

Tips to deal with problems

在緊急情況下，須通報旅行社、家屬、觀光局及海外救援公司請求協助。

In an emergency, call your agency, families, Tourism Bureau, and oversea companies for help.

➡ 團員走失

When tour group members are missing

A. 為了兼顧其他團員，要求他們在指定地點集合或將他們帶回車上

Take care of other tour group members by asking them to gather at a certain spot or bring them back to the bus.

B. 利用當地服務中心廣播協尋

Use the paging service of the service center.

C. 告訴其他團員回到出發地點，並告知導遊將繼續尋找失蹤團員

Tell other tour group members to go back to the starting spot and tell them the tour guides will look for the missing persons.

D. 告訴團員認識隊旗，如果過了一段時間，導遊還沒有回來，就應該報警

Tell the tour group members to recognize the team flag. If it's been a while and the tour guide hasn't come back, they should call the police.

➡ 班機延誤
When the flight is delayed

A. 安撫團員，並等候航空公司協調或轉搭別家航空

Calm the tourists. Wait patiently for the airline to solve the problem or take the flight from another airline.

B. 向航空公司爭取補償

Ask the airline for compensation.

C. 向航空公司領取住宿券後，帶隊前往飯店辦理入住手續

Lead the tour group members to check in at the hotel after getting the tickets for accommodation from the airline.

D. 隔天（次日）提早結束用餐，準時到機場報到

Finish the breakfast earlier the next morning and get the airport on time.

➡ 護照遺失時，如何辦理通關手續
How to go through the customs when the passport is lost

A. 到當地警察局報案

Report the case to the local police.

B. 聯絡我駐外代表處，並提供護照遺失者的個人資料

Contact the representative office of R.O.C and provide the personal information of the individual(s) who lost their passport.

C. 準備備用照片、警方簽發的護照遺失證明、護照影本以及身為旅行團成員的身分證明

Prepare back-up photos, passport lost certificate issued by the police, copies of the passport, and the proof of identity as a member of the travel group.

➡ 團員發生緊急狀況、受傷或發病

When group members are in an emergency, are injured, or suffer from the illness

A. 立即根據情況採取行動幫助成員，並詢問醫師是否需要留下做進一步的治療

Immediately take action to help the members based on the situation and ask the doctors if the members need to stay for further treatment.

B. 徵詢當事人的決定，或返臺進一步治療

Ask for the members' decision, or send them back to Taiwan for further treatment.

➡ 行程中團員意外死亡

When group members die from accident during the travel

A. 取得警方的報案證明及法醫的驗屍報告

Get the case-reporting certificate from the police and the autopsy report from the coroners.

B. 向我駐外代表處備案，並提供死者的詳細資料，例如護照號碼、出生年月日、死亡原因和地點

Report the case to the representative office of R.O.C and provide detailed information of the deceased, such as his / her passport number, birthday, cause of death, and location of death.

C. 協助處理善後，例如取得死亡證明書及保險理賠的相關事項

Help with the remaining issues, such as getting death certificate and settlement of insurance claims.

推廣觀光資源，打造成為獨特品牌—贏得旅客的心，讓他們願意前往旅遊景點，帶來新商機

Promote tourist resources that make the destination a unique brand – win the tourists' hearts and make them willing to travel to the tourist spots, which brings new commercial interests

文化之旅

Cultural tourism

文創產業正在世界各地蓬勃發展。

Cultural and Creative Industry is thriving everywhere around the world.

導遊可以介紹文化資產的歷史性。透過文物的朝代變遷，可以使本地變成具有富含文化底蘊的旅遊勝地。諸多文化資產，例如國立故宮博物院的收藏品、節慶、珍饈、舊城區、原住民部落、古早運輸系統（如鐵路系統）以及特色民宿，都可以成為旅客的主題景點，可以吸引外國旅客並促進文化互動。歷史可以為旅遊業做出大貢獻。

Tour guides can introduce the history of the culture assets. Relics passed down by different dynasties can turn the place into tourist spots rich in cultural value. Cultural assets, such as the collection in National Palace Museum, festivals, delicacy, old towns, aboriginal tribes, old transportation system (such as railway system), and accommodation can become the theme of the tourist spot, which will attract foreign tourists and facilitate cultural interaction. History can contribute a lot to tourism.

➡️ 文創園區
Cultural and creative industry park

A. 臺北和高雄文創園區受歡迎的程度顯著增長

There are parks in Taipei and Kaohsiung that have been enjoying remarkable growth in popularity.

B. 新興文創園區現正進駐臺中、花蓮和臺東

New-built parks are now at Taichung, Hualian, and Taitung.

C. 文創園區和周邊購物區商店販售的商品應該具有創造性和高品質

Products sold in the stores in the parks and the shopping districts around them should be creative and of quality.

➡️ 夜市
Night markets

A. 需認真思考更新觀光夜市的口袋名單

To renovate tourist night markets, serious considerations are needed.

B. 詳細介紹在地美食

Specify the local cuisines.

C. 重新規劃整體管理，提升品牌形象

Reorganize the overall management to promote the brand image.

➡️ 觀光工廠
Tourism factories

A. 推動觀光新亮點

Promote the novel features for tourism.

B. 結合觀光和行銷策略

Combine the trip with marketing strategies.

C. 建立評鑑和輔導機制

Establish evaluation and assistance system.

➡ 休閒農場
Leisure farms

A. 透過推廣休閒農場，將臺灣產品推向國際市場

Promote produce from Taiwan to the international market by promoting leisure farms.

B. 深入當地文化，建立農產品展示中心並定期舉行展售會

Probe into the local culture. Establish the centers for produce display and hold expositions on a regular basis.

➡ 城市行銷
Selling the cities

A. 針對自由行旅客或背包客，推廣一日遊或兩日遊行程

Promote one- or two-day trip intended for self-guided tourists or backpackers.

B. 首先將旅客帶往旅遊景點或最具特色的地點

Take the tourists to tourist spots or the most prominent sites first.

C. 帶領旅客到百貨商店的美食街或夜市

Take the tourists to the food courts in the department stores or the night markets.

D. 邀請遊客好好感受臺灣的人情味和美景

Invite the tourists to enjoy the people and the scenery in Taiwan.

PART 02

領隊篇

GATES 6-9

 情境說明 ✈

　　在出國當天,當團員興高采烈前往機場,於規定的時間內至指定地點集合向領隊報到之前,領隊早就抵達機場細心地與送機人員交接各項文件、滿懷期待地等候團員們的到來。當確認所有團員抵達後,領隊會跟大家宣布重要注意事項,並協助團員辦理登機手續及托運行李。如果是在回國當天,領隊及導遊則會送全體團員到機場,他們也會在機場引導團員辦理登機手續及托運行李。領隊及導遊此時需要用到哪些英語呢?一起來看看吧!

Warm-up

Q1: As far as you know, what are the procedures for an airport check-in?

Q2: What information should a tour leader tell his/her guests before an airport check-in?

Q3: Restricted and prohibited items (Yes or No)

No.	1.	2.	3.	4.	5.
Photo					
English	Ammunition/ Weapon	Fireworks (Firecrackers)	Matches	Diving Tanks	Camping Gas
Chinese	槍械彈藥 / 武器	煙火(鞭炮)	火柴	潛水用氧氣瓶	瓦斯罐
Yes/No					

No.	6.	7.	8.	9.	10.
Photo					
English	Peroxides	Mercury	Pesticides/ Agricultural Chemicals	Magnetized Materials	Lighter/Paint
Chinese	漂白劑	汞（水銀）	殺蟲劑 / 農藥	磁性物質	打火機 / 油漆
Yes/No					

No.	11.	12.	13.	14.	15.
Photo					
English	Power Bank/ Mobile Power Pack	Wet Battery	Charcoal	Radioactive Material	Instant Noodles
Chinese	行動電源（器）	電瓶	木炭	放射性物質	泡麵（不含豬製品）
Yes/No					

領隊篇

 Vocabulary & Phrases

1. counter [ˋkaʊntɚ] *n.* [C] a long flat table used in an airport at which passengers are served　櫃臺

2. assist [əˋsɪst] *vt.,vi.* help; aid; lend a hand　幫助；協助

3. task [tæsk] *n.* [C] job; thing; duty; work　工作；任務；事情

4. complete [kəmˋplit] *vt.* finish; end; close up　完成

5. in advance [ɪn əd`væns] *adv.ph.* beforehand; ahead of time; ahead of schedule　事先；預先

6. wait for [wet fɔr] *v.ph.* await; watch for　等待

7. document [`dɑkjəmənt] *n.* [C] paper; certificate　公文，文件；證件

8. contract [`kɑntrækt] *n.* [C] a legal or formal paper addressing the agreement(s) between two people or among a group　契約；合約
   c.f. contract [kən`trækt] *vt.,vi.*　訂契約

9. agency [`edʒənsɪ] *n.* [C] office　辦事處

10. insurance [ɪn`ʃʊrəns] *n.* [U; C] security; warrant; warranty　保險（業）

11. immigration [ˌɪmə`greʃən] *n.* [U] moving from one country to another country　移居；移民；（機場）證照查驗

12. announce [ə`naʊns] *vt.,vi.* tell; claim; say; state; report; make known　宣布；告知；布達

13. fill out [fɪl aʊt] *v.ph.* fill in; complete; write something in blanks　填寫（表格、申請書等）

14. scanner [`skænɚ] *n.* [C] a device or a machine that can examine, read, or monitor something like documents　掃描器

15. make one's way [mek wʌnz we] *v.ph.* move forward　向前走；往前走

16. punctual [`pʌŋktʃʊəl] *adj.* on time　準時的；守時的

17. be familiar with [bɪ fə`mɪljɚ wɪθ] *v.ph.* know; be acquainted with; master　熟悉；精通

18. empathetic [ˌɛmpə`θɛtɪk] = empathic *adj.* feeling someone else's feelings or emotions in a given situation　移情作用的；同理（心）的

19. thanks to [θæŋks tu] *ph.* because of; owing to; on account of　幸虧；由於

20. mindset [`maɪndˌsɛt] *n.* [C] attitude; tendency; habit　心態；傾向；習慣

21. make a difference [mek ə `dıfərəns] *v.ph.* have an influence on　有影響；有意義；有關係；有差別

22. later on [`letɚ ɑn] *ph.* at a time in the future　之後；後來；其後

23. lithium ion battery [`lɪθɪəm `aɪɑn `bætərɪ] *n.* [*C*]　鋰電池

24. power bank [`paʊɚ bæŋk] *n.* [*C*] a portable device for charging the battery of electronic devices such as mobile phones　行動電源

25. resealable [rı`siləb!] *adj.* wrapped; enclosed　可密封的

26. transparent [træns`pɛrənt] *adj.* easy to be seen　透明的

27. line up [laın ʌp] *v.ph.* be in line; wait in line　排隊

28. detector [dı`tɛktɚ] *n.* [*C*] a device for finding specific substances or materials　探測器，感應器

29. take one's seat [tek wʌnz sit] *v.ph.* sit down; be seated; seat oneself　就坐；坐下

領隊篇

 **Reading Task**

▶ Reading for Gist

_____ 1. Who might be the target readers of this article?

    (A) Travelers

    (B) Tour leaders

    (C) Customs officers

_____ 2. What might be the title of this article?

    (A) Airport check-in procedures for tour leaders

    (B) Reminders for airport check-in for travelers

    (C) Guidelines for airport check-in for ground staff

❯ Reading

Title: _____

In Taiwan, the members on a group tour usually report to their tour leader at a group check-in counter of an airline company in the airport two hours before the departure time on the departure day or the first day of the trip. To better assist the guests in the check-in process, there are a lot of tasks that need to be done by a tour leader like you. If you fail to complete those tasks in advance, it may take more time in the check-in process. Here are the guidelines for what you should do before and during the airport check-in.

1. Arrive at least 2.5 hours before departure and wait for your guests in the group check-in counter.

2. Get all the necessary documents ready, such as the contract with the local travel agency, an insurance policy, PNR (Passenger Name Record), passports of your guests, boarding passes, rooming lists, guest forms, baggage tags, etc.

3. When your guests arrive, greet them and distribute boarding passes and baggage tags to them.

4. Explain procedures for checking-in, clearing immigration and security checks to the guests.

5. Announce new seat assignments if necessary.

6. Indicate and emphasize the boarding time and boarding gate number.

7. Give reminders for "free luggage allowance" and "restricted and forbidden items" for carry-on and checked luggage.

8. Assist your guests in filling out the E/D cards (embarkation / disembarkation cards) and customs declaration cards.

9. Guide all your guests to the check-in counter to check in and provide assistance.

10. After all the suitcases go through the X-ray scanner without problems, gather all the guests and make your way to the next stop – immigration or security check.

On the departure day of a return trip, what a tour leader should do is similar while a local tour guide might share some of your work. It is possible that there is not a group check-in counter at the airport. As a result, you cannot obtain a printed boarding pass and share more boarding information with your guests in advance. In this case, you can instruct the guests to check in with their travel companion at a regular check-in counter so that their seats can be assigned next to each other.

Not everyone travels abroad often. Some might not know the ins and outs of the airport check-in procedures. That's why a professional tour leader can be a great helper. There might be a lot of hassles on the first day or the last day of the trip in an airport check-in. For example, some guests are not punctual or are not familiar with the luggage requirements. However, as a tour leader, be sure to be patient, empathetic and put on your charming smile no matter what challenges you are faced with. Why? For you, this might be just the beginning or the end of this single trip, or it is just an average ordinary day. But for the guests, this group tour might be more than just a trip. If the problems can be handled properly, this trip could be turned into an unforgettable journey of their lifetime thanks to your professional attitude and mindset. So, sit back, enjoy the ride and make a difference.

領隊篇

❯ Reading for Details

Write T for "True" or F for "False" for each statement.

_____ 1. A tour leader usually has to arrive earlier at the airport than the guests.

_____ 2. Before check-in, a tour guide usually can obtain boarding passes of the guests.

_____ 3. It's important for a tour leader to explain the departing procedures.

_____ 4. A responsible tour guide should fill out an embarkation cards for the guests.

_____ 5. For people on a group tour to check in in an airport, they always do it at a group check-in counter.

_____ 6. Professional attitude is essential to be a successful tour leader.

   p.216

❯ Listening for Gist

_____ In the following conversation, which task does the tour leader **NOT** do?

(A) Check with the ground staff about when the check-in counter is open.

(B) Remind the guests of the luggage requirements.

(C) Assist the guests in the check-in procedures.

(D) Teach the guests how to refund taxes in the airport.

> Listening for Details

1. What is the flight number? _____

2. What is the travel destination? _____

3. When is the departure time? _____

4. When is the check-in counter open? _____

5. Can the guest put a hair spray in his / her carry-on? _____

6. When is the boarding time? What is the boarding gate? _____

7. What is the seating preference of the first guest? _____

8. What is the free luggage allowance? _____

9. In the second check-in, is the luggage overweight? _____

10. After check-in, what should the guests do? _____

領隊篇

Useful Language

1. fail to V : cannot V　未能

2. it takes + 時間 (to V)…　（做某事）要花…時間

Exercise

_____ 1. Chair Wang asked me to _____ him in designing a new course.

(A) persist　　(B) assist　　(C) insist　　(D) resist

_____ 2. Tomorrow, we will enter into a _____ with Stanley for renting his tenement.

(A) content　　(B) patience　(C) contract　　(D) practice

_____ 3. Before you check in, you are required to _____ the form.

(A) fill out　　(B) cross out　(C) cut in　　(D) check out

23

_____ 4. Any passenger's luggage is required to pass through the
_____ to make sure there are no restricted or prohibited items
inside.

(A) tanner　　(B) skinner　　(C) spanner　　(D) scanner

_____ 5. If you want to interview Dr. Wang, you had better prepare questions

_____.

(A) in advance　　　　　(B) with empathy

(C) on purpose　　　　　(D) by accident

_____ 6. I hope that all of you will be _____ in submitting your papers
tomorrow.

(A) factual　　　　　(B) influential

(C) punctual　　　　　(D) potential

_____ 7. _____ your help, we had a wonderful trip to Finland last month.

(A) Thanks to　　　　　(B) According to

(C) In addition to　　　　　(D) Apart from

_____ 8. I am in the habit of saving my files or data in my computer and

_____.

(A) Citibank　　　　　(B) power bank

(C) riverbank　　　　　(D) bankruptcy

_____ 9. Please _____ to have your luggage inspected in front of the
counter.

(A) line up　　(B) look up　　(C) take a seat　　(D) stand for

_____ 10. You have to pass through _____ before you enter a country.

(A) imagination　　　　　(B) interaction

(C) punctuation　　　　　(D) immigration

Answers 🔒

Warm-up

1. No	2. No	3. No	4. No	5. No
6. No	7. No	8. No	9. No	10. No
11. Yes (carry-on bag only)	12. No	13. No	14. No	15. Yes

Reading Task

Reading for Gist

1. (B)   2. (A)

Reading for Details

1. T	2. T	3. T	4. F	5. F	6. T

Listening Task

Listening for Gist

(D)

Listening for Details

1. CI1234   2. Taipei   3. 10:30 a.m.   4. 8:30 a.m.

5. Yes (less than milliliters and in a resealable transparent plastic bag or a zipper bag)

6. 10:00 a.m.; gate13   7. window seat   8. 30 kilograms   9. No

10. They have to check the monitor and make sure all their suitcases go through the X-ray detector without any problems.

Exercise

1. (B)	2. (C)	3. (A)	4. (D)	5. (A)
6. (C)	7. (A)	8. (B)	9. (A)	10. (D)

領隊篇

情境說明 ✈

　　機場登機及行李托運辦理完畢後，領隊帶著興高采烈的團員一行人往登機門方向前進。但在登機前，為了確保飛行安全，乘客本人及其隨身行李仍必須接受海關人員檢查，在確認沒有任何問題之後，大家方能再往下一站前進。尖峰時刻安檢隊伍往往綿延數公尺，如乘客們皆能事先了解安檢相關規定，將能加快安檢的速度，減少大家等待的時間。在等候安檢前及進行安檢時，領隊需要用到的英語有哪些呢？一起來看看吧！

 **Warm-up**

1. Discussion

Q1: Do you think "security check" is necessary? Why or why not?

Q2: What things go "beep" when you walk through the scanner?

Q3: Are you embarrassed when they frisk you after you have walked through the scanner and set off the alarm?

2. Task

Circle the words in the box based on the given words.

領
隊
篇

frisk	c	c	c	e	k	r	e	r	r
carousel	a	o	c	e	k	r	e	r	o
empty	r	m	o	m	o	k	t	e	r
trigger	o	p	n	p	t	s	g	g	o
tablet	u	a	v	t	e	i	g	g	t
detector	s	n	e	y	l	r	d	i	c
cooperate	e	y	y	a	b	f	a	r	e
company	l	a	o	b	a	k	e	t	t
conveyor	a	b	r	c	t	w	f	f	e
	c	c	k	k	s	s	d	d	d

 Vocabulary & Phrases

1. frisk [frɪsk] *vt.* check; use hands or detectors to search someone's body [口語]（用手或探測器）搜（某人的）身體；搜身

2. set off [sɛt ɔf] *v.ph.* trigger; cause something accidently　觸發

3. rush hour [rʌʃ aʊr] *n.* [C] the busy time of a day when a town or a city was crowded, either when people go to work in the morning or go home after work in the afternoon　尖峰時間

4. carousel belt [ˌkærʊˋzɛl bɛlt] *n.* [C] conveyor belt; a moving strip or belt used for transporting stuff from place to place　旋轉行李輸送帶；行李輪盤

5. trigger [ˋtrɪgɚ] *vt.* touch off; start; begin　觸發

6. empty [ˋɛmptɪ] *vt.* take out all the things inside something　使變空；清空

7. head [hɛd] *vi.* go; move toward; set out　出發，往前

8. on vacation [ɑn vəˋkeʃən] *n.ph.* taking a trip to another place or a scenic spot for pleasure　渡假

9. tray [tre] *n.* [C] a flat container for carrying objects　托盤

10. tablet [`tæblɪt] *n.* [C] tablet computer; a small, flat computer that is controlled by touching the screen or by using a special pen　平板電腦

11. security guard [sɪ`kjʊrətɪ gɑrd] *n.* [C] someone whose job is to protect goods in stores, to frisk passengers to make sure whether they carry any restricted or prohibited objects, etc.　安全人員；安檢人員

 p.219

> ## Listening for Gist

_____ Why does the tour leader give this talk?

(A) To tell the guests what to do before the security check.

(B) To tell the guests what to do during the security check.

(C) To tell the guests what to do after the security check.

(D) All of the above

> ## Listening for Details

_____ 1. Why might the security line be long?

(A) Because it's rush hour.

(B) Because there is something wrong with the scanners at the checkpoint.

(C) Because the carousel belts don't function properly.

領
隊
篇

_____ 2. Which of the following is **NOT** mentioned in the talk?

(A) Passengers have to take off their shoes, jackets and belts.

(B) Passengers can leave their laptop computers in their carry-on baggage.

(C) A security guard might frisk a passenger after the alarm is triggered.

(D) Passengers have to empty their water bottles before the inspection.

_____ 3. What should the passengers do next after the security check?

(A) Proceed to gate 13 independently or with the tour leader.

(B) Get to the immigration before 10:00 a.m.

(C) Wait for the tour leader, clear immigration and proceed to the gate 13 together.

(D Board the airplane after 10:00 a.m.

Useful Language

1. cooperate with: team up with; work together　與…合作

2. take it easy: take your time　慢慢來；不用急

3. come across: run across; bump into; meet with; run into　碰到

4. stay put: stay still　保持不動（put是形容詞，口語用法，意為固定不動的）

5. keep sb. company: keep company with sb.; accompany sb.　陪伴某人
   （accompany with sb. 是錯的，accompany 是及物動詞，不加 with）

6. most of all: most important of all; most importantly　最重要的

7. take turns V-ing: do something by turns; do something one by one　輪流做…

 **Activity**

The teacher can revise the 10 instructions from the script and make them imperative sentences, which are similar to what a security guard might say at the security checkpoint.

All the students stand up and follow the instructions from the teacher.

Divide the class into groups of four or five. Each student takes turns reading an instruction out loud to the group members. The other students have to act out what the student says.

Exercise

_____ 1. Passengers _____ walking through the metal detector. It means that passengers walk through the metal detector one by one.
(A) speak ill of (B) take turns
(C) stay awake (D) look forward to

_____ 2. Don't be embarrassed when a security guard _____ you after an alarm is triggered.
(A) saves (B) invites (C) confuses (D) frisks

_____ 3. A: Where are you _____ now?
B: Paris.
(A) on vacation (B) on purpose
(C) by accident (D) by mistake

_____ 4. Any passenger is required to _____ out all his/her pockets onto a tray before he / she goes through a scanner in an airport.
(A) ridicule (B) spread (C) check (D) empty

領
隊
篇

_____ 5. In an airport, you had better _____ with security guards and take it easy when they frisk you.

(A) cooperate   (B) communicate

(C) make friends   (D) find faults

_____ 6. When our parents are older and older, we need to keep them _____ as often as we can.

(A) awake   (B) aware   (C) company   (D) complaint

_____ 7. Do college students prefer _____ and smartphones to PCs and laptops in Taiwan?

(A) couplets   (B) tablets   (C) booklets   (D) chaplets

_____ 8. Turning on the lights will _____ the alarm.

(A) take off   (B) set off   (C) see off   (D) show off

_____ 9. The tour guide told all the passengers to stay _____ and wait for his return.

(A) hut   (B) cut   (C) gut   (D) put

_____ 10. You should let your tour leader know as long as you _____ any problem on a journey.

(A) come across   (B) complain about

(C) pick up   (D) get along

Answers 🔒

Warm-up

2. Task

frisk	c	c	c	e	k	r	e	r	r
carousel	a	o	c	e	k	r	e	r	o
empty	r	m	o	m	o	k	t	e	r
trigger	o	p	n	p	t	s	g	g	o
tablet	u	a	v	t	e	i	g	g	t
detector	s	n	e	y	l	r	d	i	c
cooperate	e	y	y	a	b	f	a	r	e
company	l	a	o	b	a	k	e	t	t
conveyor	a	b	r	c	t	w	f	f	e
	c	c	k	k	s	s	d	d	d

Listening Task

Listening for Gist

(D)

Listening for Details

1. (A)　2. (B)　3. (A)

Exercise

1. (B)	2. (D)	3. (A)	4. (D)	5. (A)
6. (C)	7. (B)	8. (B)	9. (D)	10. (A)

領
隊
篇

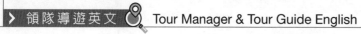

 情境說明 ✈

　　通過「安檢」及「證照查驗」後，終於可以鬆了一口氣，此時映入眼簾的是令人眼花瞭亂的免稅商店，有的團員應該已經迫不及待想去逛逛這些免稅店了。而身為領隊的你在登機前該做些什麼事呢？登機後是否就可以好好放鬆一下了呢？還有哪些事項需要留意呢？此時會用到哪些英語呢？一起來看看吧！

Warm-up

領隊篇

Q1: After security check and immigration, what should a tour leader do before boarding and after boarding?

Q2: Based on the following boarding pass, write down the related information in the box.

1	2	3	4	5	6
passenger's name	flight number	destination	boarding time	boarding date	gate number

7	8	9	10	11	12
airline company	seat number	class	gender	departure from	original boarding time

 Vocabulary & Phrases

1. request [rɪˋkwɛst] *vt.* ask; apply for; demand; beg　要求，請求

2. adjust [əˋdʒʌst] *vi.,vt.* arrange; rearrange; adapt; change　調整；適應

3. dietary [ˋdaɪəˌtɛrɪ] *adj.* of food; related to diet　飲食的

4. delay [dɪˋle] *vt.,vi.,n.* [U；C] not being on time; postpone; put off　拖延；耽擱；延誤

5. hesitate [ˋhɛzəˌtet] *vi.,vt.* stop; think too much; pause　猶豫

6. chaos [ˋkeɑs] *n.* [U] disorder; confusion; being messy　混亂

7. overstep [ˋovɚˋstɛp] *vt.* be against; exceed; surpass; go beyond　違犯；超出…的範圍

8. recharge [riˋtʃɑrdʒ] *vt.* make energetic; refresh　再充電

9. proceed [prəˋsid] *vi.* go ahead; go forward; progress; move forward　繼續進行；前往

10. remaining [rɪˋmenɪŋ] *adj.* other; rest; left　剩下的；其餘的

11. crystal [ˋkrɪst!] *adj.* bright; obvious; apparent; transparent　清澈的，透明的

Reading Task

❯ **Reading for Gist**

Put each of the following sentences in the right blanks.

(A) Adjust seat assignments if necessary

(B) Request a blanket for your guests

(C) Pay attention to boarding calls

(D) Check on your guests during the flight

(E) Always board the plane after all of your guests

❯ **Reading**

領隊篇

After clearing immigration, your guests might visit duty-free shops when they are on the way to the boarding gate. As a tour leader, you might think you can relax a bit. However, usually it's not the case. There are a couple of things you have to work on before boarding:

1. _____(1)_____ just in case that the flight is delayed or the boarding gate is changed. If the flight is delayed and it might cause you to miss your connecting flight, you have to take action and solve the potential problem. No matter what happens to your flight, you have to keep your guests updated with the latest flight information.

2. _____(2)_____. For a tour group, the seat numbers are usually arranged in alphabetical order of the English names of the passengers. Passengers can not select their seats in advance. As a result, it is likely that two friends or the whole family are separate. As a tour leader, if you don't

have time to manually rearrange the seats to suit the needs of the guests before they report to you for the airport check-in, probably it is a good time for you to work on it while waiting for boarding. Just be sure to tell your guests about their new seat numbers before boarding. Also share your seat number with them just in case they might need your assistance on board. If some of your guests have some dietary restrictions, don't forget to mark their new seat assignments because you are going to update the info for the flight attendant who is in charge of the meal services later on the flight.

3. _____(3)_____. This is extremely important because some guests might lose track of time when they are window shopping in the duty-free shops. As a tour leader, your job is to make sure they don't miss the flight. Once your guest does not turn up at the boarding gate on time, don't hesitate. Call him/her immediately. If you still can not reach the guest by phone, seek assistance from the ground staff.

After all your guests get on board, here are what you can do during the flight:

1. Make sure each of the guests is in the right seat.

2. _____(4)_____ from the flight attendant if this is a long flight.

3. Update the flight attendant in charge of meal services with the new seat assignments of your guests who have particular dietary restrictions or preferences. In this way, a chaos can be avoided when the flight attendants are serving in-flight meals.

4. _____(5)_____ from time to time and provide necessary assistance for your guests.

If you can work on the tasks above before boarding and during the flight, you are professional and that will definitely impress your guests at the beginning of the journey. However, be careful not to let your enthusiasm overstep your responsibility as a tour leader because most services on board should be provided by flight attendants, not a tour leader. Meanwhile, don't forget to seize the time on board, catch up on some sleep, recharge your batteries because you will have a lot to do after the flight arrives at the destination or if you have a connecting flight to catch.

❯ Reading for Details

Write T for "True" or F for "False" for each statement.

_____ 1. A tour leader has to pay attention to boarding calls.

_____ 2. Generally speaking, a passenger on a tour group can not select his/her seat.

_____ 3. A thoughtful tour leader might adjust the seat numbers of the guests so that they can sit together with their friends or family members.

_____ 4. A tour leader should board the plane before his/her guests and make sure all the guests are on board afterwards.

_____ 5. Some guests might not show up at the boarding gate on time because they spend too much time in duty-free shops.

_____ 6. A tour leader should serve his/her guests all the time during the flight to show his/her enthusiasm.

_____ 7. A tour leader should make sure his/her guests get the right meals, especially when they have dietary restrictions or preferences.

_____ 8. A tour leader should not rest because he/she has to check on his/her guests and see if they need any assistance.

領隊篇

Listening Task 1 p.221

> Listening for Gist

Listen to the following 4 boarding calls and write down the key information.

No.	Flight Number	Destination	Gate Number	Purposes
1				
2				
3				
4				

Listening Task 2 p.222

> Listening for Gist

_____ What is the purpose of the conversation?

(A) To hit on the flight attendant.

(B) To request a meal.

(C) To update a seating list.

> Listening for Details

_____ 1. What does the first speaker do?

(A) A flight attendant.　(B) A tour leader.　(C) A pilot.

_____ 2. Which of the following information is **NOT** on the list?

    (A) Special meals.

    (B) Old seat numbers.

    (C) Chinese names of the passengers.

_____ 3. What is the seat number of the first speaker?

    (A) 15B   (B) 50B   (C) 5B

Useful Language

1. if necessary　如果需要（原為 if it is necessary；另 if it is possible，可以 if possible 來用）

2. pay attention to: notice　注意

3. generally speaking　一般來講

   adv. + V-ing 放句首，如 strictly speaking（嚴格來講）、educationally speaking（就教育上來講）等等。

4. show up: appear; turn up　出現

5. take action: start to do something; start doing something　採取行動

6. in alphabetical order　以字母排序（in + adj + order 以…排序）

7. in case: in the event　萬一；以防萬一

8. on board: on a plane; in a car; on a boat　上船（飛機，火車）；在船上（飛機上，火車上）

9. flight attendant: workers in an airplane; steward and stewardess　空服人員（中性用詞）

10. be in charge of: be responsible for; take responsibility for　負責

11. lose track of: forget　忘記；失去…的線索（相反片語 keep track of；類似片語 lose touch with; lose sight of）

12. turn up: show up; appear　出現

13. ground staff: workers in airports　地勤（人員）

14. from time to time: sometimes; at times; on occasion; (every) now and then
有時；偶而

15. provide something for somebody　提供某人某物（也可用 provide somebody with something）

16. catch up on: do something that a person missed　趕著做；彌補

17. bound for: heading for　朝向；前往；開往（通常可用 be bound for 動身前往…，開往…；準備到…；去…）

18. be expected to: be regarded as likely; anticipate　預期；期望（類似片語 be supposed to; be obliged to）

19. on the list: items or things written on a paper　在清單上

Activity

1. Please translate the following boarding calls from Chinese to English.

(1) 請搭乘中華航空 CI1215 班機往釜山 (Busan) 的旅客至 3 號登機門登機。

_____

(2) 搭乘泰國航空 TG1688 班機往曼谷 (Bangkok) 的旅客，請至 2 號登機門登機。

_____

(3) 這是最後一次對搭乘長榮航空 BR1215 班機往吉隆坡 (Kuala Lumpur) 旅客王美玲 (Wang May-lin; May-lin Wang) 小姐的登機廣播。請搭乘長榮航空 BR1215 班機至吉隆坡的王美玲小姐立即至 3 號登機門登機。

2. Role-play the dialogue with your partner.

Exercise

_____ 1. You can use my smart phone during the journey, _____.

(A) interestingly enough   (B) if necessary

(C) on the list   (D) let alone

_____ 2. Flight attendants are _____ charge _____ the meal services on board.

(A) in…of   (B) of…of   (C) in…in   (D) of…in

_____ 3. Professor Wang _____ his students to submit their papers after class.

(A) reported   (B) rearranged

(C) rehearsed   (D) requested

_____ 4. If you feel uncomfortable, you can _____ your seat.

(A) accommodate   (B) adjust

(C) recommend   (D) digest

_____ 5. We had better _____ our camera batteries before we take a trip to Yunlin County.

(A) overstep   (B) remain   (C) expect   (D) recharge

_____ 6. I would like to make it _____ clear that I strongly value the importance of punctuality.

(A) crystal   (B) hospital   (C) fundamental   (D) environmental

_____ 7. One who _____ is lost. （當斷不斷，必受其患）

(A) congratulates   (B) hesitates

(C) formalizes   (D) civilizes

_____ 8. A teacher may try his/her best to provide opportunities _____ students to practice speaking in an English classroom.

(A) for   (B) to   (C) with   (D) by

_____ 9. A tour leader may seize the time to _____ some sleep on board.

(A) catch up on   (B) put up with

(C) get tired of   (D) look forward to

_____ 10. Instead of sitting here and doing nothing, we have to _____ to stop the boy from killing himself.

(A) enjoy ourselves   (B) fool around

(C) take action   (D) be bound for

Answers 🔒

Warm-up

1	2	3	4	5	6
passenger's name	flight number	destination	boarding time	boarding date	gate number
Wang, Ching Huang	BR0119	Kaohsiung	19: 45	April 15	51

7	8	9	10	11	12
airline company	seat number	class	gender	departure from	original boarding time
Eva Air	46A	Economy	Male	Fukuoka	19:50

領隊篇

Reading Task

Reading for Gist

(1) (C)   (2) (A)   (3) (E)   (4) (B)   (5) (D)

Reading for Details

1. T   2. T   3. T   4. F   5. T   6. F   7. T   8. F

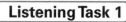
Listening Task 1

Listening for Gist

No.	Flight Number	Destination	Gate Number	Purposes
1	CI1234	Tokyo	3	Boarding
2	BR1122	Chiang Mai	13	The last boarding call
3	HA1121	Kuala Lumpur	18	Boarding priority (order)
4	TG1123	Bangkok	12	New Boarding time (8:00 a.m.) and new departure time (8:30 a.m.) due to heavy fog

Listening Task 2

Listening for Gist

(C)

Listening for Details

1. (B)   2. (C)   3. (A)

Exercise

1. (B)	2. (A)	3. (D)	4. (B)	5. (D)
6. (A)	7. (B)	8. (A)	9. (A)	10. (C)

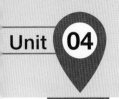

Unit 04 過境轉機

情境說明 ✈

　　出國有時未必都是搭乘直達或直飛的航班，到較遠的國家旅行常需要在國外其他機場中轉或轉機，香港、新加坡、東京、中國大陸、吉隆坡、杜拜都是常見的轉機地點。身為領隊，如果帶團時需要過境轉機，你知道有哪些重要事項要處理嗎？處理這些工作時又需要用到哪些英語呢？一起來看看吧！

 **Warm-up**

Q1: What is a transit? What is a transfer? Is there any difference between them?

Q2: What is a non-stop flight? What is a direct flight? Is there any difference between them?

Q3: What should a tour leader do during an airport transit/transfer?

Q4: Please write down the meaning of the given English terms or phrases in English or Chinese individually or in a small group.

	English	Chinese and/or English
1	make efforts to	
2	As ... suggests	
3	in contrast	
4	in other words	
5	no more than	
6	catch up with	
7	distribute something to somebody	
8	be sure to	

	English	Chinese and/or English
9	remind somebody of something	
10	turn into	
11	just a moment	
12	as a result	
13	Don't mention it.	

 Vocabulary & Phrases

1. intermediate [ˌɪntəˈmidɪət] *adj.* middle; in between　中間的，中途的

2. complicated [ˈkɑmpləˌketɪd] *adj.* complex; not simple　複雜的

3. interchangeably [ˌɪntəˈtʃendʒəblɪ] *adv.* in a way that things can be exchanged with each other　可互換地

4. disembark [ˌdɪsɪmˈbɑrk] *vi.,vt.* leave an airplane, a ship, etc. after a journey　下飛機；下船

5. differentiate [ˌdɪfəˈrɛnʃɪˌet] *vt.,vi.* separate; tell…from…; distinguish…from…　區分

6. stopover [ˈstɑpˌovə] *n.* [C] a short intermediate stay in an airplane that a passenger makes while he/she is on a longer journey to another city or destination　中途停留

7. ultimate [ˈʌltəmɪt] *adj.* total; final; eventual; last　完全的；最後的；最終的

8. scenario [sɪˈnɛrɪˌo] *n.* [C] situation; condition　情況；情形

9. troublesome [ˈtrʌb!səm] *adj.* bothersome; tough; difficult; worrisome　令人煩惱的；麻煩的；棘手的

10. time-consuming [ˈtaɪmkənˌsjumɪŋ] *adj.* taking a lot of time to do a certain thing　費時的

11. clear [klɪr] *vt.* go through; pass 　通過（海關等）

12. seamless [`simlɪs] *adj.* without any lines of joining two things 　無縫的

13. reminder [rɪ`maɪndɚ] *n.* [C] a message used to help a person remember to do something 　提醒；提醒物

14. orientation [ˌorɪɛn`teʃən] *n.* [C] training or preparation for a journey or an activity 　說明會

15. belongings [bə`lɔŋɪŋz] *n.pl.* some things belonging to someone; property; possessions; riches; assets 　財產；所有物

16. synchronize [`sɪŋkrəˌnaɪz] *vi.,vt.* occur or happen at the same time 　同時發生；同步

17. dismiss [dɪs`mɪs] *vt.* expel; send away 　解散（Class dismissed. 下課）

18. daunting [`dɔntɪŋ] *adj.* frightening; worrisome; disappointing 　令人卻步的；令人氣餒的；令人生畏的

19. disaster [dɪ`zæstɚ] *n.* [C；U] misfortune; mishap; catastrophe 　災難

20. unload [ʌn`lod] *vt.,vi.* remove 　卸（貨）；卸（客）

21. reassign [ˌriə`saɪn] *vt.* distribute again; assign again 　再分配；重新分配

領
隊
篇

 **Reading Task I**

〉 Reading for Gist

Please put each of the following headings in the right blank of this article (one is extra).

(A) General transfer procedures

(B) Transit vs. Transfer

(C) Non-stop flight vs. Direct flight

❯ Reading 1

Does a "non-stop" and "direct" flight sound the same to you? Or do you use the terms "transit" and "transfer" interchangeably?

(1)

As the term suggests, a non-stop flight goes from one airport to the destination airport without making any stops along the way. A direct flight still brings you from the airport of origin to the destination airport, but it could make a brief stop at an intermediate airport along the way. In this case, passengers may disembark the plane and board the plane at the intermediate airport just like how a bus picks up and drops off passengers. Please note that there is still only one flight number for a direct flight. For example, if a flight flies non-stop from Singapore to San Francisco, it is a non-stop flight. In contrast, if a flight flies from Singapore to San Francisco with a stop at Hong Kong Airport, it is a direct flight. Even though most people use the terms "non-stop flights" and "direct flights" interchangeably, it is still very important for a tour leader to differentiate them.

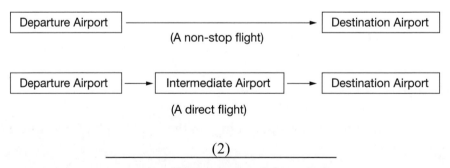

(2)

If an aircraft makes a brief stopover at an airport and continues the journey after its passengers return to the same aircraft, it is a transit. In this case, each passenger only obtains a boarding pass when he/she checks in at the departure airport and his/her luggage can be sent through to the ultimate destination. When passengers make a transit at the intermediate airport, they have to disembark the plane with their carry-on bags. Usually passengers receive transit passes from the ground staff upon their arrival at the intermediate airport and then pass security checks with their carry-on bags checked. Finally they are guided by the ground staff and proceed to the boarding gate and wait for boarding. In other words, there is no need for passengers to clear immigration, claim baggage and clear customs at the intermediate airport.

If a passenger has to take more than two different flights to get to the final destination, then it is a transfer, not a transit. When the two flights belong to the same airline company or the same alliance, usually the luggage can be sent directly all the way from the departure airport to the final destination if the transfer time takes no more than 24 hours. While two boarding passes with seat assignments are issued most of the time at the departure airport during the check-in, sometimes only the first boarding pass is issued and the second boarding pass is obtained at the transfer desk at the intermediate airport. For a transfer like this, if the first flight is delayed, passengers usually don't have to worry about missing the connecting flight because the airline companies will provide necessary assistance and solve the problem. For passengers, a transfer can be as easy as a transit at the intermediate airport because the passengers do

領
隊
篇

not have to report to the transfer desk unless they need to obtain their second boarding pass or when the first flight is delayed and they have missed their connecting flight. Otherwise, the only difference is that the passengers might have to proceed to another gate or terminal building after security checks because the connecting flight might depart from another terminal or from a different gate even in the same terminal. So, to be on the safe side, passengers should make sure that they have enough time in between flights.

Departure Airport	Intermediate Airport	
• Obtain two boarding passes • Luggage can be sent through to the final destination • Boarding (Flight TW123)	• Security check • Proceed to a new boarding gate (maybe in a different terminal) • Waiting room • Boarding a different plane (Flight T321)	Destination Airport

What if a passenger takes two flights and they don't belong to the same alliances? It is still a transfer and the procedures for baggage check-in and obtaining two boarding passes can be as simple as those in the scenario where two flights belong to the same alliances. However, it is possible that the baggage cannot be sent through to the destination airport and only one boarding pass is issued at the departure airport. In this case, upon arrival at the intermediate airport, be sure to report to the transfer desk to obtain the second boarding pass or confirm your checked luggage status with the ground staff. You might have to claim your luggage and recheck in for your luggage again. Meanwhile, in the case that your first flight is delayed and you can't catch up with the second flight, the services for connections might not be that seamless as in the case where the two flights belong to the same airline company or the same alliance.

Departure Airport

- Obtain two boarding passes
- Luggage can be sent through to the final destination
- Boarding (Flight TW123)

Intermediate Airport

- (Transfer desk)
  - (Get 2nd boarding pass)
  - (Confirm your luggage status)
- Security check
- Proceed to a new boarding gate (maybe in a different terminal)
- Waiting room
- Boarding a different plane (Flight ABC321)

Destination Airport

Here is the comparison for the three scenarios:

領
隊
篇

Number of Flight(s)	One flight	Two Flights	Two Flights
Partnership between flights	Same company	Same company or same alliance	Different companies or different alliances
Transit/transfer	Transit	Transfer	Transfer
Two boarding passes are issued at the departure airport	Yes	Yes	It depends
Luggage can be sent through to the destination airport	Yes	Yes	It depends
Get a transit pass	Yes	No	No
Security check before boarding at the intermediate airport	Yes	Yes	Yes
Boarding gate at the intermediate airport	The Same	Different	Different
Boarding in a different terminal at the intermediate airport	No	Maybe	Maybe

If one of the flights is a low-cost carrier (LCC), a transfer usually is more troublesome and time-consuming. For example, if you are flying on a low-cost carrier (LCC) and transferring to a full-service carrier (FSC), usually one boarding pass is issued and your luggage can not be sent directly all the way to the final destination. Upon your arrival at the intermediate airport, you have to clear customs, collect your baggage, and then check in for your next flight to get your next boarding pass, which takes more time. However, it is good to know that more LCCs offer seamless services for connections to partner airlines. So, it is suggested to check the transfer procedures at the intermediate airport before booking flights.

❯ Reading for Details

Write T for "True" or F for "False" for each statement.

_____ 1. A non-stop flight and a direct flight are the same. They bring you from the departure airport to the final destination without making any stops along the way.

_____ 2. A transit and a transfer are the same. When passengers have to take a connecting flight at an intermediate airport, it is called a transit or a transfer.

_____ 3. Generally speaking, a transit pass is issued to a passenger who is going to take the same flight at the same boarding gate upon their arrival.

_____ 4. Generally speaking, passengers can always get two boarding passes when they check in at the departure airport if they have a transfer or a transit at an intermediate airport.

_____ 5. Generally speaking, passengers can always have their luggage sent through to the final destination when they check in at the departure airport.

_____ 6. Generally speaking, at an intermediate airport for a transfer or a transit, the carry-on bags of the passengers have to be inspected for security reasons.

_____ 7. Generally speaking, for a transfer, passengers go to a different boarding gate for boarding the connecting flight at the intermediate airport.

_____ 8. Generally speaking, for a transit, passengers go to the same boarding gate for boarding at the intermediate airport.

_____ 9. Generally speaking, for a passenger who has to take two flights which belong to the same airline company or the same alliance for his trip, if the first flight is delayed, the passenger doesn't have to worry much about whether to miss his connecting flight because the airline company usually makes efforts to assist the passenger.

_____ 10. Generally speaking, for a passenger who has to take two flights which don't belong to the same airline company or the same alliance for his trip, it is possible that the passenger can not send his luggage through to the final destination.

_____ 11. Generally speaking, for a passenger who has to take two flights and one of the flights is a LCC, the transfer procedures usually take more time and they are usually more complicated.

領隊篇

Reading Task 2

> Reading for Gist

_____ 1. What might be the title of this article?

    (A) Mistakes passengers should avoid in a transfer or a transit.

    (B) Main tasks of tour leaders in a transfer or a transit.

    (C) Reminders for passengers in a transfer or a transit.

    (D) Main tasks for tour leaders during an airport check-in

_____ 2. Who is this article for?

    (A) Backpackers.   (B) Guests on a group tour.

    (C) Tour leaders.   (D) Pilots.

> Reading 2

Title: _____

    As a tour leader, do you know what you should do for your guests in a transit or a transfer? If you don't have a clue, this article might be just the ticket for you. Even though the transit or transfer procedures vary from airport to airport, here are some general guidelines for you to follow:

1. Before the trip, you should check how long it takes for a transfer/transit. If it takes more than 4 hours, check with the airline company whether a soft drink is provided. If it takes more than 6 hours, check with the airline company whether a snack coupon is offered. If there are no complimentary drinks or snacks, check whether this will be covered by the travel agency.

2. If two boarding passes are issued at the departure airport, you should keep all the copies of the second boarding passes for your guests just in case. Distribute it to each of your guests before the security check at the intermediate airport.

3. Gather your guests upon arrival at the intermediate airport. Confirm the transfer/transit procedures with the ground staff and update your guests with the latest information.

4. In the case of a transit, be sure to confirm if each of your guests receives a transit pass because it is required to get around at the intermediate airport for your guests.

5. Even if you get the boarding pass for the connecting flight beforehand at the departure airport, be sure to check the latest information about the boarding gate and time upon your arrival at the intermediate airport.

6. In the case of a transfer without the boarding pass for the connecting flight, prepare the PNR (Passenger Name Record), collect all the passports, visas and baggage claim tickets from your guests and go to the transfer counter for further assistance.

7. If the first flight is delayed and you have missed the connecting flight, prepare the PNR, collect all the passports, visas and baggage claim tickets from your guests and go to the transfer counter for further assistance.

8. As all carry-on bags have to be inspected either in a transit or transfer due to security reasons, be sure to remind your guests that they have to take all their personal belongings with them while disembarking the aircraft at the intermediate airport.

9. Be sure to synchronize your watch with the local time and tell your guests to do so. Guide your guests to the boarding gate for the connecting flight

領
隊
篇

or the right departure level of the terminal building, remind them of the boarding time, and ask them to report to you before boarding. Before the group is dismissed, don't forget to tell them how to contact you just in case that they cannot find you when they are lost and they cannot find the way back to the boarding gate.

10. If the transfer/transit takes a while, indicate the locations or directions of the lavatories, duty-free shops, VIP lounges or other facilities for your guests because they might be interested.

A transfer/transit is inevitable for a long journey but it seems rather daunting for travelers. If a tour leader doesn't understand the general procedures and cannot deal with some problems properly during the transfer/transit, a wonderful trip might turn into a disaster. Conversely, if a transit or transfer is as smooth as silk, a professional image can be built and more trust can be earned from the guests easily.

> Reading for Details

Write T for "True" or F for "False" for each statement.

_____ 1. Transfer or transit procedures are universal and there are no exceptions.

_____ 2. If a transfer or transit takes more than four or six hours, usually an airline company offers a drink or snack coupon to its passengers.

_____ 3. Always distribute two boarding passes to the guests at the departure airport.

_____ 4. For a transfer or transit, passengers have to take their carry-on bags with them when they get off the aircraft at the intermediate airport.

_____ 5. It is important to check the latest information on the boarding time and boarding gate at the intermediate airport because there might be changed.

_____ 6. A tour leader should proceed to a transfer desk for further assistance when a boarding pass for the connecting flight has not been issued at the departure airport or when the tour group cannot catch its connecting flight because the first flight is delayed.

_____ 7. For a transfer or a transit, it is better to ask the guests to board the connecting flight at the intermediate airport without reporting to you as a tour leader.

_____ 8. It is always a good idea for a tour leader to give an orientation about the intermediate airport to the guests because they might be interested.

_____ 9. If a tour leader doesn't know the general transfer or transit procedures, the guests might be in trouble.

領
隊
篇

 **Listening Task 1**   p.223

> Listening for Gist

_____ 1. Where is the conversation taking place?
   (A) Immigration.
   (B) Security checkpoint.
   (C) Transfer desk.
   (D) Lost and Found Counter.

_____ 2. What is the purpose of this conversation?

(A) To check in for a connecting flight.

(B) To report missing luggage.

(C) To ask for a help due to a delayed flight.

(D) To inspect personal belongings for security reasons.

❯ Listening for Details

1. What is the number of the connecting flight?_____

2. What is the destination of the connecting flight?_____

3. Why does the tour leader check the luggage status?_____

4. When is the boarding time?_____

5. What is the gate number?_____

6. Do the passengers have to go through a security checkpoint before boarding?_____

Listening Task 2 掃描 p.224

❯ Listening for Gist

_____ 1. Where is the conversation taking place?

(A) Immigration. (B) Security checkpoint.

(C) Transfer desk. (D) Lost and Found Counter.

_____ 2. What is the purpose of this conversation?

(A) To have their seats reassigned.

(B) To report missing luggage.

(C) To ask for an assistance due to a delayed flight.

(D) To inspect personal belongings for security reasons.

> Listening for Details

1. What is the number of the connecting flight?_____

2. What is the destination of the connecting flight?_____

3. What does the tour leader give to the staff?_____

4. When is the boarding time?_____

5. What is the gate number?_____

6. What are the tour leader and his guests probably going to do next?

_____

 **Useful Language**

1. upon arrival　一到達

   upon + n. = on + n./V-ing = as soon as S + V　一…就…

   Upon/On arrival at Kaohsiung, they hurried to shop.

   =On arriving at Kaohsiung, they hurried to shop.

   =As soon as they arrived at Kaohsiung, they hurried to shop.

2. whether to V: whether S + V　是否去

   I don't know whether to take a trip to Seoul next month.

   = I don't know whether I should take a trip to Seoul next month.

Activity

1. Tell your partner about the main differences between "non-stop flights" and "direct flights."

2. Tell your partner about the main differences between "a transit" and "a transfer."

3. Tell your partner about general transit procedures and what a tour leader should do in a transit.

4. Tell your partner about general transfer procedures and what a tour leader should do in a transfer.

5. Take a look at the scripts of the two dialogs and role-play each dialog with your partner.

Extension Activity & Assignments

Role-play with your partner based on the following scenario. One plays a tour leader and the other plays the airline staff at the transfer counter:

1. Number of guests: 20 people.

2. Departure Airport: Taoyuan International Airport (TPE Airport).

3. 1st Flight: BR1122 departing at 11:00 a.m. at gate 12

4. Intermediate Airport: Hong Kong International Airport

5. Original connecting flight: CX3344 departing at 14:00 at gate 4

6. The 1st flight is delayed and you can't catch your connecting flight.

7. You go to the transfer desk at the intermediate airport for assistance.

8. The tour leader hands the PNR, passports and baggage claim tickets to the staff at the transfer desk.

9. New connecting flight: CX1234 boarding at 16:00 and departing at 16:30 at gate 6.

10. The tour leader checks the luggage status with the staff at the transfer counter.

11. The staff hands the PNR, passports and boarding passes to the tour leader and gives directions to the boarding gate.

Exercise

_____ 1. It is a _____ task for us to complete a research study in six months.

(A) daunting   (B) yummy   (C) stubborn   (D) unemployed

_____ 2. It is a _____ task for writing teachers to grade or score their students' compositions every week.

(A) time-consuming   (B) briefing

(C) time-consumed   (D) briefed

_____ 3. Peter is a(n) _____ student because he always concentrates on playing an online game in class.

(A) handsome   (B) troublesome

(C) quarrelsome   (D) awesome

_____ 4. Because of time constraint, the crew are making an _____ to unload the ship.

(A) offer   (B) honesty   (C) effort   (D) integrity

_____ 5. I cannot lend my money to you because I just have _____ (=only) NT$ 100.

(A) no less than   (B) not less than

(C) no more than   (D) not more than

領
隊
篇

_____ 6. In _____ with his classmates, Gary is rather smart.

(A) compact　　(B) contract　(C) combat　　(D) contrast

_____ 7. Sophie is the smartest student in her class. _____, she is smarter than any other classmate in her class.

(A) To our surprise　　　　　(B) In other words

(C) That is to be said　　　　(D) Interestingly enough

_____ 8. The tour leader will _____ plane tickets to us right here soon.

(A) distribute　　　　　　　(B) contribute

(C) attribute　　　　　　　(D) tribute

_____ 9. It is necessary for a tour leader to give his/her guests a(n) _____ about the transit or transfer.

(A) congratulation　　　　　(B) population

(C) orientation　　　　　　 (D) concentration

_____ 10. The tour leader reminded his guests to _____ the plane and board another plane at the intermediate airport.

(A) remark　　(B) birthmark　(C) postmark　　(D) disembark

Answers 🔒

Warm-up

	English	Chinese and/or English
1	make efforts to	竭盡全力／ make every/an effort to
2	As … suggests	如…暗示；如…所示
3	in contrast	相反地／ on the contrary; conversely
4	in other words	也就是說／ that is to say
5	no more than	只有／ only; merely; nothing but
6	catch up with	趕上
7	distribute something to somebody	分發 (東西) 給 (人)
8	be sure to	確信／ be certain to
9	remind somebody of something	提醒 (人)(事情)
10	turn into	變成／ change into; become
11	just a moment	等一下／ just a minute; just a second
12	as a result	結果／ consequently; in consequence
13	Don't mention it.	不客氣／ You are welcome.; Not at all.

領
隊
篇

Reading Task 1

Reading for Gist

1. (C)　2. (B)

Reading for Details

1. F	2. F	3. T	4. F	5. F	6. T
7. T	8. T	9. T	10. T	11. T	

Reading Task 2

Reading for Gist

1. (A)   2. (C)

Reading for Details

1. F	2. T	3. F	4. T	5. T
6. T	7. F	8. T	9. T	

Listening Task 1

Listening for Gist

1. (C)   2. (A)

Listening for Details

1. CI1234   2. Istanbul

3. Because the tour leader wants to make sure the luggage is not missing and is on the connecting flight.

4. 6:30 p.m.   5. Gate 16   6. Yes

Listening Task 2

Listening for Gist

1. (C)   2. (C)

Listening for Details

1. NW4321   2. Honolulu

3. PNR, passports and baggage claim tickets of the first flight.

4. 7:30 p.m.   5. Gate 15

6. They are going through security checks first and then going to the boarding gate.

Exercise

1. (A)   2. (A)   3. (B)   4. (C)   5. (C)

6. (D)   7. (B)   8. (A)   9. (C)   10. (D)

情境說明 ✈

　　飛機終於抵達了目的地機場，團員們莫不懷著雀躍不已的心情準備下飛機，迫不及待地想感受異國的空氣、溫度、聲音及一切新奇的事物。然而下了飛機後，領隊及所有團員並不能馬上見到接機的當地導遊或司機，因為大家仍需辦理入境程序及通過相關審查。必須在確認一切沒有問題後，大家才能順利到「入境大廳」，真正開始悠閒地體驗異國的風土人情。然而，如果入境時恰巧是尖峰時段，往往隊伍難免綿延數公尺，光是入境就會耗去不少時間。此時如果乘客們能了解入境相關程序及注意事項，將能加快入境審查的速度，減少大家等待的時間。然而，在入境海關檢查及到達入境大廳之前，領隊需要用到的英語有哪些呢？一起來看看吧！

領隊篇

 **Warm-up**

Q1: What are the common arrival procedures for passengers at an airport?

Q2: What information should a tour leader tell his/her guests after landing?

Q3: Fill in the blanks based on the given terms.

(A) carousel	(B) a lost and found counter	(C) the passport cover
(D) baggage claim ticket	(E) customs declaration card	(F) the arrival hall

1. ＿＿＿＿＿	2. ＿＿＿＿＿	3. ＿＿＿＿＿
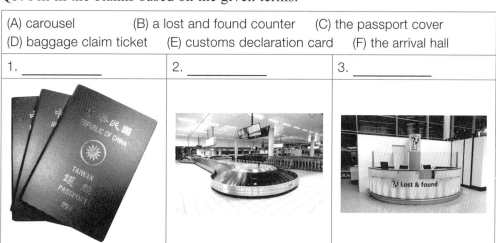		

4. _____	5. _____	6. _____
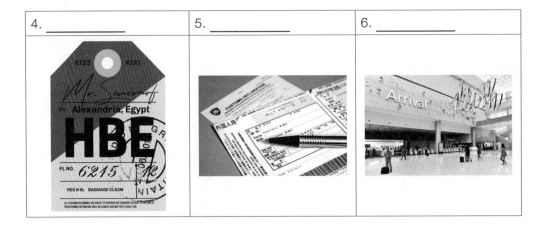		

 Vocabulary & Phrases

1. headshot [`hɛd͵ʃat] *n*. [*C*] a photo/photograph/picture of a person's head　頭照

2. fingerprint [`fɪŋɚ͵prɪnt] *n*. [*C*] the patterns of many curved lines on the ends of a person's fingers　指紋

3. decline [dɪ`klaɪn] *vt*. turn down; refuse; reject　婉拒，拒絕

4. taxi [`tæksɪ] *vt*.,*vi*. move; go forward　（飛機起降時在地面）滑行

5. potentially [pə`tɛnʃəlɪ] *adv*. possibly　可能地

6. hurdle [`hɝd!] *n*. [*C*] difficulty; obstacle; barrier; block; problem　障礙，困難

7. specify [`spɛsə͵faɪ] *vt*. make sure; make clear; clarify; make certain　確定，明確

8. hand [hænd] *vt*. submit; give; pass　面交，給，遞

> Reading for Gist

_____ 1. What might be the title of this article?

(A) Common mistakes passengers usually make when they clear immigration

(B) Common departing procedures and suggestions for tour leaders

(C) Common procedures for reporting missing luggage for passengers

(D) Common arrival procedures and tour-leading tips for tour leaders

_____ 2. According to this article, what is the order of the procedures in the airport?

(A) Customs → Baggage Claim → Immigration

(B) Customs → Immigration → Baggage Claim

(C) Immigration → Baggage Claim → Customs

(D) Baggage Claim → Customs → Immigration

> Reading

Title: _____

After an aircraft makes a landing and taxis to the gate, it is time for a tour leader like you to get ready for potentially time-consuming and daunting arrival procedures at the destination airport. As a tour leader, you should know the following guidelines like the back of your hand, including clearing immigration, baggage claim, report missing luggage and clearing customs:

1. Before landing, it is always a good idea to tell your guests to stay together as a tour group and not to make a beeline for the immigration by themselves right after entering the terminal building.

2. After entering the terminal building, be sure to bring all of your guests together, do a head count and explain the arrival procedures. If some of them have to relieve themselves, indicate the directions to the lavatory and patiently wait for them to come back before proceeding to the immigration.

3. Tell your guests that they are on vacation and they should kick back and be patient because the arrival procedures might take longer than expected.

4. Before clearing immigration, remind your guests that photography or video recording is prohibited in the restricted area. Then, indicate where to line up. After that, tell them to remove the passport covers, get their boarding passes, visas and arrival cards (disembarkation cards) ready, and wait for their turns. Immigration officers might take a head shot of each passenger and take their fingerprints in some countries. Finally, don't forget to tell them which aisle you will be on and ask them to call your name if something comes up.

5. It is a good idea for a tour leader to stay behind the tour group just in case your guests need your assistance while going through the immigration. However, in the case of having a group visa, a tour leader should stay ahead of the line, present the group visa list and talk to the immigration officer first.

6. It is more efficient if you can assign one or two experienced travelers to be the first to go through the immigration and indicate how to find the information on which carousel the luggage will be on. In this way, they can also share the information and guide other guests to claim their luggage before you can.

7. Be attentive and see if there is any guest that needs your assistance while going through the immigration. Make sure no one is left behind before making your way to the baggage claim area.

8. In the baggage claim area, guide your guests to take all the suitcases with the same luggage tag provided by your travel agency off the carousel. Then ask your guests to identify their suitcases that match their baggage claim tickets. If a guest cannot locate his/her suitcase, accompany him/her to the lost and found counter, report missing luggage and calm him/her down.

9. Before clearing customs, remind your guests to present the customs declaration cards and take the right channel. Usually the green channel is for nothing to declare while the red channel is for something to declare. Also ask one or two experienced travelers to look for the local guide in the arrival area before you can. If one of your guests is stopped by a customs officer for further inspection, reach out and provide assistance immediately.

領隊篇

The arrival procedures may be lengthy and there might be some hurdles before you and your guests can arrive at the arrival hall and meet the local tour guide or tour bus driver, especially when it is rush hour in the airport. However, if you can understand the common arrival procedures and how to solve some potential problems, and give your guests a heads up in advance, I believe, some confusion will be avoid, more time can be saved, and you will definitely look professional in the eye of your guests.

> Reading for Details

Write T for "True" or F for "False" for each statement.

_____ 1. It's a good idea for the guests to proceed to the immigration individually right after they get off the plane as long as their tour leader tells them about the procedures beforehand.

_____ 2. Generally speaking, travelers have to submit two forms: an arrival card and a customs declaration card.

_____ 3. When an immigration officer asks you to take a headshot or take fingerprints, it's OK for a passenger to decline.

_____ 4. A tour leader should be the first to go through the immigration all the time and wait for his/her guests in the baggage claim area.

_____ 5. If one guest cannot locate his/her luggage on the carousel, a tour leader should accompany the guest to report lost luggage at the lost and found counter.

_____ 6. The guests can confirm if they are taking the right suitcases off the carousel by checking their baggage claim tickets.

_____ 7. Always guide the guests through the green channel while clearing customs.

   p.225

＞ Listening for Gist

_____ 1. Where is the conversation taking place?

(A) At a check-in counter.

(B) At an immigration.

(C) At a security checkpoint.

(D) At a lost and found counter.

_____ 2. What does the second speaker do?

(A) A tour guide. (B) A tour leader.

(C) An interpreter. (D) A tourist.

領隊篇

＞ Listening for Details

1. Where is the second speaker from?_____

2. What kind of visa is presented?_____

3. How many people are there in the tour group?_____

4. How long are the people going to stay in the country?_____

5. Where are the people going to stay?_____

6. Why does the second speaker want to stay behind the group?_____

7. What does the second speaker give the first speaker during the conversation?_____

8. What will the first speaker give the second speaker later? Why?

_____

   p.226

> Listening for Gist

_____ 1. Where is the conversation taking place?

(A) At a check-in counter.

(B) At an immigration.

(C) At a security checkpoint.

(D) At a lost and found counter.

_____ 2. What is the purpose of this conversation?

(A) To report missing luggage.

(B) To fill out a claim form.

(C) To ask where to claim luggage.

(D) To complain about poor inflight services.

> Listening for Details

1. What is the flight number?_____

2. How long did they wait before they went to the counter?

_____

3. Where is the missing item now?_____

4. What information should be provided in the claim form?

_____

5. How soon will they get back the item? Do they have to go to the airport to

claim it?_____

 **Useful Language**

1. get off　下飛機；下車（相反詞為 get on）

2. get ready　準備好了（用法：get/be ready for + n./V-ing; get ready to + V）

3. do a head count　數人頭（用法：do/make/take a count of sb./sth.）

4. make a beeline for　直奔（用法：make a beeline for sb. /sth.）

5. on vacation　在度假（用法：go/be on vacation；比較：vocation 是行業或職業）

6. kick back: relax; keep calm　[俚語] 放（輕）鬆，保持平靜

7. than expected　比預期的還…（than 當「準關係代名詞」，中間可省略掉 it was/it is/ they were 等等）

8. heads up　當心，小心（give sb. a heads up 叮嚀某（些）人小心）

9. the Philippines　菲律賓（菲律賓是由很多島組成的，所以字尾有 s）

10. step aside　往旁邊站；讓開（= give way；相反詞為 stay on）

11. complain about　抱怨（用法：complain to sb. about sth. 向某人抱怨某事）

12. ASAP　盡快地（是 as soon as possible 的縮寫）

 **Activity**

1. Please briefly describe general arrival procedures at the destination airport.

2. Among the nine guidelines in Reading Task, which three do you think are important? Why?

3. Role-play the dialogue in Listening Task 1 with your partner.

4. Role-play the dialogue in Listening Task 2 with your partner.

Extension Activity & Assignments

Role-play with your partner based on the following scenario. One plays a tour leader and the other plays the clerk at the lost and found counter. You guys are going to report missing luggage. Prepare an authentic claim form to fill out in this exercise.

1. Flight number: CI2431 (From Kaohsiung).

2. The tour leader hands the baggage claim ticket to the clerk.

3. The luggage is still in Kaohsiung now.

4. The clerk asks the guest to fill out the claim form.

5. You will stay at the Marriott Hotel downtown for four nights.

6. Check when the luggage will arrive and how it can be claimed.

7. The suitcase should arrive in two days. The airline company will deliver it to your hotel once it arrives.

Exercise

_____ 1. I cannot meet you in Tainan today because I am on _____ in Sydney now.
   (A) vocation   (B) vacation
   (C) provocation   (D) cation

_____ 2. Peter _____ to take a trip to Hawaii with his friends in the summer break, saying that he did not have enough money to do it.
   (A) declined   (B) reclined
   (C) inclined   (D) acclaimed

_____ 3. Passengers had better _____ and be patient because the arrival procedures could take them longer time than expected.

(A) fall behind   (B) go crazy

(C) kick back   (D) mull over

_____ 4. A _____ is a picture or photo of a person's head.

(A) headache   (B) heads-up

(C) headset   (D) headshot

_____ 5. A tour leader had best accompany his/her guests to report their lost luggage at the lost and _____ counter.

(A) fined   (B) found

(C) fainted   (D) frowned

_____ 6. It's a joy to see a plane making a landing and _____ to the gate in an airport.

(A) taxing   (B) taxiing

(C) faxing   (D) axing

_____ 7. This trip was so amazing that I got nothing to _____ about.

(A) explain   (B) obtain

(C) complain   (D) contain

_____ 8. A tour leader needs to overcome any _____ that his guests encounter in a journey.

(A) cuddle   (B) model

(C) hurdle   (D) middle

_____ 9. The notorious travel agency has scared away many _____ guests.

(A) potential   (B) confidential

(C) influential   (D) inertial

領
隊
篇

_____ 10. When travelers clear customs, they have to show the customs
_____ cards and take the right channel.

(A) indication   (B) presentation

(C) confirmation   (D) declaration

Answers 🔒

Warm-up

1. (C)　　　2. (A)　　　3. (B)　　　4. (D)　　　5. (E)　　　6. (F)

Reading Task

Reading for Gist

1. (D)　2. (C)

Reading for Details

1. F　　　2. T　　　3. F　　　4. F　　　5. T　　　6. T　　　7. F

Listening Task 1

Listening for Gist

1. (B)　2. (B)

Listening for Details

1.　Taiwan　　　　2.　A group visa　　　　　3.　Twenty people

4.　Five days　　　5.　Friday Boracay Resort

6.　Because he wants to make sure there is no problem with each of the guests while clearing immigration. If there is a problem, he can step in and provide assistance more easily.

7.　A passport, an arrival card, and a group visa.

8.　The immigration officer won't return the group visa to the tour leader until the identity of each guest of the tour group is checked.

領隊篇

Listening Task 2

Listening for Gist

1. (D)　2. (A)

Listening for Details

1. CI1234.　　　　　2. Almost 45 minutes.　　　　　3. In Hong Kong.

4. The type and color of the suitcase, phone number and the place to be reached.

5. By tomorrow evening. No. The suitcase will be delivered to the Hilton Hotel.

Exercise

1. (B)	2. (A)	3. (C)	4. (D)	5. (B)
6. (B)	7. (C)	8. (C)	9. (A)	10. (D)

Unit 06 辦理旅館入住手續

情境說明 ✈

　　一天的行程結束後進到旅館大廳，團員們莫不想早點進入房間休息，但領隊及導遊卻依舊在旅館櫃臺忙著辦理入住手續。為了讓團員們熟悉當晚入住的旅館設施及相關注意事項，領隊及導遊可還有不少事項要跟團員們交待及宣布呢？到底領隊及導遊在旅館在忙些什麼，需要用到哪些英語呢？一起來看看吧！

 **Warm-up**

1. Brainstorming

Q1: What information should a tour guide or tour leader tell his/her guests in a hotel check-in?

Q2: As a guest, what questions might you ask a tour guide or tour leader in a hotel check-in?

2. Wheel of Fortune

1. _ _ _ _ _ e _

2. _ _ _ _y

3. _ _ _ _ _ _ _ _ e

4. _ _ _ _ _ _ _ _ _ r

5. _ _ _ _ _ _ i _ _

6. _ _ _ _ r _ _ _ _ _ _ r

7. f _ _ _ _ _ _ _ _

8. _ _ _ _ a _ _ _

9. _ _ _ _ _ _

10. _ a _ _ _ _ _ _

Vocabulary & Phrases

1. manager [`mænɪdʒɚ] *n.* [*C*] leader; governor　（商店、公司等的）負責人；主任，經理

2. distribute [dɪ`strɪbjʊt] *vt.* give; allot; spread　分發；分配 (+ to / among)

3. attention [ə`tɛnʃən] *n.* [*U*] notice; care; concern; focus; concentration　注意；注意力；專心

4. facility [fə`sɪlətɪ] *n.* [*C*] equipment; building; structure; room; office　設施，設備

5. gym [dʒɪm] *n.* [*C*] a place for people to exercise or play sports　體育館（gymnasium 的縮寫）；健身房

6. respectively [rɪ`spɛktɪvlɪ] *adv.* each; individually; personally　分別地，各自地

7. coupon [`kupɑn] *n.* [*C*] a ticket or paper used for a financial discount or rebate when buying something　贈券；減價優待券

8. password [`pæs͵wɝd] *n.* [*C*] a combination of letters or numbers or both used to prove a person's identity or who he/she is　密碼

9. nightstand [`naɪt͵stænd] *n.* [*C*] night table; a table beside a bed in a room　床頭櫃（放在床頭邊的小桌）

10. mineral water [`mɪnərəl `wɔtɚ] *n.* [*U*] natural underground water with dissolved minerals　礦泉水

11. complimentary [ˌkɑmpləˋmɛntərɪ] *adj.* free; for nothing　[美] 贈送的 ; 免費的

12. wake-up call [ˋwekˌʌp kɔl] *n.* [*C*] a phone call that a counter staff will call you up in a hotel at a certain time you arrange　電話喚醒服務

13. snorkel [ˋsnɔrkl̩] *vi.* dive with a tube　浮潛

14. lobby [ˋlɑbɪ] *n.* [*C*] a large room; entrance; passageway　大廳 ; 走廊 ; 入口

15. gear [gɪr] *n.* [*C* ; *U*] equipment; furnishing; facilities　設備，裝置 ; 家用器具

16. sunblock [ˋsʌnblɑk] *n.* [*C*] a cream or lotion used to protect the skin from sunburn　防曬油

17. depart [dɪˋpɑrt] *vi.* leave; exit; go away; set out　出發 ; 離開

18. housekeeper [ˋhaʊsˌkipɚ] *n.* [*C*] a person, usually a woman, dealing with arranging and cleaning another person's house or room in a hotel　（旅館，醫院等的）清潔人員

19. non-smoking [ˌnɑnˋsmokɪŋ] *adj.* smoke-free; smoking which is not allowed　禁止吸菸的 ; 非吸菸的

20. elevator [ˋɛləˌvetɚ] *n.* [*C*] lift; a device like a small room that carries people or goods directly up and down in high buildings such as hotels　[美] 電梯 ; 升降機 ; 起重機

21. toilet [ˋtɔɪlɪt] *n.* [*C*] restroom; bathroom; lavatory; washroom　廁所，洗手間，盥洗室

22. assistance [əˋsɪstəns] *n.* [*C*] help; aid; support; favor　援助，幫助 (+in)

   p.227

> Listening for Gist

_____ Which of the following topics is NOT mentioned in the conversation?

(A) Hotel facilities

(B) Time for a wake-up call

(C) How to make an in-house call

(D) How to go to a night market

> Listening for Details

1. What are the room numbers of the tour guide and tour leader?

_____

2. How many nights are they going to stay at this hotel?

_____

3. How late is the gym open?_____

4. When is breakfast time? Is a coupon required?_____

5. If a guest makes an in-house call, what number should be dialed first?

_____

6. By what time should the guests wait at the lobby tomorrow morning?

_____

7. What gears should the guests bring tomorrow morning?

_____

8. How much should the guests tip the bell captain for one piece of luggage?

_____

9. Why does the tour leader give the guests the business card of the hotel?

_____

10. What should the guests check after they get into their rooms?

_____

 **Useful Language**

領
隊
篇

1. room type　房型（包括 single room, double room, twin room, triple room, extra bed 等）

2. hotel facilities　飯店設施（包括 gym, spa, health club, fitness center, conference room, business center, mini bar 等）

3. breakfast coupon= breakfast voucher= breakfast ticket　餐券

4. extension number　內線號碼；分機號碼

Activity

Form a group of three and role-play the dialogue.

Extension Activity & Assignments

Form a group of three and role play based on the following scenario:

1. 3rd floor: Gym (8:00 a.m. ~ 11:00 p.m.)(a room key is required)

2. 4th floor: Restaurant (Breakfast: 6:30 a.m.~9:30 a.m.) (a coupon is required)

3. 5th floor: swimming pool (8:00 a.m.~11:00 p.m.) (a room key should be presented)

4. Wi-Fi: Free in the lobby and in rooms. The password is "ilovetraveling."

5. Complimentary items: two bottles of water in the mini bar.

6. Luggage: Bell captain will take care of it.

7. Wake-up call: 7:30 a.m.

8. Gathering time: 9:00 a.m. tomorrow in the lobby

9. Next-day itinerary & reminders: Temple tours. Don't wear shorts and tank tops. Sandals are OK.

10. Room number (T/L & T/G): Room 910 & Room 912

Exercise

_____ 1. It was a wonderful experience to jump into the sea for _____ in Kenting last summer.
    (A) snorkeling   (B) struggling
    (C) shuffling   (D) skating

_____ 2. It is a _____ that often clears our hotel room every morning.
    (A) manager   (B) plumber   (C) housekeeper (D) mariner

_____ 3. If necessary, I could help you _____ the room keys to all the guests.
    (A) contribute   (B) distribute (C) attribute   (D) reattribute

_____ 4. Our tour leader/guide will make an announcement in the hotel _____ after dinner.
    (A) hobby   (B) chubby   (C) hubby   (D) lobby

_____ 5. Students should pay _____ when their teacher is teaching.
(A) attention (B) prevention
(C) convention (D) invention

_____ 6. The hotel _____ interest me very much because they include a gym, a heated swimming pool, a bar, and some spas.
(A) facilities (B) activities (C) possibilities (D) authorities

_____ 7. On entering a hotel room, I tend to find a _____ to connect to the hotel Wi-Fi.
(A) keyword (B) password (C) account (D) discount

_____ 8. I often go to the _____ soon after I eat vegetarian food for lunch or dinner.
(A) fillet (B) bullet (C) violet (D) toilet

_____ 9. The hotel _____ is very helpful for me to carry my luggage to my 11th floor room.
(A) calculator (B) facilitator (C) elevator (D) contributor

_____ 10. One or two bottles of _____ in the hotel freezer are free, but the beverages are not.
(A) mineral water (B) coca cola
(C) orange juice (D) chicken soup

Answers 🔒

Warm-up

2. Wheel of Fortune

1. snorkel　　2. lobby　　3. distribute　　4. housekeeper

5. attention　　6. mineral water　7. facilities　　8. elevator

9. toilet　　10. password

Listening Task

Listening for Gist

(D)

Listening for Details

1. Tour guide: Room 812; Tour leader: Room 712

2. Two nights

3. 10:00 p.m.

4. From 6:30 a.m.to 10:30 a.m.; Yes, a coupon is required

5. One

6. 8:30 a.m.

7. Swimming gears, sunblock and towel

8. One dollar

9. Just in case that the guests get lost or can't find their way back to the hotel. They can take a taxi and show it to the taxi driver.

10. Check if there is hot shower and if the toilet is working properly

Exercise

1. (A)　　　2. (C)　　　3. (B)　　　4. (D)　　　5. (A)

6. (A)　　　7. (B)　　　8. (D)　　　9. (C)　　　10. (A)

領隊篇

Unit 07 餐廳用餐

情境說明

　　由於每個地方的飲食與其氣候、歷史及文化習習相關，因此品嘗美食往往成為出國旅行體驗當地文化非常重要的一環。然而，因為每一團的預算或團費不盡相同，所以每個旅行團所安排的餐廳等級、菜色也都不盡相同，但一般而言，都會以體驗當地有特色的餐點為主，中式餐廳為輔，一方面讓喜歡嚐鮮的團員能品嘗當地料理，另一方面也讓容易水土不服的團員們吃到熟悉的家鄉味。然而，為了讓團員吃得開心，領隊在餐廳時需要用到的英語有哪些呢？一起來看看吧！

1. Warm-up questions

Q1: What food do you like to eat? Make a list.

Q2: Do you think it's important to taste exotic cuisines during an overseas trip? Why or why not? What about Chinese or Taiwanese food?

Q3: What tasks should a tour leader do before and after the tour group arrives at the restaurant?

2. Please explain the given English terms in Chinese and/or English.

English terms	Chinese or/and English Translation
a peak season	
a through guide	
beat the crowd	
dress code	
on the spot	
Bon appetit	
for free	

Vocabulary & Phrases

1. exotic [ɛg`zɑtɪk] *adj.* foreign　異國情調的；外來的

2. cuisine [kwɪ`zin] *n.* [U] a cooking style; food　烹飪（法）；菜餚

3. overseas [`ovɚ`siz] *adv.* abroad　在海（國）外

   adj. foreign; exotic; abroad　（在）海（國）外的

4. hassle-free [`hæs! fri] *adj.* free from/of dispute or trouble　免於激烈爭論
   （口角、麻煩）的（*n.*-free 意為免於…或無…的，如 anxiety-free 免於
   （無）焦慮的）

5. handle [`hænd!] *vt.* cope/deal with; overcome; manage　處理

6. reflect [rɪ`flɛkt] *vt.* show; present; indicate　反映

7. distinctive [dɪ`stɪŋktɪv] *adj.* special; characteristic; distinguishing　有特色
   的，特殊的

8. foody [`fudɪ] *n.* [C] gourmet　[美式口語] 美食家

9. etiquette [`ɛtɪˌkɛt] *n.* [*U*] manners; curtesy　禮節；規矩

10. faux pas [fɔ`pɑ] *n.ph.* bad manners; impoliteness; rudeness　[法語] 失禮

11. utensil [ju`tɛns!] *n.* [*C*] device; tool　器具，餐具

12. accommodate [ə`kɑməˌdet] *vt.* offer; have room for; supply; provide　可容納；能提供膳宿；（飛機等）可搭載

13. budget [`bʌdʒɪt] *n.* [*C*] arranged money; ration　預算；經費

14. flat [flæt] *adj.* (a drink) has stopped having bubbles　（啤酒等）沒有氣泡的：If a drink is flat, it has stopped being fizzy (=with bubbles).

15. linger [`lɪŋgɚ] *vi.,vt.* stay; delay; wander　繼續逗留，徘徊；緩慢度過

16. happy camper [`hæpɪ `kæmpɚ] *n.* [*C*] one who is happy with his / her situation　快樂或開心的人

17. refill [ri`fɪl] *vt.* fill again　再裝滿，再灌滿

18. tab [tæb] *n.* [*C*] expense; the total money for food, meals, beverages, etc. in a restaurant or hotel　（待付）帳款，費用

19. stunningly [`stʌnɪŋlɪ] *adv.* amazingly; very good; great　極好地；令人目眩地

20. terribly [`tɛrəbəlɪ] *adv.* rather; very much　[口語] 很，非常

 **Reading Task**

❯ Reading for Gist

Skim and scan the article. Match each of the following headings with the right paragraph.

Answers	Numbers	Headings
	1	(A) Handle dining problems properly
	2	(B) Create a seating plan beforehand
	3	(C) Confirm the dining time and meal orders
	4	(D) Be attentive during the meal
	5	(E) Equip your guests with basic dining etiquette and meal information

> **Reading**

Local food can reflect a distinctive national or cultural identity. For overseas travelers, trying exotic cuisines is essential to understand and experience local culture during a trip. If a tour leader or a through guide could do something to ensure that his or her guests have a wonderful dining experience, this would definitely spice up the trip, especially for foodies.

Here are a couple of things a tour leader or a through guide can do:

1. _____

Be sure to call the restaurant two or three hours before the meal and confirm the number of diners, meal orders, dietary restrictions, seating arrangements, and arrival time. During peak season, it is very likely that there is no available table during normal dining hours. So, it is extremely critical to ensure the best arrival time for your tour group. In other words, to beat the crowd and arrive at the restaurant in time, sometimes there is no choice but to advance or push back the dining time. In this case, don't forget to keep your guests in the loop and explain the changes to avoid customer complaints.

2. _____

When in Rome, do as the Romans do. As dining etiquette varies from country to country, it is always a good idea to educate your guests by walking them through some cultural faux pas they should avoid at a restaurant. For example, dress code, how to use utensils properly, how to use a napkin, how to ask a server for help, and how loudly a person should talk, etc. On top of that, don't forget to help your guests set the right expectations for the meal, such as the portion and flavor of the meal, the price info of alcohol and beverages, and the speed of service in the restaurant. If you can bring those up to your guests, some misunderstandings will be avoided.

3. _____

A table in a western restaurant usually accommodates four to six people while a round table in a Chinese restaurant usually can have a maximum capacity of 10 people. Meanwhile, some guests have dietary restrictions. It is better for a tour leader to have a seating plan beforehand and communicate with the restaurants in advance. In this way, your guests can enjoy a hassle-free meal.

4. _____

Always take your seat and have your meal after two or three meals are served to your guests or after you make sure things are on the right track. Be attentive and keep an eye open for your guests even during the meal because your guests might need your assistance when they cannot communicate with the servers effectively. If you dine in a different room, be sure to come back to your guests before they finish the meal just in case they are looking for you. If your guests are still hungry or don't seem to be full enough, you might want to consider adding one or two dishes for them if the extra cost is within your budget.

5. _____

During the meal, some problems might come up. For example, it takes longer than expected before the meal is served. The dish is not what your guest ordered. There is something strange or funny in the dish. The beer is flat or the spoon is dirty. If something like this happens and a tour leader can step in and provide assistance timely on the spot, the problems won't linger in the mind of your guest for too long and you might potentially turn a customer complaint into customer satisfaction.

It's no picnic to satisfy your guests with each meal along the journey. However, if you can help them set the right expectations before the meal, provide professional and thoughtful assistance during the meal, and collect feedback after the meal from your guests, almost each guest will still be a happy camper even though some dishes might not appeal to their appetite. Bon appetit!

❯ Reading for Details

Write T for "True" or F for "False" for each statement.

_____ 1. For most travelers, it is not that important to taste local cuisines.

_____ 2. It is important to confirm some reservation details with the restaurant before the meal.

_____ 3. During peak season, a travel itinerary might be adjusted in order to bring your guests to dine at a restaurant in time.

_____ 4. Never provide assistance for your guests during the meal because it's not your job and you might make the work of the servers more complicated.

_____ 5. If your guests are still hungry after the meal, be flexible and always order more meals to make them happy.

_____ 6. Customer dissatisfaction can be reduced if you can help your guests set the right expectations before the meal.

_____ 7. To make a good seating plan beforehand is helpful to bring your guests a hassle-free dining experience.

_____ 8. Once the guests are seated, a tour leader should take his/her seat right away and let the servers do their jobs.

_____ 9. If a customer complaint is handled properly, it might lead to customer satisfaction.

   p.230

> Listening for Gist

_____ Which of the following topics is NOT mentioned in this conversation?

(A) The number of the guests.

(B) Dietary restrictions.

(C) Dining problems.

(D) The location of the bathroom.

領隊篇

> Listening for Details

1. What is the name of the restaurant?_____

2. What is the name of the tour group?_____

3. How many people are there in this tour group, excluding the tour leader?

   _____

4. Where are the tables for this tour group?_____

5. Do the guests have any dietary restrictions? If yes, what is it?

   _____

6. How many dishes are there for the meal?_____

7. Does the tour leader dine in the same room with the guests?

   _____

8. Can the guests get a refill for their drinks for free?_____

9. What problems are there during the meal?_____

10. How does the tour leader pay?_____

Useful Language

1. lead to: result in　導致；引起（lead to 也有「通往」的意思，如 All roads lead to Rome. = Every road leads to Rome. 條條大路通羅馬）

2. spice up: add flavors in cooking, baking, etc.; to make a trip or life more interesting and meaningful　調味；增加情趣

3. there is no choice but to V　沒有選擇餘地；不得不

4. push back: postpone; put off　把⋯向後推；延期

5. keep people in the loop: keep people informed about what's going on　讓人們得知相關資訊與最新進度

6. When in Rome, do as the Romans do.　入境隨俗

7. vary from country to country: vary from one country to another　因國家而異

8. ask sb. for help　要求某人幫助

9. on top of that: besides that; aside/apart from that/in addition to that　除…之外；此外

10. bring up: talk about; mention; tell　提起…；談到

11. be on the right track: be settled down　上軌道；處理妥善

12. keep an eye open: notice; pay attention to　[口] 留心或注意

13. step in: get involved; interfere　介入

14. It's no picnic to V...　做…不是一件輕鬆的事情（no picnic 意指「不是一件輕鬆的事情」）

15. appeal to + n.: attract; cause　引起

16. excluding + n.　不包括（原為 which exclude + n. 省略 which, exclude 變成 excluding）

17. Do you mind + V-ing...?　你介意…嗎？（mind 後面接動名詞）

18. Put it on my tab.: I will pay the whole amount later, say at the end of the day, week, etc.　帳或消費算我的

領隊篇

Activity

1. Among the 5 tips in Reading Task, which three do you think are important? Why?

2. Role-play the dialog in Listening Task with your partner.

 Extension Activity & Assignments

Step 1: What are other common customer complaints at a restaurant? Talk with your partner and write down as many as possible.

Step 2: As a tour leader, what can you do to properly handle each of the complaints in step 1?

Step 3: Use the part with customer complaints in Listening Task as a model and create a dialog with your partner. Don't forget to include two customer complaints in step 1 and their solutions in step 2 in this dialog.

Step 4: Practice the dialog with your partner.

Step 5: Perform your dialog in front of another pair without looking at your script. The listeners are expected to answer the following questions:

Q1: What are the customer complaints and solutions?

Q2: What do you think of their performance?

Step 6: Take turns.

Exercise

_____ 1. Sophia is a gourmet, so she likes to try _____ food, especially in foreign countries.

(A) exotic　　(B) critic　　(C) political　　(D) practical

_____ 2. Such local food as stinky tofu can reflect a _____ cultural identity in Taiwan.

(A) distinctive　(B) functional (C) defeating　　(D) anti-social

_____ 3. Each room in this hotel can _____ two to three tourists.

(A) moderate　　　　　　(B) considerate

(C) accommodate　　　　(D) candidate

_____ 4. Social _____ dictates that people cannot speak or laugh too loud in a restaurant or museum.

(A) etiquette　(B) banquet　(C) tablet　(D) booklet

_____ 5. A wonderful meal experience that a through guide offers to his or her guests could _____ their travel.

(A) build up　(B) spice up　(C) get on　(D) depend on

_____ 6. We missed the airplane, and _____ we lost our passports.

(A) on top of that　(B) namely

(C) that is to say　(D) in other words

_____ 7. It's _____ (=not easy) to appeal to each guest with meals along the journey.

(A) no critic　(B) no trap　(C) no fault　(D) no picnic

_____ 8. It's very important to keep your guests in the _____ to tell them what things they should keep in their minds before visiting a museum.

(A) coop　(B) goop　(C) hoop　(D) loop

_____ 9. If you want to request more rice or a refill for drinks, please feel free to do it and put it on my _____.

(A) cab　(B) dab　(C) gab　(D) tab

_____ 10. In the famous restaurant, all the guests enjoyed their meals and had a(n) _____ dining experience.

(A) hassle-free　(B) suspicious

(C) illegal　(D) symbiotic

領隊篇

Answers 🔒

Warm-up

2. Please explain the given English terms in Chinese and/or English.

English terms	Chinese or/and English Translation
a peak season	旺季
a through guide	領隊兼導遊
beat the crowd	避開人群
dress code	服裝規定
on the spot	當場
Bon appetit	祝用餐愉快 =Good appetite
for free	免費 =for nothing; free of charge

Reading Task

Reading for Gist

1. (C)　　　2. (E)　　　3. (B)　　　4. (D)　　　5. (A)

Reading for Details

1. F　　　2. T　　　3. T　　　4. F　　　5. F

6. T　　　7. T　　　8. F　　　9. T

Listening Task

Listening for Gist

(D)

Listening for Details

1. Moonlight Restaurant   2. Supreme Tour   3. 24 guests

4. By the window (They can overlook the night view)

5. Yes. Some of them don't eat beef.

6. Six dishes.

7. No. In a different room.

8. They can get a refill, but it's not free of charge.

9. There are two problems. One is that the dishes for Table One take too long to be served. The other is that the wrong dish is served. (The guests at Table One don't eat beef, but a beef dish is served.)

10. He pays with a voucher.

領
隊
篇

Exercise

1. (A)	2. (A)	3. (C)	4. (A)	5. (B)
6. (A)	7. (D)	8. (D)	9. (D)	10. (A)

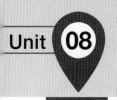

Unit 08 置入性自費行程

情境說明

　　出國旅行活動內容五花八門，然而並非每項都是老少咸宜的活動，因此有些行程或活動會被列為「自費行程」，未列入既定行程當中，而是由「領隊」或「當地導遊」在旅途中推薦或介紹「自費行程」詳細內容，如有團員們感興趣報名，行程空檔中將安排相關「自費活動」讓團員們體驗。然而，領隊在推薦「自費行程」是否有任何需要留意的地方呢？此時，會使用到的英語有哪些呢？一起來看看吧！

1. Discussion

Q1: Do you think it's important to have optional tours in a group tour? Why or why not?

Q2: As far as you know, what are some common optional tours? Give examples.

Q3: Have you ever signed up for any optional tours before? Share your experience with your partner.

2. Choose the best English/Chinese explanation for the English terms or idioms.

Answer	terms/idioms	English/Chinese explanation
	1. optional tours	(A) 置入性自費行程；額外可選擇的自費行程
	2. package tours	(B) 套裝行程
	3. far and foremost	(C) first of all; to begin with; at first; in the beginning
	4. set a deadline	(D) 訂下最後期限
	5. the first priority	(E) 第一優先（權）; the first choice/option
	6. pros and cons	(F) 贊成與反對

 Vocabulary & Phrases

1. default [dɪ`fɔlt] *n.* [U] not obeying a contract 違約

2. lower [`loɚ] *vt.* drop; reduce; relieve; decrease 放下；放低；減低

3. flexibility [ˌflɛksə`bɪlətɪ] *n.* [U] the possibility of being able to alter or be altered in a specific condition 彈性；可塑性

4. festive [`fɛstɪv] *adj.* merry; joyous; holiday-related 節慶的

5. trek [trɛk] *n.* [U], *vi.,vt.* hiking; traveling; moving slowly 艱苦跋涉；緩慢地行進

6. skydiving [`skaɪˌdaɪvɪŋ] *n.* [U] jumping out of a plane and then floating to the ground with a parachute 特技跳傘；空中跳傘

7. bungee jumping [`bʌndʒi `dʒʌmpɪŋ] *n.* [U] an activity in which a player jumps out off a high spot with one end fixed at a jumping-off point and the other end of an elastic rope tied to his/her body or ankles 高空彈跳

8. price-conscious [`praɪs`kɑnʃəs] *adj.* being aware of whether things are cheap or expensive 節省的；對價格有感的

9. helicopter [`hɛlɪkɑptɚ] *n.* [C] a kind of aircraft 直升機

10. scuba diving [`skubə ˌdaɪvɪŋ] *n.* [*U*] an activity in which a person uses special breathing equipment to swim under water　戴水肺的潛水

11. commission [kə`mɪʃən] *n.* [*U*] additional money; compensation; fee; payment　佣金

12. articulate [ɑr`tɪkjəlɪt] *adj.* clear; not chaotic　清楚的；清晰的

13. left-out [lɛft aʊt] *adj.* alienated; alone　被排擠的

14. rehearse [rɪ`hɝs] *vi.,vt.* repeat; train; practice　演練，練習，排練

p.232

領隊篇

▶ Listening for Gist

_____ 1. What is the topic of the presentation?

(A) A package tour.

(B) An optional tour.

(C) A group tour.

_____ 2. Who is the presentation for?

(A) Tour leaders.

(B) College students.

(C) Tour guides.

_____ 3. Which of the following is not the main point of the presentation?

(A) What is an optional tour?

(B) Why does an optional tour exist?

(C) How do you avoid customer complaints?

_____ 4. What does the speaker do?

(A) A teacher.

(B) A student.

(C) A tour leader.

_____ 5. How long is the presentation?

(A) Five minutes.

(B) Seven minutes.

(C) Ten minutes.

_____ 6. When are the listeners allowed to ask questions?

(A) At any time.

(B) In the Q&A session.

(C) They can't ask questions.

> Listening for Details

Write T for "True" or F for "False" for each statement.

_____ 1. An optional tour is the tour included in a "default" itinerary in a group tour.

_____ 2. Optional tours give people more opportunities to experience some activities they might not be able to have in their own home countries.

_____ 3. Optional tours can effectively lower the costs of package tours and attract more potential customers.

_____ 4. Optional tours can provide more flexibility for travel agencies and guests.

_____ 5. The reason why most guests don't like optional tours is that optional tours are usually associated with hidden costs.

_____ 6. Tour leaders and local tour guides usually find it easy to promote optional tours.

_____ 7. A tour leader should give a brief introduction to optional tours to the guests during an orientation.

_____ 8. To attract more guests to sign up, a tour leader should not talk much about the risks of the optional tours.

_____ 9. A considerate tour leader or tour guide also cares about the guests who don't sign up for optional tours and makes sure they are not ignored.

_____ 10. "Optional tour" is a new concept in the tourism industry.

Useful Language

1. as far as you know　就你所知（句型為 As far as sb. know(s)，常放句首）

2. sign up　報名；簽名

3. be associated with: have something with　與…有關

4. major in: specialize in　專長

5. divide ... into　把…分成

6. fill you in on　對某人提供有關事宜（片語為 to fill sb. in on sth.）

7. when it comes to V-ing/n.　當提到…時（常放句首）

8. sunrise volcano trekking　日出火山健行（(n.+) n.（名詞）+ V-ing（動名詞）= n.（名詞），比如 mountain climbing（登山）、bungee jumping（高空彈跳）、scuba diving（戴水肺的潛水）等）

9. to sum up: in a word; to conclude; in conclusion　總而言之（通常放句首）

領隊篇

 **Activity**

1. Which key points in the presentation do you think are important? Why?

2. Use your own words to talk about the pros and cons of optional tours?

3. In your opinion, to attract more guests to sign up, what should a tour leader or local tour guide do when he/she promotes optional tours?

 Extension Activity & Assignments

Step 1: Form a group of three. Select a travel destination for your group tour and discover some popular optional tours in a group tour like this.

Step 2: Each group has to discuss and decide which optional tour to promote.

Step 3: Each group has to think about how to promote this optional tour in English to the guests on a tour bus. Be sure to include the following info:

(1) The name of the optional tour

(2) The duration of the optional tour

(3) The procedures, details and the reminders of the optional tour

(4) The price of the optional tour

(5) The deadline for the registration

(6) What will non-participants do during the optional tour?

Step 4: Each member should say a few lines and work together to complete this introduction. Practice your introduction and rehearse with your group members as a group.

Step 5: Introduce your optional tour in front of another group without looking at the script. The listeners are expected to answer the following questions:

Q1: What is the name of the optional tour?

Q2: How long will the optional tour last?

Q3: What is the optional tour all about?

Q4: How much is the optional tour?

Q5: When is the deadline for the registration?

Q6: What will non-participants do during the optional tour?

Q7: Are you interested in this optional tour? Why or why not?

Step 6: Take turns.

領
隊
篇

Exercise

_____ 1. _____, the capital of the United States is Washington DC, not New York.

    (A) Aside from me   (B) As far as I know

    (C) As soon as possible   (D) Apart from me

_____ 2. A person's success is usually _____ with his/her attitude.

    (A) associated   (B) associating

    (C) appreciated   (D) appreciating

_____ 3. Gary _____ tourism in college and he would like to be a tour guide or tour leader after graduation.

    (A) turns into   (B) looks into

    (C) majors in   (D) tunes in

_____ 4. Most _____ consumers know how much things cost and compare prices of things in different stores.

(A) price-conscious　　　　(B) left-out

(C) literature-related　　　　(D) open-minded

_____ 5. A person works on _____ in his/her job. That is to say, s/he is paid based on the amount s/he sells in his/her job.

(A) committee　　　　(B) commitment

(C) commission　　　　(D) communication

_____ 6. The student actors and actresses are _____ each scene in preparation for next week's graduation performance.

(A) purchasing　(B) reminding　(C) punishing　(D) rehearsing

_____ 7. When it comes to _____ group tours, Taiwanese tour leaders usually know how to make it.

(A) promising　　　　(B) pronouncing

(C) prospering　　　　(D) promoting

_____ 8. In America, the celebration of Christmas makes all the cities and counties in _____ mood.

(A) festive　　　　(B) disgusting

(C) alienated　　　　(D) punctual

_____ 9. A tour leader's announcement should be _____, or the tour guests could not understand what s/he says.

(A) punctuate　(B) articulate　(C) partial　(D) artificial

_____ 10. I am not afraid to take a plane, but I am afraid of taking a _____ tour because it is small like a toy in my mind.

(A) volcano　　　　(B) helicopter

(C) glacier　　　　(D) scuba

Answers 🔒

Warm-up

2. Choose the best English/Chinese explanation for the English terms or idioms.

1. (A)　　2. (B)　　3. (C)　　4. (D)　　5. (E)　　6. (F)

Listening Task

Listening for Gist

1. (B)　　2. (B)　　3. (C)　　4. (C)　　5. (B)　　6. (B)

Listening for Details

1. F	2. T	3. T	4. T	5. T
6. F	7. T	8. F	9. T	10. F

Exercise

1. (B)	2. (A)	3. (C)	4. (A)	5. (C)
6. (D)	7. (D)	8. (A)	9. (B)	10. (B)

領
隊
篇

Unit 09 購物行程

情境說明

　　一般人出國都會採購伴手禮或紀念品以便回國贈送親友，為了滿足團員這方面的需求，團體行程中往往會安排購物站，一方面讓團員有足夠的時間購買當地特產，另一方面也能讓領隊或導遊因團員購物而賺取些許佣金。然而，「購物行程」卻也常讓領隊或導遊遭客訴，到底原因是什麼呢？在推薦「購物行程」時領隊該留意什麼呢？這個階段領隊需要用到的英語有哪些呢？一起來看看吧！

1. Discussion

Q1: Do you usually buy souvenirs or local specialties when you travel abroad? Why or why not?

Q2: Do you like "shopping tours" arranged by a travel agency when you travel with a group? Why or why not?

Q3: What should a tour leader do before and during a shopping tour?

2. Write down the following English terms or idioms in Chinese and/or English.

No.	English terms/idioms	Chinese and/or English explanation
1	local specialty	
2	shopping tours	
3	time-consuming	
4	a one-stop service	
5	How come?	
6.	in exchange for	
7	in other words	
8	in the mean time	
9	a win-win situation	
10	a three-win situation	
11	Honesty is the best policy.	
12	be skeptical about	
13	the local tax refund policy	
14	after-sale service	
15	keep track of time	
16	nutritional supplements	
17	Turkey	

 Vocabulary & Phrases

1. souvenir [`suvəˌnɪr] *n.* [C] keepsake; memento　紀念品（物）；伴手禮

2. shelf [ʃɛlf] *n.* [C] (*pl.* shelves) bracket　架子

3. refund [rɪ`fʌnd] *n.* [U] repaying; paying (money) back　退還，歸還（金錢）；退錢

4. replacement [rɪ`plesmənt] *n.* [*U*] substitute　代替，取代；更換；歸還替換品；換貨

5. effectively [ɪ`fɛktɪvlɪ] *adv.* usefully; efficiently　有效地

6. economical [ˌikə`nɑmɪk!] *adj.* frugal; saving; thrifty　經濟的；節約的；節儉的；經濟實惠的

7. competitive [kəm`pɛtətɪv] *adj.* competing; rival　競爭（性）的；有競爭力的

8. sponsorship [`spɑnsɚˌʃɪp] *n.* [*U*] help; support　資助；贊助

9. rental [`rɛnt!] *n.* [*U; C*] the act of renting a car, a scooter, or an apartment　租賃（業）；出租

10. tactfully [`tæktfəlɪ] *adv.* carefully; considerately; empathically　機智地；巧妙地；圓融地

11. incorporate [ɪn`kɔrpəˌret] *vi.,vt.* combine; join; merge　融入 (+in/into)；把…合併 (+with)

12. intrigued [ɪn`trigd] *adj.* interested; excited; fascinated　好奇的；被迷住了的

13. indigenous [ɪn`dɪdʒɪnəs] *adj.* local; native; original　土產的；本地的；與生俱有的

14. cosmetic [kɑz`mɛtɪk] *adj.* improving a person's appearance by using certain substances　化妝（用）的；化妝品的

15. stimulate [`stɪmjəˌlet] *vt.* encourage; push; motivate　刺激；激勵；促使 (+to/into)

16. fantastic [fæn`tæstɪk] *adj.* wonderful; great; amazing; awesome　很棒的

17. constructive [kən`strʌktɪv] *adj.* helpful; useful; creative　建設性的；有幫助的

領隊篇

Listening Task 掃描 p.236

❯ Listening for Gist

_____ 1. Where can you hear this passage?

(A) A TV station. (B) A radio station.

(C) A business meeting. (D) A presentation.

_____ 2. Who are the target listeners of this passage?

(A) People who love traveling.

(B) People who love traveling and shopping.

(C) Experienced tour leaders.

(C) Inexperienced travelers.

3. Tick the topics that are mentioned in this passage.

Answer	Number	Topic
	(A)	Why are there shopping tours?
	(B)	Can shopping tours bring more income for tour leaders or tour leaders?
	(C)	Why do most consumers dislike shopping tours?
	(D)	What should a tour leader do before a shopping tour?
	(E)	What should a tour leader do during a shopping tour?

❯ Listening for Details

Write T for "True" or F for "False" for each statement.

_____ 1. The name of the program is "KIIS."

_____ 2. The show is on from 8:00 a.m. to 10:00 a.m.

_____ 3. The show is playing after Chinese New Year.

_____ 4. The special guest is an inexperienced tour guide.

_____ 5. People can call into the show and ask questions.

_____ 6. "Shopping tours" makes shopping easier and less time-consuming for guests.

_____ 7. Generally speaking, people have to worry about the quality of products offered by the souvenir shops or factories from "shopping tours."

_____ 8. After a guest buys a product from "shopping tours," the product can't be returned or replaced if there is a problem.

_____ 9. Generally speaking, "shopping tours" can bring down the costs of a group tour or a package tour.

_____ 10. Generally speaking, a tour leader or a tour guide can earn some commissions if his/her guests purchase products at those shopping stops.

_____ 11. To earn more commissions, a tour leader should make his/her guests stay in the shopping stops as long as possible.

_____ 12. The special guest provides three strategies on how to promote "shopping tours" on a tour bus.

_____ 13. The host traveled to Turkey with the special guest last year.

領隊篇

Useful Language

1. keep you company: accompany you　陪（伴）你（不可用 accompany with you）

2. be around the corner: be approaching; to be coming　…近了

3. cut to the chase: talk about the most important thing instead of unimportant things　言歸正傳；回到主題；開門見山

4. do some shopping: do the shopping; shop; go shopping　買東西；購物

5. out of curiosity: because of curiosity; because of a strong desire to know about something　出於（自）好奇

6. Chances are that+ 子句 : (The) chances are (that) S + V; It is possible that S + V; It is likely that S +V...　可能

7. at a lower price: using less money　用較低的價格（介系詞 at 接價格 price）

8. make a profit: make profits; make money; earn money　獲利；賺錢

9. on a commission basis: on the basis of money; on the basis of profit　以佣金為基礎（出發點）（片語用法為 on a ＿＿＿＿ basis）

10. Most important of all: Most importantly　最重要的

11. focus on: concentrate on; be absorbed in; give much attention to one specific person, object or matter　集中；聚焦於

 **Activity**

Interview at least three of your fellow classmates by asking the following questions.

Q1: Would you like to sign up for a group tour with shopping tours? Why or why not?

Q2: If you were a tour leader, would you like to lead a group tour with shopping tours? Why or why not?

Q3: After listening to the passage, which about shopping tours surprises you? Why?

Q4: Among the suggestions for potential tour leaders on how to promote shopping tours before and during shopping tours, which suggestions do you find constructive? Why?

Q5: Among the three strategies for tour leaders to promote shopping tours on a tour bus, which strategy do you think is the most important? Why?

領
隊
篇

 Extension Activity & Assignments

> Pair Work

Task: Share info on one shopping stop in an orientation of a group tour with your guests.

Step 1: Work together with your partner and check common shopping tours of a group tour to Seoul or Busan in Korea. Select two shopping stops. Each of you will have to make an introduction to one shopping stop and its products respectively.

Step 2: Follow the suggestions from the listening and think about what you are going to say in an orientation in English. Work on your scripts.

Step 3: Practice your introduction with your partner.

Step 4: Perform both of the introductions in front of another pair without looking at your scripts. The listeners can ask questions about the shopping tours if they want. The listeners are expected to answer the following questions:

Q1: What products are promoted in the shopping tours?

Q2: What detailed information about the products do you know?

Q3: How do you like their performance?

Step 5: Take turns.

Exercise

_____ 1. When traveling abroad, tourists usually buy _____ or gifts, such as candies and candles.

(A) souvenirs　(B) pioneers　(C) helicopters　(D) sponsors

_____ 2. My name is Gary and I am your tour leader, so I will _____ from Monday to Sunday.

(A) keep you accompany　　(B) accompany with you

(C) accompany you　　　　(D) company with you

_____ 3. The winter break is just _____. What plan do you make for the break?

(A) up and down　　　　(B) around the corner

(C) far and foremost　　　(D) to and fro

_____ 4. Tourists are expected to visit souvenir shops and factories and _____ . (Choose one WRONG option.)

(A) do some shopping　　　(B) do the shopping

(C) do a lot of shopping　　(D) do many shopping

_____ 5. Professor Chang said in class, "_____ is the best policy, so no cheating in the mid-term exam."

(A) Loyalty　　　　　　　(B) Community

(C) Beauty　　　　　　　(D) Honesty

_____ 6. Any announcement a tour leader makes should be clear, or his/her guests might be _____ about his/her ability to express.

(A) typical　　(B) skeptical　(C) cosmetic　　(D) symmetric

_____ 7. _____ are that Gary has traveled around more than twenty countries, such as Iceland and Finland.

(A) Cosmetics　(B) Practices　(C) Critics　　(D) Chances

_____ 8. Kids tend to like touching things such as a plug just out of _____ .

(A) curiosity　(B) sincerity　(C) creativity　(D) dishonesty

_____ 9. Don't beat around the bush and just cut to the _____.

(A) chase　　(B) phase　　(C) phrase　　(D) rephrase

_____ 10. Claire would like to give Gary her dissertation in _____ for his thesis.

(A) responsibility　　　　(B) exchange

(C) respondent　　　　　(D) egoism

領
隊
篇

Answers 🔒

Warm-up

2. Write down the following English terms or idioms in Chinese and/or English.

No.	English terms/idioms	Chinese and/or English explanation
1	local specialty	something amazing in a specific place（地方）特產
2	shopping tours	購物行程
3	time-consuming	耗時的；曠日廢時的
4	a one-stop service	一站式服務
5	How come?	Why?
6.	in exchange for	以…換取，（以…作為）交換
7	in other words	that is to say 換句話說
8	in the mean time	at the same time 同時
9	a win-win situation	雙贏
10	a three-win situation	三贏
11	Honesty is the best policy.	誠實為上策；誠實為最佳政策
12	be skeptical about	doubt 對…懷疑
13	the local tax refund policy	當地退稅政策
14	after-sale service	售後服務
15	keep track of time	留意時間；掌控好時間
16	nutritional supplements	營養補給品
17	Turkey	土耳其（國名）

Listening Task

Listening for Gist

1. (B)   2. (B)

3.

Answer	Number	Topic
✓	(A)	Why are there shopping tours?
✓	(B)	Can shopping tours bring more income for tour leaders or tour leaders?
	(C)	Why do most consumers dislike shopping tours?
✓	(D)	What should a tour leader do before a shopping tour?
✓	(E)	What should a tour leader do during a shopping tour?

領隊篇

Listening for Details

1. F	2. T	3. F	4. F	5. T	6. T	7. F

8. F	9. T	10. T	11. F	12. T	13. T

Exercise

1. (A)	2. (C)	3. (B)	4. (D)	5. (D)
6. (B)	7. (D)	8. (A)	9. (A)	10. (B)

情境說明

　　一趟出國旅程要圓滿順利需要許多單位的配合，例如航空公司、旅行社、餐廳、遊覽車公司、購物站、領隊及導遊等等。任何一個環節出錯或有天災人禍，都可能對整趟旅程投入變數。當突發狀況發生時，身為領隊雖然不見得是該一肩扛起所有責任的人，但卻往往是身在第一線必須臨機應變、處理問題、安撫團員情緒的人。具備良好的危機應變能力的領隊，往往能妥適處理問題，將危機化為轉機。如領隊能在國外順利解決問題，除了能讓團員滿意，減少客訴外，也不會將問題帶回臺灣，造成旅行社同事們後續處理的困擾。帶團時常見的突發狀況有哪些呢？身為專業的領隊又該如何處理這些突發狀況呢？一起來看看吧！

1. Discussion

Q1: What emergencies might occur during an overseas tour? Did any of them happen to you before?

Q2: To deal with emergencies, what abilities should a tour leader have? Why?

2. Translate the given English words into Chinese and then circle them in the box.

English	Chinese											
		e	t	p	i	m	e	d	i	c	i	n	e
diarrhea		a	d	i	a	r	r	h	e	a	d	p	d
headache		e	h	c	a	d	a	e	h	h	a	o	f
stomachache		f	m	k	l	k	m	s	m	e	l	r	l
flu		t	e	p	y	g	r	e	l	l	a	c	u
treatment		s	t	o	m	a	c	h	a	c	h	e	i
medicine		r	n	c	u	l	e	t	t	f	e	k	r
allergy		d	i	k	c	l	d	u	a	l	r	e	r
fracture		e	t	e	a	g	r	o	a	r	g	t	h
pickpocket		a	p	t	r	e	a	t	m	e	n	t	e

Vocabulary & Phrases

1. gigantic [dʒaɪˋgæntɪk] *adj.* huge; vast; enormous　巨大的

2. bas-relief [ˋbæsrɪˌlif] *n.* [C] an artistic sculpture in which the shapes are cut from the surrounding stone to make them slightly raised from the flat surface　浮雕

3. diarrhea [ˌdaɪəˋriə] *n.* [U] an illness in which one's waste matter is so watery that it is excreted even more frequently than normal　腹瀉；拉肚子

4. empathy [ˋɛmpəθɪ] *n.* [U] the ability to understand someone else's feelings, experiences, situations, etc.　同理心

5. assembly point [əˋsɛmblɪ pɔɪnt] *n.* [U] a given place for a group of people to gather　集合地點

6. fork road [fɔrk rod] *n.* [C] either of two parts divided by a road　岔路

7. announcement [ə`naʊnsmənt] *n*. [U; C] something that somebody says publicly or information about something that somebody gives officially　通知；宣布；廣播

8. request [rɪ`kwɛst] *vt*. beg; coax; file; demand; ask for something　要求，請求

9. compensation [ˌkɑmpən`seʃən] *n*. [U] repayment; reimbursement; money paid to someone in exchange for something lost or damaged　補償（金）

10. entitle [ɪn`taɪt!] *vt*. empower; designate; authorize; enable; give someone the right to do something　給…權利（資格）（用法為 be entitled to）；有權利（資格）

11. file [faɪl] *vi*. request; ask for something　提出（申請等）

12. necessity [nə`sɛsətɪ] *n*. [C] something that people need, especially in daily life　必需品 (+of/for)

13. allergic [ə`lɝdʒɪk] *adj*. (over) sensitive　（對…）過敏的（用法為 be allergic to）

14. treatment [`tritmənt] *n*. [U; C] the use of drugs for curing one of an illness　治療

15. reimbursement [ˌriɪm`bɝsmənt] *n*. [U] compensation; the money paid back to someone who has spent or lost it earlier　退款；補償；賠償；核銷費用

16. outpatient [`aʊtˌpeʃənt] *n*. [C] someone who is treated in a hospital but does not stay overnight there　門診病人

17. front desk [frʌnt dɛsk] *n*. [C] a counter near the gate of a hotel or an office building　服務臺

18. traffic congestion [`træfɪk kən`dʒɛstʃən] *n*. [U] a traffic condition in which roads are crowded with vehicles and the moving speed is slow, especially in the rush hour　塞車

領隊篇

Listening Task

> Listening for Gist   p.241~243

Listen to the first part of each conversation and match each of them with its problem.

Answer	Part	Possible Problem
	1	(A) The flight is delayed.
	2	(B) A guest is lost.
	3	(C) A guest doesn't feel well.
	4	(D) Help a guest report missing luggage

> Listening for Details   p.243~250

Listen to each complete passage and write down how the tour leader handles each problem.

No.	Action Taken	Possible Action
(1) Problem 1		(A) Express empathy (B) Calm down the guest
(2) Problem 2		(C) Find out more details on the problem (D) Diagnose the problem
(3) Problem 3		(E) Make a suggestion (F) Seek further assistance & Take action
(4) Problem 4		(G) Report the progress

Useful Language

1. blow sb. away: surprise sb.; make sb. surprised　震驚，驚訝，驚喜

2. must have + pp.　過去必定發生…（是對於過去肯定推測的用法）

3. relate to: be related to; be associated with　涉及；與…相關；與…有關

4. stay + adj.　保持…(keep + adj.)：stay calm　保持冷靜；stay put　留在原地

5. That's nice of you.　你人真好（形容人的特質用 of）

6. branch office　分公司

7. National Health Insurance Bureau　衛生福利部中央健康保險署

8. What a relief!　鬆了一口氣，終於解脫了（用法：What a + n.!，如：What a shame! 真丟臉；真倒楣）

Activity

1. Does the tour leader in Listening 1 handle the problem properly? Why or why not? If you were the tour leader, what would you do?

2. Does the tour leader in Listening 2 handle the problem properly? Why or why not? If you were the tour leader, what would you do?

3. Does the tour leader in Listening 3 handle the problem properly? Why or why not? If you were the tour leader, what would you do?

4. Does the tour leader in Listening 4 handle the problem properly? Why or why not? If you were the tour leader, what would you do?

5. Form a group of 4 or 5 and discuss some general strategies for handling an emergency as a tour leader.

Step 1

Step 2

Step 3

 Extension Activity & Assignments

❯ Pair Work

Create a dialog with your partner and handle one of the following problems as a tour leader. Be sure to use the strategies to take care of each problem effectively.

1. One guest loses his boarding pass after he clears immigration in the airport.

2. One guest cannot find his passport after purchasing some products from duty-free shops in the city center. There are still two days left for this trip.

3. On the way to your next tourist attraction, the tour bus you are taking has a breakdown and it doesn't seem to work properly any time soon.

4. On the way to your next scenic spot, there is traffic congestion. Your guests on the tour bus are getting more impatient. There is a chance that you might not be able to make it to the evening show after you visit this scenic spot.

5. After checking-in at a hotel, one guest calls you and complains about the bad smell inside the room. He wants to move to another room. However, it's all booked out in the hotel tonight after you check with the hotel staff.

Exercise

_____ 1. The dinner was so spicy that I had _____ and it almost killed me.

(A) diarrhea　　(B) orchestra　(C) dichotomy　(D) abracadabra

_____ 2. Some people are _____ to air pollution in Taiwan, especially in the winter.

(A) mechanic　(B) lyric　　(C) magic　　(D) allergic

_____ 3. Many people were late for the meeting because of traffic _____ .

(A) conjunction　　　　(B) congestion

(C) composition　　　　(D) contribution

_____ 4. A good tour leader must have _____ with his/her guests' problems such as illness.

(A) empathy　　　　　(B) bibliotherapy

(C) philosophy　　　　(D) therapy

_____ 5. The bas-reliefs on the walls of the exhibition room are really fantastic and they do _____ me _____ .

(A) pick ... up　　　　(B) blow ... away

(C) let ... out　　　　(D) single ... out

_____ 6. After one hour, remember to come back to this _____ point.

(A) resemble　(B) shamble　(C) assembly　(D) humbly

_____ 7. Whenever you get lost in this area, remember to stay calm and stay _____ .

(A) cut　　　(B) hut　　　(C) nut　　　(D) put

領隊篇

_____ 8. As long as the flight is delayed for more than four hours, we can _____ compensation.

(A) request   (B) guest   (C) banquet   (D) conquest

_____ 9. A(n) _____, not a refund, is the act of paying back money to someone who has spent beforehand or lost earlier.

(A) remembrance   (B) reimbursement

(C) embracement   (D) enforcement

_____ 10. Morrie has tried many _____ for his ALS (Amyotrophic Lateral Sclerosis).

(A) enhancements   (B) basements

(C) embarrassments   (D) treatments

Answers 🔐

Warm-up

2. Translate the given English words into Chinese and then circle them in the box.

English	Chinese	e	t	p	i	m	e	d	i	c	i	n	e
diarrhea	腹瀉	a	d	i	a	r	r	h	e	a	d	p	d
headache	頭痛	e	h	c	a	d	a	e	h	h	a	o	f
stomachache	胃痛	f	m	k	l	k	m	s	m	e	l	r	l
flu	流感	t	e	p	y	g	r	e	l	l	a	c	u
treatment	治療	s	t	o	m	a	c	h	a	c	h	e	i
medicine	藥	r	n	c	u	l	e	t	t	f	e	k	r
allergy	過敏	d	i	k	c	l	d	u	a	l	r	e	r
fracture	骨折	e	t	e	a	g	r	o	a	r	g	t	h
pickpocket	扒手	a	p	t	r	e	a	t	m	e	n	t	e

領隊篇

Listening Task

Listening for Gist

1. (B)　　　　2. (A)　　　　3. (D)　　　　4. (C)

Listening for Details

(1) (A)(B)(C)(E)(F)(G)　(2) (A)(C)(E)(F)(G)　(3) (A)(B)(C)(E)(F)　(4) (C)(E)

Exercise

1. (A)　　　2. (D)　　　3. (B)　　　4. (A)　　　5. (B)

6. (C)　　　7. (D)　　　8. (A)　　　9. (B)　　　10. (D)

導遊篇

PART 03

GATES 6-9

Located in New Taipei City, Jiufen used to be the center of gold-mining in Taiwan. This small village is next to the mountains, and faces the ocean. During the early years of the Qing Dynasty, the isolated village housed nine families. A lack of transportation gave the residents there a hard time reaching an outside market for purchasing daily supplies. Therefore, whenever one of the nine families went to the market for grocery shopping, "nine servings or nine pieces" was requested. In this way, all the nine families could have sufficient daily supplies. This is how Jiufen, literally meaning "nine pieces" in Mandarin, became the name of the village.

In 1890, some workmen discovered flakes of gold while constructing the new Taipei-Keelung railway. In 1893, a rich placer deposit was discovered in the hills of Jiufen, and then several kilograms of gold was produced a day over there. The gold rush resulted in Jiufen's rapid development and the flourish reached a peak during the Japanese Colonial Era.

During World War II, the town housed a Japanese prisoner of war camp where Allied soldiers captured in Singapore (mainly British) were forced to work in the gold mines. The town began to wane when the gold mining activities declined after World War II. The mine was shut off in 1971 and Jiufen was mostly forgotten ever since then.

Jiufen is the setting of a Taiwanese film titled "A City of Sadness" by Taiwanese director Hou Hsiao-hsien. "A City of Sadness" was the first film to discuss the politically controversial "February 28 Incident of 1947," and it won the Golden Lion Award at the 1989 Venice Film Festival. Jiufen, where the film was set, revived due to the film's popularity. Therefore, from the beginning of the 1990s, Jiufen experienced a tourist boom and that has shaped the town into an attraction easily accessible from Taipei City as a nice day trip destination. In 2001, Jiufen also became popular due to its resemblance to the downtown in the Japanese anime movie "Spirited Away" by Studio Ghibli. Many Japanese travel magazines and guide books recommended Jiufen and Jiufen has become a must-visit place among Japanese tourists. However, Miyazaki himself denied that Jiufen was the city in the movie.

The Jiufen Old Street usually refers to the areas of Shuqi Road and Jishan Street. Shuqi Road was once called Baojia Road and it was used by the troops during the Qing Dynasty for military purposes. It was a stone-paved road and it used to be the major gateway for the local residents to reach the port for their living supplies. Now Shuqi Road is filled with a variety of tea houses, coffee shops, lodgings, and craft stores.

Jishan Street was the major business street in Jiufen where grocery stores, restaurants and entertainment places were located. Due to the frequent rains in Jiufen, the stores on the street built the rain canopy outside, which formed a faint alley, and it is also known as "Dark Alley." Jishan Street is still the liveliest street now with lots of local snacks, such as Glutinous Rice Cake, Taro Glutinous Rice Cake, Hongzao Meatball, and cold and hot Taro Rice Balls. The street is filled with delicious snacks. Coming to Shuqi Road, you may spend time drinking a couple of good tea in a tea house while enjoying the scenery. As it is very crowded on weekends, to beat the crowd, it's suggested to come here on weekdays if you want to relax and truly enjoy some serenity.

導遊篇

Shengping Theater was the first theater in northern Taiwan, and also the biggest theater during the Japanese Colonial Era. The history of Shengping Theater can be traced back to 1916 when it was open thanks to the land provided by Yan, Yun-Nian and the funds raised by the government. After it collapsed in 1927, the theater was rebuilt at the present site in 1934. It was renamed to Shengping Theater after Taiwan's restoration. The 1930s was the golden age of Jiufen because a lot of people came to Jiufen for the gold mine. As a result, Shengping Theater became the most important entertainment spot for the gold diggers. In 1951, the theater was converted into reinforced concrete construction. The theater was almost destroyed by the typhoon and was closed in 1986. In 2011, the theater was renovated and reopened to the public.

Jiufen Taro Ball is a symbolic local snack. It was developed by Madam Tsai in the 1940s by accident. Originally, Madam Tsai made taro balls only for her family. Due to rave reviews and positive feedback, she started to sell taro balls in her grocery store. The original purpose of making the taro balls was to go with the shaved ice in summer or hot soup in winter. Although now Jiufen Taro Balls can be found easily all over Taiwan, they still do not have exactly the same flavor and texture as found in Jiufen.

There are two super famous Yuyuan shops in the Jiufen Old Street. The first one is Grandma Lai's Yuyuan. It occupies 3 full shops in the old street: one is for making and selling the taro balls while the other two shops are for diners to eat their purchased taro balls. Ah Gan Yi Yuyuan is another famous shop that sells taro balls. If you are at the intersection of Jishan Street and Shuqi Road, just walk up in the direction of Jiufen elementary school, and eventually you'll find Ah Gan Yi Yuyuan on your right. What's so special about Ah Gan Yee Yuyuan? You should come here because it has huge windows with great views of the mountains and the ocean.

At the end of Jishan Street, you can see Jiufen Teahouse. Jiufen Teahouse was once a meeting place for many great Taiwanese writers and artists after it was first open. You can choose your favorite tea and tea snacks from the menu and sit there for as long as you like. Just take a break and wander around to look at the paintings and other wonderful artwork by local artists. There is also a gallery on the lower level with more beautiful ceramics. Don't miss out on them.

There are many small alleys connecting Jishan Street and Shuqi Road in order to save time for the local residents to walk from one street to another. These small alleys in the front or the back of the house are named "Penetrating House Alley." They are so unique because they are so narrow that they can only accommodate one person. What is more interesting is that you may be walking through someone's living room or gate without even noticing it.

Because of the humid and rainy climate, the town residents built houses with a tilted roof to facilitate drainage. The roof has been painted with a layer of asphalt which formed a unique scene of the black roofed Jiufen mountain village. The correct name of the Jiufen black roof is "Black Oil Felt Roof." The oil felt is not only water and wind resistant, but also durable, low-cost, and easy to maintain.

Make sure you visit Jiufen in good physical condition since the stairways can be very steep. Do not forget to wear a good pair of running shoes because walking is going to be the main mode of transportation for you to explore Jiufen and get around. Finally, you might want to bring your umbrella as it could also rain a lot.

導
遊
篇

Geographically, Yehliu is situated in northern Taiwan between Jinshan and Wanli. The total distance measured from the entrance of the Yehliu Geopark to the end of the cape is about 1.7 km; the widest area in between is shorter than 300 m. Yehlieu is famous for its varieties of landscapes and in 1964 was appointed as a scenic area.

There are three different explanations regarding the name of "Yehliu:" 1. An abbreviation of a Spanish word; 2. A term translated from the Pinpu language; 3. A term describing the situation of local residents to steal the rice from the rice traders during transportation. Rice traders often mentioned "the rice was stolen by the savages" (whereas "steal" and "savage" are pronounced similar to Yeh (savage) and liu (steal) in Taiwanese).

Yehliu Geopark is divided into three areas, where areas 1 and 2 are tourists' "must-see" areas. The first area contains mushroom rocks, ginger rocks and candlestick-shaped rocks. We may learn the development process of mushroom rocks in area 1, as well as witness the appearance of ginger rocks and potholes. On top of that, the famous candlestick-shaped rocks and the ice cream rock are presented in this area too.

The second area is similar to the first one, where the mushroom rock and the ginger rock are the main focuses, but they are fewer in numbers. You may see Queen's Head Rock, Dragon's Head Rock, and Gorilla Rock located in this area. Since the area is near the coast, rocks that develop into four different kinds of formations can be seen in this area: Elephant Rock, Fairy's Shoe, Earth Rock and Peanut Rock.

The third area is the wave-cut platform located on the other side of Yehliu. This area is much narrower than the second area; one side of the platform is closely adjacent to steep cliffs while down below the other side is a scene of torrent waves. Several rocks of sea erosion can be seen in this area, including the 24-Filial Piety Rock, Pearl Rock and Marine Bird Rock. The third area also includes the major ecology reserve of Yehliu Geopark. The place is suitable for geological study and field research.

Cuesta (Monocline Structure)

Cuesta refers to a kind of ridge featuring a stiff slope on one side and a gentle slope on the other side. It was uplifted by the orogenic movement and then collapsed by weathering and erosion. Each year, the place is under the influences of Northeast monsoon and wave erosion for over a six-month period. Because of differential erosion, many small monoclines are exposed on the coastal area as well as a huge monocline which can be viewed from the Tourist Center.

Joints

During the formation process of sea cape, the rock layer is extruded by external force that causes the development of cracks. These cracks are called joints. Joints can be developed in various sizes; for example, they can be as small as the bean curd rocks (tofu rocks) or as large as the sea grooves. Some of them even can be served as brides that connect both sides of the land.

Mushroom Rocks

Here you can see about 180 rocks in the shape of mushroom. The mushroom rocks can be divided into three types according to the different appearances on the head and neck of the rock: "thick-neck rock," "thin-neck rock," and "neckless rock." Among them, the famous Queen's Head Rock now becomes the landmark of Yehliu Geology Park. Originally these mushroom rocks had gone through sea erosion and, as time went by, the hard concretion came out because of the impact of wind, sun, rain, sea-water and strong northeast monsoon.

The so called "Queen's Head" is in fact a mushroom rock. It is formed due to the differential erosion caused by seawater during earth crust movement. When comparing its height with the crust's rising rate, it is assessed that the

導
遊
篇

age of the rock is about 4,000 years old. It gets the title because its shape was formed after the top of the rock fell apart in 1962. From some angle, it looks like the side face of the ancient Egyptian queen Nefertiti or England's Queen Elizabeth I. However, it is expected to be broken in the next few years.

Potholes

Yehliu has a large area with different types of potholes. These potholes appear on the wave-cut platform and have a strong link with salt weathering. The potholes are continuously eroded and cut by the stones carried by the waves. Over time, these potholes become larger and deeper.

Candlestick-shaped Rocks

Candlestick-shaped rocks were carved by sea erosion. After the softer surface had been removed, the ball-like concretion stood out in the shape of a candlewick. Meanwhile, sea erosion had not only created a circular trench on the top but also eroded downward to shape a cone candlestick.

Ginger Rocks

Ginger rocks are distributed on a particular layer of the rock formations of Yehliu. Ginger rocks are similar to mushroom rocks in structure, but have a different shape. After the softer surface had been washed away as a result of long period sea erosion, the hard calcium concretion of rock was further squeezed by earth movement to take the shape of gingers. The Fairy's Shoe is the most famous among them. You would almost believe that it was left in a hurry by a fairy.

Camel Rock

When looking toward the South East of Yehliu Geopark, you may notice a strange rock standing beside the harbor. The rock looks like a camel resting with its face looking toward Yehliu, and it's called Camel Rock. By the way, it also looks like the figure of a snail.

Princess' Head Rock

There is a Successor of The Queen's Head- Princess' Head in the park. The successor is chosen to distract the attention of the Queen's Head and prevent the Queen's Head from accelerating its damage resulting from tourists' touch.

Ice Cream Rock

The Ice Cream Rock is formed as a result of differential erosion. When looking at it with face toward the hill, its shape is like the yummy ice cream people love to eat in summer days.

Fried Drumstick-shaped Rocks

The shape of the ginger rock is like a fried drumstick.

Fossils

There are plenty of fossils in the rock bedding, including the sea urchin fossil, which belongs to the species of "sand dollar" sea urchins from the early Miocene era. Moreover, the traces of early creature lives were reserved in the sedimentary rocks, which are called "trace fossils."

導
遊
篇

Japanese Geisha

The shape of the mushroom rock is like the figure of an elegant, attractive Japanese geisha.

Carp Rock and Parrot Rock

A rock in a shape of the eyes of the fish is situated on the left rear side of the candlestick-shaped rock; therefore people call it Carp Rock. On the hill opposite to the Carp Rock, a rock in the shape of a parrot lying down toward the sea can be seen.

Taiwan Rock

The Taiwan Rock stands right behind the first sea groove bridge, and its shape is similar to Taiwan. You may notice the pattern in the center of the rock is where the real Central Mountain Range of Taiwan is located.

Statue of Mr. Lin Tien-chen

In March 1964, when Mr. Lin tried to help a college student who visited Yehliu and fell into the sea. Unfortunately, both Mr. Lin and the student lost their lives. Statue of Mr. Lin Tien-chen is a reminder of his brave actions.

Sea Cave

As the sea waves continue to hit on rocks along the coast, the rocks on the coast will be worn away and a sea cave will be formed. "Lover's Cave" is one of the biggest sea caves as developed in the case.

Sea Groove

Sea groove is formed as the surface of joint is eroded by sea waves while the joint is developed in a position vertical to the cape. The small bridges set up in the park are meant to connect two lands where sea grooves are formed below.

Elephant Rock

The Elephant Rock is the lime concretion while being formed under the influences of differential erosion. Legend says that the fairy forgot to bring the elephant back to the heaven. Finally, the elephant stood there waiting to be taken home and rejected to go ashore.

Fairy's Shoe

Legend has it that this shoe was left accidently by a fairy that came down to earth. The Fairy's Shoe belongs to ginger rock, and is formed due to seawater erosion on rock layer that contains rocks of different hardness, along with the impact caused by stratum extrusion.

Peanut Rock

The Peanut Rock is situated on the left hand side of the Fairy's Shoe. Concretion with special shape is eroded by seawater and rises above sea level. It was formed in a figure similar to a peanut and thus it's called the Peanut Rock.

Pearl Rock

As the Pearl Rock situated below the Fairy's Shoe is a beautifully formed globe concretion, it's also called the Earth Rock.

Chessboard Rocks (Bean curd rocks or tofu rocks)

In the coastal area between the Fairy's Shoe and the lighthouse lies complete Chessboard Rocks. Such rocks were pressed and squeezed as a result of earth crust movement and weathering to show chessboard-like joints. After long-term sea erosion, these cracks form small lines of pattern, just like pieces of delicious tofu.

導遊篇

Dragon's Head Rock

A dragon's head rock is a unique-formed mushroom rock, with one side featuring an image of a dragon's head.

Gorilla Rock

This rock is formed in the shape of a giant gorilla squatting down to worship the dragon king.

Pineapple Bun

On the back of the Gorilla Rock, there stands a particular shape of concretion near the sea. The joints resemble the texture of a pineapple bun.

 Useful Vocabulary and Phrases

1. literally [ˈlɪtərəlɪ] *adv.* using the real or original meaning of a word or phrase 照字面地

2. flake [flek] *n.* [C] a small, thin piece of something 薄片

3. placer [ˈplæsɚ] *n.* [C] deposit of earth, sand, containing valuable mineral in particles, especially by the side of a river [礦物學]（含金）砂礦

4. asphalt [ˈæsfælt] *n.* [U] a black, sticky substance, that forms a strong surface when it becomes hard 瀝青；柏油

5. differential erosion [ˌdɪfəˈrɛnʃəl ɪˈroʒən] *n.* [U] it occurs at irregular or varying rates, caused by the differences in the resistance and hardness of surface materials [地質學] 差異侵蝕

6. crustal movement [ˈkrʌst! ˈmuvmənt] *n.* [U] the moving of earth's crust [地質學] 地殼運動

7. texture [ˈtɛkstʃɚ] *n*. [U] mouthfeel　口感

8. stratum extrusion [ˈstrætəm ɪkˈstruʒən] *n*. [U] the process of forming a layer of rock by forcing or pushing it out　地層擠壓

9. candlewick [ˈkændəlˌwɪk] *n*. [C] a piece of string in the center of a candle 燭心

10. filial piety [ˈfɪliəl ˈpaɪətɪ] *n*. [U] translation of Chinese Hsiao; affectionate loyalty and respect, esp. to parents　孝順

Exercises

_____ 1. Founded during the Qing Dynasty, this small town was a relatively isolated village until the discovery of _____.

(A) copper　　(B) iron　　(C) coal　　(D) gold

_____ 2. The _____ was the first cinema in Taiwan, opened in 1914 to provide some entertainment for the miners in Jiufen and Jinguashi.

(A) Shengping Theater　　　(B) Neiwan Theater

(C) National Theater　　　(D) Shilin Theater

_____ 3. Jiufen's _____ is said to be the most famous, which is a traditional Taiwanese cuisine dessert.

(A) sweet potato balls　　　(B) oyster omelet

(C) taro ball　　　(D) bubble tea

_____ 4. The coastal town of _____ is said to be the inspiration for the Miyazaki classic Spirited Away. However, Miyazaki himself denied that it was the city of the movie.

(A) Jinguashi　　(B) Jiufen　　(C) Shifen　　(D) Yehliu

導遊篇

_____ 5. Jishan Street was the major business street in Jiufen, which is known for a _____.

(A) long alley   (B) narrow alley

(C) small alley   (D) dark alley

_____ 6. Yehliu, situated in northern Taiwan between Jinshan and Wanli, is a famous _____.

(A) waterpark   (B) geopark

(C) theme park   (D) amusement park

_____ 7. Here you can see about 180 rocks in the shape of a(n) _____. Among them, the famous Queen's Head now becomes the landmark of Yehliu Geology Park.

(A) ginger   (B) candle   (C) mushroom   (D) ice cream

_____ 8. There are plenty of fossils in the rock bedding. These fossils are _____.

(A) sea stars   (B) sea urchins

(C) sea cucumbers   (D) seahorses

_____ 9. The Fairy's Shoe belongs to _____.

(A) mushroom rock   (B) potholes

(C) ginger rocks   (D) chessboard rocks

_____ 10. The stones carried by the waves continuously erode and cut the rocks, and over time these rocks become larger and deeper. These rocks are _____.

(A) ice cream rocks   (B) elephant rocks

(C) ginger rocks   (D) potholes

Answers

1. (D)   2. (A)   3. (C)   4. (B)   5. (D)   6. (B)   7. (C)   8. (B)   9. (C)   10. (D)

Shilin Night Market ✈

Shilin Night Market is located in Shilin District, Taipei, the former place of residence of Ketagalan of Pingpu tribe. It is regarded as one of the largest and most popular night markets, especially when it comes to street food. Shihlin Night Market lies next to metro Jiantan Station. Shilin Market, opened in 1913, has been designated a historic monument by the city government. With the influx of customers, many new businesses and food vendors began to establish themselves in the area and Shilin Night Market was born.

Due to ventilation, sanitation, public safety, and fire hazard concerns, the old Shilin Market structure was demolished in October of 2002 by the Taipei City Government and the food vendors formerly based within the old structure were relocated to a new temporary structure a few hundred meters away, next to the metro Jiantan Station. The renovated site was re-opened in December of 2011. The new Shilin Market was rebuilt into a building with two floors above ground and three floors below ground. The food court was moved back to the ground floor of the new Shilin Market.

Shilin Night Market encompasses two distinct sections. One section centers on the Shilin Market building on Jihe Road with most of the food vendors and small restaurants and surrounding shops selling non-food items. The other section centers on Yangming Movie Theater and it's a full-blown snack market covering a few blocks and extending in all directions to as far as Wen Lin, Ji He, Da Dong and Da Nan roads. The areas are home to some of the best local delicacies, such as Shilin big sausages and Shanghai pan-fried buns. Also, people will find shops or stalls selling non-food items, such as clothing, smartphone accessories, souvenirs, toys, household goods, and games. Shilin

導
遊
篇

Night Market has become a renowned place for great foods. Because the night market is close to many schools, students are the main customer group. Goods are sold at relatively low prices as compared to regular stores.

In recent years, freshly cut fruits have become popular at the Shilin Night Market, with some vendors suspected of overcharging their customers. To avoid misunderstandings, the city government asked the fruit vendors to provide four pieces of transparent information before a purchase decision by a customer. First, "How much for each fruit?" Secondly, WEIGH the chosen fruit. Thirdly, PAY the total price. Finally, OKAY to cut the fruit now. These steps must be explicitly displayed in both Chinese and English. If a fruit vendor cuts the fruits before indicating the total price or seeking a confirmation from a customer, the vendor will be fined.

Mom and Pop stalls at Taiwanese night markets have garnered some international attention as most recently the Michelin Guide Taipei 2019 awarded 24 night market stalls the Bib Gourmand distinction, an honor that signifies "good quality, good value cooking" for eateries offering a three course meal with the total price not exceeding NT$1,300. Among the 24 stalls, there are three in Shilin Night Market, including Hai You Pork Ribs Soup, Chung Chia Sheng Jian Bao, and Good Friend Cold Noodles of Shilin Night Market.

Hai You Pork Ribs Soup is very famous for its Chinese medicinal ribs. As awarded as a Michelin Bib Gourmand shop, Hai You Pork Ribs Soup has been in operations for over 45 years. It is known for its herbal style Pork Rib and Chicken Drumstick Soup, cooked by using a secret recipe with over 15 herbs. Hai You adjusts its medicinal herbs as seasons change. The winter is an especially good time for a bowl of steaming hot ribs. The soups at Hai You are simmered for hours with Chinese herbs considered to be medicinal. Definitely don't miss out on the herbal soups when you enjoy their famous herbal-stewed pork ribs.

With Shanghainese origins, one of the famous stalls at Shilin is Chung Chia Shanghai Sheng Jian Bao (or Shanghai pan-fried pork buns). From a distance, you can see a long line of customers waiting for famous Sheng Jian Bao. As some patiently waiting customers like to note, "You cannot say you have really been to Shilin Night Market until you have Sheng Jian Bao." These delicacies come with either a vegetable filling of cabbage or a meat filling of pork. The smell of the bun's crispy bottoms and cabbage or pork-filled insides permeates Shilin Night Market, enticing not only locals already familiar with the scent, but also visitors who are immediately lured. But be careful when biting a freshly-cooked bun, because you don't want to get burned by the hot juice inside.

"Good Friend Cold Noodles" used to be a pharmacy and sell cold noodles on the side. Due to its popular demand, it decided to shut down the pharmacy and has focused on its noodle business. As a simple-looking dish, the cold noodles of Good Friend are dressed in a thick, rich sesame sauce and julienned cucumbers. This dish is so ubiquitous that even local convenience stores sell it. Good Friend offers a true, authentic version of the staple with high-quality ingredients. Be sure to taste their egg drop miso soup as well.

導遊篇

Taiwanese fried chicken shop "Hot Star Large Fried Chicken" is a homegrown brand in Shilin Night Market. The main feature is that its fried chicken is ridiculously huge – measuring up to 30cm long, bigger than a palm, and almost the size of a face. The outside is coated evenly with batter. This huge piece of chicken is deep fried till it is golden brown and the meat is tender and juicy. It is then sprinkled with flavoring powder (a mixture of white pepper and five spices) and red pepper powder before being served. The local Hot Star store will not cut the meat, even if its customers request it.

Ningxia Night Market

Ningxia Road runs about 300 meters. There are stalls along the street side and mid-street, and beyond the street side are the shop façades. Ningxia Night Market has over 200 stands, and the vast majority sells foods. With more than 60 years of history, some vendors have been in operation in the same spot for 30 to 40 years, and even have passed the family torch to the next generation. Ningxia Night Market used to sell garments and accessories, but with the emergence of large department stores, traditional snack food vendors quickly replaced the garment stores, resulting in the Ningxia Night Market we have today.

To heighten the quality of the visitor's shopping experience, the city government has established a pedestrian-only venue and worked closely with the vendors to introduce a grease interceptor that could keep grease from entering the sewage system, thus eliminating hygiene-related problems. In 2008, another public-health program was launched to promote the use of eco-friendly chopsticks. In October of 2014, Ningxia Night Market became the first in Taiwan to ban smoking, and violators would be subject to a fine upwards of NT$10,000. In 2019, the Environmental Protection Administration convened a press conference to launch an anti-plastic campaign calling for people to reduce plastic consumption in their daily lives. Besides, in recent years, many businesses have voluntarily reduced their plastic usage. For example, nearly all of the vendors at Taipei's Ningxia Night Market have switched to using eco-friendly tableware. As a result, their waste removal fee has fallen from NT$300,000 10 years ago to NT$150,000 today. When you sit down at Ningxia Night Market, the tableware you use is made of galvanized iron, porcelain, or glass. Because of all the environmentally-friendly measures above, without doubt, Ningxia Night Market can be proud enough to declare itself to be the city's most "eco-friendly night market."

To promote Ningxia Night Market and fulfilling people's wish of tasting all the Taiwanese street foods at once, vendors came out the idea to hold a Taiwanese banquet (Pan-toh), where you can enjoy more than 20 kinds of vendors' cuisines. As all of the vendors sell cuisines for more than 50 years, and all the total age combined is more than 1000 years, that's how it got the name "Chien Sui Feast" (Millennium Feast; a thousand years old banquet). Due to its popular demand, the night market association reminds visitors to make a reservation in advance.

In 2019, American actor Will Smith and director Ang Lee came to Taiwan to promote the new film "Gemini Man," They toured Ningxia Night Market and sampled a number of popular Taiwanese dishes. During his visit to the night market, Smith tried sesame oil chicken and watermelon milk. Smith then tried some of the game stalls, including a BB gun balloon game, where he shot with great accuracy, wowing the crowd with every direct hit.

The owners of food stalls and restaurants in and around the night market have begun offering services in English, Japanese, Korean and French, and have begun cooperating with travel Web site Klook to promote their businesses. All signs at the night market are in at least two languages — Chinese and English. The owners of some stalls can speak each language a little, which makes them more approachable for foreigners. The vendors also conscientiously post calorie counts for their offerings. Ningxia Night Market was selected as the "Favorite Night Market in Taipei" in the 2015 Taipei Night Market Festival. In 2019, Ningxia Night Market was also the first night market in Taipei to include electronic payment methods, including Easy Card.

Ningxia Night Market has a good variety of great cuisines to choose from, being home to two Bib Gourmand recipients and one honorable mention. Liu Yu Zi's fried taro balls come from a little food stall in Ningxia Night Market.

導
遊
篇

If it weren't for the long line, you probably wouldn't even know that these bite-sized snacks made it on the Michelin Bib Gourmand list too. You know a place is good when all the locals swear that the long line is worth the wait. Watch how Liu Yu Zi's famous deep-fried taro balls are made, and then be sure to taste the original taro ball as well as the salted egg yolk filled balls.

There are a lot of stalls serving shredded chicken on the rice in Ningxia Night Market, but only "Fang Chia Shredded Chicken on the Rice" won the Michelin Guide Taipei 2019 Bib Gourmand selection. The shredded chicken is tender, and the chicken oil mixed soy sauce over hot rice tastes so delicious and is not too greasy. Fang Chia specializes in two simple dishes: shredded chicken rice and braised tofu. They're both "must eats" and complement each other so well.

For over 60 years, "Rong's Pig Liver" has been serving fresh pork liver soup. As the pork liver tastes so tender without any blood smell that you can always see people line up before the stall. It was listed in the Michelin Guide Taipei Bib Gourmand selection in 2019. Besides the fresh pork liver soup, its zongzi (rice dumpling), a triangular-shaped sticky rice ball wrapped in bamboo leaves, is also highly recommended because it contains a moist egg yolk and fresh mushrooms and it's tasty. Don't forget to add the sweet hot sauce when you taste it.

You can reach Ningxia Night Market via Red Line 2 and get off at Shuanglian station, Exit 1. Turn left onto Minsheng West Road heading west, and then take a walk for six to eight minutes until you see the night market on the left side.

Din Tai Fung ✈

Originally founded by Yang Bingyi as a cooking oil retail business in 1958, "Din Tai Fung" was a combination of the name of its founder's previous employer's company, "Heng Tai Fung" and his new supplier's company name, "Din Mei Oils." In 1972, Din Tai Fung was reborn as a xiaolongbao and noodle restaurant. Today Din Tai Fung has grown from a mom-and-pop restaurant to an internationally recognized brand.

Din Tai Fung is known internationally for its xiaolongbao. The quality always remains the same. Xiaolongbao is to Din Tai Fung as the Big Mac is to McDonald's. The original restaurant is located on Xinyi Road in Taipei. In 1996, its first international branch was opened in Tokyo, and its first North American store was opened in Arcadia, California, in 2000. The first European branch was opened in London in December of 2018. Din Tai Fung was named one of the top ten restaurants in the world by The New York Times in January, 1993. Further international recognition came in 2010, when Din Tai Fung won a Michelin Star in Hong Kong. CNN has also honored Din Tai Fung as one of the best golden chain restaurants in the world.

Over the years, Din Tai Fung has discovered that the skin must be 18 folds, which is the golden ratio where the skin is thick enough to hold the pork and hot liquids hidden inside. The xiaolongbao is so special because there's soup inside the dumpling, which makes it so hard to make. The xiaolongbao skin is made up of very basic ingredients: flour, water, and the fermented starter. They go in the mixer, and we put it in the machine for several minutes. It takes about six to ten times to knead the dough to create that perfect xiaolongbao skin.

導遊篇

Xiaolongbao is a really difficult thing to make, especially up to Din Tai Fung's standards, because Din Tai Fung really wants every dumping to be the same. So it takes three to six months for someone to even learn the basics of how to make the xiaolongbao. And it takes years and years to truly master the craft of making it. Every single dumpling is weighed down to the gram, including every single dumpling skin. The ideal weight that Din Tai Fung is going for is five grams. Din Tai Fung doesn't give a green light unless it's between 4.8 and 5.2 grams.

A big part of the flavor of the soup dumpling comes from the soup itself. And Din Tai Fung makes the soup from a really rich bone broth of chicken and pork. And from there, Din Tai Fung has to figure out how to get the soup into the dumpling. And the way Din Tai Fung does this is by gelatinizing the soup. In this way, the soup can be wrapped up in a dumpling. When it's steamed, it turns back into soup.

The English translation of xiaolongbao is soup dumpling. But literally, "xiao" means small, "long" means basket, and "bao" means dumpling. In other words, it literally means "little dumpling in a basket." Do you know there is a proper way to eat xiaolongbao? First, pour some soy sauce and vinegar into a small dish with julienned ginger. The suggested ratio was one part soy sauce to three parts vinegar. Then, use your chopsticks to pick the dumping up and dip it into the sauce. After that, use your chopsticks, or your teeth, to puncture a small hole into the side of the dumpling. This will release the soup broth into your spoon. Finally, you can eat your dumpling and finish it off with drinking the broth.

The sanitation in Ding Tai Fung is better than that in most restaurants in Taiwan and it is obvious to see that--first in the kitchen, and then the tables are wiped very clean. For safety and consistency, the management seeks out private channels for staples such as flour, pork and chicken. Besides that, it lets customers watch through glass as a dozen cooks in white suits bang out orders of dumplings served in traditional bamboo containers.

The key to perfect services lies in attention to detail. The staff at Din Tai Fung seeks to put the customer's needs first. Even the tiniest detail embodies Din Tai Fung's service philosophy and brand values. Daily sales targets are not everything. Instead, Din Tai Fung's main aim is to provide customers with the best possible service, strengthen brand visibility, and achieve sustainable growth.

Yong Kang Beef Noodle ⋙

Beef noodles can be said to be one of the essence of Taiwanese food culture. The taste attracts countless tourists to Taiwan. If you ask the Taiwanese to name one type of food that can represent Taiwan, I think most of them will tell you "beef noodles."

Because Taiwanese farmers regard cattle as their loyal helpers, beef was not part of the traditional diets, but starting in the 1960s, after the ROC army veterans started selling this typical Sichuan dish, it gradually became more and more popular. Yong Kang Beef Noodles was founded in 1963 by Mr. Cheng, who was originally from Sichuan in China. After he finished his military duties, Mr. Cheng decided to open a small stall at Yong Kang Street and sell beef noodles. After Mr. Cheng retired in the 1970s, the place was handed over to Mr. Lo, the current owner. Yong Kang Beef Noodle is around a 10-minute walk from the nearest Dongmen station in Da'an District. Yong Kang Beef Noodle has been listed as the first Taipei Michelin Bib Gourmand, which recognizes cheap and delicious food and Yong Kang Beef Noodle is also a constant winner of the "Taipei Beef Noodle Festival."

導遊篇

Occupying two floors of a building, Yong Kang Beef Noodle is perpetually packed and a long line outside the restaurant is a common sight here. There are two kinds of beef noodles. One has hearty and aromatic broth, and people could feel its distinct and unique herbal taste (Hong Shao). In Chinese, "beef noodles" is usually prefixed with the word "Hong Shao"("red cooked") because the meat is first browned in a pan (braised), and then simmered for many hours in a liquid containing reddish-brown substances. The ingredients include handmade fermented bean paste, soy sauce, brown sugar, caramel and various spices. The resulting tender and tasty beef is served with noodles and a vegetable or two. The other one is "Beef noodles stewed in clear broth" and it has a cleaner soup base with a less intense flavor and you could appreciate the natural flavors of the beef better. In comparison, the beef chunks in the Clear Broth version are much tenderer and almost melting in your mouth.

Yong Kang's signature dish is "Sichuan-style spicy red broth with beef and tendon soup." The broth in crimson red is using many different kinds of seasoning, such as five-spice powder, star anise, peppercorn, Chinese medicine and, of course, some of their secret ingredients. The pickled vegetable goes well with the broth and it also helps to cut through the robust flavors and any sense of "oiliness" from the broth. The meat is perfectly braised, tender and still retains a good bite texture. The tendon is equally well cooked to slightly "chewy" and both the meat and tendon fully absorb the essence of the broth. Beef tendon is regarded as a delicacy, so this version of beef noodles is substantially more expensive. Yong Kang Beef Noodle only accepts cash, so make sure you bring enough cash with you.

While you're waiting for your food, near the door there is a station where you can order a variety of side dishes. Don't be deceived by the so-called "side" dishes. If made with care, some side dishes can add unexpectedly welcome flavors to your meal. Some side dishes are being served before the noodles, including Steamed Hog Spareribs, Steamed Hog Large Intestines, pickled cucumbers, Kimchi, etc.

 Useful Vocabulary and Phrases

1. simmer [ˋsɪmɚ] *vt.,vi.* cook food gently at or just below the boiling point 用文火慢慢地煮

2. permeate [ˋpɝməˏet] *vt.,vi.* spread through something　滲透

3. julienne [ˋdʒuljən] *adj.* (vegetables, meat, etc.) cut into short thin strips 切成絲的

4. gelatinize [dʒɪˋlætəˏnaɪz] *vt.,vi.* convert into gelatinous form or jelly　使成膠狀

5. chewy [ˋtʃuɪ] *adj.* (of food) needing to be bitten a lot before it is swallowed 耐嚼的

6. essence [ˋɛsəns] *n.* [U] the most important thing　精髓

7. façade [fəˋsad] *n.* [C] the front of a building　建築物的正面

8. galvanized [ˋgælvəˏnaɪz] *adj.* (metal) covered with a thin layer of zinc　鍍鋅的

9. sample [ˋsæmp!] *vt.* taste a small amount of food　品嘗

10. shredded [ˋʃrɛdɪd] *adj.* prepared by cutting　切成絲的

導遊篇

Exercises

_____ 1. Din Tai Fung's two Hong Kong locations have each received

_____.

(A) One Michelin star

(B) Academy Award

(C) Golden Globe Awards

(D) The World's 50 Best Restaurants.

_____ 2. According to the recipe, you need to mix all the _____ together and place them in a shallow dish.

(A) qualifications   (B) introductions

(C) ingredients   (D) achievements.

_____ 3. Din Tai Fung was originally founded as a(n) _____ retail business in 1958. However, it was reborn as a steamed dumpling and noodle restaurant in 1972.

(A) coconut oil   (B) cooking oil

(C) olive oil   (D) avocado oil

_____ 4. The Shihlin Night Market lies next to metro _____ station.

(A) Taipei   (B) Jiantan   (C) Shilin   (D) Beitou

_____ 5. Which of the following shops is not being listed on the Bib Gourmand?

(A) Fang Chia Shredded Chicken on the Rice

(B) Hot Star Fried Chicken

(C) Hai You Pork Ribs Soup

(D) Rong's Pig Liver

_____ 6. As the patiently waiting customers like to note, "You haven't been to Shi Lin Night Market if you haven't had _____."

(A) Chung Chia Sheng Jian Bao

(B) Hot Star Fried Chican

(C) Hai You Pork Ribs Soup

(D) Good Friend Cold Noodles

_____ 7. Yong Kang's signature dish is _____ spicy red broth with beef and tendon soup.

(A) Taiwan-style　　　　　(B) Sichuan-style

(C) Tainan-style　　　　　(D) Beijing -style

_____ 8. What is Din Tai Fung's signature dish?

(A) Xiaolongbao.　　　　　(B) Beef Noodle Soups.

(C) Fried Chicken.　　　　　(D) Peking Roast Duck.

_____ 9. To promote Ningxia Night Market and fulfill people's wish of tasting all the Taiwanese street foods at once, vendors came out the idea to hold a _____.

(A)Ten Year Feast　　　　　(B) One Year Feast

(C) Hundred Year Feast　　　　　(D) Millennium Feast

_____ 10. In 2019, Ningxia Night Market was also the first night market in Taipei to use _____.

(A) credit card　(B) Line Pay　(C) Easy Card　(D) Apple Pay

導
遊
篇

Answers

1. (A)　　2. (C)　　3. (B)　　4. (B)　　5. (B)　　6. (A)　　7. (B)　　8. (A)　　9. (D)　　10. (C)

National Palace Museum ✈

The development of the National Palace Museum (NPM) is closely tied with modern Chinese history. Late Oct. 1924, General Feng Yuxiang launched the Beijing coup. On Nov. 4, Prime Minister Huang Fu passed a law, requesting that Emperor Puyi and the Qing royal family leave the Forbidden City in one day. On the National Day of the Republic of China, Oct. 10, 1925, the NPM was officially founded. In 1931, the Japanese Army launched the September 18 Incident, posing a serious threat to northeastern China. The nationalist government decided to relocate the collection of the most precious artifacts to the south. In 1933, the NPM moved the artifacts southward to Shanghai. In 1936, all of the artifacts were relocated from Shanghai to a warehouse in Nanjing. In 1937, the Marco Polo Bridge Incident took place, forcing the NPM to once again relocate its artifacts in three batches to three separate locations away from the battle areas. The NPM artifacts finally were relocated to the west. After winning the war in Aug. 1945, the NPM artifacts previously relocated to the west were shipped back to Beijing by means of sea transport. The artifacts were returned in full by the end of 1947. In 1948, the Chinese Communist Party began gaining an upper hand in the civil war, when the NPM artifacts were relocated to Taiwan and subsequently became a markedly important part of Taiwan's culture.

After the containers arrived at Taiwan, all the artifacts, except for those from the Institute of History and Philology, Academia Sinica, were stored at the warehouse of the Taichung Sugar Factory of the Taiwan Sugar Corporation; artifacts of the Institute of History and Philology, Academia

導遊篇

Sinica were kept in Yangmei. In March 1953, the Joint Management Office constructed a small cave in a mountain near the Beigou Storehouse so that the most precious artifacts could be immediately stored in times of an emergency. In Sept. 1954, nspection of all the artifacts sent to Taiwan was completed. Although the artifacts were delivered at a time of war and via various means of both sea and land transport, they sustained only minimal damage. In Dec. 1956, the Beigou Gallery was completed and opened to visitors in March 1957. Realizing that the location of Beigou was too isolated to draw domestic and foreign visitors, the Taiwanese government soon decided to build a new museum in Waishuanghsi, a suburb in Taipei. In Aug. 1965, construction of the NPM building was completed. On Nov. 12, 1965, the new NPM in Taipei opened to the public. The NPM's artifact collection in comprised of artifacts inherited from the Song, Yuan, Ming, and Qing Courts. As in June 2020, the entire collection is composed of 698,629 objects. The objects in the Museum's collection are great in both number and variety.

Bronze

The Bronze Age of China started in the late Xia Dynasty, lasting about 1,500 years through several dynasties from the Shang to Western Zhou and then to the Eastern Zhou. During these eras, only the ruling class was allowed to use the precious bronze vessels. Worship and warfare are the first and foremost affairs of a country. Bronze was mainly cast into ritual objects, in addition to weaponry, to offer sacrifices to ancestors for their blessing of family.

After a long period of experience and experimentation, humans discovered that by mixing copper with a small amount of tin, they could create bronze, a material that was stronger and more durable than ceramics. By using different techniques like "piecemolding" and "lost-wax casting," bronze could be shaped into forms larger, heavier, and more complex than those of pottery. It was also possible to decorate the surface of bronze with magnificent decorations and patterns.

During the Shang and Chou Dynasties, approximately contemporaneous with the Chinese Bronze Age, piece-mold casting (piecemolding) was the dominant technique. The primary technique employed in the West, the lost-wax casting enabled the casting of more detailed forms and decorations, including even openwork designs. China developed the lost-wax casting during the late Spring and Autumn period, using it in conjunction with the piece-mold casting (piecemolding). The emergence of lost-wax casting marked a new phase in the artistic history of Chinese bronze.

The kings and nobles of ancient China considered brilliant bronze to be as precious as gold, a substance of auspicious power, and thus referred to it as "auspicious metal." If bronze was originally golden in color, why are the bronzes that we see today all green? The answer is that the ancient bronze artifacts which survive today were all buried in the earth for centuries. This exposure caused oxidization on their surface, leaving a green patina.

Bronzes have three main use categories of water, wine, and food vessels. We can see how they would have been used from a virtual scene of an ancient feast. In ancient times, in preparation for any important event such as pre-worship or attending a banquet, the kings and guests would be required to wash their hands in a ceremony known as the "wo kwan chih li"（沃盥之禮）, or handcleansing rite. During the ceremony they would use two bronze water vessels. The yi（匜）would be used to pour water over the hands, and this water would be collected in the pan（盤，a basin below）.

Following the hand-cleansing rite, the banquet guests would proceed into the main hall, where they would be met with a lively scene of cups

導
遊
篇

clashing and toasts being made! Alcohol was an indispensable part of life during the Shang Dynasty, and in fact a majority of the bronzes dating back to this dynasty are wine vessels. The chueh and ku were two of the most basic units of the Shang Dynasty bronze sets. The Shang people were defeated by the Chou, who believed the downfall of the Shang Dynasty had its roots in their indulgence in alcohol. The new Chou rulers thus issued a directive, advising the people to avoid drinking too much. This change is reflected in the development of bronzes over the course of the Chou Dynasty, when wine vessels became rarer in favor of water and food containers.

The ding was one of the most important bronze food vessels, often used to cook meat. In fact, the remains of this meat can still be seen in some of the unearthed ding. Scholars believe that food was first cooked in the larger ding and then distributed into smaller ones to be eaten. Dings were not, however, the only type of vessels to be used for cooking. For example, lis were used to cook gruel, and yans were used as steamers. The common characteristic of the three bronze food vessels lies in their three legs. This design meant that they could be placed over a fire, and in fact some vessels show residue of ash and flame on their bases. A successful feast needs more than just wine. No banquet would be the same without music and song! Perhaps the most attention has been paid to the sets of bronze bells. A set excavated from the Hubei, China of Warring States period tomb of Tseng Hou Yi represents the largest, most complete set yet found, and certainly the most impressive set of ancient Chinese bronze musical instruments known today.

What are bronze inscriptions? Bronze inscriptions are writings either cast or carved onto bronzes. Ancient bronzes were originally a shiny gold color, and for this reason the cast or inscribed writings found on them are sometimes referred to as chinwen, meaning "golden characters." Because these texts were generally cast or inscribed on the surfaces of ritual ding cauldrons or bells, they are sometimes also called chung ting wen (inscriptions on bells and cauldrons). There are three main reasons that these inscriptions are so important to us today: 1. They are intimately related to the origins of writing in China. 2. They are an invaluable primary historical resource for understanding the Shang and Chou Dynasties of Ancient China. 3. They can be used to date the vessels on which they are found, and also to distinguish authentic works from the forgeries. The Mao Gong Ding, San pan and Zong Zhou Zhong are among the most important historical artifacts within the National Palace Museum's collection of bronzes, primarily because of the lengthy inscriptions cast onto them. These inscriptions not only demonstrate the dignified and refined nature of the "large seal script"（大篆） style of calligraphy, they are also very important historical documents for scholars researching the Western Chou period.

Mao Gong Ding

Mao Gong Ding (The cauldron of Duke Mao) is considered an important national treasure because of the inscription on the inside. The Mao Gong Ding, one of the most discussed bronze vessels in the world, has an inscription of 500 characters arranged in 32 lines, the longest inscription on the currently existing Chinese bronzes. From the contents of the inscription, scholars believe that the Mao Gong Ding must have been cast in the first year of the reign of King Hsuan. The first part of the inscription is an injunction from King Xuan to the Duke of Mao. The inscription describes how King Xuan cherished the way in which Kings Wen and Wu followed the Mandate of Heaven and established the Chou Dynasty, but he was more circumspect and concerned about the Mandate of Heaven he inherited from his ancestors. The latter part of the inscription details the rewards bestowed by King Xuan on the Duke of Mao. It also

導遊篇

expresses King Xuan's earnest instructions, expectations, and faith in the Duke of Mao in taking on important responsibilities. At the end of the inscription, the Duke expresses his thanks to the king and the hope that the cauldron will be handed down from generation to generation. Because the "large seal script" （大篆） has already reached a mature stage, the inscription on the Mao Gong Ding has influenced many calligraphers since being unearthed.

The San Pan

The San Pan (Pan water vessel of San) was unearthed during the reign of the Emperor Kangxi in the Qing Dynasty and presented to the court as a birthday present in 1809 to celebrate the fiftieth birthday of Emperor Jiaqing. It became one of the most important pieces in the imperial collection. The San Pan was cast when King Li was on the throne. This bronze is valuable not only for the high degree of craftsmanship that it displays, but also because documents territorial disputes between vassal states during the late Western Chou.

The inscription on the San pan consists of 350 characters arranged in 19 columns. The inscription describes how the vassal state of Ce ceded land to the San clan during the Western Chou period, after the state of Ce attacked lands of the San clan and then sought to offer compensation for its infringement. The inscription also indicates that the authority of the Chou king was weakening, since it shows that the allocation of land was no longer totally in the hands of the monarch. The vassal states were becoming increasingly aggressive in taking territory, and the well-field system was disintegrating. The only option open to the king was to send an official, Chung Nung, to oversee the proceedings. The role of a king changed from a ruler to an observer. Land distributions were no longer fully under the control of the king, and sending a government official was merely a way to give the impression of due process, a superficial expression of authority. San pan was probably the fairest political contract in history.

Zong Zhou Zhong

Zong Zhou Zhong (Bell of Zhou) was commissioned by King Li of the late Western Chou to perform the ceremony of ancestral worship. Also known as Bell of Hu, only a handful of the Western Chou bronzes currently known to exist were commissioned by a Chou king. The inscription on the Zong Zhou Zhong consists of 17 lines with 123 characters on the bronze, detailing how King Li led his forces on an expedition to the south, securing promises of loyalty from 26 kingdoms in the south and east. The long inscription commences from the middle of the front, continues on the lower left then turns to the lower right of the other side. The inscription seeks the blessing of his ancestors for his descendants, and asks them to bring peace and prosperity to the kingdom. The Zong Zhou Zhong is an excellent example of this type of oval bronze bell. The piece has 36 short pillar-shaped protrusions arranged along both sides of the bell. The center of the lower body is decorated with a two-dragon pattern. In addition, the lower body is where the bell is struck. Striking the bell creates two different sounds depending on whether the center or the side of bell's lower area is struck, which is why it is sometimes referred to as a "dual-tone bell."

導遊篇

Chinese Jade

Jade has always been the material most highly prized by the Chinese. It was also widely believed that objects of a certain shape or decorated with certain patterns were equally magical. Ancestors of the Chinese believed that jade was rich in "power" or "energy," which is why they frequently used jades as ceremonial items when offering sacrifices to the gods.

Jade Pig-dragon

Scholars have debated the proper name for these objects. Some have called them "pig-dragons" and others "bear-dragons." Pigs are essential farm animals, while bears were objects of worship by the ancient inhabitants of northeastern China. This unusually shaped pig-dragon is a jade object from the Hongshan Culture. Its round form recalls the jade chueh earrings of the Xinglonghua culture. The pig-dragon has bat ears, a wrinkled nose, and an arched mouth, and it resembles an animal embryo. Prehistoric people may have believed that an embryo represented the life force, and created this formal design as a symbol of vitality.

Jade wo and Jade han

The Han Dynasty had its own unique burial and funeral customs. The most common jades buried along with the deceased are Jade wo and Jade han. Ancient Chinese people were convinced that jade could protect the bodies of the deceased from decaying. This custom was a way to show love for the deceased as it prevented the deceased from leaving this life empty-handed. In the tombs of Han Dynasty nobles, the most common shape of Jade wo was that of a pig, like this "Pair of jade pigs covered by gold sheet." （金片包玉豬） The jade pigs were held in the hands of the deceased, extending wishes for the prosperity of his descendants. They were modeled in a simple style, and the eyes, ears and legs were roughly outlined with no further carving, because funerary objects needed not be very refined. Based on archaeological research, such objects were intended for use by the highest noblemen. The fact that they were wrapped in gold foil demonstrates the high social status of their owners.

This pair of gold foiled jade pigs is the only example that has been found to date; therefore they are cultural relics of great importance.

Also, when their loved ones passed away, they would place a "jade han" in the mouth of the dead to show their love and affection. In the Han Dynasty, the cicada was the most popular form. After incubation, a cicada bores into the ground and stays in the soil for a long period of time. It comes out of the ground when it has become fully mature. People of the Han Dynasty therefore saw cicadas as a symbol of life as they believed that cicadas could come back to life again after they died. Placing a "jade cicada" in the mouth of the dead was a way to show that they hoped the deceased would resurrect like the cicadas.

Jade Bixie (Auspicious Beast)

Ancient people believed that Bixie could repel wickedness. In fact, its name means "to ward off evil" in Chinese. This was why people placed Bixie along with other fierce stone animals in front of the spirit road leading up to tombs. It's like the Sphinx in front of the pyramids in Egypt. A Bixie is an animal derived from the lion. A Jade Bixie is actually a mythological animal. According to specialists, its creation was probably influenced by statues of winged beasts from West Asia. The Qing Emperor Qianlong was particularly fond of this piece, so much so that he commissioned a special base and had a poem engraved into the chest of the beast and on its bottom.

導
遊
篇

Jadeite Cabbage

This piece is almost completely identical to a piece of bokchoy cabbage. The figure was carved from a single piece of half-white, half-green jadeite which contained numerous imperfections such as cracks and discolored blotches. These flaws were incorporated into the sculpture and became the veins in the cabbage's stalks and leaves.

The Jadeite Cabbage is considered by many to be the "most famous masterpiece" in the entire National Palace Museum. The Jadeite Cabbage, the Meat-shaped Stone, and the Mao Gong Ding, are considered to be Three Treasures of the National Palace Museum. Despite their popularity with museum-goers and frequent representation as a national treasure, they are in fact only designated as a significant antiquity, having less rarity and value than required for categorization as a national treasure under the Cultural Heritage Preservation Act.

The sculptor of the Jadeite Cabbage is unknown. It was first displayed in the Forbidden City's Yonghe Palace, the residence of the Qing Empire's Guangxu Emperor's Consort Jin who probably received it as part of her dowry for her wedding to Guangxu. This Jadeite Cabbage was a dowry gift to symbolize her purity and offer blessings for bearing many children. Let's also not forget the two insects that have alighted on the vegetable leaves! They are a locust and a katydid, which are traditional auspicious symbols for having numerous children in Chinese culture.

The Meat-shaped Stone

At first glance, this meat-shaped piece of stone looks like a luscious, mouth-watering piece of "Dongpo pork." The Meat-shaped Stone, along with the Jadeite Cabbage and the Mao Gong Ding, is today is considered by many to be one of the Three Treasures of the National Palace Museum. Although the Meat-shaped Stone is of only moderate importance from the point of view of art history, it is a very popular favorite of visitors.

The stone was carved into the shape of a piece of Dongpo pork during the Qing Dynasty from agate. It is a naturally occurring stone that accumulates in layers over many years. With time, different impurities will result in the production of various colors and hues to the layers. The craftsman who carved the stone with great precision and stained the skin, which resulted in a realistic looking piece of stone with multiple layers appearing like layers of fat and meat.

Ceramics

Ceramics are sign of civilization. From processing the clay, shaping the forms, and applying the glazes to firing the products in kilns, raw materials go through many changes as soft clay becomes durable ceramic. There are two primary categories of Chinese ceramics, low-temperature-fired pottery or táo（陶，about 950~1200°C）and high-temperature-fired porcelain or cí（瓷，about 1250~1400°C）. The forms, glazes and decorative patterns on ceramics are diverse and varied because they were created under different cultural and social conditions. Emperors, officials, potters and users of ceramics all contributed to the formation of various period styles in China.

Most ceramics in the National Palace Museum collection were inherited from the Qing imperial court and passed through many places before being moved to Taiwan. Originally from the palaces in Beijing, Rehe and Shenyang, these ceramics possess a distinct accession number that can help trace the original location at which each piece was once stored or displayed. It makes the collection of the National Palace Museum unique and distinct from other public and private museums. Even though the Museum does not have many pre-Song Dynasty ceramics, it boasts many famous wares unparalleled anywhere in the world, including renowned Song wares, doucai porcelains of the Chenghua reign in the Ming Dynasty, painted enamel porcelains of the Qing Dynasty as well as official wares of various Ming and Qing Dynasty reigns.

導遊篇

The "Song to Yuan Dynasties" exhibit explores the decorations and beauty of various wares from different kilns. The "Ming Dynasty" section theme narrates the establishment of the Jingdezhen imperial kilns, as porcelain production became a state affair and local civilian kilns competed for market share. The "Qing Dynasty" section shows how three emperors, Kangxi, Yongzheng, and Qianlong, personally gave orders for the imperial kilns, the influence of official models reaching a peak at that time. As the dynasty began to decline, the styles of folk art began to extend into late Qing imperial wares.

Ru ware

Although Ru ware was only produced for a short period, it is traditionally considered to be one of the "Five Great Wares" of the Song Dynasty. It is traditionally estimated that only about 70 complete examples of Ru ware have survived, so it is highly treasured. Ru ware was made at Ruzhou in Henan Province in China. The glaze of Ru ware has been described as "sky blue mixed with light opaque green, resembling jade."

Jingdezhen

A famous ceramics-producing center is located in present-day Jiangxi Province in China. The kilns at Jingdezhen have been active since the Five Dynasties period (907~960). In the Northern and Southern Song Dynasties (960~1279) their main product was blue-white（qinghua 青花） ware, a type of porcelain with a blue-tinted white glaze. In the Yuan Dynasty (1279~1368) Jingdezhen produced underglaze blue and underglaze red porcelain. By the end of that dynasty it had become the main ceramic production center of China. In the Ming (1368~1644) and Qing (1644~1911) Dynasties official kilns were established. They produced porcelain of the finest quality for the imperial court. Thus the name Jingdezhen is synonymous with "porcelain capital" in Chinese culture.

Falangcai

When this craft arrived in China from the West in the late 17th century, it quickly became a favorite among the Qing emperors and gradually developed into a new form that combined different techniques of Eastern and Western decorative art. Falangcai is a type of porcelain with painted enamel. Painted enamel involves painting the surface of a vessel with enamel glaze, placing the piece in a kiln, and then firing at a low temperature.

Wine cup with doucai polychrome decoration of chicken in a garden

This wine cup was made around the 1460s, during the reign of the Ming Emperor Cheng Hua. The cup is delicate, small, and brightly colored. It combines the doucai decorating technique developed during the Xuan De Era with a new form created by the official kilns of the period. What is doucai （contrasting colors, 鬥 彩 ）? It is a type of decoration on porcelain that has both underglaze blue and overglaze polychrome components. The outlines of the decoration are painted in cobalt and fired under a transparent glaze at a high temperature. After the first firing, the other colors are painted over the transparent glaze, within the cobalt-blue outlines, and the object is fired again at a lower temperature. The colors contrast, hence the Chinese name doucai (contrasting colors). The exterior wall features two finely painted compositions of chickens with their chicks. The two groups are separated by peonies, orchids and rocks. In both cases, a rooster and a hen lead their chicks to find food together in the wild. In this piece, the numerous doucai colors include tones of red, yellow, brown and green. This is a heartwarming scene of domestic bliss. This treasured piece was admired by emperors and literati alike. According to a late Ming archive, a pair of such fine, almost translucent miniature cups were once purchased by the emperor for 100 thousand cash. If these pieces

導
遊
篇

sold such a high price in their own time their current value must be beyond all reckoning!

Lotus-shaped warming bowl in light bluish-green glaze, Ru ware

This ten-petal lotus bowl has gently curved sides, a subtly flaring rim, smooth transition from one petal to the next, and a relatively tall ring foot. The blue-green glaze, from rim to the base, is uniformly thin and opaque, with fine crackling. During firing, this piece was supported by five tiny points underneath the ring foot, and these are the only parts of the body not covered by the glaze.

Pottery figure of a standing lady with painted colors

During the Tang Dynasty, particular emphasis was placed on elaborate funerary ritual which often included large quantities of grave goods. As a result, Tang burial frequently included large numbers of earthenware tomb figurines. This female figure is one example. The young woman has a plump figure; long, attenuated brows and lashes; a small peach-shaped mouth; round face; and a composed expression. Her tall, elaborate hairdo, with descending strands that encircle her cheeks, is a hairstyle that was particularly popular in the late Tang. The woman wears a long, broad robe, with her right hand held up before her chest and her left hand extended slightly down. Pointy-tipped shoes protrude from beneath the hem of her robe.

Pillow in the shape of a recumbent child with white glaze, Ding ware

The Ding kilns were renowned northern kilns during the Song Dynasty located in modern-day Quyang County, Hebei Province. The kilns mainly produced white porcelains. Because the ancient name for the place was Dingzhou, it was called Ding ware.

Did the Chinese make a pillow in the form of a baby? Only three pillows in the shape of a recumbent child are known to exist. This is because there is a strong desire to continue the male family line in China. The ancient Chinese used to say that if you slept on one of these little boy pillows, you had a better chance of having a son. So this cute pillow actually symbolizes the values placed on having sons. The glaze on this piece is ivory white and smooth, with the head and body comprising two molds fixed together and the facial features added later. If one picks up the piece, it becomes clear that there is a small piece of clay inside that makes a faint rattling sound when moved. The bottom of the pillow has been inscribed with a poem written by the Qianlong Emperor in the spring of 1773.

Narcissus basin in bluish-green glaze, Ru ware

This oval dish has deep, slightly flaring sides, a flat base, and four cloud-shaped feet. The body is very thin on the sides, becoming slightly thicker on the base and feet. It is covered all over in a light blue, highly lustrous glaze, which shows a hint of green at the base and light pink at the rim and the corners. During firing, the piece would have been supported from underneath by small points on the feet, and on these parts the cream color of the body could have been seen where the glaze did not cover them.

The glaze over the whole piece has a wonderful smooth quality, without any crackles, a very rare feature among existing examples. People praised "Those with 'crab-claw' (crackle) patterns as divine, but those without as truly superb." Ru ware is known for its elegant tianqing or "heavenly blue" color of the glaze as well as its refined, handsome form.

導遊篇

This "Celadon Narcissus Basin with Light Bluish-Green Glaze" can be regarded as "the masterpiece of the masterpieces" among the numerous Chinese ceramics.

Revolving vase with swimming fish in cobalt blue glaze

Revolving vases were made as composites pieces, though from the exterior they appear as a single work. The body is divided into internal and external sections, the former being covered with light green glaze on which is painted fallen flowers, water plants, and swimming fish. Because this is a composite vase, rotating the neck of the piece causes the inner vase to revolve at which point one can see different goldfish swim through the openings of the outer vase. By rotating the neck of the piece, the vase spins and through the openings of the outer vase creates the impression of fish swimming and playing in the water. Whether such an innovation was influenced by the traditional Chinese merry-go-round or western spinning tops with wind-up springs, the firing process required making individual components and then assembling them. One gains a better understanding of the whole vessel from the integrated complete piece.

Monk's cap ewer with ruby red glaze

This distinctive vessel type is known as a monk's cap ewer because of the unusual shape of its mouth. Red glazed vessels of this sort were particularly treasured by the Qing imperial family. An imperial painting also depicts a scene showing one on the wardrobe of a consort of the Yongzheng Emperor. Chinese ceramic artisans succeeded in firing deep red glaze for the first time in the early fifteenth century, during the Yongle era of the Ming Dynasty. During the Xuande reign, the glaze became thicker and richer, taking on a ruby-red hue. However, because the technique used for firing these wares was highly unstable, many were discarded and very few examples have survived. The glaze is thin and clear around the mouth, handle, and edge of the vessel's foot, revealing the white body within. This quality is one of the characteristic features of Xuande period red wares, and it serves to frame and accentuate the richness of the red.

🔊 Useful Vocabulary and Phrases

1. patina [ˋpætənə] *n.* [U] a blue-green layer that forms on copper, brass or bronze　（銅器表面的）銅綠，銅鏽

2. directive [dɪˋrɛktɪv] *n.* [C] an official instruction　指令，命令

3. bestow [bɪˋsto] *vt.* give something as an honor or present　贈予；給予

4. vassal [ˋvæsəl] *n.* [C] a country that is controlled by a more powerful country, and has to provide military support or pay money to it when needed　附庸國，諸侯

5. luscious [ˋlʌʃəs] *adj.* having a pleasant sweet taste or containing a lot of juice　汁液豐富的

6. resurrect [ˌrɛzəˋrɛkt] *vt.* bring someone back to life　使復活，使起死回生

7. recumbent [rɪˋkʌmbənt] *adj.* lying down　臥式的，躺著的

8. glaze [glez] *n.* [U] a substance used to polish something　釉，釉料

9. kiln [kɪln] *n.* [C] a type of large oven used for making bricks and clay objects hard after they have been shaped　窯

10. well-field system [ˋwɛl-fild ˋsɪstəm] *n.* [C] a Chinese land distribution method, existing between the ninth century BC (late Western Chou Dynasty) to around the end of the Warring States period. Its name comes from the Chinese character 井 (jing), which means "well" and looks like the # symbol　井田制度

導
遊
篇

Exercises

_____ 1. _____, San pan and Zong Zhou Zhong are among the most important historical artifacts within the National Palace Museum's collection of bronzes,

(A) Chueh (B) Narcissus basin

(C) Ku (D) The Mao Gong Ding

_____ 2. Ancient people believed that _____ could repel wickedness. In fact, its name means "to ward off evil."

(A) bixie (B) jadeite

(C) mao gong ding (D) jade pi

_____ 3. The meat-shaped stone was carved during the Qing Dynasty from _____.

(A) jasper (B) jade (C) gold (D) stone

_____ 4. Which insect is a traditional metaphor for having numerous children?

(A) Butterfly. (B) Locust. (C) Ant. (D) Bee.

_____ 5. How many pillows in the shape of a recumbent child are known to exist?

(A) Two. (B) Three. (C) Four. (D) Five.

_____ 6. A type of decoration on porcelain that has both underglaze blue and overglaze polychrome components. What kind of decoration technique is this?

(A) Falangcai（琺瑯彩）

(B) Tri-colored（Tangcancai, Tang tricolor pottery，唐三彩）

(C) Doucai（contrasting colors，鬥彩）

(D) Blue-white（qingbai 青花）

_____ 7. During the Shang and Chou Dynasties, approximately contemporaneous with the Chinese Bronze Age, _____ was the dominant technique.

(A) piece-mold casting　　　　(B) overglaze

(C) lost-wax process　　　　(D) underglaze

_____ 8. _____ was probably the fairest political contract in history.

(A) Mao gong ding　　　　(B) Song hu

(C) San pan　　　　(D) Zong zhou zhong

_____ 9. A famous ceramics-producing center located in present day Jiangxi Province in China. The kilns at _____ have been active since the Five Dynasties period.

(A) Nanchang　(B) Yichun　(C) Jiujiang　(D) Jingdezhen

_____ 10. Zong Zhou Zhong (Bell of Chou), was commissioned by _____ of the late Western Chou to perform in the ceremony of ancestral worship. Also known as Bell of Hu, only a handful of the Western Chou bronzes currently known to exist were commissioned by a Chou king.

(A) King Xuan　(B) King Li　(C) King Wen　(D) King Wu

導遊篇

Answers

1. (D)　2. (A)　3. (A)　4. (B)　5. (B)　6. (C)　7. (A)　8. (C)　9. (D)　10. (B)

臺南孔廟、鹽水蜂炮與炸寒單

Tainan Confucius Temple ✈

Confucius is known to every person of Chinese descent. Confucius lived in what's now northeastern China 2,500 years ago. Taiwan's first Confucius Temple is located in Tainan and it holds a ceremony at 5:00 a.m. on September 28 each year. The ceremony celebrates the birthday of the Chinese educator and philosopher, which is also Teacher's Day in Taiwan. The Tainan Confucius Temple is the only institution in Taiwan that still practices the offering of three different animals, which are goat, pig and ox, to worship Confucius, while other Confucius temples present the three sacrifices, but replace the animals with pastry in animal shapes. When visiting the Confucius Temple, do not forget to ask the great teacher himself for some words of wisdom! Every year once the ceremony is complete, throngs of people will head to the main hall to pull a "wisdom hair" from a cow. And it is said that this hair helps bring wisdom for the following year. When considering pulling a wisdom hair, please remember to bring your own transparent plastic bag or red envelope to place the hair, and upon returning home make sure to dry the hair in the sun. Otherwise, the moisture within the hair will damage it over time.

The temple has gone through several different transformations and has had to be rebuilt several times due to the turbulent nature of Taiwan's political and colonial history. Even though not all of the buildings we see today are over 350 years old, the fact remains that this temple has played an instrumental role in Taiwan's history. Tainan Confucius Temple was established in 1665 during the Kingdom of Tungning. Tungning Kingdom's ruler, Zheng Jing, the eldest son of Koxinga, built the temple at the suggestion of his Chief of General Staff Chen Yong-hua. The Kingdom of Tungning, a government founded by

導遊篇

Koxinga, remained between 1661 and 1683 as part of a loyalist movement to restore the Ming Dynasty. In the Qing Dynasty, it served as a school for Taiwan's tóngsheng, literally "child students," regardless of age, also referred to as rútóng (Confucian apprentices), the entry-level examinees. The temple was also known as the First Academy of Taiwan, and served as a vanguard for Confucianism in Taiwan while gaining a reputation for cultivating intellectuals. In 1997, Tainan Confucius Temple was designated as a national historic site.

At the entrance to the temple stands a dismounting stele. Placed at the entrance on imperial orders in 1687, it is the oldest and best-preserved dismounting stele among the four remaining steles in Taiwan. The red-painted granite stele has incised Chinese characters on the right and Manchu script on the left. The stele reads "all civil and military officials, soldiers, and citizens must dismount from their horses here" to pay respects to Confucius.

Tainan Confucius Temple has undergone several major renovations over the past three centuries. It is one of the finest examples of traditional architecture in Taiwan, as well as the most complete traditional Minnan (Southern China) architectural complex in Tainan. It is composed of an academy (The Hall of Edification) on the left and a temple on the right. The temple layout consists of three rows of buildings joined by two long wings running from the front to the back to create two interior courtyard areas. The first row includes the Dacheng Gate, the Shrine of Distinguished Officials, the Shrine of Respected Village Scholars, the Shrine of Bereaved Sons, and the Shrine of Fidelity and Piety. The Dacheng Gate has a wooden framework supported by six columns. Unlike most temples, no door gods are painted on the doors of a Confucian temple. Instead, 108 metal studs are installed. Couplets, usually found at the entrance of a traditional Chinese building, do not appear at the Dacheng Gate. This is done in veneration of Confucius; it signifies that his greatness is beyond words. The Dacheng Hall is the second row. The wings on either side of the Dacheng Hall are dedicated to eighty-one ancient sages and seventy-seven ancient Confucians. The Ritual Implement Storeroom and the Musical Instrument Storeroom are located to the north of the East and West Wings. Implements and instruments used in Confucian rites are stored in these two locations. Behind the Dacheng Hall is the third row, Chung Sheng Shrine.

The present appearance of the Dacheng Hall dates from its 1977 renovation. It is the tallest building in the temple complex. Its location—right in the middle of the complex and surrounded by the other buildings— reveals its significance. The hall sits in the middle of a granite courtyard with a large elevated platform in front of it as well as on the sides. Inside the Dacheng Hall is a very simple shrine set up with the Confucius Spirit Tablet（神位） on a nice red table with several plaques above it. One of the common features of all Confucius temples is that there is no imagery or statues of Confucius. This is a rule that goes back almost 500 years to the Ming Dynasty when the emperor decreed that all Confucius temples should be uniform and only have "spirit tablets"（神位） rather than images of the sage. Hanging inside the Dacheng Hall are horizontal inscription plaques (horizontal described boards) presented in praise of Confucius by every emperor since the Kangxi Emperor of the Qing Dynasty), till today, the Tainan Confucius Temple of Taiwan owns the most complete royal horizontal described boards of all leaders with the sole exception of Puyi, the last emperor of China.

The platform in front of the Dacheng Hall is also called Tanchih. Every Confucius temple has this platform as the stage for Yi Dance, performed in the Confucius Ceremony. There is an imperial road inlaid in the wall of the platform in front of the Dacheng Hall, carved with chess, piano, calligraphy

導
遊
篇

and dragon heads. In ancient times, ordinary people were not allowed to walk on the imperial road. Only when the new champion of imperial examination and the emperor worshipped the Confucius, they could walk through this imperial road to the Dacheng Hall. In fact, the emperor and the champion went up on the sedan chair, and the person who carried the sedan chair walked up the stairs. There is a nine-story pagoda in the center of the ridge which is said to have the power of driving away evil.

There is one Tungtien pillar or Hiding Scripture cylinder at each end of the ridge of the Dacheng Hall. And there are hornless dragons on them and sea-tortoises below them. It is said that this is to commemorate that Confucius is the model of perfection. Another legend says that it is to commemorate the cylinders that were used to hide books when Qin Shi Huang, the first emperor of Qin, ordered the books to be burnt and scholars to be buried alive.

There are water dragons and weed decorations in the sloped ridge of the Dacheng Hall. It is said that the water dragon can quell Chu lung, the fire god, and so guard against fire. There are owls on the roof of the Dacheng Hall. Owls were originally one of the fiercest birds. However, there goes a legend about the owl. It says that when a flock of owls flew over the place where Confucius was teaching, they were moved and perched to listen to the teaching. The owls on the roof of the Dacheng Hall exactly illustrate the all-encompassing characteristic of Confucius. He teaches without any discrimination.

Chung Sheng Shrine is a windowless room made of wood with eighteen columns supporting a swallowtail gable roof. The main shrine is dedicated to five generations of Confucius' ancestors. The shrine was constructed in 1723. In fact, this kind of arrangement has its roots in the Chinese clan ethics that have existed for several thousand years. The layout of Confucius temples is also very similar to that of a clan ancestral temple. The Chongsheng Shrine is as wide as five normal-sized rooms. The beams in the Chongsheng Shrine are the same as the ones in the Yimen Gate: one can see the beams and the carvings of the melon pillar. The frame has three beams and five short pillars. The melon pillars are carved into pumpkins or papayas, and look very round and substantial, both powerful and beautiful. The carved lions on the top, which seem to carry the beams on their shoulders, look as if they were real lions.

Located on the other side of the Confucius Temple, the Hall of Edification or "Minglun Hall" was the most common name for Confucian lecture halls. It consists of a main gate with a courtyard and the main building, which is usually open and has excellent air circulation. These halls were used as classrooms in the Qing Dynasty prefectural schools. Students were expected to study Confucian ethics and virtues, as well as human relationships under the patriarchal system. Inside the hall is a horizontal stone tablet inscribed with school rules, from the days when it served as a center for Confucian studies.

The Yanshui Beehive Firecrackers Festival ✈

導遊篇

The Yanshui Beehive Firecrackers Festival in the south of Taiwan, the Pingxi Sky Lantern festival in the north and the Bombing Lord Handan in the east are the island's three major activities on the day of the Lantern Festival in Taiwan. The tradition in Yanshui is to hold the firecrackers festival on the 15th day of the first lunar month. There are many legends regarding the origin of Yanshui Beehive Rockets. Some say it was created to greet the Jiaqing Emperor when he visited Taiwan, while others say it was for a firecrackers competition. However, the most popular version is that the origins of the Yanshui Beehive Firecrackers Festival is tied to a cholera epidemic that swept through the Yanshui region in 1885. The congregation decided to carry the holy palanquin with Lord Guan's statue from Yanshui's Lord Guan Temple （Yanshui Wu Temple 鹽水武廟） in procession around the area from the 13th to the 15th days of the first lunar month. The believers set off beehive firecrackers to ward off epidemic diseases. This was the start of the 130-year long tradition.

People invented rocket towers and multi-directional models along with a whole variety of other creative designs to show respect to the god. In the past, the firecrackers used to greet the palanquin during the Yanshui Festival were regular firecrackers and strings of firecrackers. In 1945, shortly after World War II, bottle rockets appeared. In 1984, rocket towers first emerged. Encouraged by the traditional belief that more exploding firecrackers would bring greater prosperity and wealth, the event grew larger. Packed with exciting light and sound, the highly entertaining celebration has become a major tourist attraction. In recent years, the international press has crowned Yanshui's Beehive Rockets with an array of titles: one of the top three folk celebrations in the world, one of the ten most dangerous festivals in the world, and one of the ten best festivals in the world.

The early version of the rocket tower was simply made with several wood planks. The rockets could only fly in one or two directions. This gradually evolved into a large rocket tower, or gun deck, with a metal base and several levels and layers. The top is covered with a metal net onto which the bottle rockets can be affixed to fire in any direction. The rockets can also blast off at multiple angles. Thousands, even hundreds of thousands of rockets are connected with the main fuse placed in the center of the tower. In 1984, the design of the rocket tower grew in sophistication and the paper wads were replaced with plastic, making the whistling sound even louder. They are placed indoors and the gun deck is rolled out and ignited in praise of the deity upon arrival of the holy palanquin carrying Lord Guan's statue.

Originally a one-day event on the day of the Lantern Festival, the activity has now been extended into a two-day event that alternates between two areas. The first procession begins on the morning of the 14th day of the first lunar month and ends on the deep night of the next day. The routes are determined in advance during a council meeting. Those who wish to ignite rocket towers during the event must register. When the holy palanquin approaches their doors, the owners roll the gun decks out, remove the red paper covering, and peel off the red seal. After praying and burning joss paper in front of the deity, the palanquin is moved forward three times and backward three times, symbolizing Lord Guan's acceptance of the birthday wishes.

But what sets the Yanshui Firecrackers Festival apart is the fact that the firecrackers (bottle rockets to be more precise) are shot directly at participants! That's right. Anyone who is brave enough is welcome to join in and get bashed with a fiery barrage of rockets. Sounds intriguing! To protect against injury, it is advised that a participant (should) complete his safety outfit by purchasing some protective gear, including a helmet that covers his whole head and face, a scarf or towel around the neck to prevent stray rockets from flying up into his clothing, a cotton or denim jacket, long pants, gloves, and flats or sneakers. It is unsafe to wear a rubber raincoat or fabrics that are prone to melting.

導遊篇

The Firecracker Bombing of Lord Handan

The Lantern Festival falls on the first full moon night after the Lunar New Year. It is also a time when many distinctive religious events are held all over Taiwan to celebrate the New Year. The event that can measure up to the Yanshui Beehive Firecrackers Festival is the Firecracker Bombing of Lord Handan in Taitung City. This is perhaps the most important annual folk-religion event on Taiwan's East Coast, and certainly the most important in Taitung City.

It is most widely believed that Handan is one of the Daoist Five Gods of Wealth, and ordinary people call him the Military God of Wealth. The deified Zhao Gongming, a Shang Dynasty general, became a god named Handan （寒單） after death. Firecrackers were set off for warmth around a man who volunteers to be his living manifestation during the Bombing Handan parade. The Firecracker Bombing of Lord Handan folk event has been held in Taitung for over fifty years. In the early years, followers of Lord Handan took turns enshrining the deity in their homes. In 1989, Taitung's Xuanwu Temple was established to create a permanent place for the worship of Lord Handan. The Firecracker Bombing of Lord Handan event began in 1951. At one point, it was banned by the authorities for being too disruptive but worshippers later managed to get the event reinstated. In 1998, organizers began collaborating with the Taitung County Government, and the event has since expanded to one of the highlights of The Firecracker Bombing Festival celebrations. As a result, the Firecracker Bombing of Lord Handan Festival has become one of Taitung County's most iconic cultural events. The Taitung County Government designated it a cultural asset in 2007.

The Firecracker Bombing of Lord Handan Festival has become extremely popular in recent years. The length of the festival differs every year, but it normally lasts for five or six days. The organizers hold a seminar and give a presentation about the history and origins of Taitung's Firecracker Bombing of Lord Handan event on the 12th and 13th days of the first lunar month. Small-scale firecracker bombing of Lord Handan activities are also held to give the public a first-hand experience of what the event is like. Xuanwu Temple begins the preparations for Lord Handan's inspection tours from the 12th to

14th days of the first lunar month, erecting a temporary shrine at Haibin Park, extending invitations to other deities, preparing the palanquin, and inviting the troupes. Divination blocks are cast to decide the order of the palanquins holding the various deities' statues to be carried in the procession. Following the ceremony, an offering of the three sacrificial offering meats (chicken, pork, and fish), vegetarian foods, and fruit is made.

The highlight of the Firecracker Bombing of Lord Handan event takes place on the 15th and 16th days of the first lunar month, when Lord Handan is bombarded with firecrackers during both public inspection tours and private bombardment events. Troupes taking part in Taitung's Lantern Festival Blessing Procession accompany Lord Handan's palanquin during the public inspection tours. Along the route, the men playing the role of Lord Handan are bombarded with firecrackers prepared by business owners and spectators. Business owners can also register with Xuanwu Temple in advance for Lord Handan to be bombarded with firecrackers in front of their stores or offices. To provide international exchange students studying in Taitung with an opportunity to experience this unique tradition first hand, they are also invited to take on the role of Lord Handan on the afternoon of the 15th day of the first lunar month.

Every year, people volunteer to play the role of Lord Handan during the firecracker bombing event because those doing so are said to receive blessings from the deity. The number of impersonators varies each year in accordance with the endurance level of the participants. The majority of volunteers are young men, although at times veterans of the event will join them if needed. The appearance of Lord Handan is governed by tradition. Volunteers wear a marshal's seal around their neck and a yellow headscarf. They are bare-chested and wear red shorts. A wet towel covers their mouths and noses, and cotton

導遊篇

balls are used as earplugs. The volunteers also carry bunches of leafy sprigs from a banyan tree (Taoists believe the branches and leaves of the banyan tree can protect against demons) to shield themselves against the firecrackers and block burning ash cinders.

A statue of Lord Handan is strapped to the top of the palanquin, which is preceded by a gong troupe. When the procession arrives at a given destination, the bearers select a windward spot to prepare the palanquin and the volunteers for firecracker bombardment. At the leader's command, the volunteer set to board the palanquin prays to the Lord Handan statue for safety before getting on. The palanquin bearers then lift the sedan chair up, perform the "three steps forward, three steps backward" ritual for the homes and shops of that particular spot, and make a circuit around the area.

How is Lord Handan bombarded with firecrackers? Firecrackers are bound together in rows of three to five to form a bunch, and a detonator attached with a rubber band. The artillery men take the bunches and form a circle around the palanquin. They light the firecrackers and bombard Lord Handan as he is carried around the circle. When one volunteer can endure no more, another takes his place. At certain special sites, the volunteers all stand atop the palanquin to be bombarded with firecrackers together. This is the most common bombing method. The information on the route and schedule of the Firecracker Bombing of Lord Handan event is adjusted annually and is announced online. Those wishing to watch the event or take part in event-related activities or international exchange student activities are advised to wear long-sleeved shirts, long pants, hats, protective eyewear, face masks, and earplugs for their own safety.

Useful Vocabulary and Phrases

1. dismount [dɪsˋmaʊnt] *vi.* get off a horse　下馬

2. edification [ˏɛdəfəˋkeʃən] *n.* [U] the improvement of the mind and understanding, especially by learning　教化

3. piety [ˋpaɪətɪ] *n.* [U] strong belief in a religion that is shown in the way someone lives　虔誠

4. congregation [ˏkɑŋgrɪˋgeʃən] *n.* [C] a group of people gathered together for religious worship　會眾

5. palanquin [ˏpælənˋkin] *n.* [C] a structure formerly used in East Asia for transporting one person　轎子

6. plank [plæŋk] *n.* [C] a long, narrow, flat piece of wood or similar material　板

7. procession [prəˋsɛʃən] *n.* [C] a line of people who are all walking or traveling in the same direction　遊行

8. detonator [ˋdɛtəˏnetɚ] *n.* [C] a device used to cause an explosive to detonate　引信

9. troupe [trup] *n.* [C] a group of performers such as singers or dancers who work and travel together　（巡迴）劇團

10. couplet [ˋkʌplɪt] *n.* [C] two lines of poetry next to each other　楹聯

導遊篇

Exercises

_____ 1. _____ in the south of Taiwan, the Sky Lantern festival in the north and the Bombing Lord Handan in the east are the island's three major activities on the day of the Lantern Festival in Taiwan

(A) The Sky Lantern festival

(B) The Yanshui Beehive Firecrackers Festival

(C) Ku

(D) The Bombing Lord Handan

_____ 2. It is the _____ Confucius Temple of Taiwan to own the most complete royal horizontal described boards of all dynasties.

(A) Tainan   (B) Taipei   (C) Taitung   (D) Taichung

_____ 3. The _____ is dedicated to five generations of Confucius' ancestors.

(A) Dachng Hall   (B) Chung Sheng Shrine

(C) Edification Hall   (D) King Wu

_____ 4. Every Confucius temple has this platform as the stage for _____, performed in the Confucius Ceremony.

(A) Yi Dance   (B) ballet   (C) street dance   (D) breakdance

_____ 5. On September 28, people celebrate the birthday of the Confucius, which is also _____ in Taiwan.

(A) Labor's Day   (B) Army's Day

(C) Teacher's Day   (D) Father's Day

_____ 6. The Bombing of _____ Festival has been held in Taitung for over fifty years.

(A) Lord Guan   (B) Matsu   (C) Guanin   (D) Lord Handan

_____ 7. There is one _____ at each end of the ridge of the Dacheng Hall.

(A) clay owl   (B) pagoda

(C) lightning rod   (D) Tungtien pillar

_____ 8. In recent years, the international press has crowned _____ with an title: one of the top three folk celebrations in the world.

(A) The Bombing of Lord Handan

(B) Yanshui's Beehive Rockets

(C) Sky Lantern Festival

(D) Dragon Boat Festival

_____ 9. Lord Handan is the _____, the deified Zhao Gongming, a Shang Dynasty general.

(A) Military God of Wealth   (B) God of Medicine

(C) God of Sea   (D) God of flower

_____ 10. The appearance of Lord Handan is governed by tradition. Volunteers are bare-chested and wear _____ shorts.

(A) white   (B) red   (C) yellow   (D) black

導
遊
篇

Answers

1. (B)   2. (A)   3. (B)   4. (A)   5. (C)   6. (D)   7. (D)   8. (B)   9. (A)   10. (B)

Manka Lungshan Temple ✉

Located in Taipei's Wanhua District, the Manka Lungshan temple was founded in 1738 but has been rebuilt several times. It was dedicated to the Buddhist Goddess of Mercy (Guanyin in Chinese) along with other Taoist deities, including the sea goddess Mazu and the Saint of War Lord Guan. In Taiwan, there is a saying, "Tainan first, Lugang second, and Manka third." This phrase states that of the three major cities in the Qing Dynasty. Manka (known as Wanhua today) is the oldest district of Taipei City. The name Manka, which means canoe in the language of the Taiwanese indigenous people (the Pingpu tribe) clearly suggests Manka was a place known for convenient shipping transportation and its proximity to the Tamsui River at the time. The temple has been destroyed either in full or in part in numerous earthquakes and heavy rainfalls, but Taipei residents have consistently rebuilt and renovated it.

During Japanese colonial period, parts of the temple were used as a school, a military camp, and offices. In 1919, after termites extensively destroyed the wooden structure, Abbot Fu-chih and local intellectuals organized a fundraising campaign to reconstruct the crumbling temple. They employed Wang Yi-Shun, a master of temple-building in southern Fukien, as the architect. This temple, therefore, has become a masterpiece of Mr. Wang in Taiwan. He made it a beautiful temple and laid the foundation for the current Lungshan Temple's appearance today. During World War II, in 1945, the Lungshan Temple was hit and damaged by American bombers, and further restoration did not take place until 1955 due to the severe economic repercussions from the war. In 2018, the Lungshan Temple was designated as a national historical site in Taipei City.

導遊篇

Immigrants from the three counties Chin-chiang, Nan-an and Hui-an of Fukien came to Manka at the beginning of the eighteenth century. As they were pious followers of the ancient Lungshan Temple in their home town, they erected this one as a branch temple at Manka and named it after the root temple when they created a new settlement here in Taipei. The present Lungshan Temple consists of three halls: the fore hall, the main hall and the rear hall. The fore hall is used as the entrance and the space for people to worship. The main hall is in the center of the whole complex with a statue of Guanyin as the main god of the temple. The rear hall mainly houses the Taoist gods and is divided into three parts. The center is for the veneration of Mazu, the goddess of marine voyages. The left is dedicated to the gods of literature, or patrons of examinations for civil service in the old days. The right is for the Lord Guan, the Saint of War. The Lungshan Temple houses hundreds of statues of Buddhist, Taoist, and Confucian deities.

The structure of the fore hall is subdivided into the Sanchuan Hall, the Dragon Gate Chamber, and the Tiger Gate Chamber. The Sanchuan Hall is beautifully decorated with artistic carvings and the green and white stones of its walls form a pleasing symmetry. Since the construction occurred in early 20th century, Mr. Wang had already known something about western architecture. He put small concrete gables on top of the front walls as decorative screens and added Corinthian capitals on some columns as ornaments. All of these characteristics make the Lungshan Temple a landmark of traditional Chinese architecture of its time in Taiwan.

The dragon columns located by the front entrance of the Sanchuan Hall are the only pair of cast bronze dragon columns in Taiwan. The cement molds for the columns were made in 1920 by Ang Khun-hok of Xiamen, and the columns themselves were cast by Li Lu-xing of the Taipei Iron Workshop.

The dragon's bodies have distinctive patterning, the columns are decorated with representations of characters from the Ming Dynasty novel Investiture of the Gods (Fengsheng Bang), and the bases were cast with depictions of ocean waves and carp, showing the intelligence and engineering skills behind the designs of these enterprising craftsmen.

The caisson ceiling design is exclusively used for important buildings in Chinese tradition. The octagonal caisson ceiling in the Lungshan Temple's front hall is composed of 32 sets of interlocking wood brackets aligned toward the center with cross vaults interlacing diagonally between the brackets. The delicately-structured double caisson ceiling has an inner layer and an outer layer and is a masterpiece of carpenter Mr. Wang Yi-shun. The joining of the walls and roof did not employ any nails. Covered by overtapping tiles, the temple roof is decorated with figures of dragons, phoenixes and other auspicious creatures.

Generally, the bell and drum towers of traditional temples are independent structures. The bell tower is located on the east side of the temple and the drum tower is located on the west side of the temple. The bell and drum towers are decorated with sedan-chair styled roofs or a hexagonal shape like that of a helmet. These were Taiwan's first bell and drum towers to be built in this architectural style, and they influenced the design of many other temples in Taiwan. The towers' current facades are also the work of Wang Yi-shun.

An image of "silly barbarians" was caston the golden censer or corner of the wall at the Lungshan Temple. As for why the craftsmen put the silly barbarians in the corner of the wall or on the top of the incense burner, there are four different explanations: 1. Silly barbarians are black slaves introduced by the Dutch. 2. In the past, the Han people often called the Pingpu people with a lot of power " barbarians." 3. According to legend, the folks were dissatisfied

導
遊
篇

with the Dutch's high-handed rule, so the craftsmen put the Dutch on the wall or on the top of the furnace to support the heavy corners or incense burner. 4. According to legend, there is a person who likes to criticize the craftsmen's works, and often makes the craftsmen very unhappy. Later, if the person criticized the craftsmen's works without any reason, the craftsmen would make a barbarian's face based on the people who liked to criticize. So we must not offend the craftsman. The number of censers at the Lungshan Temple, with which Taiwanese people place their burning incense sticks as an offering, has been reduced from seven to three since mid-2015 in an effort to cut the levels of harmful PM2.5 particles inside the temple. The Lungshan Temple decided to join the government's green initiative and trimmed down the number of incense burners in use at the temple from three to one starting in 2017 and will reduce that to zero in March of 2020.

In the Lungshan Temple's main hall, the spiral caisson ceiling is located at the top of the roof, surrounded by four golden columns. The caisson ceiling is composed of 32 sets of interlocking wood brackets. The caisson ceiling was originally composed of 16 sets of interlocking wood brackets designed by master carpenter Wang Yi-shun in a counterclockwise direction. However, the ceiling pattern was altered and reconstructed in its present clockwise direction after World War Two in 1945. There is a sculpture of　Buddha that stands in the main hall which was carved in 1925 by Taiwan's first known sculptor, Huang Tu-sui. The sculpture is based on a famous painting by Liang Kai of the Southern Song Dynasty. The original sculpture was burnt during World War II; the present sculpture is a replica made by the Council for Cultural Affairs of the Executive Yuan, the present-day Ministry of Culture.

The Lungshan Temple has always maintained its basic function as a Buddhist temple, but many Taoist deities in the rear hall show the tolerant mentality of the local people in their religious life. Nearby you can also find people asking for blessings in matters of love, marriage, and childbirth. Well, there are actually many gods to whom worshippers can pray to at the temple, but Yue Lao (god of matchmaking) is the one that attracts the interest of tourists the most. Single locals will come to pray to the deity in the hopes that their loves or lovers will marry them and stay with them forever. They can even take a piece of red string that they can put on the wrist of their loved one that in theory will bind them together forever.

Divination blocks, transliterated as throwing poe like tossing a coin and called Bwa Bwei in Taiwanese, are two crescent-shaped red blocks. The divination blocks are used by Taoists as a form of divination, or talking to the gods. They are not only used in temples, but also in homes. If there are no divination blocks for people to use, coins can be used instead. People stand in front of the deity and briefly introduce themselves. They typically tell the deity their name, birthday, and address. After that, they toss the divination blocks into the air, let them land on the ground, and check out the results.

There are two sides to the block, one round side and one flat side. If the blocks both land round-side up, it's an "angry answer." It means the god does not agree to grant your request. If the blocks both land flat-side up, it's a "laughing answer." But it doesn't mean a "yes." The god smiles but does not reply, meaning that the explanation is unclear, or it is not the right time to ask the question. If the blocks land one side up and the other same side down, then it's a "divine answer." This means "yes," representing the approval of the god in the matter of your prayers. There is another rare occasion when the blocks might stand erect on the floor. This implies that the deity does not understand your question. Generally speaking, believers throw deviation blocks to ask the deity for something. However, if believers ask for nothing, their divination

導遊篇

blocks can more easily "kia bui/bwei," (stand erect) and this is seen as a miracle by believers.

Dalongdong Baoan Temple ✈

The Dalongdong Baoan Temple (also known as the Taipei Baoan Temple) is a Taiwanese folk religion temple built in the Datong District of Taipei, Taiwan. Dalongdong is one of the oldest areas in downtown Taipei, situated near the intersection between the Keelung and Tamsui Rivers. The present temple was originally built by clan members from Tongan, Fujian, who immigrated to Taipei in the early 19th century and gave the temple the name Baoan in order to "protect those of Tongan people." The temple then became a spiritual center for the Tongan people living in Dalongdong.

In 1709, the Qing government issued the first reclamation license to the Chen Lai-chang reclamation firm. Dalongdong was already part of its northern frontiers. The 44-kan (shop) block is considered Dalongdong's earliest business district, now known as Hami Street. It is said that after the completion of the Baoan Temple, the unused building materials were purchased at discounted prices by rich households like the Wangs, Chengs, Kaos, and Chens. They used the materials to build two rows –a total of 44 shops– on the left side of the Baoan Temple; a shop was called a kan. The Taipei Confucius Temple is located adjacent to the Baoan Temple.

The history of the Baoan Temple goes back to 1742 in "Toaliongtong" (modern-day Dalongdong), when new immigrants moving to Taiwan constructed a small shrine to worship the Baosheng Emperor on the site where the current temple exists. As the population grew in the area, the wooden shrine became insufficient and plans were made to construct a much larger temple after funds were raised. The construction of the temple began in 1805 and it was completed in 1830.

The Baoan Temple is a Taoist temple whose main deity is the Baosheng Emperor, the God of Medicine. The Baosheng Emperor is the god that people pray to for the good health of themselves and their families, making him an important figure within Taoism with over three hundred temples or shrines dedicated to him in Taiwan alone. The Baosheng Emperor, also known as Da Dao Gong or Wu Zhen Ren, is a god of medicine worshiped in the Minnan region of China. Originally a skilled doctor and Taoist practitioner named Wu Tao, he was credited with a number of miracles and deified after his death. In 1150, a temple was built in his name in Baijiao Village, Fujian Province, which Emperor Gaozong of the Song Dynasty honored with the title Ciji Temple.

During his lifetime, the Baosheng Emperor even performed some medical miracles. For instance, he applied eye drops to a dragon's eye and removed a foreign object from a tiger's throat. It is said that in the Song Dynasty a tiger once ate a woman. Since her hairpin pierced his throat, he felt in great pain. The tiger asked Master Wu for help. Master Wu rebuked him "It is the punishment from Heaven for killing people and animals. I can't save you." The tiger did not leave, just stayed and lowered his head to repent for what he had done. Touched by his sincerity, Master Wu then cured him. To thank Master Wu for his kindness, the tiger stayed by his side from then on. When the tiger was alive, he served Master Wu as his ride. Thus, Master Wu transformed the fierce tiger into a deity. Since then, on every April 16, the ceremony of "General Tiger" is observed. When Song Kaozong was the crown prince and sent to be a hostage at the Jin Court, it was the Baosheng Emperor's divine presence that saved Kaozong and escorted him back to China. After Kaozong had ascended the throne, he ordered the founding of a temple (the ancestral temple for the Baosheng Emperor) and bestowed the title of Great Tao Immortal on the Baosheng Emperor. Ming Cheng-tzu's Empress Wen suffered from a breast ailment and her imperial doctors had no cure. The Baosheng Emperor appeared as a Taoist priest and came to the rescue. He felt the empress's pulse through a silk string and then cured her. Cheng-tzu wanted to compensate the Baosheng Emperor with gold, but he declined and rode away on a crane. Cheng-tzu then expressed his appreciation by conferring the title of Emperor.

Throughout the 20th century during the Japanese colonial period, the temple underwent numerous improvements and extensions, which resulted in the present temple. In 2018, the Baoan temple was designated as a national historical site in Taipei City. Because of the natural damage and the serious damage caused by termites. In 1995, the Baoan Temple's then-Vice President Liao Wu-Zhi raised funds himself and found old craftsmen to repair the temple in a traditional way. Due to the strict adherence to the "Cultural Assets Preservation Act" during the repair process, the adherence to the principle of "repairing the old as before" and making full use of the assistance of modern technology, the restoration of the Baoan Temple was singled out for recognition by UNESCO, receiving the 2003 Asia-Pacific Award for Cultural Heritage Conservation. The Baoan Temple is the only temple in Taiwan to have received the UNESCO Asia-Pacific Award for Cultural Heritage Conservation.

This 3,000-ping temple marks the nation's largest temple for the Baosheng Emperor. The temple is oriented to the south. The main structure in the middle includes Sanchuan Dian (the front hall), the main hall, and the rear hall. On the sides are the east and west wing and the Bell and Drum Towers. All combined, they form a complete, three-hall "huí" shape. The main hall is the tallest; next in sequence are the rear hall, the front hall, and the east and west wings. Such hierarchy is in line with Confucian rituals and Taoist formations.

On the walls of the Baoan Temple's east and west gates, there are windows of book scrolls and bamboo nodes. The stone window frames are carved into book scrolls; within the frames there are stone-carved bamboo plants. An odd number of bamboo plants stands for "yang," and an even number of bamboo plants stands for "yin;" such is for the harmony between yin and yang.

On both sides of the Baoan Temple's main gate stand two stone lions: one male and one female. Usually, the female lion keeps her mouth shut and the male one keeps his open. It is said that the craftsman made a mistake by leaving the lioness's mouth open; and he had to take a cut in his salary due to the breach of contract. The make-up of these two stone lions is somewhat different from conventional ones. With huge eyeballs, big tails, curly hair, wide-open mouths, chipped horns, and flat heads, this is what ancient people called "ren beast" or "qilin." It is said that ren beast or qilin are ritual animals.

The octagonal dragon columns of Sanchuan Hall are the earliest stone carving work of the Baoan Temple. They were completed in the Jiaqing Period of the Qing Dynasty (1804).The dragon column of the Taiwanese temple is also known as the "pán long column," which refers to the dragon that has not ascended to heaven. Since the dragon columns of the Sanchuan Hall were completed in the middle of the Qing Dynasty, its style is relatively simple. The dragon is one of the four beasts. Legend has it that the dragon has nine characteristics, namely, the head of a camel, the antler of a deer, the bristles of a lion, the mouth of a cow, the nose of a dog, the body of a snake, the scales of fish, the talons of an eagle, and the eyes of a shrimp.

導遊篇

In 1983, Liu Jia-Zheng re-painted two door gods, Qin Shubao and Yuchi Gong, on the main gate of the Sanchuan Hall. His drawing techniques on door gods' eyes attracted many people's attention. It is through "the four eyes techniques" that viewers can watch the door gods from any angle, and they all have the feeling of being stared at by the door gods.

The Bell and Drum Towers were built on top of the East and West Wings. Their roofs are of the gablet double-roof style. The square-shape towers are rather unique, differing from the conventional hexagon towers in Taiwan. The Bell and Drum Towers are a place where the competition is played. The East and West are designed by two masters. The East Wing Bell Tower and the West Wing Drum Tower feature works of masters Chen Ying-Bin and Guo Ta respectively; they present different styles for woodcarving designs and colored-drawing patterns. On the exteriors of the Bell and Drum Towers, there are horizontal tablets inscribed with "jing fa" (tolling at the sight of a whale) and "tuo-pong" (alligator-skin drums beats loudly) respectively. Judging from the names of the Bell and Drum Towers, designating the Baoan Temple as the most literary temple in Taiwan is well deserved.

The corridor walls surrounding the main hall of the Baoan Temple feature colored mural paintings. These murals paintings are the works of Pan Lishui, a well-known painter from Tainan. The murals were completed in 1973. Pan Lishui studied ink painting with his father since childhood, especially figure painting. His father, Pan Chunyuan, is also a well-known folk painter. In 1993, Pan Lishui was awarded the National Artist Award from the Ministry of Education and was also the first folk painter to receive this award. The stories of colored mural paintings were inspired by ancient Chinese tales and historical events. There are seven paintings with these subjects: "Han Xin is insulted by crawling under another person's groin," "the eight hammers fight Lu Wenlong at Zhuxian Town," "Zhong Kui welcomes his sister back home," "the Eight Immortals' big adventure in the East Sea," "Hua Mulan substitutes for her father as a soldier," "Three heroes fight with Lu Bu at Hulao Pass," and "the virtuous Mother Xu."

The renovation during Japanese colonial period (around 1917) was conducted by Zhangzhou carpenters Chen Ying-Bin and Guo Ta 　—each working on one half of the temple's main hall. The two masters showcased their own unique skills in the highly refined woodwork. It is also a kind of construction method which is called "the match" (competition between two master carpenters). However, no matter how the work is divided, the craftsmen have to follow a certain basic size specification such as height and width to construct, so it will not affect the integrity of the temple. The reason why the competition is so important is because the biggest goal of winning the game is to win the word of mouth and to attract more cooperation opportunities in other temples, especially in the era when the social environment is relatively closed. The economic motives may play the most important role. The final results are highly artistic and valuable, such as the woodcarvings on the panels that support the cross beams on the sides of Sanchuan Hall, and the woodcarving "the Eight Immortals' big adventures in the East Sea" on the wood bracket of the Main Halls' double eaves.

Since 1994, from early March to early May, the birthday celebration of the Baosheng Emperor (The Baosheng Culture Festival) has been transformed from a traditional temple event into a vibrant cultural festival. A series of events is organized each year, including a three-day worship ritual, theatrical plays traditionally performed by local clans, the Baosheng Emperor's grand birthday banquet, performances by a folk art troupe (yìzhèn), and more.

導
遊
篇

Useful Vocabulary and Phrases

1. deify [`diə͵faɪ] *vt.* make someone or something into a god 神化，將…尊奉為神

2. divination [͵dɪvə`neʃən] *n.* [U] forseeing what will happen in the future 占卜

3. replica [`rɛplɪkə] *n.* [C] an exact copy of an object 複製品

4. gable [`geb!] *n.* [C] the top end of the wall of a building, in the shape of a triangle 山牆

5. caisson [`kesən] *n.* [C] referred to as a caisson ceiling, or spider web ceiling, an architectural feature typically found in the ceiling of temples and palaces, usually at the center and directly above the main throne 藻井

6. reclamation [͵rɛklə`meʃən] *n.* [U] making land suitable for building or farming （對土地的）開墾

7. scale [skel] *n.* [C] one of the many very small, flat pieces that cover the skin of fish, snakes, etc. 魚鱗

8. talon [`tælən] *n.* [C] a sharp nail on the foot of a bird that it uses to hunt animals 爪

9. mural [`mjʊrəl] *n.* [C] a large picture that has been painted on the wall of a building 壁畫

10. antler [`æntlɚ] *n.* [C] a horn with parts like branches that grows on the head of a deer 鹿角

Exercises

_____ 1. Manka, known as Wanhua today, is the oldest district of Taipei City. The name Manka, which means _____ in the language of the Taiwanese indigenous people (Pingpu tribe).

(A) witch　　　(B) canoe　　(C) cat　　　　(D) cow

_____ 2. During World War Two, in 1945, Lungshan Temple was hit and damaged by _____ bombers.

(A) German　　(B) Spanish　(C) American　(D) French

_____ 3. The dragon columns of the Lungshan Temple are Taiwan's only pair of _____ dragon columns.

(A) stone　　　(B) wood　　(C) gold　　　(D) bronze

_____ 4. Which is the major deity of the Lungshan Temple?

(A) Guanyu.　　　　　　　(B) Mazu.

(C) Guanyin.　　　　　　　(D) Baosheng Emperor.

_____ 5. There are two sides to the block, one round side and one flat side. If the blocks both land round-side up, it's a _____.

(A) laughing answer　　　　(B) divine answer

(C) kia bui　　　　　　　　(D) angry answer

_____ 6. The mural paintings of Baoan Temple are the works of _____ a well-known painter from Tainan.

(A) Wang Yi-Shun　　　　　(B) Pan Chun-Yuan

(C) Pan Li-Shui　　　　　　(D) Liu Jia-Zheng

_____ 7. Dalongdong Baoan Temple (also known as the Taipei Baoan Temple) is a Taiwanese folk religion temple built in the _____ District of Taipei, Taiwan.

(A) Shinyi　　(B) Datong　(C) Wanhwa　(D)Shilin

導遊篇

8. The major deity of Baoan Temple is _____.

    (A) Lord Guan   (B) the Baosheng Emperor

    (C) Mazu   (D) Guanyin

9. In 1983, _____ re-painted the door gods, Qin Shubao and Yuchi Gong, on the main gate of the Sanchuan Hall.

    (A) Guan Yu   (B) Wang Yishun

    (C) Pan Lishui   (D) Liu Jia-Zheng

10. Which is the only temple in Taiwan to have received the UNESCO Asia-Pacific Award for Cultural Heritage Conservation?

    (A) Baoan Temple.   (B) Lungshan Temple.

    (C) Mazu Temple.   (D) Guanyin Temple.

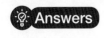

Answers

1. (B)　2. (C)　3. (D)　4. (C)　5. (D)　6. (C)　7. (B)　8. (B)　9. (D)　10. (A)

PART 04

附　錄

GATES 6-9

Unit 1

 **Listening Task** p.22

A: Tour leader B: Ground staff C&D: Guests

A: Hi. My name is Gary and I'm a tour leader. We are flying to Taipei on flight CI1234. Can you tell me when the check-in counter will be open?

B: It will be open 2 hours before departure. The departure time of CI1234 is 10: 30 a.m. It is 8:20 a.m. right now. So, you should be able to check in for your flight in 10 minutes.

A: That's good to hear. So, is there a group check-in counter here?

B: Not really. But you and your guests can check in from counter 11 to counter 13 later on. For passengers who would like to sit together, they can check in together.

A: Great. Thanks for your help.

B: No problem.

The tour leader is talking to all the guests

A: Hello. Can I have your attention, please? We will be checking in at counter 11 after it is open in 10 minutes. Before then, I'd like you to check if you put any lithium ion batteries, power banks, or valuable items in your checked luggage. If you did, please make sure to move them to your carry-on bag. For liquid, aerosol or gel items, such as drinks, skin-care products, toothpastes, or hair sprays, if each of them is less than 100 milliliters, then you can store them in a resealable transparent plastic bag or a zipper bag, and put them in your carry-on bag. Otherwise, be sure to put them in your checked baggage. Please don't hesitate to ask if you are not sure about what to do.

Before the guests check their carry-on bags and checked luggage

A: The counter is open now. Please line up here and get your passport ready. I'll be in front of the counter assisting you. After you check in, don't forget to check the monitor over there and make sure all your suitcases go through the X-ray detector without any problems. Finally, please take your seat in this area until we all finish the check-in procedures. Thank you for your cooperation.

At 8: 30 a.m. at the check-in counter

A: Hi. This is my guest and he would like to check in.

B: OK. Can I see his passport?

A: Sure. Here you go.

B: Does he like a window seat or an aisle seat?

A: A window seat, please.

B: Certainly. Does he have any luggage to check?

A: Yes, just one piece.

B: Can you put it on the scale, please?

A: Sure.

B: Here are the passport, boarding pass, and baggage claim ticket. The boarding time is 10:00 a.m. at gate 13.

A: OK. Thanks.

B: No problem. Next.

附
錄

A: They would like to check in together.

B: OK. Can I have the passports, please?

A: Here you are.

B: Two seats together?

A: Yes. One window seat and one middle seat.

B: You've got it. Any luggage?

A: Yes. Two pieces.

B: OK. Put the luggage on the scale, please.

C: OK. Wow. It weighs 50 kilograms. Is it overweight? Do I have to pay any overweight charge?

B: The free luggage allowance is 30 kilograms for each person. There are two of you. So, you are entitled to 60 kilograms. It is not overweight.

D: What a relief!

B: OK. Here are the passports, boarding passes, and baggage claim tickets. The boarding time is 10:00 a.m. at gate 13.

A: Thank you so much.

Unit 2

 **Listening Task** p.29

Hello. Can I have your attention please? Now we are heading to the security checkpoint together. As you can see, there are so many people right now because it's rush hour. So, the security line can be long and is moving slowly. To get through it faster, here is what we can do:

1. Relax and stay patient because we are on vacation.
2. Present your passport and boarding pass to the security guard at the entrance.
3. Empty your pockets and put all metal objects in the tray.
4. Remove your shoes, jacket, and belt, and put them in the tray.
5. Take your tablet, laptop computer, and mobile phone out of your carry-on bag and put them in the basket.
6. Empty your water bottle before the inspection.
7. Put all the carry-on baggage on the conveyor.
8. Step through the metal detector. If the alarm is set off, stay calm. The security guard might ask you to stand still and raise your arms before they frisk you. If that happens, just cooperate with them and take it easy.
9. If they ask you to open your suitcase from the conveyor belt, just follow the instructions.
10. After the inspection, don't forget to pick up your suitcase.

附
錄

Just in case, I will stay behind our group all the time. If you come across any problems, please let me know. If you are an experienced traveler, after you go through the security check, you can have your passport and boarding pass ready and make your way to the immigration and then the boarding gate. Or you can stay put and wait for me. I'll keep you company all the way to the boarding gate. Anyway, don't forget to arrive at gate 13 before 10:00 a.m. Most of all, please report to me before boarding. That's all you have to know at this moment. Any questions? If there is no question, let's get going.

Unit 3

Listening Task 1 p.40

Boarding Call 1

Passengers on China Airlines flight CI1234 to Tokyo, please proceed to gate 3 for boarding. Passengers on China Airlines flight CI1234 to Tokyo, please proceed to gate 3 for boarding.

Boarding Call 2

This is the last boarding call for passengers on Eva Air flight BR1122 bound for Chiang Mai. For passengers on EVA Air flight BR1122 departing for Chiang Mai, please proceed to gate 13 for boarding immediately.

Boarding Call 3

Ladies and gentlemen, thank you for your patience. Happy Airlines flight HA1221 to Kuala Lumpur will now be boarding at gate 18. Please have your boarding pass ready.

We invite those passengers with small children or those requiring special assistance to the boarding gate.

We now invite all first class and business class passengers to board.

We now invite passengers from rows 35 through 70 to board.

We now accept all remaining passengers to board.

Boarding Call 4

Attention. Flight TG1123 to Bangkok, scheduled to depart at 7:00 a.m. at gate 12, has been delayed due to heavy fog outside. The flight is expected to depart at half past eight. The new boarding time is 8:00 a.m. Sorry to cause you any inconvenience and thanks for your patience.

附
錄

   p.40

A: Tour leader B: Flight attendant

A: Excuse me. I'm a tour leader. I'd like to update our seating list for my guests who requested special meals. Do you know who I should talk to?

B: I'm in charge of the in-flight meal services. You are talking to the right person.

A: Great. Here is the list. As you can see, here are the English names of the passengers and the special meals they requested. You can find their old and new seat numbers right here.

B: Wonderful. It's crystal clear. Can I keep the list?

A: Certainly.

B: Thanks for the update. I'll make sure our colleagues serve the right meals to them.

A: That would be great. Thanks. If there is any question on this, you can find me at 15B.

B: OK. No problem.

Unit 4

 **Listening Task 1** p.59

A: Good afternoon. Can I help you?

B: Yes. I'm a tour leader. We are here to check in for our connecting flight.

A: May I have your tickets and passports, please?

B: Certainly. Here are the PNR, all the passports, and the baggage claim tickets of our first flight.

A: Thanks. There are 26 of you on flight CI1234 to Istanbul. Is that correct?

B: Yes, it is. Can we have our seats close to each other?

A: I'll do my best.

B: That would be great. Thanks. BTW, can you also check the baggage status? I'd like to make sure that our baggage is not missing.

A: Of course. Just a moment, please. As I can see, the luggage has been unloaded from your last flight earlier and it is on the connecting flight CI1234.

B: That's good to hear. Thanks for the confirmation.

A: No problem, sir. So, here are your PNR, passports, and boarding passes. The boarding time is 6:30 p.m. at gate 16. The departure time is 7:00 p.m.

B: Would you please tell me the way to the gate?

A: Sure. Just go straight, turn right and then take the elevator up. You will have to pass the security check first and you won't miss the sign to your gate.

B: Thanks for the information.

A: No problem. Have a nice flight.

附
錄

 p.60

A: Good afternoon. What can I help you with?

B: I'm a tour leader. Our first flight CI1234 from Taipei was delayed and as a result we couldn't catch up our connecting flight NW1234 right here to Honolulu. Can you give us a helping hand?

A: I'll see what I can do. Sir, can I have your tickets and passports?

B: Sure. Here are the PNR, all the passports, and the baggage claim tickets of our first flight.

A: Thanks. There are 23 of you. Is that correct?

B: Yes.

A: Actually we have a flight bound for Honolulu and it departs at 8:00 p.m. Currently there are still 30 vacancies. So, if it's acceptable, then I'll put you on this flight. The flight number is NW4321.

B: That would be great. We'll take it. BTW, can you also help us make sure that our luggage has arrived and will be moved to this new connecting flight?

A: Certainly. So, here are your PNR, passports, and boarding passes. The boarding time is 7:30 p.m. at gate 15. The departure time is 8:00 p.m.

B: Would you please tell me the way to the gate?

A: Sure. Just go straight, turn right and then take the elevator up. You will have to pass the security checkpoint first and you will see the sign to your gate.

B: Thanks for the information and your assistance. You just saved our trip.

A: Don't mention it. Have a nice flight to all of you.

Unit 5

   p.75

A: Good afternoon. Welcome to the Philippines. May I see your passport and arrival card, please?

B: Sure. Here you go. I'm the leader of the tour group. Here is our group visa.

A: Thanks. Where are you guys from?

B: We are from Taiwan.

A: How many people are there in your group?

B: There are 20 of us. All of them are behind me. Do I have to collect all the passports for you?

A: No, you don't. Actually, each passenger has to clear immigration individually.

B: Got it.

A: How long is this trip?

B: Five days.

A: Where are you guys going to stay?

B: Fridays Boracay Resort.

A: Please look at the camera and put your fingers on the device.

B: Sure. Can I stay behind my group just in case that my guests need any assistance when they clear immigration?

A: Certainly. Or you can step aside and wait for them over there. Here is your passport. I'll return the group visa to you later.

B: Thanks.

A: No problem. Next.

附

錄

   p.76

A: Hi. I'm a tour leader. My guest's baggage seems to be missing. We waited for the luggage to show up in the baggage claim area for almost 45 minutes earlier, but it didn't arrive. We'd like to report lost luggage.

B: Yes, sir. What flight were you on?

A: Flight CI1234 from Taipei. Here is the baggage claim ticket.

B: Let me see. Our computer says that the suitcase is now in Hong Kong.

A: Hong Kong?

B: Yes. We are sorry about the mistake. Please fill out this claim form. Specify the type and color of the suitcase. Be sure to include a phone number and indicate where we can reach you or your guest.

A: OK. When can we get the suitcase?

B: I think we can deliver the suitcase to you by tomorrow evening. Where will you be at that time?

A: We will be in the Hilton Hotel downtown.

B: OK. Once we get it, we will deliver it to the Hilton Hotel ASAP. Sorry to cause you any inconvenience.

Unit 6

 **Listening Task** p.86

A: T/G B: T/L C: Guest

A: Here is the list with all the room numbers for our guests. There are five double rooms and three twin rooms. Is that correct?

B: Yes, it is. Which room is the largest or has the best view?

A: The space of each room is almost the same, but room 912 has the best ocean view. Maybe you can save it for the manager.

B: Good idea. Let me put it down on the rooming list. So, what's your room number?

A: Room 812. What about yours?

B: I'll stay with one of the guests in room 712.

A: Got it. Here are the room keys. Would you like me to help you distribute them to our guests?

B: Thanks for asking. But I think I can manage it. Before that, I need to spend some time on the rooming list. So, why don't you share something about the hotel with our guests and tell them about our plans for tomorrow morning?

A: Sure. Ladies and gentlemen, can I have your attention, please? We are going to stay at this hotel for two nights. Leo will tell you about your room number and give the room key to you later. Now, let me tell you something about the hotel facilities and our plans for tomorrow. In this hotel, there are a gym and a heated swimming pool. They are on the 4th floor and 7th floor respectively. They are both open from 8:00 a.m. to 10:00 p.m. If you want to go to the gym or the swimming pool, all you have to do is to

附

錄

present your room key. The restaurant is on the third floor. Breakfast time is from 6:30 a.m. to 10:30 a.m. You'll have to present a coupon before you can enter the restaurant. Leo will give you the coupon later. If you want to go on the Internet, you'll need a password before you can connect to the Wi-Fi network. The password can be located on the nightstand in your room. There are two bottles of mineral water on the table in each room and they are complimentary. If you want to make an in-house call, please dial "one" first and then the room number. For example, if you would like to call room 302, you should dial 1302. Leo is going to stay at room 712, and my room number is 812. If you have any questions, just give us a call. Our wake-up call tomorrow is at 7:00 a.m. We are going snorkeling tomorrow morning. Be sure to come down to the lobby at 8:30 with your swimming gears, sunblocks and towels. We are departing at 8:35 tomorrow. Don't be late.

C: What about our luggage? Should we take the luggage to the room on our own?

A: Just leave your luggage here. The bell captain will deliver the luggage to your room. Don't forget to tip the bell captain. One dollar for one piece of luggage.

C: OK. When we go out, do we have to return the room key to the front desk?

A: You don't have to. But please make sure the key is with you at all times when you are out.

C: Do we need to leave a tip on the table before we go out tomorrow morning?

A: Yes, you are encouraged to leave one dollar for housekeepers because they will clean your room tomorrow. Now, Leo is going to tell you about your room number.

B:　Sorry to have kept you waiting. When you hear your name and room number, please come collect your room key and breakfast coupons. Each of you will have two coupons because we are going to stay here for two nights. Besides that, each of you will have the business card of this hotel. Just in case that you get lost or you can't find your way back to the hotel, you can take a taxi and show it to the taxi driver. After you get your room key, breakfast coupons, and the business card, you can take the elevator over there to your room. All the rooms are non-smoking rooms. The first thing you have to do after you enter your room is to check if there is hot shower and if the toilet is working properly. In five minutes, John and I will go to each room and see if you need any assistance. So, if there is a problem with the room facilities, please let us know then. Now, let me distribute the room keys and coupons to you.

Unit 7

 p.99

A: Host B: Tour Leader C: Server

A:　Good evening, sir. Welcome to Moonlight Restaurant. Do you have a reservation?

B:　Yes. I'm the tour leader with Supreme Tour.

A:　How many people are there in your party?

B:　There are 25 of us.

A:　I can see your reservation on the computer, sir. We are expecting you. The four tables by the window are ready for your group. So, are all your guests here?

B:　They just got off the tour bus and they will be here in a minute after going to the bathroom in the parking lot. Do you mind showing me the way to our tables?

A:　Certainly. This way, please. There will be six people for each table. Table No.1 is for people who don't eat beef. Pork or chicken will be served to them instead. Your meal will be served in another room down the hall. Here we are. Your guests can overlook the night view from here. So, what do you think? Will the tables be OK?

B:　They are more than OK. Thanks for reserving the best spot for us. I'm sure they are going to love it. Can you show me the menu?

A:　Here you go. Here are the six dishes you ordered for each table.

B:　Great. If any of the guests requests more rice or a refill for their drinks, please do that and put it on my tab.

A:　Certainly. The guests seem to have arrived at the entrance. Let's bring them in, shall we?

B: Sure. Let's go.

After the guests are seated and the first two dishes are served

B: Excuse me. The first two dishes were served to all the tables, except for Table One, 10 minutes ago. Why is it taking so long for Table One?

C: I'm very sorry, sir. I'll check the order with the chef right away.

B: Thanks.

After the first dish is served to Table One

B: Excuse me. Is this beef?

C: Yes, it is.

B: My guests at Table One don't eat beef. I was told this was a non-beef table.

C: Oh. I'm really sorry for the mistake. I'll bring chicken or pork instead.

B: OK.

After the guests are full and done with their meals

A: Sir, did your guests enjoy today's meal?

B: They seemed to like it. The night view is stunningly beautiful. But for the non-beef table, it took a bit longer before the first dish was served. After the dish finally arrived, it was beef.

A: We are terribly sorry for this mistake. We will be more careful next time.

B: OK.

A: Can I have your voucher for this group?

B: Of course. Here you are.

A: Please sign here.

B: Here you go.

A: Thanks and we are looking forward to serving you again soon.

附
錄

Unit 8

p.109

Good morning. It's my pleasure to give this presentation to you today. First of all, please allow me to introduce myself. My name is Anderson Newman. I'm a tour leader and I work for Happy Tours. I know all of you major in tourism in college and some of you might become tour leaders or tour guides in the future. So, I'm so excited that I can share some hands-on experience with you. The aim of this presentation is to talk about "optional tours" in a group tour. I've divided this presentation into three parts. First of all, I'm going to talk about "What are optional tours?" And then, I'm going to share "Why do optional tours exist?" Finally, I'm going to fill you in on what a tour leader should keep in mind when it comes to promoting optional tours. This presentation will take about seven minutes. If you have any questions, please hold your questions until the end of the presentation. Thanks.

So, what is an optional tour? An optional tour is an activity that is not included in a "default" or "standard" itinerary. In other words, it is an alternative option for people to get to explore local culture or special activities during a group tour.

After you know what an optional tour is, maybe you are wondering why optional tours exist and why it is not included in a tour package in the first place.

As a tour leader, I know not every guest likes "optional tours." People tend to associate it with "extra costs" or "hidden costs" in a group tour. That's why sometimes even a tour leader or tour guide doesn't feel comfortable or finds it challenging to promote "optional tours" to the guests. However, "optional tours" exist for two reasons.

First, "optional tours" can provide guests with more flexibility in a group tour. As we know, each country has its distinctive culture and activities. It is always fun to see them with your own eyes or be part of them during your journey. For example, festive or religious activities, water sports, adventurous activities, musicals, operas, folklore performances, massages, sunrise volcano trekking, cooking classes, and the list goes on and on. However, not all the activities are to everyone's liking. For example, an opera can be interesting for some people but dull for others. Similarly, bungee jumping or skydiving can be considered risky or dangerous by some people, but super exciting or intriguing by others. So, if those activities can be moved from a "standard" itinerary to an "optional tours" list for guests to choose from, the guests can just sign up for whatever they like to do without hard feelings.

Second, "optional tours" can bring down the costs of a package tour and attract price-conscious guests. For a travel agency, it is very important to keep its package tours competitive. However, in some countries, the costs of some activities are high, such as a helicopter tour, glacier trekking, or discovery / discover scuba diving. If those activities are part of the "default itinerary," the prices don't look pretty at all. On the contrary, if those expensive tours can be removed from a "default" tour package, the overall costs can be effectively reduced. As a result, price-sensitive consumers might be interested in the package tour and more competitiveness can be enhanced.

Now that we have talked about "What are optional tours" and "Why optional tours exist," let's move on to "What a tour leader should keep in mind when it comes to promoting optional tours?"

附
錄

Before a group tour, usually an orientation will be held. In the orientation, a tour leader should give a brief introduction to the optional tours to the guests, including the connections between the optional tours and local customs or cultures. In this way, the guests might be intrigued and sign up during the tour. However, don't forget to give some heads-up if there are potential risks in some particular activities. After all, safety is first and foremost and it should be the number one concern even though more registrations for optional tours can generate more commissions for a tour leader.

During a group tour, it's OK for a tour leader or a local tour guide to be articulate and encourage the guests to sign up for the optional tours, especially those activities they don't usually have the opportunity to experience in their home countries. However, don't just focus on how fun or interesting each optional tour is as the guests usually want to know more about the procedures and duration of an optional tour. Finally don't forget to give them some time to consider and tell them when the registration will be open. After the number of the participants is calculated, it's always a good idea to tell your guests that you are going to make a reservation for the activity first and set a deadline for the final registration.

Don't expect that every guest would sign up for optional tours. It is usually the case that the non-participants have to wait while those participants are having fun. Those non-participants might feel bored and ignored. As a thoughtful tour leader, be sure to check what those non-participants would like to do. For example, ask them if they would like to go back to the hotel, go window shopping in a nearby department store or a market, or enjoy some coffee in a café. In this way, they wouldn't feel left-out.

To sum up, optional tours have been part of a group tour for many years in this industry. While optional tours can bring more extra income for a tour leader, it also might bring some customer complaints. If a tour leader can build the right mentality about why optional tours exist, practice how to promote optional tours properly and remember that the safety of the guests is the first priority, I believe it will create a win-win situation. That's all for my presentation today. Hopefully it is useful for you. Thanks for listening. Now it's the Q&A session. At this moment, I'm very interested in hearing any questions you may have. Any questions?

Unit 9

 p.120

DJ: Welcome back to today's "Morning Show" on KIIS Radio, your favorite radio station in Taiwan. My name is Jack and I'll keep you company from 8:00 a.m. to 10:00 a.m. The Chinese New Year holiday is just around the corner. Are you excited? If you plan on traveling overseas and you love shopping during the upcoming nine-day holiday, you are in the right place. Why? Because right now in our studio we have a special guest, who is a certified and experienced tour leader. He's going to talk about "shopping tours" and share more insight with us. If you have any questions, just feel free to give us a call at 25189999. We will answer any questions you may have. Hi, Jerry. Welcome to "Morning Show." How are you doing?

Jerry: Pretty good. Thanks for having me.

DJ: It's our pleasure. So, let's cut to the chase and talk about "shopping tours."

Jerry: OK.

DJ: First of all, what are "shopping tours?"

Jerry: "Shopping tour" is a tour arranged by a travel agency, usually in a package tour or group tour. For example, if you are on a group tour, some souvenir shops and factories are part of the itinerary and you are expected to visit them and do some shopping.

DJ: OK. Just out of curiosity, why do we need those shopping tours? When we travel, we can shop at any time at any places, right?

Jerry: I know where you are coming from. Actually, one of the reasons why there are shopping tours is that they make it easier or more convenient for travelers to buy souvenirs or local specialties for their friends or family members. It's like a one-stop service. When you are in a souvenir shop arranged by a travel agency, usually the most popular items are on the shelves. For people who have no idea about what souvenirs to choose from, this can save them a lot of time. Besides, those shops or factories are selected or recommended by a local travel agency. So you don't have to worry about the quality of the products. According to the laws in Taiwan, if there are any defects or problems with the products, you can contact your travel agency for more assistance, such as a refund or a replacement, within one month after the purchase.

DJ: That sounds great. So, what are some other reasons for including shopping tours in a group tour?

Jerry: That's a good question. Another reason is that "shopping tours" can effectively lower the costs of a package tour.

DJ: Why is that?

Jerry: As we know, most people are price-sensitive, tend to compare prices and choose a more economical package tour. So, if a travel agency can offer its package tours at more competitive prices, chances are that more people might be interested or even sign up. If a group tour includes some "shopping tours," its price can be reduced and become more competitive.

DJ: How come?

Jerry: Because of sponsorship. Those shopping stops, such as a souvenir shop or factory, sponsor part of the travel expenses for group tours. For example, the rental fee for a tour bus. So, it helps lower the overall costs of a group tour. However, usually the sponsorship is in exchange for a visit to the souvenir shop and factory by the tourists because the guests might make a purchase once they enter those shopping stops. In other

附

錄

words, if a person signs up for a group tour at a lower price, usually he or she is expected to visit those shopping stops and stay there for a while.

DJ: I see. No wonder sometimes my friends told me they didn't have to take too much money out of their pockets when they signed up for an overseas group tour.

Jerry: Exactly. If a person can travel abroad at a more economical price, buy good quality of products at a souvenir shop or factory for his friends or family, and, in the meantime, the souvenir shop can make a profit, isn't that great?

DJ: You are right. It's more like a win-win situation.

Jerry: You can say that again.

DJ: What about tour leaders or tour guides? Do tour leaders or tour guides also make some money from the shopping tours?

Jerry: Yes. If the guests make a purchase in those shopping stops, the tour leader or tour guide can also make some money on a commission basis.

DJ: Then it's not just a win-win situation. It's more like a three-win situation.

Jerry: Yes, if you put it that way.

DJ: As you know, some of our listeners always want to be tour leaders. So, do you have any suggestions for those future tour leaders about promoting shopping tours?

Jerry: Yes. Before the group tour, be sure to tell your guests detailed information on the shopping tours of this trip in an orientation. Honesty is the best policy. Don't be shy to talk about this because the guests usually know what they have signed up for. If you choose not to talk about it, your guests might be skeptical about whether there is a hidden agenda in the itinerary. Besides, don't forget to share the local tax refund policy and emphasize the after-sale service provided by you and the travel agency. That is to say, your guests can always seek further assistance from you or the travel agency within 30 days of the purchase once there are product defects or problems.

DJ: What about during the shopping tour?

Jerry: When your guests are in the souvenir shop and have any questions about the products, let the staff of the shop do the talking because they know better about their products. Most important of all, keep track of time and don't keep your guests in the shopping stops longer than they should, especially when there is no sign of more purchases from your guests. This might upset a local tour guide. However, if you make this mistake, more customer complaints will be on the way.

DJ: Those are good suggestions. Now let's open the phone line and take questions from our listeners. Hello, KIIS Radio. Who is this?

Listener: This is Mary from Taipei.

DJ: Hi, Mary. What question do you have for our guest Jerry today?

Listener: Well, I'm a tour leader and I've been in this industry for 3 years. But I always find it challenging to promote shopping tours to my guests when we are on a tour bus. If you could share some tips or strategies with us, that would be great.

Jerry: I'm glad that you brought this up. In my experience, you can try three different strategies. First, when you share local history, customs or lifestyles with your guests, you can tactfully incorporate local specialties and famous products. Second, you can be a model to demonstrate those products and how useful they are. For example, if you are going to

附
錄

promote a scarf or leather jacket, you can wear it from the first day of the tour. Some guests might be intrigued and ask you for more info on the products. And then you can use their question as an opening to give a brief introduction to the product. Usually it can arouse more curiosity or interest from your guests. Finally, I have to say that most people are price sensitive. If a product is indigenous and is a famous global brand, its local price is usually lower than its international price. For example, some popular cosmetic products, bags, nutritional supplements, etc. So, when you promote those products, you can focus on the price comparison. It should be able to stimulate the purchase desire of your guests more easily.

DJ: Jerry, the three strategies are fantastic. I was on your tour group to Turkey last year. Come to think of it, you used all the three strategies to promote some products and I was not even aware of it at all. Good job, Jerry.

Jerry: Haha. I'll take it as a compliment, Jack.

DJ: It is indeed. Mary, hopefully you are still listening and find Jerry's tips useful. Now let's take another call.

Unit 10

＞ First Part of Listening 1

 p.132

A: Tour Leader B: Guest 1 C: Guest 2 D: Staff of the temple E: Mr. Lee

A: Welcome back, guys. How do you like this temple?

B: This temple is gigantic. The bas-reliefs on the walls are amazing. I saw them online before. But when I saw them with my own eyes, they really blew me away.

A: That's how I felt when I was here for the very first time. They are amazing, aren't they?

B: Yes, they are.

C: Jerry, my father was with me earlier. But now I can't seem to find him. He must have been lost on the way back. There are so many rocks on the trails. We also have to climb up and down along the way. I'm afraid that he might fall down somewhere or get trapped. What should we do now?

A: You must be very worried. I can relate to your feelings. Please tell me where and when you last saw your father?

C: Do you remember there was a giant tree on our way back here? He was with me there and we even took a picture together about 20 minutes ago. Let me show you the photo on my cell phone.

A: Yeah. I remember this giant tree. Now I need you to stay calm and stay put with other guests just in case your father comes back. I'll share this photo with some staff of the temple and we will look for him together. Whoever has located him will give an update in our Line group.

C: OK. I'll do that. Sorry to cause any delay or inconvenience to you or other guests.

A: No worries. Now the most important thing is to find your father.

附
錄

> First Part of Listening 2 p.132

A: Guest B: Tour Leader C: Ground staff

A:　Hey, Gary. It's 5:30 p.m. already. When are we boarding?

B:　The boarding time is 5:20 p.m. You must be wondering why we are still waiting. I believe there must be a delay. Let me check with the ground staff first and get back to you. I'll be right back.

The tour leader is talking to ground staff at the boarding counter

B:　Hi. My name is Gary and I'm a tour leader. The boarding time of this flight is 5:20 p.m. But now it's 5:32 already. I'm just wondering if there is a delay.

> First Part of Listening 3 p.132

A: Guest B: Tour Leader C: Clerk at Lost and Found Counter

A:　Hey, Gary. We have been waiting for the luggage for 30 minutes. I can't seem to find my luggage. What should I do?

B:　As all the people except you have got their luggage, and now it's all empty on the carousel, I think there is a chance that your luggage is missing.

A:　Really? I can't believe this. It's only the first day of the trip and my luggage is missing. How LUCKY!

B:　I'm sorry that this happened to you. I understand how you feel. You must feel a bit angry and frustrated. Please don't worry because 98 percent of the luggage will come back eventually. Why don't we go to the "Lost and found" counter and report missing luggage first?

A:　OK.

▶ First Part of Listening 4

 p.132

A: Guest B: Tour Leader

A: Hello. Is Gary there?

B: Speaking. May I ask who's calling?

A: This is Jerry.

B: Hi, Jerry. What can I do for you?

A: I don't know if it's just me or the dinner was too spicy. After dinner, my stomach was upset and I have been to the bathroom a couple of times. I guess I have diarrhea. It's killing me. I'm just wondering if you happen to have any medicine with you?

▶ Listening 1

 p.132

A: Tour Leader B: Guest 1 C: Guest 2 D: Staff of the temple E: Mr. Lee

A: Welcome back, guys. How do you like this temple?

B: This temple is gigantic. The bas-reliefs on the walls are amazing. I saw them online before. But when I saw them with my own eyes, they really blew me away.

A: That's how I felt when I was here for the very first time. They are amazing, aren't they?

B: Yes, they are.

C: Jerry, my father was with me earlier. But now I can't seem to find him. He must have been lost on the way back. There are so many rocks on the trails. We also have to climb up and down along the way. I'm afraid that he might fall down somewhere or get trapped. What should we do now?

A: You must be very worried. I can relate to your feelings. Please tell me where and when you last saw your father?

附

錄

C: Do you remember there was a giant tree on our way back here? He was with me there and we even took a picture together about 20 minutes ago. Let me show you the photo on my cell phone.

A: Yeah. I remember this giant tree. Now I need you to stay calm and stay put with other guests just in case your father comes back. I'll share this photo with some staff of the temple and we will look for him together. Whoever has located him will give an update in our Line group.

C: OK. I'll do that. Sorry to cause any delay or inconvenience to you or other guests.

A: No worries. Now the most important thing is to find your father.

The tour leader is talking to the staff of the temple

A: Excuse me. I'm a tour leader. One of my guests might be lost because he hasn't found his way back to our assembly point. He is in his 80s. We are afraid that something might happen to him. Can you do me a favor and help us find him?

D: Sure. Where and when did you guys last see him?

A: About 30 minutes ago he was still with his daughter near this giant tree.

D: I see. There is a fork road behind the giant tree. He must have turned right and taken the wrong path. If we go there, maybe we can find him.

A: Good idea. Let's go.

After a while...

A: There you are. Mr. Lee, we've been looking all over for you. Is everything OK?

E: Hi, Jerry. Thank God that you found me. Everything is OK except that I got lost earlier and I couldn't find my daughter. Actually, I was a bit nervous earlier. But you always told us to look for something obvious and wait patiently if we get lost. That's why I decided to come back to the giant tree.

A: I'm glad that you remember that. Good job! Now, let me give your daughter an update in our LINE group first. He's very worried about you.

> **Listening 2** p.132

A: Guest B: Tour Leader C: Ground staff

A: Hey, Gary! It's 5:30 p.m. already. When are we boarding?

B: The boarding time is 5:20 p.m. You must be wondering why we are still waiting. I believe there must be a delay. Let me check with the ground staff first and get back to you. I'll be right back.

The tour leader is talking to ground staff at the boarding counter

B: Hi. My name is Gary and I'm a tour leader. The boarding time of this flight is 5:20 p.m. But now it's 5:32 already. I'm just wondering if there is a delay.

C: Yes, there will be a slight delay. Actually, we are just about to make an announcement and give an update on the new boarding time. Because the airplane just made a landing earlier and all the baggage is being loaded to the aircraft at this moment, there will be a departure delay. We are sorry about the inconvenience.

B: Do you know how long it will take?

C: We should be boarding at 10 to 6.

B: OK. Thanks.

C: No problem.

The tour leader is breaking the news to the guests of the tour group

附
錄

B: Hello, everyone. Can I have you attention, please? I just checked with the ground staff at the boarding counter. The airplane just made a landing at the airport a while ago. As the baggage is being loaded right now, there will be a slight departure delay. The new boarding time is 10 to 6. Now it is 5:40 p.m. If there is a change to the boarding time again, I'll give you an update. Thanks for your patience.

A: Hi, Gary. As the flight is delayed, do you think we can request compensation from our travel insurance?

B: That's a good question. Generally speaking, people are entitled to file a claim for compensation in the event where the flight is delayed for more than four hours. In our case, it's still too early to do that at this moment. However, you can always check your travel insurance policy just in case.

A: Thanks for the suggestion. I will.

B: Excuse me. I have to send a message and tell our local tour guide in Bangkok that our flight is delayed. In this way, he can adjust our itinerary today.

A: OK.

> **Listening 3** 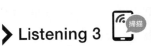 p.132

A: Guest B: Tour Leader C: Clerk at Lost and Found Counter

A: Hey, Gary. We have been waiting for the luggage for 30 minutes. I can't seem to find my luggage. What should I do?

B: As all the people except you have got their luggage, and now it's all empty on the carousel, I think there is a chance that your luggage is missing.

A: Really? I can't believe this. It's only the first day of the trip and my luggage is missing. How LUCKY!

B: I'm sorry that this happened to you. I understand how you feel. You must feel a bit angry and frustrated. Please don't worry because 98 percent of the luggage will come back eventually. Why don't we go to the "Lost and found" counter and report missing luggage first?

A: OK.

The tour leader is talking to the staff at the Lost and Found Counter

B: Hi. My name is Gary and I'm a tour leader. My guest's luggage seems to be missing. We'd like to report lost luggage.

C: Yes, sir. What flight were you on?

B: Flight CI2123 from Taipei.

C: Does your guest have the "baggage claim ticket?"

B: Here you go.

C: Please fill out this claim form first. Be sure to specify the type and color of the suitcase. Don't forget to include a phone number and an address where we can reach you.

B: OK. So, do you know where the luggage is?

C: According to the computer record, this luggage is in Hong Kong. There must be a mistake. We apologize for the mistake.

B: When can we get the luggage back?

C: I think we will put it on the next flight from Hong Kong to Bangkok and deliver the suitcase to you by tomorrow evening. Where will you be at that time?

B: We will be at the Hilton Hotel.

C: OK. Once we get the suitcase, we will give you a call and deliver it to the Hilton Hotel ASAP. Sorry to cause you any inconvenience.

附

錄

B: Thanks for your help.

A: Thanks for your help, Gary.

B: No problem. This is what I should do as a tour leader.

A: So, do you think I can request compensation from our travel insurance for the missing luggage?

B: I'm glad that you asked me. I was about to tell you about it. Generally speaking, an insurance company or an airline company will pay compensation for delayed or missing luggage. But the definitions of "delayed luggage" and "missing luggage" are quite different.

A: Can you be more specific?

B: Sure. 12 hours after you submit the claim form and you still haven't got your luggage, it's considered "delayed luggage." After 24 hours, it's considered "missing luggage."

A: So, after 12 hours, are they going to cover anything that I need?

B: Not really. Usually they only cover necessities, such as underwear, socks and all that.

A: Thanks for the info. I guess now all I can do is to wait for their further notice.

B: Actually, you can also check your insurance policy first. Maybe you can get more compensation. If you have any questions, let me know.

A: OK.

> **Listening 4**  p.132

A: Guest B: Tour Leader

A: Hello. Is Gary there?

B: Speaking. May I ask who's calling?

A: This is Jerry.

B: Hi, Jerry. What can I do for you?

A: I don't know if it's just me or the dinner was too spicy. After dinner, my stomach was upset and I have been to the bathroom a couple of times. I guess I have diarrhea. It's killing me. I'm just wondering if you happen to have any medicine with you.

B: I'm sorry to hear about that, Jerry. Unfortunately, I don't have any medicine like that with me. Besides, we are not allowed to provide our guests with any medicine.

A: How come?

B: Because we don't know what medication a guest is allergic to. If he or she takes the wrong medication, we might put his or her life on the line.

A: That makes sense.

B: If you still don't feel well, I suggest you go to see a doctor. I'll keep you company. No worries.

A: That's very nice of you. Thanks. However, as far as I know, it is costly to seek medical treatment when we are abroad, isn't it?

B: You are right. Usually it's more expensive. But health is the most important thing.

A: I know. So, does the insurance that comes with our group tour cover our overseas medical expenses?

B: Not that I know of. The inclusive insurance only covers medical expenses in the event of an accident, not diarrhea. Did you buy any travel insurance for this trip?

A: Not really.

附

錄

B: I see. But don't worry about the money. Our national health insurance in Taiwan covers part of our overseas medical expenses. All we need to do is to request some medical proof, such as "a certificate of diagnosis," from the hospital after the treatment. After we go back to Taiwan, we can contact any branch office of the National Health Insurance Bureau and apply for a reimbursement within six months from the date of outpatient, emergency treatment or discharge.

A: That's good to know. What a relief!

B: So, should I ask the Front Desk to call us a cab now?

A: That's OK. I think it's too much trouble. I feel better now. If I still have the runs, I'll give you a call. You've been working so hard the whole day. You should get some rest.

B: OK. Be sure to let me know if you still don't feel well, OK? I'm here for you.

A: Thanks, I will. Have a good night.

B: Get well soon.

領隊篇 Unit 1

❯ Reading 閱讀

標題：_____

　　在臺灣，在出發當天或旅行的第一天，旅行團團員通常會於出發前 2 個小時在機場的航空公司團體報到櫃檯向他們的旅行團領隊報到。為了在辦理報到手續上給團員更好的協助，有很多任務需要像你這樣的領隊去完成。如果你無法事先完成那些任務，那麼可能會在辦理報到手續上花費更多的時間。以下是你到機場辦理報到手續之前和期間應該做的準則：

1. 出發前至少兩個半小時到達（機場），並在團體報到櫃檯等候你的團員。

2. 備好所有必要的文件，譬如與當地旅行社的契約、保單、團員姓名紀錄、團員訂位紀錄、團員的護照、登機證、分房表、團員資料表、行李條等等。

3. 當你的團員到達時，歡迎他們並且分發登機證和行李條給他們。

4. 向團員說明辦理報到手續、辦理出境審查和安全檢查的程序。

5. 如有必要，宣布新的座位號碼。

6. 指出並強調登機時間和登機門號碼。

7. 提醒隨身和託運行李的「免費行李限制」以及「限制和違禁物品」。

8. 協助你的團員填寫 E / D 卡（出入境卡）和海關申報卡。

9. 帶你的團員到報到櫃檯報到並提供協助。

10. 在所有的行李沒有問題的通過 X 光機掃描後，集合所有的團員前往下一站──出境查證或安全檢查。

附錄

在回程出發當天，領隊應該做的事情與此類似，而當地導遊可能會分擔你的一些工作。機場可能沒有團體報到櫃檯。因此，你無法事先取得已列印的登機證，與團員分享更多的登機資訊。在這種情況下，您可以指導團員與他們的旅行同伴一起在一般的報到櫃檯辦理報到手續，以便他們可以被分配到彼此相鄰的座位。

並非每個人都經常出國旅行。有些人可能不知道機場辦理報到手續的細節。那就是為什麼專業的領隊可以成為極佳的助手。第一天或最後一天在機場辦理報到手續可能會有很多麻煩。例如，一些團員不準時或不熟悉行李要求。但是，作為領隊，無論面對什麼挑戰，都要保持耐心，有同理心，並展現出迷人的笑容。為什麼呢？對你而言，這可能僅僅是這次旅行的開始或結束，或者只是平常普通的一天。但是對團員來說，這趟跟團旅遊可能不僅僅是一次旅行。如果問題能夠處理得宜，那麼由於你專業的態度和心態，這趟旅行可能會變成他們一生中難忘的旅程。因此，倚著靠背舒服地坐下來，享受這趟旅途，準備發揮你的影響力為這趟旅程帶來改變吧！

▶ Listening 聽力

A：領隊　B：地勤人員　C&D：團員

A：嗨！我叫蓋瑞。我是領隊。我們將搭航班 CI1234 飛臺北。你能告訴我報到櫃檯何時會開始作業呢？

B：它會在出發前兩個小時開始。CI1234 出發時間是上午 10:30。現在是 8:20。所以，10 分鐘之後你的航班應該可以辦理報到了。

A：太好了。所以，有團體報到櫃檯嗎？

B：沒有。但稍後你和你的團員可以在 11 到 13 號櫃檯辦理報到手續。想坐在一起的乘客可以一起辦理報到。

A：太好了。謝謝你的幫助。

B：不客氣。

領隊正在和團員說話

A：哈囉。請注意到我這裡來。10 分鐘後我們會在 11 號櫃檯辦理報到。在此之前，檢查一下你們是否把鋰電池、行動電源，或貴重物品放在你們的託運行李裡。如果有，請把它們移到你的隨身行李裡。對於液體、噴霧劑或凝膠物品，如飲料、護膚產品、牙膏或髮膠，如果它們每樣少於 100 毫升，則可以將它們放在可密封的透明塑膠袋或夾鍊袋中，並放入隨身行李裡。否則，請務必將其放入你的託運行李裡。如你不確定該怎麼做時，請盡管發問。

在團員檢查隨身和託運行李之前

A：報到櫃檯現在開始作業了。請在這兒排隊並準備好你的護照。我會在櫃檯前協助你們。報到後不要忘了去看那邊的螢幕，確認你的行李箱通過 X 光機無誤。最後，請在這區域稍坐，直到我們都完成報到手續。謝謝你們的合作。

上午 8:30 在報到櫃檯

A：嗨！這位是我的團員，他要辦理報到。

B：好的。我能看你的護照嗎？

A：是的，在這裡。

B：他喜歡靠窗或走道的座位？

A：靠窗的座位。

B：沒問題。他有任何行李要託運嗎？

A：有的，只有一件。

B：請你把它放在磅秤上。

A：好的。

附錄

253

B：這是護照、登機證和行李託運收據。登機時間是上午 10 點在 13 號登機門。

A：好，謝謝！

B：沒問題。下一位。

A：他們想要一起辦理報到。

B：好。可以給我護照嗎？

A：給你。

B：兩個位置在一起？

A：是的。一個靠窗座位，一個靠中間座位。

B：知道了。有任何行李嗎？

A：是的，兩件。

B：好。請把行李放在磅秤上。

C：好。哇！50 公斤重。超重了嗎？我要付任何超重的費用嗎？

B：免費行李限額是每位 30 公斤。你們是兩位，所以你們可以到 60 公斤。它沒有超重。

D：好佳在（真是令人鬆了一口氣）！

B：好的。這是護照、登機證和行李託運收據。登機時間是上午 10 點在 13 號登機門。

A：真是多謝你了。

領隊篇 Unit 2

➤ Listening 聽力

　　哈囉！請注意這邊。我們即將前往安檢站了。因為是尖峰時間，你們可以看到很多人在那邊排隊，所以隊伍前進緩慢又大排長龍。為了節省時間快速通過安檢，以下有幾個小撇步：

1. 放輕鬆及保持耐心，因為我們正在度假。
2. 在入口出示你的護照跟登機證。
3. 口袋清空並將金屬物品放在托盤中。
4. 脫鞋、外套和皮帶，並將它們放在托盤中
5. 將平板電腦、筆電和手機從隨身包拿出來放到籃子裡。
6. 在檢查前將瓶子內的水清空。
7. 將隨身行李放上輸送帶。
8. 走過金屬探測器。假使途中探測器響了，請保持冷靜。安檢人員會在搜身前請你站直雙手舉高。搜身過程中請保持放鬆跟配合。
9. 假如安檢人員請你打開輸送帶上的行李箱做檢查，請遵循他們的指示。
10. 檢查完畢，請記得帶走你的行李。

　　以防萬一，我（領隊）會一直待在隊伍後面。遇到任何問題，請務必告訴我。如果你常出國旅行，過安檢站後你就可帶著你的護照跟登機證往登機門去了，或者你也可以待在原地等我。我（領隊）會陪著你們一起到登機門。總之，不要忘了在 10 點前抵達 13 號登機門。更重要的是，登機前請先找我報到。以上有問題嗎？如沒問題，我們就出發吧！

附錄

領隊篇 Unit 3

> Reading 閱讀

　　在通關（通過證照查驗）後，團員在前往登機門的路上，可以去免稅商店逛逛。身為領隊，也許你以為可以稍微放鬆，然而實際狀況並非如此，在登機前仍然有許多事要完成。

1. 隨時注意登機廣播以防班機延遲或是更換登機門。假如班機延遲，有可能會使你無法順利登上轉接班機，你必須要採取行動解決這些可能會發生的問題。無論你的班機發生了什麼問題，要跟你的團員告知最新的航班資訊。

2. 必要時適當調整座位分配。以旅行團來說，座位通常是依乘客英文名字的字母順序來排的。乘客不能事先選座位，所以會導致朋友間或是家人無法坐在一起。身為領隊，萬一你沒有時間在團員機場報到前重新安排符合團員需求的座位，那在登機前的這段時間很適合拿來做這件事。在登機前告知團員他們新的座號，也告訴他們你的座號，以備他們在飛機上需要你的協助。假如你的團員有飲食上的限制，別忘了在調整座位後重新註記他們的新座位號碼，因為你必須跟負責餐食的空服員更新這些資訊。

3. 總是在你的團員們都登機後你才登機。這是非常重要的，因為總有團員在免稅店逛到忘了時間。領隊的工作之一就是要確保你的團員不要錯過班機。一旦你的團員沒有準時出現在登機門，不要猶豫，立刻打電話給他／她。萬一用電話聯繫不上該名團員，請地勤人員協尋。

　　在你的團員都順利登機後，這裡有列出幾項你能在飛機飛行中做的事：

1. 確認所有團員坐在正確的座位。

2. 假使飛行時間很長，為每位團員跟空服員要一條毯子。

3. 在換座位後，告知負責餐食服務的空服員有特殊飲食需求團員的新座位號碼。這樣能避免空服員送錯餐。

4. 在飛行途中不時地注意團員的狀況，以便提供必要協助。

　　假如你能在登機前跟飛行途中完成這些工作，代表你十分專業且會在旅行一開始就在團員心中留下好印象。但是千萬要注意，不要因為太熱情做出超過領隊範圍的事，因為在飛機上就讓空服員做他們該做的事。同時，別忘了把握時間，補個眠、好好充個電等等，因為無論抵達目的地之後還是需要轉機，你都還有很多事情要做。

⟩ Listening 聽力 2

A：領隊　B：空服員

A：不好意思。我是領隊，我想要更新一下我們的座位表，因為我的團員有特殊飲食需求。你知道要跟誰說嗎？

B：喔！我就是負責飛機餐配送的人，你找對人了。

A：太棒了。這是新的座位清單，你可以看到他們的英文名字跟他們點的特殊餐食。新的跟舊的座位號碼在這裡。

B：太好了！真是太清楚了！這張紙條我可以留著嗎？

A：當然。

B：謝謝你的告知。我會確認同事們送正確的餐點給他們。

A：太好了，謝謝。還有其他問題的話，可以來 15B 找我。

B：好的，沒問題。

附
錄

領隊篇 Unit 4

▶ Reading 閱讀 1

「直達」和「直飛」航班對你來說聽起來都一樣嗎？或者是你將術語「中轉」（原機過境）和「轉機」交替使用呢？

-----------------------------(1)-----------------------------

顧名思義，直達航班是從一個機場到目的地機場，一路上沒有任何停靠。直飛航班是帶你從起點的機場到目的地機場，但沿途可能會在中途機場短暫停留。在這種情況下，乘客可能會下飛機，然後在中途機場登上飛機，就像客運巴士接送乘客上下車一樣。請注意，直飛航班只有一個航班編號。例如，如果有航班從新加坡飛到舊金山且中途未停靠任何地方，那就是直達航班。相較之下，如果航班是從新加坡飛往舊金山，在香港機場有停靠，則為直飛航班。即使大多數人會將「直達航班」和「直飛航班」這兩術語交替使用，但對於領隊來說，能區分兩者的不同點仍是非常重要的。

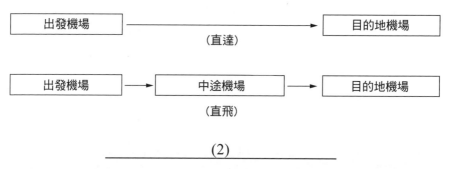

-----------------------------(2)-----------------------------

如果飛機在機場短暫停靠，並在乘客返回搭同一班飛機後繼續飛行，就是原機過境。在這種情況下，每位乘客在他／她出發機場辦理報到手續時只取得一張登機證，而且他／她的行李可以寄送到最終目的地。當乘客在中途機場過境時，必須攜帶隨身行李下飛機。通常，乘客到達中途機場後會從地勤人員那裡收到過境通行證，然後通過安全檢查和隨身行李受檢。最後，他們在地勤人員的引導下前往登機門等待登機。換句話說，乘客在中途機場無須辦理入境審查、領取行李以及接受海關行李檢查。

出發機場		中途機場		目的地機場
• 取得兩張登機證 • 行李可運送到目的地 • 登機（航班TW123）	→	• 取得過境通行證 • 安全檢查 • 候機室 • 同一登機門登機 　（航班TW123）	→	

　　如果乘客必須搭乘兩個以上的不同航班才能到達最終目的地，那就是轉機，而非原機過境。當兩航班屬於同一家航空公司或同一聯盟時，只要是轉機時間不超過 24 小時，通常就可以將行李直接從出發機場運送到最終目的地。雖然在辦理報到時，大多數都會在出發機場核發兩張已劃位的登機證，但有時只有核發第一張登機證，第二張登機證則是在中途機場的轉機櫃檯取得。像這樣轉機，如果第一班航班延誤了，乘客通常不必擔心錯過轉機航班，因為航空公司會提供必要的協助並解決問題。對乘客來說，轉機如同中途機場過境（中轉）一樣容易，因為乘客無須到轉機櫃檯報到，除非他們需要取得第二張登機證，或當第一班航班誤點而錯過了轉機的航班。否則唯一的區別是在進行安檢後，乘客可能不得不前往另一登機門或航廈，因為轉機航班可能會從另一航廈，或甚至從同一航廈的另一登機門離開。所以，為了安全起見，乘客應確保兩航班之間要有足夠的時間轉機。

出發機場		中途機場		目的地機場
• 取得兩張登機證 • 行李可運送到目的地 • 登機（航班TW123）	→	• 安全檢查 • 前往新登機門 　（可能不同航廈） • 候機室 • 登上不同飛機 　（航班T321）	→	

附錄

如果乘客搭乘兩航班且它們不屬於同一聯盟怎麼辦？這仍然是轉機，辦理行李托運和取得兩張登機證的手續，會和搭兩航班屬同一聯盟的情況一樣簡單。但是，有可能無法將行李運送至目的地機場，在出發機場也可能僅核發一張登機證。這種情況下，在到達中途機場後，一定要到轉機櫃檯報到，以取得第二張登機證，或與地勤人員確認你的托運行李狀況。你可能需要領回行李，然後再次重新辦理行李托運。同時，在你第一個航班誤點且你無法趕上第二個航班的情況下，轉機服務可能不會像隸屬同一家航空公司或同一聯盟的兩航班那樣無縫接軌。

出發機場
- 取得兩張登機證
- 行李可運送到目的地
- 登機（航班TW123）

中途機場
- （轉機櫃檯）
  - （取第2張登機證）
  - （確認行李狀況）
- 安全檢查
- 前往新登機門（可能不同航廈）
- 候機室
- 登上不同飛機（航班ABC321）

目的地機場

　　比較三種狀況如下：

航班	一個航班	兩個航班	兩個航班
航班間合作關係	同一航空公司	同一航空公司或同一聯盟	不同航空公司或不同聯盟
原機過境／轉機	原機過境（中轉）	轉機	轉機
出發機場核發兩張登機證	是	是	視情況
行李托運到最終目的地	是	是	視情況
有過境通行證	是	否	否

航班	一個航班	兩個航班	兩個航班
在中途機場登機前需安檢	是	是	是
在中途機場是同一登機門	同	不同	不同
在中途機場不同航廈登機	否	可能	可能

　　如果其中一個航班是廉價航空公司 (LCC)，轉機通常會比較麻煩且耗時。例如，如果你乘坐廉價航空公司 (LCC)，轉機搭乘傳統航空公司 (FSC)，通常只會核發一張登機證，而且你的行李無法直接運送到最終目的地。到達中途機場後，你必須通過海關行李檢查、領取行李，然後辦理下一個航班的報到手續，以取得下一張登機證，這需要更多時間。不過，很高興知道有更多的廉價航空公司為轉機與合作的航空公司提供無縫銜接的服務。因此，建議在預訂航班之前確認中途機場的轉機手續。

＞ Reading 閱讀 2

標題：＿＿＿＿＿＿＿＿＿＿＿＿＿＿＿＿

　　作為領隊，你知道在原機過境或轉機中應該為團員做什麼嗎？如果你沒有頭緒，本文可能正是你所需要的。即使原機過境或轉機的程序因機場而異，這裡有一般準則供你遵循：

1. 行前，你應該確認轉機或原機過境需花多久時間。如果超過 4 小時，與航空公司確認是否供應不含酒精的飲料。如超過 6 小時，與航空公司確認是否提供點心折價券。如果沒有免費的飲料或點心，確認旅行社是否願意承擔。

2. 如果出發機場核發兩張登機證，以防萬一，你應該為你的團員保存第二張登機證。在中途機場安檢前，再將第二張登機證分發給每位團員。

附錄

3. 抵達中途機場時集合你的團員。與地勤人員確認轉機／原機過境手續，並將最新資訊告知團員。

4. 以原機過境來說，務必確認每位團員都收到過境通行證，因為你的團員在中途機場走動時將需要它。

5. 即使你事先在出發機場取得了轉機的登機證，務必在到達中途機場時查看登機門和登機時間的最新訊息。

6. 如果轉機時無登機證，請準備PNR（團員名單），向團員收取所有護照，簽證和行李提領票根，並前往轉機櫃檯尋求進一步協助。

7. 如果第一班航班誤點而你錯過了轉機航班，請準備PNR，向團員收取護照、簽證和行李提領票根，然後前往轉機櫃檯尋求進一步的協助。

8. 基於安全理由，在原機過境或轉機過程中所有隨身行李必須受檢，務必提醒你的團員在中途機場下飛機時必須帶好所有個人隨身物品。

9. 務必將你的手錶與當地的時間同步，告訴團員也要如此做。引導你的團員前往登機門轉機，或到航廈正確的離境樓層，提醒他們登機時間，並請他們登機前向你報到。旅行團解散前，不要忘了告訴他們，萬一他們迷路找不到你，以及找不到回到登機門的路時，要如何與你聯絡。

10. 轉機／原機過境需要一段時間，要為你的團員指出洗手間、免稅商店、貴賓休息室或其他設施的位置或方向，因為他們可能會有興趣。

　　一段長時間的旅程，轉機／原機過境是不可避免的，但是那似乎會令旅行者卻步。如果領隊不瞭解轉機／原機過境的一般手續，無法妥善處理一些問題，一趟精彩的旅程將會變成一場災難。相反地，如果原機過境或轉機相當順暢（像絲綢般的順暢），則可以建立領隊的專業形象，並輕鬆贏得團員更多的信任。

> Listening 聽力 1

A：午安。需要幫忙嗎？

B：是的，我是領隊。我們來這裡辦理轉機報到手續。

A：請給我你們的機票和護照。

B：當然。這是 PNR（團員名單）所有的護照和我們第一班航班的行李提領票根。

A：謝謝。到伊斯坦堡航班 CI1234 有 26 位，正確嗎？

B：是的，沒錯。我們的座位互相可以靠近一點嗎？

A：我會盡力。

B：那就太好了。謝謝。另外，可以確認行李的狀況嗎？我想要確認我們的行李有沒有遺失。

A：當然。請等一下。就我所知，行李稍早已經從你們上一班航班卸下來，現在行李已在轉機航班 CI1234 了。

B：太好了。謝謝你的確認。

A：沒問題，先生。所以，這是你的 PNR（團員名單）和登機證。登機時間是下午 6:30 在 16 號登機門。起飛的時間是下午 7:00。

B：請問登機門往哪走？

A：好的。直走，右轉然後搭電梯上樓。你會先經過安檢，再來你一定會看到往登機門的標示。

B：謝謝你的資訊。

A：不客氣。一路順風。

> Listening 聽力 2

A：午安。我能幫上你什麼忙嗎？

B：我是領隊。我們從臺北起飛的航班 CI1234 誤點，結果我們無法趕上我們的轉機航班 NW1234 去檀香山。你能幫我們嗎？

A：我看看我能做什麼。先生，能給我你們的機票和護照嗎？

B：當然。這是 PNR（團員名單）、所有的護照和我們第一班航班的行李提領票根。

A：謝謝。你們是 23 位，對嗎？

B：是的。

A：事實上，我們有一班飛往檀香山的航班，它會在 20:00 起飛。現在還有 30 個空位。如果可以接受的話，我將安排你們搭上這航班。航班編號是 NW4321。

B：那真是太好了。我們接受。可以的話，你能幫我們確認我們的行李是否已經到達，並且將會搬到新的轉機航班上呢？

A：當然可以。這是你們的 PNR、護照和登機證。登機時間是下午 7:30 在 15 號登機門。起飛時間是下午 8:00。

B：請告訴我登機門的方向？

A：好的。直走，右轉，然後搭電梯上樓。你會先經過安檢，再來你將會看到往登機門的標示。

B：感謝你的資訊和協助。你剛剛拯救了我們的旅行。

A：不客氣。祝你們旅途愉快。

領隊篇 Unit 5

＞ Reading 閱讀

標題：_____

　　飛機降落並滑行至登機口後，這時候像你這樣的領隊要準備好在目的地機場辦理可能耗時且讓人害怕的入境程序。作為領隊，你應該對以下準則瞭若指掌，包括入境審查、領取行李、行李掛失和海關行李檢查：

1. 在降落之前，最好告訴你的團員，在進入航廈後要跟團員集體行動，不要自己直奔移民局（入境審查）。

2. 進入航廈後，務必集合所有團員，統計人數並且說明入境程序。如果他們之中有人必須上廁所，指出洗手間的方向，並耐心等待他們回來後再前往移民局（入境查證）。

3. 告訴你的團員他們正在休假中，他們應該放輕鬆並耐心等待，因為入境程序可能比預期要花更長的時間。

4. 在入境審查之前，請提醒團員管制區內禁止拍照或錄影。然後，指示排隊的位置。之後，告訴他們取下護照套，準備好登機證，簽證和入境登記表，並等候輪到他們。某些國家的移民官可能會拍攝每位團員的大頭照，採取他們的指紋。最後，不要忘了告訴他們你的走道。如果有什麼事情發生，要他們叫你。

5. 對於領隊來說，最好是留在旅行團後面，以免你的團員在入境審查時需要你的協助。但是，在獲得團體簽證的情況下，領隊應保持在隊伍的前面，出示團體簽證清單並先與移民官員交談。

6. 如果你可以指派一個或兩個有經驗的團員率先通過入境審查，並告知如何找到行李及行動轉盤的資訊，這樣會更有效率。如此一來，他們也可以分享這些資訊，並在你之前引導其他團員領取行李。

附錄

7. 細心觀察是否有團員在通過入境審查過程中需要你的協助。在你前往行李提領區之前確認所有人都跟上。

8. 在行李提領區,引導你的團員將所有與旅行社提供的行李箱標籤相同的行李箱從轉盤上取下。然後,請團員確認他們的行李箱是否符合他們的行李提領票根。如果團員找不到他/她的行李箱,陪同他/她到失物招領櫃檯,申報行李遺失,並讓他/她冷靜下來。

9. 在海關行李檢查之前,提醒您的團員出示海關申報卡並選擇正確的通道。通常,綠色通道是沒有物品要申報,而紅色通道則是有物品要申報。還有,請一位或兩位有經驗的團員到入境接機大廳後找一下當地導遊。如果你有團員被海關人員攔下做進一步的檢查,你要立即伸出援手並提供協助。

入境程序可能很漫長,在你和你的團員到達入境接機大廳與當地導遊或遊覽車司機會面之前,也可能會有一些障礙,尤其是在機場尖峰時間。然而,如果你能了解常見的入境程序,以及如何解決一些潛在的問題,並事先提醒你的團員,我相信你可避開一些混亂,節省更多的時間,而且你在你團員的眼裡看起來肯定是專業的。

▶ Listening 聽力 1

A:午安。歡迎來到菲律賓。請問我可以看你的護照和入境登記表嗎?

B:當然,請看!我是旅行團的領隊,這是我們的團體簽證。

A:謝謝!你們是從哪裡來的?

B:我們來自臺灣。

A:你們團員有多少人?

B:我們有 20 人,他們都在我後面。我必須收集所有的護照給你嗎?

A:不,不用。事實上,每個團員必須個別入境審查。

B：了解！

A：這趟旅程多久？

B：5 天。

A：你們會在哪停留？

B：長灘島星期五渡假村

A：請看著照相機，並把手指放在機器上。

B：好的。我可以留在我的旅行團後面，以備我的團員在入境查證時需要我的協助嗎？

A：當然可以的。或者你可以站在一邊等他們。這是你的護照。我稍後會把團體簽證還給你。

B：謝謝！

A：沒問題！下一位。

❯ Listening 聽力 2

A：嗨，我是領隊。我團員的行李好像不見了。我們在行李提領區等行李，等了快 45 分鐘，但行李都沒有到。我們想要申報行李遺失。

B：是的，先生。請問你們搭哪班飛機？

A：從臺北起飛的班機 CI1234。這是行李提領票根。

B：我看看。我們的電腦顯示您的手提箱現在在香港。

A：香港？

B：是的，我們對於這樣的錯誤感到抱歉。煩請填寫這份行李遺失表。詳細說明手提箱的款式和顏色。務必包含電話號碼並告知我們可以聯繫到你或你團員的地方。

A：好的。我們何時可以拿到手提箱呢？

B：我想我們可以明天傍晚把手提箱送給你。那時你會在哪裡？

A：我們會在市區的希爾頓飯店。

B：好的。一旦我們拿到手提箱，我們會盡快把它送到希爾頓飯店。很抱
　　歉給你帶來不便。

領隊篇 Unit 6

▶ Listening 聽力

A：導遊　B：領隊　C：團員

A：這是所有團員的房號。五間單床雙人房跟三間雙床雙人房對嗎？

B：對的。哪間房間是最大或風景最好的？

A：每間房間都差不多大，但 912 號房有最好的海景，也許你可以保留給經理。

B：好主意！讓我寫下來。請問你住的房號是？

A：812 號房，你呢？

B：我會和另一位團員住 712 號房。

A：了解。這是房間鑰匙，需要我幫忙分配給其他團員嗎？

B：謝謝，沒關係，我能自己處理。在那之前我需要在分房表上花點時間。你不妨先跟團員們介紹這間旅館並告知我們明早的行程。

A：OK，各位先聽這邊。我們會在這間旅館住兩晚，Leo 等會會告訴你們的房號並且給你們房卡。我先為各位介紹旅館的設施和我們明天的行程。這間旅館附設健身房跟溫水游泳池它們分別在 4 樓和 7 樓。健身房跟游泳池從早上 8 點開到晚上 10 點，帶著你的房卡前往就能使用了。餐廳在三樓，早餐供應的時段是從 6 點半到 10 點半，Leo 等等會發餐券給你們，進去前先出示你的餐券。假如你需要上網，這邊的 WI-FI 都需要密碼才能連上，密碼在各位房間的床頭櫃上。桌上兩瓶水是免費的。假如你要打內線電話，先按 1 再按房號。比如我現在要打去 302 號房，就按 1302。Leo 會在 712 號房，我則會在 812 號房。有任何問題，可打給我們。明早 7 點 morning call。明早我們會去浮潛。記得 8 點半準時在大廳集合，帶上你的游泳裝備、防曬乳跟毛巾，我們會在 8 點 35 準時出發，別遲到。

附錄

C：那我們的行李該怎麼辦，我們要自己帶到房間嗎？

A：行李放在這就好，行李員會把它們送到你們的房間。不要忘了給小費，一件行李一塊錢。

C：那我們出去的時候要把房卡放在櫃臺嗎？

A：不用喔。但外出的時候要隨身攜帶你的房卡。

C：我們明早離開的時候需要留小費嗎？

A：可以啊。建議你給清潔人員一元美金小費，因為他們明天會打掃你的房間。接下來 Leo 會告訴你們每個人的房號。

B：抱歉讓你們久等了！當你們聽到你們的名字跟房號時，請來領取房卡跟餐券。每個人都會拿到兩張餐券，因為我們會在這裡住兩晚。等等你們都會拿到旅館的名片，萬一你們外出找不到回旅館的路，你可以搭計程車回來秀名片給司機看。拿完房卡、餐券跟名片，你們就可以搭那裡的電梯到各自的房間了。所有房間禁止吸菸。進房後第一件事先確認有沒有熱水，看馬桶是否能用，五分鐘後 John 和我會去每間房間看看你們有沒有需要幫助的。有任何房間的問題，請讓我們知道，現在開始發房卡跟餐券。

領隊篇 Unit 7

▶ Reading 閱讀

當地食物可以反映獨特的國家或文化特徵。對於海外的團員，在旅途中嘗試異國料理來了解和體驗當地文化是至關重要的。如果領隊或導遊能做些什麼以確保他或她的團員有個美好的用餐體驗，這無疑會為旅程增添樂趣，特別是對美食家來說。

有幾件領隊或導遊可做的事：

1. 用餐 2 到 3 小時前一定要打電話給餐廳，確認用餐人數、餐點、飲食限制、座位安排和到達時間。旺季時，在正常用餐時間很可能沒有空的桌子，所以確保你的旅行團在最佳的時間到達就非常的重要。換句話說，為了避免擁擠能即時到達餐廳，有時只好提前或延後用餐時間。在這情況下，不要忘記要讓團員了解理由，並解釋變動的原因，以避免客訴。

2. 入境隨俗。由於用餐禮儀因國家而異，告知團員避免因不熟悉當地文化而失望總是個好主意。例如：服裝規定、如何適當地使用餐具、如何使用餐巾、如何請服務生幫忙，以及講話應有的音量等等。此外，不要忘了協助你的團員設定好對餐點的期待。例如，餐點的分量和風味，酒和飲料的價格資訊，以及餐廳的服務速度。如果你能對團員提及這些資訊，將可避免一些誤會。

3. 西式餐廳的餐桌通常可供 4 到 6 人，而中式餐館的圓桌通常最多可容納 10 人。同時，有些團員有飲食限制。領隊最好事先安排好座位，並提前與餐廳溝通。這樣，你的團員就可以盡情無障礙地享受餐點。

4. 在 2 或 3 道菜後或確定事情已步上正軌後，你才坐到自己的位子上用餐。在用餐時也要留意你的團員，因為當團員無法有效地和服務人員溝通時，可能需要你的協助。如果你在不同房間用餐，務必要在團員用完餐之前回來，免得他們正在找你。如果團員仍然肚子餓或似乎沒吃飽，而額外的費用在你的預算之內，你可以考慮為他們添加一、兩道菜。

附錄

5. 用餐時，有些問題可能會出現。例如，出菜的時間比預期的久。餐點不是團員點的。菜裡有一些稀奇古怪的東西。啤酒沒氣了或湯匙髒了。諸如此類的事情發生後，如領隊可以在現場適時地介入和提供協助，這些問題將不會停留在你團員的腦海裡太久，你反而可能將客訴變成客戶滿意。

　　旅途中要每一餐都滿足你的團員不是件輕鬆的工作。然而，如果你能在餐前協助團員設定好應有的期待，用餐期間提供專業和周到的協助，並在餐後收集團員的回饋，幾乎每位團員仍會開心，儘管有些菜不合他們的胃口。祝用餐愉快！

> **Listening 聽力**

A：餐廳接待員　B：領隊　C：服務生

A：先生，晚安。歡迎來到「月光餐廳」。有訂位嗎？

B：有的。我是「極致旅遊」的領隊。

A：你們總共有多少人呢？

B：我們有 25 人。

A：先生，我在電腦上有看到你的訂位。我們正期待你們的到來。4 張靠窗的桌子已為你們準備好了。所以，你的團員都到了嗎？

B：他們剛下車，去停車場的廁所，待會就會到。你能告訴我我們的座位在哪裡嗎？

A：當然。這邊請。每張桌子可坐 6 位。1 號桌是給不吃牛肉的人。餐點將改為豬肉或雞肉。你的餐點將在大廳盡頭的另一個房間供應。我們到了。團員可以從這裡俯瞰夜景。那麼，你覺得呢？桌子還可以嗎？

B：好極了。感謝你為我們保留最好的位置。我確定他們會喜歡的。可以給我看菜單嗎？

A：在這裡。這是你為每桌訂的 6 道菜。

B：太好了。如果任何團員要求加飯或續杯，請照做並記在我的帳上。

A：當然。團員似乎已到了門口。我們去帶他們進來，好嗎？

B：好的。我們走。

（在團員就座和前兩道菜上完之後）

B：不好意思！ 10 分鐘前各桌都已上了兩道菜，除了 1 號桌外。為什麼 1 號桌要那麼久？

C：非常抱歉，先生。我馬上和廚師確認餐點。

B：謝謝。

（在上第一道菜給 1 號桌後）

B：不好意思。這是牛肉嗎？

C：是的，是牛肉

B：1 號桌的團員不吃牛肉。有人告訴我這桌是沒有牛肉的。

C：喔！我為這錯誤感到非常抱歉。我會換上雞肉或豬肉。

B：好吧！

（在所有團員吃飽並用完餐之後）

A：先生，你的團員們還滿意今天的餐點嗎？

B：他們好像喜歡。夜景非常漂亮。但沒有牛肉那桌，第一道菜出菜時間有點久，好不容易出菜後，最後來的卻是牛肉。

A：我們對於這樣的錯誤深感抱歉，下次我們會更加小心。

B：好吧！

A：可以給我這個旅行團的 voucher（商家用來跟旅行社請款的憑證）嗎？

B：當然。給你。

附
錄

A：請在這裡簽名。

B：好的。

A：謝謝，我們期待很快能再次為你服務。

領隊篇 Unit 8

Listening 聽力

　　早安。今天很高興跟大家做簡報。首先，請容我自我介紹。我叫安德森 · 紐曼。我是領隊，為「快樂旅遊」工作。我知道你們在大學裡都主修觀光，有些人未來可能成為領隊或導遊。所以我很興奮能與你們分享一些實務經歷。本次演講的目的是要談團體旅遊中的「自費行程」。我將演講分成三個部分。首先，我要談的是「什麼是自費行程？」，然後我將分享「為什麼有自費行程的存在？」，最後，我將向你們介紹領隊在推廣自費行程時應該謹記些什麼。這場簡報大約 7 分鐘。如果你有任何問題，請在 Q&A 再提出。謝謝！

　　所以，什麼是自費行程？自費行程是不包含在「預定」或「標準」行程中的活動。換句話說，它是在團體遊旅期間人們可探索當地文化或特殊活動的替代選擇。

　　在你知道什麼是自費行程之後，可能會想知道為什麼會有自費行程，以及為何一開始就未包含在旅遊套裝行程中。

　　身為領隊，我知道不是每個團員都喜歡「自費行程」。團員容易把「自費行程」與團體旅遊裡的「額外費用」或「隱藏費用」聯想在一起。這就是為什麼有時候甚至領隊或導遊都會感到不自在或覺得向團員推廣「自費行程」是一種挑戰。然而，「自費行程」的存在有兩個原因。

　　首先，「自費行程」可以為團員提供更多團體旅遊的靈活性。就我們所知，每個國家都有其獨特的文化和活動。在旅程中親眼看到或成為他們的一部分總是很有趣的。例如：節慶或宗教活動、水上運動、冒險活動、音樂劇、歌劇、民俗表演、按摩、日出火山健行、烹飪課程等等不勝枚舉。然而，並不是所有活動都受到每個人的喜愛。例如：歌劇對某些人來說可能很有趣，但對其他人來說卻很沉悶。同樣地，高空彈跳或跳傘被某些人認為是冒險或危險的，但其他人卻超級刺激或覺得有趣。因此，如果這些

活動可以從「標準行程」移到「自費行程」清單裡供團員選擇，團員就可以自在地報名參加任何他們喜歡的活動。

　　第二，「自費行程」可降低套裝旅遊行程的成本，並吸引對價格敏感的團員。例如：對旅行社而言，保有競爭力的套裝旅遊行程是很重要的。然而，某些國家有一些活動的費用很高，比如直升機之旅、冰川健行，或體驗潛水。如果這些活動是「預定」行程的一部分，價格一點都不好看。相反地，如果這些昂貴的旅遊行程可以從「預定」的套裝旅遊行程移除，整體成本將能有效地降低。因此，對價格敏感的消費者可能對套裝旅遊行程感興趣，更可提高競爭力。

　　即然我們已經討論了「什麼是自費行程？」和「為什麼有自費行程存在？」，現在讓我們繼續討論「在推廣自費行程時，領隊應該謹記些什麼？」

　　團體旅遊前，通常會開一個行前會議。在會議中，領隊應該扼要地介紹自費行程給團員，包括自費行程與當地習俗或文化之間的關聯。這樣，團員可能會感興趣並在旅途中報名參加。然而，不要忘記提醒有些特殊活動會有潛在的風險。儘管越多團員登記報名自費行程可增加領隊的傭金，但安全畢竟是最重要且應該是第一考量的因素。

　　團體旅遊途中，領隊或當地導遊可以明確表達且鼓勵團員報名參加自費行程，尤其是團員在自己國家裡不太有機會可以體驗的活動。儘管如此，不要只聚焦於每項自費行程有多好玩或多有趣，因為團員通常會想知道更多有關於自費行程的流程和時間長短。最後，不要忘了給團員一些考慮的時間，並告訴他們何時開始登記報名。在統計要參加的人數後，最好告訴你的團員你會先預約活動，和設定最後登記報名的截止時間。

　　不要指望每位團員都會報名參加自費行程。通常情況會是沒有參加的人必須等待那些有參加且正玩得開心的人。那些沒有參加的人可能會感到無聊和被忽視。作為考慮周到的領隊，一定要了解沒報名的人想做什麼。

例如：問他們是否想回飯店、到附近的百貨公司或市場逛逛，或是在咖啡館裡喝咖啡。如此，他們就不會感到被冷落了。

　　總而言之，自費行程被當作團體旅遊的一部分在這產業裡已行之有年。雖然自費行程可以為領隊帶來更多額外的收入，但它也可能會帶來一些客訴。如果領隊對於為何有自費行程的存在能建立正確的思維，練習如何適當地推廣自費行程，並記得團員的安全為首要，我相信必能創造雙贏的局面。我今天的演講內容到此。希望對你們會有所幫助。感謝聆聽！現在是 Q&A 時間。此刻，我非常有興趣聽到你們的問題。有任何問題嗎？

附
錄

領隊篇 Unit 9

> Listening 聽力

DJ：歡迎回到今天 KIIS 廣播的「晨間秀」，臺灣你最愛廣播電臺。我是 Jack，將在早上 8:00 到 10:00 陪伴你。春節假期即將到來，你是否感到興奮呢？如果接下來的 9 天連假你有國外旅遊的規劃，而且你喜歡購物，那你來對地方了。為什麼呢？因為現在我們的播音間有一位特別來賓，他是擁有領隊執照及經驗豐富的領隊。待會兒他將與我們討論「購物行程」及分享更多見解。如果你有任何疑問，歡迎撥打 25189999 這支電話給我們，我們會盡力回答你的提問。Hi，Jerry，歡迎來到「晨間秀」，你好嗎？

Jerry：很棒！謝謝邀請我來這個節目。

DJ：這是我們的榮幸！讓我們直接切入正題來談一下「購物行程」吧！

Jerry：好的。

DJ：首先，請問何謂「購物行程」？

Jerry：「購物行程」是由旅行社所安排的行程，通常存在於「套裝行程」或「團體行程」。舉例來說，如果你跟團，紀念用品店或工廠會是行程的一部分，你也預期會造訪它們，進行購物。

DJ：好！好奇地問一下，為什麼需要「購物行程」呢？旅行期間我們隨時隨地都可購物，不是嗎？

Jerry：我懂你的意思！事實上，其中一個原因是「購物行程」讓團員為他們的朋友或家人採購紀念品或當地特產更加地容易及便利，如同「一站式」服務一樣。當你來到旅行社安排的紀念用品店時，通常架子上都是最受歡迎的品項。對於不知道要買什麼紀念品的人而言，這樣子能節省他們很多時間。此外，由於這些紀念用品店或工廠都是由旅行社精選或推薦的，所以你不必擔心產品的品質。根據臺灣的法律，在購買後的一個月內，如果該產品有任何瑕疵或問題，你可聯繫旅行社請求退錢、換貨等方面的協助。

DJ：聽起來很棒！所以，在跟團的行程中包含「購物行程」是否仍有其他的原因呢？

Jerry：這是一個好問題！另一個理由是「購物行程」能有效降低套裝行程的成本。

DJ：怎麼說呢？

Jerry：如我們所知，大部分人對價格敏感，傾向於比價後選擇較經濟實惠的套裝行程。所以，如果旅行社能針對套裝行程提供較具競爭力的價格，大部分人較可能感興趣、甚至報名。如果團體行程包含購物行程，價格就能夠降低、變得較有競爭力。

DJ：為什麼？

Jerry：因為贊助的關係。這些購物站，例如紀念用品店或工廠，都有針對團費贊助部分費用。例如，租遊覽車的費用，所以這有助降低跟團的整體費用。然而，通常這些贊助是以遊客拜訪這些紀念用品店或工廠作為交換條件，因為團員進去購物站後可能會進行採購。換句話說，如果有人報名較低價的團，通常他（她）會被期待造訪這些購物站而且待在那兒一會兒。

DJ：了解！難怪有時候我的朋友們告訴我，他們報名參加國外的團不必從自己口袋掏出太多錢。

Jerry：是的。如果一個人能以較經濟實惠的價格出國旅遊、在紀念用品店或工廠為他的朋友或家人購買品質好的產品，同時購物站也能獲利，這樣子不是很好嗎？

DJ：對！創造雙贏！

Jerry：非常同意！

DJ：那領隊或導遊呢？領隊或導遊能從「購物行程」中賺到錢嗎？

附
錄

Jerry：可以的。如果團員有在這些購物站購物，領隊或導遊也能賺到一些佣金。

DJ：那就不是只有雙贏了，是三贏！

Jerry：這麼說也對。

DJ：你知道我們有不少聽眾都想當領隊。對於這些未來的領隊，在推銷「購物行程」方面，你有什麼建議嗎？

Jerry：有的。行前會議時，你務必告知團員們該趟旅程中有關「購物行程」方面的詳細資訊，因為「誠實為上策」。千萬不要羞於談論這個話題，因為團員通常都知道他們報名的是什麼旅行團。如果你決定不談這個話題，團員們反而可能會懷疑行程表中是否有隱藏行程。此外，別忘了要跟團員們分享當地的退稅規定及強調你及旅行社提供的售後服務，即「如果產品有瑕疵或問題，團員們在購物後的 30 天內，可跟你或旅行社尋求進一步協助」。

DJ：那在「購物行程」進行當中呢？

Jerry：當你的團員在紀念用品站對產品有任何疑問時，請店員直接跟團員講解，因為他們較了解他們的產品。最重要的是要掌握時間，尤其當團員沒有要再繼續購物的跡象時，千萬不要讓你的團員們在購物站內待超過「應該的時間」。也許這樣子做會讓地陪（當地導遊）不開心，但如果你犯了這個錯，將有更多客訴，反而得不償失。

DJ：這些都是很棒的建議。現在讓我們來接電話，接受聽眾們的提問。Hello，KIIS 廣播電臺，請問你是？

聽眾：我是來自臺北的 Mary。

DJ：嗨，Mary。你有什麼問題要問今天的來賓 Jerry 呢？

聽眾：我是領隊，在這個行業 3 年了，但我總覺得在遊覽車上要跟團員們推銷「購物行程」很有挑戰性。如果你能跟我們分享一些祕訣或策略，那就太棒了！

Jerry：我很開心你提這個問題！以我的經驗而言，你可以嘗試 3 種策略。
　　　　首先，當你在跟團員分享當地歷史、風俗習慣或生活方式時，不妨
　　　　技巧性地將當地特產、名產導入。接下來，你也可以當模特兒展示
　　　　這些產品的實用性。例如，如果你將推銷「圍巾」或「皮衣」，你
　　　　可以在行程第一天就將圍巾或皮衣穿在身上。有的團員也許會感興
　　　　趣，跟你詢問更多有關這些產品的資訊。然後，你可以將團員的提
　　　　問作為簡短介紹產品前的開場白。通常這樣子能引起團員的好奇心
　　　　或興趣。最後，我必須說大多數的人對價格較敏感。如果一個產品
　　　　是當地才有的或它是全球有名的品牌，通常它的當地價格都會比國
　　　　際價格來得低。例如，有些受歡迎的化妝品、包包、保健食品等等。
　　　　所以，當你在推銷這些產品時，你可以聚焦在比較價格方面。這樣
　　　　子應該能更容易挑起你團員們的購物慾。

DJ：這三個策略真的很棒！去年我參加你的土耳其團，現在想起來，當初
　　　你就運用了這三個策略推銷一些產品，而我一點也沒有察覺。做得好，
　　　Jerry ！

Jerry：呵呵！ Jack，我會將你剛說的話視為稱讚！

DJ：的確是稱讚！ Mary，希望你仍在收聽我們的節目而且覺得 Jerry 的祕
　　　訣有用。現在我們來接聽下一通電話。

附
錄

領隊篇 Unit 10

❯ Listening 聽力 1（第一部分）

A：領隊　B：團員 1　C：團員 2　D：寺廟員工　E：李先生

A：歡迎大家回來！你們覺得這座寺廟如何？

B：這座廟好大。牆上的浮雕超棒的！我曾在網路上看過這些浮雕，但親眼目睹時，仍令我目瞪口呆！

A：我第一次來這兒時也是這種感覺！它們真的超棒的，是吧？

B：是的！

C：Jerry，我父親稍早跟我在一起。但現在我似乎找不到他。他一定是在回程路上迷路了。沿途的步道上有許多岩石，我們必須爬上爬下的，我怕他也許在某個地方跌倒了或是困住了。現在該怎麼辦？

A：你現在一定很擔心！我能體會你的感受！請告訴我你最後看到你父親的地點及時間為何？

C：你還記得在回來的路上有一棵大樹嗎？大約 20 分鐘前我們在那兒，我們甚至還拍了合照。我給你看一下我手機中的照片。

A：是的！那棵大樹。現在我需要你保持冷靜，跟其他團員待在這兒，以免你父親回來找不到人。我會將這張照片與寺廟員工分享，一起尋找你父親。無論是誰找到他都會在 Line 群組上更新訊息。

C：好的！對你及其他團員造成不便，真的很抱歉！

A：沒事！現在最重要的是找到你父親。

▶ Listening 聽力 2（第一部分）

A：團員　B：領隊　C：地勤人員

A：嗨，Gary！現在已經下午 5:30 了，我們何時登機呢？

B：登機時間是 5:20。你一定很納悶為何我們仍在等候。我覺得班機一定有延誤。讓我跟地勤人員確認一下後再回覆你！我稍後回來！

（領隊在登機櫃臺跟地勤人員談話中）

B：嗨！我是領隊，我的名字叫 Gary。這個航班的登機時間為 5:20，但現在已經 5:32 了，請問是否有延誤呢？

▶ Listening 聽力 3（第一部分）

A：團員　B：領隊　C：失物招領櫃臺員工

A：嗨，Gary。我們已經等行李 30 分鐘了，但似乎沒有看到我的行李。現在該怎麼辦？

B：除了你之外，所有的人都已經拿到行李了，而行李轉盤上空無一物，我想你的行李可能遺失了。

A：真的嗎？真令人不敢置信！才行程第一天我的行李就不見了，還真是「幸運」呀！

B：很遺憾這件事發生在你身上。我了解你的感受，你一定覺得有點氣憤或沮喪是吧？請別擔心！因為98% 的行李最後都會回來。咱們先去「失物招領」櫃臺掛失，你覺得如何？

A：好的！

▶ Listening 聽力 4（第一部分）

A：團員　B：領隊

A：Hello，請問 Gary 在嗎？

B：我就是。請問哪裡找？

附錄

A：我是 Jerry。

B：嗨，Jerry。有什麼可以為你服務的嗎？

A：不知道是我自己的問題還是晚餐太辣的關係，晚餐後我的肚子就不太舒服，而且我已經去廁所好幾次了。我猜我拉肚子了，真難受！不知道你那兒是否剛好有藥呢？

▶ Listening 聽力 1（完整版）

A：領隊　B：團員 1　C：團員 2　D：寺廟員工　E：李先生

A：歡迎大家回來！你們覺得這座寺廟如何？

B：這座廟好大。牆上的浮雕超棒的！我曾在網路上看過這些浮雕，但親眼目睹時，仍令我目瞪口呆！

A：我第一次來這兒時也是這種感覺！它們真的超棒的，是吧？

B：是的！

C：Jerry，我父親稍早跟我在一起。但現在我似乎找不到他。他一定是在回程路上迷路了。沿途的步道上有許多岩石，我們必須爬上爬下的，我怕他也許在某個地方跌倒了或是困住了。現在該怎麼辦？

A：你現在一定很擔心！我能體會你的感受！請告訴我你最後看到你父親的地點及時間為何？

C：你還記得在回來的路上有一棵大樹嗎？大約 20 分鐘前我們在那兒，我們甚至還拍了合照。我給你看一下我手機中的照片。

A：是的！我記得那棵大樹。現在我需要你保持冷靜，跟其他團員待在這兒，以免你父親回來找不到人。我會將這張照片與寺廟員工分享，一起尋找你父親。無論是誰找到他都會在 Line 群組上更新訊息。

C：好的！對你及其他團員造成不便，真的很抱歉！

A：沒事！現在最重要的是找到你父親。

（領隊跟寺廟員工交談中）

A：不好意思！我是領隊，我有一個團員尚未回到我們的集合點，可能走失了。他大概 80 多歲，我們擔心他會有狀況。不知道你是否可以幫我們尋找他嗎？

D：當然可以！你們上次看見他的地點及時間為何？

A：大約 30 分鐘前，他與他的女兒在這棵大樹附近。

D：了解！過了這棵大樹後有叉路，他一定是右轉、走錯路了！ 如果我們去那兒，也許能找到他！

A：好主意！咱們走！

（過了一會兒…）

A：李先生，原來你在這兒！我們為了找你四處都找遍了。一切還好嗎？

E：嗨，Jerry，感謝老天你們找到我了！除了我剛剛迷路、找不到我女兒外，一切沒事！事實上，我剛剛有點緊張，但你總是告訴我們，如果迷路了就要找一個明顯物體，然後耐心等候！這也就是為何我決定回到這棵大樹的原因。

A：我很開心你記得這件事！做得好！現在讓我在 Line 群組上跟你女兒報平安，他非常擔心你！

❯ Listening 聽力 2（完整版）

A：團員　B：領隊　C：地勤人員

A：嗨，Gary ！現在已經下午 5:30 了，我們何時登機呢？

B：登機時間是 5:20。你一定很納悶為何我們仍在等候。我覺得班機一定有延誤。讓我跟地勤人員確認一下後再回覆你！我稍後回來！

（領隊在登機櫃臺跟地勤人員談話中）

B：嗨！我是領隊，我的名字叫 Gary。這個航班的登機時間為 5:20，但現在已經 5:32 了，請問是否有延誤呢？

C：是的。將有些許延誤！事實上，我們即將要廣播跟大家報告新的登機時間。由於該航班稍早才降落，此刻正在將行李運送到飛機上，以至於造成出發有些許延遲。對於所造成的不便，深感抱歉！

B：你知道要花多久時間嗎？

C：登機時間為 5:50。

B：OK。謝謝！

C：不客氣！

（領隊正在將消息告知團員中）

B：大家好！請大家注意一下，我有事情要宣布！我剛剛跟登機櫃臺的地勤人員確認，這班班機不久前才在機場降落。因為目前行李正在運送到飛機當中，所以出發會有些許延遲。新的登機時間為 5:50。現在時間為 5:40。如果登機時有任何更動，我會再跟大家報告。感謝你們的耐心等候！

A：嗨，Gary。因為班機延誤，所以你覺得我們能申請旅遊險的理賠嗎？

B：這是個好問題！一般而言，如班機延誤超過 4 小時，大家就符合申請理賠的資格。以我們現在的狀況，要申請理賠還太早。然而，以防萬一，你可跟你的保險業務員確認一下保單規定。

A：謝謝你的建議！我會的！

B：不好意思！我必須要傳訊息告訴曼谷的當地導遊說我們的班機延誤。這樣子，他才能調整我們今天的行程。

A：OK。

> ### Listening 聽力 3（完整版）

　　　　　　　　　　　　　　　　　A：團員　B：領隊　C：失物招領櫃臺員工

A：嗨，Gary。我們已經等行李 30 分鐘了，但似乎沒有看到我的行李。現在該怎麼辦？

B：除了你之外，所有的人都已經拿到行李了，而行李轉盤上空無一物，我想你的行李可能遺失了。

A：真的嗎？真令人不敢置信！才行程第一天我的行李就不見了，還真是「幸運」呀！

B：很遺憾這件事發生在你身上。我了解你的感受，你一定覺得有點氣憤或沮喪是吧？請別擔心！因為 98% 的行李最後都會回來。咱們先去「失物招領」櫃臺掛失，你覺得如何？

A：好的！

（領隊正在與失物招領櫃臺人員談話中）

B：嗨！我的名字是 Gary，是一名領隊！ 我團員的行李好像遺失了，我們想掛失！

C：好的！你們搭哪個航班呢？

B：CI2123，從臺北來的班機。

C：你的團員有「行李提領票根」嗎？

B：給你。

C：煩請先填寫這張掛失表單，務必敘明行李箱的樣式及顏色，包含我們能與你取得聯繫的電話及地址等資訊。

B：OK。所以，你知道目前行李在哪兒嗎？

C：根據電腦紀錄，目前行李在香港。一定某個地方有出錯，很抱歉！

B：何時我們能取回行李呢？

C：我相信這個行李將會放在下一個從香港到曼谷的航班，明天傍晚前會把行李運送給你。請問到時候你們人會在哪兒呢？

B：我們會在希爾頓飯店。

C：好的！我們一拿到行李就會致電給你，並盡快將它送至希爾頓飯店。對於造成的任何不便，深感抱歉！

B：感謝你的協助！

附錄

A：Gary，謝謝你的幫忙！

B：不客氣！這是我身為領隊的分內工作！

A：所以你覺得我是否能針對行李遺失的部分申請旅遊險理賠呢？

B：我很高興你問我這個問題。我剛剛才準備要跟你說明呢！一般而言，保險公司或航空公司會針對行李延誤或遺失理賠。但是「行李延誤」及「行李遺失」的定義不太相同。

A：你可以再仔細說明一下嗎？

B：當然可以！如你在送交掛失申請單後的 12 小時後仍未拿到行李，視為「行李延誤」。超過 24 小時後，則視為「行李遺失」！

A：所以，12 小時之後，他們將支付任何我需要的東西費用嗎？

B：不完全是！通常他們只會支付例如衣褲、襪子等必需品。

A：謝謝你提供的資訊！我想現在我能做的事就是等待他們的進一步通知！

B：事實上，你也可以先核對你的保單。說不定你能獲得更多補償也不一定。如你有任何問題，再跟我說！

A：好的。

▶ Listening 聽力 4（完整版）

A：團員　B: 領隊

A：Hello，請問 Gary 在嗎？

B：我就是。請問哪裡找？

A：我是 Jerry。

B：嗨，Jerry。有什麼可以為你服務的嗎？

A：不知道是我自己的問題還是晚餐太辣的關係，晚餐後我的肚子就不太舒服，而且我已經去廁所好幾次了。我猜我拉肚子了，真難受！不知道你那兒是否剛好有藥呢？

B：聽到這狀況很遺憾，Jerry。很不幸的，我沒有任何那樣子的藥物。此外，我們不允許提供任何藥物給團員。

A：為什麼？

B：因為我們不知道團員對哪些藥物過敏。如果服錯藥物，我們將置他（她）的生命於危險之中。

A：合理！

B：如果你仍覺得不舒服，我建議你去看醫生。我陪你去，不用擔心！

A：你人真好！謝謝你！然而，就我所知，當我們人在國外就醫的費用很高，不是嗎？

B：是的！通常較貴。但是健康是最重要的事！

A：我懂！所以，我們的團體保險有涵蓋海外醫療費用嗎？

B：據我所知沒有。團體保險只有涵蓋因意外引起的醫療費用，沒有涵蓋腹瀉。你有為這次的旅行買旅遊險嗎？

A：並沒有！

B：了解！但別擔心錢的問題！臺灣的健保有涵蓋部分海外費用，我們只需在治療後跟該醫院要求例如「診斷證明書」的醫療證明即可。回到臺灣後，於海外門診、急診或出院 6 個月內，聯繫健保局任一分支單位申請「醫療費用核退」。

A：很高興知道這項資訊！真是讓人鬆了一口氣！

B：所以，我應該請飯店服務臺幫我們叫計程車嗎？

A：沒關係！這樣子太麻煩了！我現在覺得好多了！如果我仍拉肚子，我再打電話給你。你整天認真工作，應該休息一下。

B：好的！如果你覺得不舒服，一定要讓我知道，好嗎？我一直都在！

A：謝謝，我會的！晚安！

B：祝早日康復！

導遊篇 Unit 1

▶ 九份

　　座落在新北市，九份曾經是黃金開採的重心。這個小鎮的位置背山面海。在清領的早期，九份曾經有九戶人家。因為交通的貧乏，導致去市場採買日常用品非常不方便。因此，每次去採買時，就必須將物品分成九份來運送。之後，九份（字面上國語的意思是九份）就成為這個村落的名字。

　　在 1890 年有工人在興建臺北到基隆間的鐵路時發現金片。在 1893 年，豐富的金礦在九份山上被發現，每天能產生幾公斤的黃金。九份就因為黃金熱潮而興盛，而且在日治時期達到高點。

　　在二次大戰期間，曾經在九份附近有一座日本的戰俘營，主要是來自在新加坡被俘虜的英國籍聯軍軍人，這些軍人被迫去挖金礦。二次大戰之後，當挖黃金的熱潮過了之後，九份經歷了快速的衰退。終於在 1971 年完全結束挖礦的工作。從此以後九份幾乎被遺忘。

　　九份是臺灣導演侯孝賢的電影《悲情城市》的拍片場景，這是首部探討臺灣政治爭議事件二二八事件的電影，1989 年獲得威尼斯影展的金獅獎。九份就因為此片的大賣，獲得重生。在 2001 年，九份再次因為和宮崎駿的吉卜力製作公司的動畫《神隱少女》中的場景類似，九份又吸引很多遊客，尤其是日本人。許多日本的雜誌和導覽書推薦九份。九份也成為日本遊客必訪的景點。然而宮崎駿否認九份是動畫電影中的城市。

　　遊客口中的九份老街，指的就是豎崎路與基山街所組成的二個區域。豎崎路早期是一條保甲路，做為清兵守備的道路。它是一條縱向的石階路，是當時九份居民往返港口及民生補給運輸的主要通道。現在的豎崎路沿途林立著無數的茶館、咖啡屋、民宿及各式藝品店，十分熱鬧。

　　基山街則是昔日九份最重要的商業街，當年民生用品、餐廳飲食及消費娛樂，所有的店鋪都匯集在這裡。由於九份多雨，街道兩旁的商家遂搭起頂棚避雨，形成幽暗的巷弄，而有了暗街仔之稱。基山街現今仍然是九份最熱鬧的街道，兩旁的小吃店交錯林立，有草仔粿、芋仔粿、紅糟肉圓及冷熱芋圓等等，到處充斥著各種美味小吃。吃美食嘗美味。來到豎崎路肯定不要錯過的，就是找一間茶館邊泡茶邊賞景，好好渡過悠閒的時光。不過假日人太多，若能平日來到九份，才比較能感受到那份悠閒。

昇平戲院是北臺灣第一間戲院，也是日本殖民時期最大的戲院。昇平戲院在 1916 年開幕，顏雲年提供土地，政府負責募款。在 1927 年戲院倒塌之後，1934 年在現在的地點重建完成。在臺灣光復之後被正式命名為昇平戲院。1930 年代是九份的黃金年代。很多人為了金礦而來到九份。昇平戲院成為黃金挖礦者最重要的娛樂場所。1951 年戲院被建造成加強混凝土結構。1986 年戲院幾乎被颱風摧毀，而不得不關閉。2011 年戲院重新翻修之後，再次對大眾開放。

九份芋圓是由創始人蔡女士在 1940 年代，無心插柳的情況下，意外成了九份地方小吃的代名詞。最初只是做給自家人吃，因受好評，才開始做起生意在自己的雜貨店販賣，在夏天時賣冷的芋圓冰，冬天則是賣熱的芋圓湯。沒想到這一做，就讓九份芋圓驚豔全臺。雖然目前全臺都吃的到九份芋圓，但仍不及當地的香氣與口感嚼勁。

九份老街有兩家超級有名的芋圓店。第一家是賴阿婆芋圓，他們在老街有三家店面，一家是製作和販賣芋圓的地方，另外兩個店面則是用餐的地方。阿柑姨芋圓是另一家有名的芋圓店。如果在基山街與豎崎路的交叉路口，往九份國小的方向走，最後會發現阿柑姨芋圓在右手邊。阿柑姨芋圓有何特別呢？你應該造訪阿柑姨芋圓店，因為它有大面窗，可以看到山與海的壯觀美景。

在基山街底，九份茶坊自開放以來就曾經是許多重要臺灣的作家與藝術家聚會的地方。我們可以從菜單選擇喜歡的茶與茶點，自在的坐在裡面享用。並欣賞在地藝術家的畫作及其他美妙的藝術作品。在地下層是展示許多陶瓷作品的藝廊，可別錯過了！

九份有許多小巷子與基山街及豎崎路互相連接，為了節省時間與通行的便利，這些小巷子穿梭在房子的前門或後院，因此被稱之為「穿屋巷」。穿屋巷有的十分狹窄，只能容一人錯身而過，可以說是十分的特別。很有意思的是，有時候走著走著，就不小心穿過別人家的大廳或房門口。

為了因應潮濕多雨的氣候，山城居民採用方便排水的斜房頂，還特別在屋頂上漆一層柏油，因此高低錯落的黑屋頂就成了九份山城的特色之一。這些黑屋頂正確的名稱叫做「黑油毛氈屋頂」。油毛氈不僅防風防雨、堅固耐用，還有價格便宜及容易維護等優點。

要確保遊九份是身體強健的，因為階梯是很陡的，所以不要忘了一雙好的運動鞋，因為走路將會是你探索九份最主要的交通方式。最後，同時雨傘也是必備的，因為九份經常下雨。

▶ 野柳

地理上，野柳座落在北臺灣，在金山和萬里之間，自野柳地質公園入口到海岬的末端，長約 1.7 公里，期間最寬的地方不及 300 公尺。野柳是以多種地景而聞名，在 1964 年被指定為風景區。

野柳地名的由來普遍有三種說法：1. 野柳地名來自於西班牙文的縮寫，2. 從平埔族的語言翻譯而來，3. 形容地方老百姓在米糧運輸過程中，會去偷糧商的米。因此米商在交談中常會說：又被「野」人給「柳」去了（臺語），因故而得名。

野柳地質公園內可概分為三區，第一區和第二區是團員必看的區域。第一區屬於蕈狀岩、薑石及燭臺石的主要集中區。在第一區中可看到蕈狀岩的發育過程，同時也有豐富的薑石及壺穴，著名的燭臺石與冰淇淋石也位在本區。

第二區的地景與第一區相似，皆以蕈狀岩及薑石為主，但數量比第一區少，著名的女王頭、龍頭石與金剛石皆位於本區。第二區靠近海邊可看到四種形狀特別的岩石，分別取名為：象石、仙女鞋、地球石和花生石。

　　第三區是野柳另一側的海蝕平臺，比第二區狹窄，平臺一側緊貼峭壁，另一側則是急湧的海浪，幾個海水侵蝕後所造成的石頭也在此區，較特殊的有二十四孝石、珠石、瑪伶鳥石。第三區同時也是野柳地質公園內重要的生態保育護區。此區適合從事地質研究及田野調查。

單面山

　　一邊坡度陡急、另一邊坡度較為和緩的山形即稱為單面山。形成的原因主要是因為地層先被地殼運動抬升而形成。而後再經過風化及侵蝕作用而崩塌形成的地形。每年此區遭受東北季風和海浪侵蝕的影響，長達六個月。因為差異侵蝕的原因，許多小的單面山在海岸線附近形成，同時巨大的單面山也能從旅遊中心的方向清楚的看到。

節理

　　在海岬形成的過程中，由於岩層受到推擠，形成一道道裂縫，這些裂縫稱為節理。節理的大小寬深，沒有一定的規律，有的間距僅數公分，有的可寬達數公尺。以野柳為例，間距小者如豆腐岩，大者如海蝕溝，有的還要以橋梁溝通兩邊。

蕈狀石

　　在這裡有超過 180 個蕈狀石，同時也是岩石進化因為不同的頭部與頸部的外型，而有三種不同的類型，從粗頸石、細頸石到無頸石。其中的女王頭雍容尊貴的形態，早已成為野柳地質公園的象徵。最早，這些蕈狀岩因受海水日夜的侵蝕，隨著時間的流逝，砂岩裡質地堅硬的結核，慢慢的露出，再經風吹、日曬、雨淋、海浪以及強烈東北季風的吹打而形成蕈狀石。

　　所謂女王頭實際上是屬於蕈狀岩的一種。在地殼抬升的過程中，因受到海水的差異侵蝕而逐漸形成今日的面貌。若以其高度比對臺灣北部地殼平均上升速度推算，估計女王頭的芳齡已經將近 4,000 歲。其實女王頭就是蕈狀岩，在 1962 年間因頂部結核上的節理斷裂，從某一角度觀看時，很像古埃及皇后娜芙蒂蒂或英國伊莉莎白一世的側面頭像，因此而得名。然而，未來幾年女王頭很可能會斷掉。

壺穴

野柳有許多的海蝕壺穴，壺穴是圓形的洞穴，從海蝕平臺表面的凹穴開始發育，並且與海水的侵蝕有很大的關係。壺穴受海浪攜帶的石粒在海蝕平臺上不斷進行侵蝕與切割作用，經過長時間的侵蝕會使壺穴逐漸擴大與深化。

燭臺石

是由海水的侵蝕所形成。在較軟的平面被移除之後。岩層裡較堅硬的球形結核，就在海水侵蝕下逐漸露出，成為燭心的形狀，且在周圍沖激出環狀溝槽，而海水會沿環槽向下侵蝕、切割出圓錐形的燭臺。

薑石

是分布在野柳的特殊石頭岩層。薑石是和蕈狀岩的結構相同，但是在形狀上不同。周邊較鬆軟的岩層，因海水長期侵蝕而剝落之後，岩層中較堅硬的鈣質結核岩塊，因為地層進一步擠壓出縱橫交錯的裂縫，所以留下表面形狀類似老薑的外觀。其中仙女鞋為最有名，就像仙女因為行色匆匆而遺留在人間的鞋子。

駱駝岩

從野柳地質公園往東南方向看，在漁港旁邊有個奇特的岩石，外型酷似一隻單峰駱駝面朝野柳坐著休息，故稱為駱駝岩。不過這隻駱駝，似乎也蠻像蝸牛呢！

公主頭

是女王頭的繼承者，公主頭也在公園裡。是為了分散對女王頭的注意力，也避免對女王頭的觸摸而加速損壞。

冰淇淋石

因岩石差異侵蝕的結果，形成造型奇特的樣子。若從海岸面對山壁的方向看，就像炎炎夏日中最受歡迎的冰淇淋。

炸雞腿石

形狀特殊的薑石，形狀就像一隻好吃的炸雞腿。

化石

在岩層中有許多化石存在，包括海膽化石，這些是屬於中新世早期的沙錢海膽化石。此外，這些在沉積岩中所遺留下來早期生物居住的痕跡，就稱為生痕化石。

日本藝妓

形狀特殊的蕈狀岩，就像一位優雅的日本藝妓的樣子。

鯉魚石與鸚鵡石

位於燭臺石左後方，岩石上的形狀很像魚的眼睛，故被稱為鯉魚石。鯉魚石正對面的山壁，可以看到一個鸚鵡形狀的岩石，正面向大海的方向。

臺灣石

是位於第一座海蝕溝橋旁的特殊地景，由於差異侵蝕作用影響下，雕刻出狀似臺灣島的奇岩異石。臺灣石不但形狀上跟臺灣島相似，連中央山脈的位置也相當神似呢！

附錄

林添禎雕像

民國 53 年 3 月一名前來野柳遊玩的大學生因天氣惡劣跌落大海而被海浪捲走，林添禎先生為救學生，不顧自身安危，躍入海中，但因風浪過大，兩人皆不幸被大浪吞噬。後人為紀念其捨身救人的精神，豎立其雕像供後人悼念。

海蝕洞

海浪持續侵蝕在海岸邊的岩石，造成海蝕洞。「情人洞」便是一個規模巨大的海蝕洞之一。

海蝕溝

形成的原因是由於結理與岬角延伸的方向垂直，結理的表面受海浪侵蝕而逐漸擴大成海蝕溝。在野柳地質公園中有許多小橋是為了跨越這些海蝕溝所設置的。

象石

象石是質地較堅硬的石灰質結核，在差異侵蝕作用下所形成的特殊地景。相傳是仙女忘了把大象騎回天庭，最後，大象仍等待著仙女回來接牠，因而拒絕上岸。

仙女鞋

傳言是天上的仙女下凡來人間，不小心遺忘在海岸的鞋子。屬於薑石的一種，形成原因是因為岩層中含有較堅硬的鈣質岩塊，在這些鈣質岩塊周邊較為鬆軟的岩層，受海水長期侵蝕而剝落，加上地層擠壓出縱橫交錯的裂縫，留下了鞋子的造型。

花生石

位於仙女鞋的左方，岩層中形狀特殊的結核，經過海水侵蝕後，而突出於海邊，由於其外型如同花生，故被稱為花生石。

珠石（地球石）

位於仙女鞋的下方，由於其形狀為完整的圓球形結核，有如明珠一般，稱為珠石，也稱為地球石。

棋盤石（豆腐岩）

位在仙女鞋與燈塔間的海岸，排列著一整排的溝紋平整的岩石，這是野柳外形最為完整的棋盤石，俗稱豆腐岩。棋盤石的成因，是岩石受地層變動的壓力推擠，產生棋盤狀的節理，這些節理裂縫長時間受海水侵蝕，切割出相互垂直的紋路，就像一塊塊美味的豆腐。

龍頭石

為一獨特的蕈狀石，一側的形狀就像龍頭。

金剛石

從第二區的測速臺方向看來，像一隻大金剛蹲坐在地上向龍王請安。

菠蘿麵包

在金剛石後方靠近海邊的方向，有個形狀相當特殊的結核。在這顆結核的上方，因具有數組交錯的節理發育，乍看之下還蠻像菠蘿麵包的呢！

附
錄

導遊篇 Unit 2

> 士林夜市

　　士林夜市，位於臺北市士林區，是以前平埔族的凱達格蘭族居住的地方。它被認為是最大而且最受歡迎的夜市，尤其是在街邊美食方面。士林夜市就在劍潭站旁邊。士林市場最早在 1913 年就成立，也被臺北市政府指定為市定古蹟。由於大量消費者的湧入，生意人和攤販開始聚集在此地，士林夜市也因應而生。

　　2002 年 10 月，由於通風、衛生、公共安全及火災等問題，舊的士林市場被臺北市政府拆除，原士林市場攤販移至位於距離數百公尺遠的臺北捷運劍潭站對面的士林臨時市場。臺北市政府於將原士林市場拆除改建，2011 年 12 月，新的士林市場改建完成。舊士林市場改建成地上 2 層、地下 3 層的建築物。士林市場在士林臨時市場的美食類攤位將遷回新的士林市場地下一樓。

　　士林夜市主要分成兩大區域。有一區主要以基河路上的士林市場為主，包含大部分是美食攤商及小餐廳，其他周邊區域以非美食商家為主。另一區以陽明戲院為中心，已經是一個完全成熟發展涵蓋幾條街區的小吃市場，這個區域最遠可以延伸到文林路、基河路、大東路、大南路，這個區域是許多著名美食起家的地方，例如士林大香腸、士林生煎包等，同時周邊也有許多非美食的攤商，像是賣衣服、手機配件、紀念品、玩具、家庭用品和玩遊戲。士林夜市主要已經是販賣許多精彩食物有名的地方。因為夜市離許多的學校很近，學生是主要消費族群，所以商品的價格跟其他地方比較起來是相對便宜的。

　　最近幾年在士林夜市裡水果攤賣現切水果很受歡迎，也有些被懷疑賣太貴給消費者。市政府要求水果攤商在賣水果給消費者之前必須有四項說明：首先是多少錢，第二是秤重水果，第三是付錢，最後才是切水果。以上的說明必須以中文及英文呈現，如攤商沒有事先講價格或在切水果前沒有得到消費者的確認，攤商會被罰錢。

　　在臺灣許多夫妻檔形式來經營的小店也得到國際性的注意，最近的 2019 米其林指南有 24 家夜市美食獲得必比登推薦的殊榮。必比登推薦名單特別強調好品質好價格的美食，標準是店家所提供的三道餐點，總價不能超過新臺幣 1300 元。在這 24 家榜上有名的夜市美食中，士林夜市就有三家店，包括海友十全排骨、鍾家原上海生煎包、好朋友涼麵名列其中。

　　士林夜市的海友十全排骨就是以中藥味聞名。海友十全排骨已經經營超過 45 年，其中以排骨及雞腿所烹調的 15 種草藥湯底的神祕食譜最為人所知。海友也會根據季節的轉變，調整草藥的味道，特別是冬天，也是喝一碗熱湯，最好的時機。這碗湯經過數小時的中草藥熬煮，已經有藥用的效果，千萬不要忘了吃著名草藥熬煮的豬肋排的同時，也品嚐美味的湯。

　　原本來自上海，「鍾家原上海生煎包」是士林夜市的著名美食。從老遠就可看到消費者排長隊在等著買上海生煎包。就像耐心地等待的消費者所說的「如果沒吃過生煎包，就不算有到士林夜市。」生煎包有兩種內餡，一種是高麗菜，一種是包肉的。生煎包煎的香脆底部和充滿高麗菜或包肉的內餡，所釋放出的香氣滲透了士林夜市，吸引不僅是在地人已經熟悉的味道，也立刻吸引陌生訪客的造訪。在咬剛煎好的生煎包時要留意不要被裡面的湯汁燙到。

　　「好朋友涼麵」以前是藥房，僅在房間的一半賣涼麵，後來因為涼麵極受歡迎的關係，最後關掉藥房，全力經營獲利的涼麵生意。看起來簡單的美食涼麵，「好朋友涼麵」以芝麻糊當調味醬，和切成絲的小黃瓜。「好朋友涼麵」好吃到連在地的便利商店也在賣。「好朋友涼麵」是真材實料，也要記得喝他們的蛋花味噌湯。

　　臺灣的炸雞排店「豪大大雞排」是在士林夜市起家的。主要的特色是炸雞排超級大到有 30 公分長，甚至比手掌大，幾乎是人臉的大小，外面均勻的用麵糊包裹，大雞排油炸到呈現金黃色，肉質多汁又柔軟，最後灑上調味粉（混合白胡椒粉及五香粉），也有紅色胡椒粉。「豪大大雞排」不會為消費者切雞排，即使是消費者要求。

附錄

▶ 寧夏夜市

　　寧夏路約占有 300 公尺，有攤販沿著街邊或是在馬路的正中間開店，還有店家在遠離街邊的商店的正面營業。寧夏夜市有超過 200 攤營業，大部分都是賣吃的。寧夏夜市擁有超過 60 年的歷史，有些攤商已經在同一個地方經營超過三、四十年，甚至有同一家族的第二代出來經營。寧夏夜市以前是賣衣服及配件的商家居多，但是在大型百貨公司興起之後，傳統的美食攤販就快速取代賣衣服的店家，導致寧夏夜市呈現如今的樣貌。

　　為了加強訪客良好的逛街經驗，市政府建立了只有行人專用的走道，同時與攤商密切合作，推出油脂截留的裝置，以避免油脂進入汙水系統，如此也消除了衛生相關問題。2008 年另一個公衛相關的議題被提起，為了推動使用生態友善的筷子。寧夏夜市在 2014 年 10 月，成為臺灣首個夜市禁煙的地方，只要有遊客邊逛夜市邊吸菸。最高可開罰 1 萬元。2019 年，環保署舉行記者會，開始推動限塑的活動。此活動呼籲人們減少日常生活中對塑膠製品的消費。事實上最近幾年很多企業已經自發性減少對塑膠製品的使用。例如：在寧夏夜市幾乎所有的攤商已經轉換使用生態友善的餐具。結果降低了廢棄物清理費用從十年前的 30 萬，減為一年 15 萬。現在當你在寧夏夜市坐下來用餐，使用的餐具已經是用鍍鋅的鐵所製作，瓷器或玻璃的材質。由於前述採取的環保措施，無疑地，寧夏夜市可驕傲地宣稱自己是臺北市最生態友善的夜市。

　　為了推廣寧夏夜市及滿足人們希望一次吃完臺灣的街邊美食的願望，攤商想到一個主意，要用臺灣式的「辦桌」，讓消費者能同時品嘗 20 道美食。他們發起了辦桌的發想，由於每一攤幾乎都是超過 50 年歷史的小吃，綜合加總小吃攤的年齡，超過千歲以上是綽綽有餘，故名為「千歲宴」。由於「千歲宴」很受消費者歡迎，夜市管理協會提醒消費者要提前預約。

　　2019 年，美國男星威爾史密斯和導演李安來臺灣推廣新電影《雙子殺手》，他們來到寧夏夜市逛，品嘗臺灣受歡迎的美食。史密斯吃了麻油雞，喝了西瓜牛奶。史密斯接著玩夜市裡的遊戲，包括 BB 槍射氣球的遊戲，因為射得非常準確，每次命中都引來群眾的歡呼。

　　夜市攤商與餐廳的主人已經開始使用英文、日文、韓文、法文、提供服務，也和旅遊網站 Klook 一起合作推廣生意。所有夜市的招牌至少有中文與英文兩種語言，某些攤商也都會講一些外語，對外國團員有消費的方便性。攤商也持續為他們的美食貼上有關多少卡路里的標示。2015 年臺北夜市節的活動，寧夏夜市被選為最受歡迎夜市。2019 年，臺北市寧夏夜市創全國之先，成為第一個可刷悠遊卡的夜市。

　　寧夏夜市有許多美食可以選擇，包括以下三家，名列米其林必比登推薦名單。「劉芋仔蛋黃芋餅」是來自於寧夏夜市的一個小攤位。如果不是看到大排長龍的隊伍，你不會知道這個一口吃的小吃也名列米其林必比登推薦名單。如果有些地方是很好的，也就是當所有在地人都說排長隊伍是值得等待的。看「劉芋仔」如何油炸製作有名的芋丸。然後一定要吃原味的香酥芋丸及鹹的蛋黃芋餅。

　　寧夏夜市有許多家賣雞肉飯，但是只有「方家雞肉」名列 2019 米其林必比登推薦名單。雞肉飯的雞肉很軟嫩，雞油混合醬油淋在熱飯上，吃起來非常美味而不會太油膩。「方家雞肉飯」主要是以雞肉飯及滷豆腐聞名，它們是兩個必吃的品項，而且口味是互補。

　　「豬肝榮仔」已經賣新鮮豬肝湯超過 60 年的歷史，豬肝嘗起來非常柔軟，而沒有任何血腥的味道，所以經常會看到攤位前大排長龍。「豬肝榮仔」也名列米其林指南 2019 必比登推介的名單中。除了新鮮的豬肝湯外，他們的粽子也很推薦，這粽子用竹葉包裹糯米，以及蛋黃和香菇，非常美味。當你吃粽子時，別忘了要加甜辣醬。

　　要到寧夏夜市可搭捷運紅線到雙連站下車，從一號出口出來，左轉進民生西路往西直走，約走 6 到 8 分鐘，直到看到夜市。

附錄

鼎泰豐

「鼎泰豐」在 1958 年由楊秉彝創立，原先是以油行起家，那麼新店名要取什麼好呢？創辦人楊秉彝先生想了想，他是向「鼎美油行」批的油，而自己又出身於「恆泰豐」，不如就取名為「鼎泰豐」。在 1972 年，鼎泰豐重新以小籠包和麵食對外開放。如今鼎泰豐已經從一間爸爸媽媽經營的小吃店，成長為一間國際知名的品牌。

「鼎泰豐」在國際上以小籠包而知名，品質都維持一樣。小籠包對「鼎泰豐」的意義，就像大麥克漢堡對「麥當勞」的意義一樣。第一家「鼎泰豐」是開在臺北市的信義路上。1996 年，第一家國際分店是開在東京，美國是 2000 年開在加州的阿卡迪亞。2018 年 12 月在歐洲的倫敦開第一家店。1993 年 1 月「鼎泰豐」被紐約時報評選為全世界十大餐廳之一。2010 年香港的「鼎泰豐」分店得到了米其林一星的證明。CNN 也評選「鼎泰豐」為全世界最佳連鎖餐廳之一。

這些年來，「鼎泰豐」發現 18 摺是小籠包外皮的黃金比例，讓每個小籠包都能夠厚到能支撐隱藏在湯包裡的豬肉湯汁。小籠包的特別之處在於裡頭有湯汁，所以製作上相當困難。小籠包的麵皮材料很基本：麵粉、水、以及發酵麵種。這些材料放到攪拌機中，在機器中攪拌幾次。麵糰前前後後大概要揉壓 6 到 10 次，才能製作出完美的「鼎泰豐」小籠包麵皮。

小籠包的製程真的很不容易，要做出達到「鼎泰豐」水準的小籠包更是難上加難，因為「鼎泰豐」希望做出來的小籠包都是一樣的。要學會製作小籠包的皮毛，就要花上 3 到 6 個月。之後年復一年不斷練習，才能真正掌握這項技藝。每個湯包都會秤重，以克計算，而這包括每一張麵皮。所以「鼎泰豐」選擇的理想重量是 5 公克，介於 4.8 到 5.2 公克才算符合要求。

湯包的滋味，很大一部分來自本身的湯汁。「鼎泰豐」用雞骨和豬大骨熬製出濃郁高湯。然後，「鼎泰豐」必須找到方法把高湯弄到湯包裡。他們的做法是把高湯製成高湯凍。如此一來，就可以包進湯包裡。高湯凍一經蒸煮，就會變回湯汁。

「小籠包」的英文翻譯是 soup dumpling（湯包）。從字面上來說，「小」對應到英文的 small，「籠」對應到 basket，「包」對應到 dumpling。所以就字面翻譯而言，「小籠包」就是 little dumpling in a basket（在竹籠裡的小湯包）。你知道該如何正確吃小籠包嗎？首先是將醬油、醋及切碎的薑片倒在小碟中，攪拌在一起，建議的比例是一份的醬油，三份的醋。接下來，用筷子將小籠包沾醬汁，接著用筷子或牙齒戳破麵皮小洞，讓湯汁流出，最後先吸盡湯汁後再吃下小籠包。

「鼎泰豐」的衛生條件比臺灣大部分餐廳更好，首先是廚房，其次是桌面擦得很乾淨，為了安全及穩定性，管理階層尋找私人管道維持大宗物質，像是麵粉、豬肉和雞肉的穩定供應。同時也讓消費者透過玻璃看到廚師穿著白色製服，製作小籠包，放進傳統的竹籠裡出訂單給團員。

細節是最完美的服務。「鼎泰豐」的員工，以客戶需求為第一優先，期許每一個細節都能累積出「鼎泰豐」的服務哲學與品牌價值。創造每日的業績目標並非絕對。而是消費者的需求得到滿足。「鼎泰豐」的主要目標是提供消費者最可能的優秀服務。加強品牌能見度，及達成永續的成長。

❯ 永康牛肉麵

牛肉麵被說是臺灣食物文化的精髓之一。味道吸引無數的團員來朝聖。如果你問臺灣人哪一道菜最能代表臺灣，他可能跟你說是牛肉麵。

因為臺灣的農民認為牛是忠誠的協助者。所以牛肉一直不是傳統美食的一部分。但是在 1960 年代開始，國軍的退伍軍人開始賣四川牛肉麵。也逐漸的越來越受歡迎。永康牛肉麵在 1963 年由來自中國四川的鄭先生創立。從軍方退伍後，他決定在永康街開一家小店賣牛肉麵。在 1970 年代，鄭先生退休後，將店轉移給現在的經營者羅先生。距離「永康牛肉麵」最近的是大安區東門捷運站，只有約 10 分鐘的路程。「永康牛肉麵」也被列入米其林必比登推薦名單，此名單推薦的是便宜又美味的食物，同時也是「臺北牛肉麵節」的常勝軍。

　　座落在一棟建築物的二個樓層，經常擠滿人而且外面有人在排隊是普遍的現象。總共有兩種口味的牛肉麵，有一種是更豐富且濃郁的湯頭；人們可以感受到卓越而獨特的草藥味道（紅燒）。在中文裡，牛肉麵的前面經常以紅燒的字眼為起首，因為牛肉先在鍋中燉煮，如此在紅色的湯汁中燉數小時，這些湯汁的成分中包含手工豆瓣醬油紅糖焦糖和各種香料，結果成就了美味而且柔軟的牛肉，並搭配麵與一、兩樣蔬菜，就是紅燒牛肉麵。其他一種是清燉牛肉麵是較清淡的湯頭為底，口味並不強烈，所以比較可以品嘗到牛肉本身的自然風味。比較兩者。清燉牛肉麵的版本，牛肉塊更柔嫩，更是入口即化。

　　「永康牛肉麵」的招牌菜是四川口味的辣紅燒湯頭的牛肉與牛筋麵。深紅色湯頭使用不同的調味料包括五香粉、八角、胡椒、中草藥還有許多神祕的成分，酸菜和湯頭的搭配很好，也會降低湯頭過度濃郁的味道和油膩感。肉經過完美的燉煮，柔軟而且仍然保持很好的口感，牛筋也被處理得很好，有嚼勁而且都充分吸收湯頭的美味。牛筋被認為是美味的佳餚，所以這個部位做成的牛肉麵，也賣得比較貴。「永康牛肉麵」只收現金，要記得帶足夠的現金。

　　當你在等待上菜的時候，在門口附近有一個小區，有許多小菜可以取用，也不要被所謂小菜的字眼所騙，如果小心搭配，小菜會帶來用餐未預期的美味。這些未上牛肉麵前的小菜包括：粉蒸排骨、粉蒸肥腸、醃小黃瓜、泡菜等。

導遊篇 Unit 3

▶ 故宮博物院

　　故宮博物院的發展與近代中國歷史息息相關。1924 年 10 月下旬，將領馮玉祥發動北京政變；內閣總理黃郛於 11 月 4 日內閣會議中通過法律，要求溥儀自即日起移出紫禁城。在 1925 年的 10 月 10 日國慶日當天，故宮博物院宣告故宮博物院成立。1931 年，日本軍隊發動九一八事變以後，對中國東北造成嚴重威脅。國民政府決定將故宮文物南遷。1933 年故宮國寶文物、往南遷到上海。1936 年，故宮又將存放上海的文物運至南京新建的庫房存放。1937 年，七七事變爆發，故宮將文物精品分成三批運往遠離戰區的地方，最後落腳在中國大陸的西方。1945 年 8 月，日本投降；故宮將文物用海路的方式運回北京，1947 年底所有精品都回到北京。然而，內戰爆發了。1948 年國共戰爭形勢逆轉，故宮決定挑選文物精品運往臺灣。從此以後，故宮文物也就成為臺灣文化中很重要的一部分。

　　故宮文物抵達臺灣之後，除了來自中研院歷史與哲學研究所的藏品之外，所有的藏品都被暫存在臺中的臺糖倉庫，而中研院歷史與哲學研究所的藏品則被保存在楊梅。1953 年 3 月，聯管處就在臺中縣霧峰鄉北溝庫房附近山地開建小規模山洞，以備必要時將最精華文物存入。1954 年 9 月，歷時四年之遷臺文物的清點檢查完畢；文物雖經戰時水陸輾轉播遷，惟損傷極少。1956 年 12 月，北溝陳列室落成，次年 3 月開放參觀。然而因為北溝的位置相當偏遠，難以吸引國內及外國觀光客，臺灣政府很快決定在臺北市近郊的外雙溪興建新的博物館。1965 年 8 月新館興建完成。12 月開放參觀。臺北故宮的藏品主要源自宋、元、明、清四朝宮廷收藏。收藏的文物，不僅數量龐大，而且品類豐富，累計至今各項數量如下：以上截至 2020 年 6 月 30 日止，全院的典藏量，總計 698,629 件。

青銅器

中國青銅時代開始於夏代晚期，經商、西周、至東周，前後一千五百年左右。珍貴的青銅鑄器只有貴族才能使用，所謂「國之大事，在祀與戎」，青銅除了部分用來鑄造兵器外，主要鑄成祭祀容器，以盛裝祭品、獻祭祖先，祈求家族生命之綿延不絕。

經過長期不斷製作與經驗的累積，人們懂得將銅與少量的錫熔合在一起，製作成比陶器更加堅固耐用與持久的青銅器。透過「塊範法」和「失蠟法」等不同的技術，可以鑄造出比陶器更複雜、更巨大厚重的器形，也可以鑄造出更精緻的紋飾。

在商周時期，幾乎與中國青銅時期重疊，塊範法就是當時最重要的青銅器鑄造方式。失蠟法是西方主要採用的青銅器鑄造法，不但可以鑄造出更繁複的青銅器造型，甚至能做出鏤空的效果，也能使紋飾更精緻、更多變化。中國在春秋時代晚期也發展出失蠟法，並將失蠟法和塊範法相互搭配運用，為中國青銅藝術開創出一片嶄新天地。

中國古代的君王貴族認為，閃亮奪目的銅器就如同黃金一般的珍貴，而且具有吉祥的象徵，因此給它一個特別的名稱，叫為「吉金」。既然青銅器原本是接近橙黃色的，那現在為什麼把它們稱為「青銅器」呢？這是因為古時候鑄造出來的銅器，埋在地下很久以後，會起一種氧化作用，以致表面會產生綠色的鏽斑。

青銅容器依功能來分類，大致可以分為水器、酒器與食器三大類。讓我們透過一個虛擬的古代貴族宴客場景，看看當時各種不同青銅容器的功用。古代君王貴族在各種重要的場合，如祭祀或參與宴會前，必須先完成「洗手」的禮儀。這樣的禮儀稱為「沃盥之禮」。行「沃盥之禮」時，通常以青銅匜和盤一起搭配使用，先用匜裝水，傾倒到手上洗淨一番，底下則以盤承接洗過的水。

當我們行完「沃盥之禮」，進入宴客廳堂時，只見杯觥交錯！商代人對酒非常重視，它是生活中不可缺少的飲料，酒器是目前商代青銅器中數量最多的器類。酒器裡面的爵和觚，則是商代青銅器系統中最基本的組合。周人伐商，取代商朝政權之後，認為商人是因為縱酒導致亡國，所以周王發表「酒誥」宣言，勸導人民切勿飲酒過度。這樣的情形明顯反映在青銅容器的發展上：在商代發展鼎盛的酒器，到了周代逐漸式微，食器與水器便成為日後青銅器發展的重心。

　　青銅食器中最重要的就是鼎，鼎通常用來烹煮各種肉類，所以有些出土的青銅鼎內，還可以看到這些肉類的殘留物。有學者推測可能是在祭祀與宴客場合中，先用最大的鼎煮食肉類，煮好後再分裝到各個小鼎之中。青銅容器裡，用來烹煮食物的器物除了鼎之外，最常見的還有用來煮粥的鬲，和用來蒸食物的甗。這三種青銅器最大的共同特徵就是有三足的造型，足下可以生火煮食，因此有些器物還可以在器腹底下看見殘留的煙灰痕跡。在熱鬧的宴會場合當中，除了美酒佳餚之外，當然還少不了歌舞樂聲的助興！因此除了必備的青銅容器之外，樂器也不可缺少。青銅樂器中，又以成組使用的編鐘最引人注目。中國湖北出土的戰國時期曾侯乙墓的編鐘，組件數量完備龐大，是現在可以見到氣勢最恢宏的青銅樂器組合。

　　什麼是青銅器銘文？青銅器銘文是指鑄造或刻寫在青銅器上的文字。它最早出現在商代前期的青銅器上，因為青銅器的顏色原本是閃耀著金屬光澤的，所以又稱為「金文」，又因為以前大多鑄造在鐘和鼎上，所以又叫做「鐘鼎文」。青銅器銘文具有的三個重要價值：第一，青銅器銘文與漢字的起源有關；第二，青銅器銘文是探討商周歷史的第一手史料；第三，青銅器銘文是青銅器辨偽和斷代的依據之一。毛公鼎、散盤與宗周鐘在國立故宮博物院收藏的青銅器中是非常重要的文物。這三件青銅器的珍貴之處，在於器身上所銘鑄的長篇銘文。毛公鼎、散盤與宗周鐘上的銘文，不但展現了大篆書法端莊與優美的一面，同時也是專家學者研究西周歷史的重要史料。

毛公鼎

　　毛公鼎以其器腹內壁的銘文而為國之重寶。也是全世界最被討論的青銅器之一。銘文全長共 32 行，500 字，為迄今所知最長的中國青銅器銘文。學者相信從銘文內容來看，毛公鼎應該是在宣王繼位的第一年所製作。銘文內容見證了西周「宣王中興」的歷史，銘文前段為宣王對毛公的訓誥之辭，文中敘述宣王於即位之初緬懷周文王、武王如何享有天命、開創國家，他即位後對其所繼承的天命也戒慎恐懼。後段詳載宣王贈予毛公的豐厚賞賜。也表達宣王對毛公承擔重責大任的指示、期待、與信任。毛公於文末亦表達了對宣王的感謝，並願以此鼎傳之於後世。「大篆」書體在這篇銘文中，可以說已經發展到最成熟的階段。自出土以來，毛公鼎影響了許多書法家。

散盤

　　散氏盤也稱散盤，於清康熙年間出土，在 1809 年嘉慶皇帝五十大壽時，散氏盤是以貢品入宮中的壽禮，從此成為內府重器。散盤為西周厲王在位時鑄造的作品，此件作品不但是一件極為珍貴的工藝佳作，也是一件象徵西周晚期諸侯國爭奪疆土的歷史信物。

　　散盤的銘文，鑄在盤內，共 19 行，350 個字，銘文內容再現曾經存在西周時期，兩個小國的一段疆土之爭。記述西周時夨（音「ㄗㄜˋ」）國向散國轉讓田地的過程。起因是夨國侵犯了散國，所以用田地來賠償散國。除此之外也象徵了西周晚期王室權力的削弱，土地的分配權已不再是周王室所主導，各諸侯國兼併土地的風氣日漸盛行，井田制度正面臨著瓦解的危機。因此在當時，周王室所能做的就只是派一位史官仲農去見證諸侯之間的私自協議。周王室的角色已經改變從統治者變成見證者。土地糾紛的裁決權，已非周天子所能掌控的，而派官員去見證，其實只是為了維持表面的權威與尊嚴罷了。散盤可能是一篇歷史上最具分量的政治的契約書。

宗周鐘

　　宗周鐘，為西周厲王所製作用來祭祀祖先的樂器，又名「胡鐘」。宗周鐘是西周晚期厲王自作用器，在目前所知的西周銅器中，周王自作器屈指可數。銘文共 17 行，123 字，這篇銘文記載的是周厲王收服南方及東方的 26 個小國的故事。銘文自鐘體正中鉦部讀起，接著往鐘的左邊，再轉至鐘的另一邊。厲王在銘文中為了祈禱先王們賜福給後代子孫，保佑國泰民安。宗周鐘，呈標準的合瓦式造型。整個鐘身最突出的裝飾是三十六枚短柱型的突出物，及下半部裝飾的雙龍紋。除此之外底部雙龍處是敲擊揚聲所在，宗周鐘可在正中部位與側邊敲出兩個不同頻率的音響，故可稱為雙音鐘。

玉器

　　玉器一直被中國人認為是貴重的物品。同時人們也普遍的相信某些形狀的物體或裝飾有某些圖案，也是具有神奇的力量。古人相信美玉都蘊含豐富的能量，也就是精氣，因此用「玉帛」作為祭祀神明的禮器。

玉豬龍

　　學術界對於這類玉器的名稱曾經有些爭論，有人稱它作「豬龍」，也有人稱它為「熊龍」。豬是農村中重要的牲畜，而熊卻是東北居民崇拜的動物。這件造型奇特的玉豬龍是紅山文化中的玉器。看起來圓圓胖胖的，輪廓有點類似興隆洼的玉玦耳環。玉豬龍有招風耳，又皺起了鼻頭，拱起了嘴，具有動物胚胎的模樣。或許是因為史前的先民相信胚胎最具有生命的元氣，就用這種造型來象徵生命力。

玉握與玉唅

　　漢朝的人有自己獨特的喪葬習俗。古代人死時，最普遍的與亡者埋在一起的玉有玉握與玉唅。古人相信以玉陪葬可以使死者的身體不朽。這樣的習俗代表對已逝親人的心意，避免已逝親人離開時是空手的。在漢朝貴族的墓葬中，最普遍的玉握的形狀是豬，就像這件「金片包玉豬」。玉豬的製作目的是作為墓主人手握之用，故為一對，寓意子孫昌盛。此對玉豬作工簡單，僅約略琢磨出眼、耳、四肢的輪廓後，並未有進一步的複雜工序。而是因為喪葬玉本來就不需要精細的製作。然而製作粗略簡約並不代表使用者階級較低，依目前考古所見，此乃最高等級貴族專用喪葬用玉。而玉豬身軀包覆金箔，正足徵墓主人不凡的地位。金片包玉豬目前僅此一對，實為重要文物。

　　同時，當親人過世時，多以玉唅放入死者的嘴中，代表對親人的心意。當古代人心所愛的人過世時，含在口中的玉就叫做玉唅，漢代流行以蟬為造型。由於蟬的幼蟲在孵化成長後，藏在土中很長一段時間，會離開地底，羽化為成蟬，漢代的人因此將蟬視為具有生命力的象徵，將玉蟬放入死者的嘴中，希望死者可以像蟬一樣，早日復活。

玉辟邪

　　古時候的人相信辟邪能趕走邪惡靈，就如同中文字面上的意義一樣「驅逐邪魔」。這也是為什麼人們將辟邪與其他凶猛的石雕動物擺放在前往墓穴兩旁的道路上，就像埃及的人面獅身像一樣。辟邪是從獅子的形象衍生出來的動物。玉辟邪是神祕的動物。根據專家的說法是漢代帶翼神獸的形象，最初可能受到來自於西亞地區的影響。本件玉辟邪流傳至清代時，乾隆皇帝相當喜愛，特地為其製作底座，並寫詩篆刻在胸口和座底之下。

翠玉白菜

　　這件與真實白菜相似度幾乎百分百的作品，是由翠玉所雕琢而成。這件作品是雕刻在一件單一的半白半綠的玉，而這塊玉也有一些瑕疵，例如裂縫與變色的斑點，這些瑕疵被整合進雕刻裡，成為白菜的莖與葉的葉脈。

　　翠玉白菜一直被稱為是整個國立故宮博物院最有名的藏品，並且和肉形石、毛公鼎等三樣藏品，一起被認為是國立故宮博物院的三樣國寶級的藏品之一。雖然在博物館愛好者間享有高知名度而經常被錯誤解讀為國寶，實際上翠玉白菜只是被認定是著名的古董，而沒有文化資產保存法中所規範的國寶物件所須具備的稀有性與價值的條件。

　　此件作品的作者是未知的。原先被放置於紫禁城的永和宮，永和宮為光緒皇帝妃子瑾妃的寢宮，因此有人推測此器為瑾妃的嫁妝，象徵其清白，並企求多子多孫。別忘了看看菜葉上停留的兩隻昆蟲，它們可是寓意多子多孫的蝗蟲和螽斯，是中國文化中多子多孫的吉祥象徵。

肉形石

　　第一眼看到這件肉形石，就像一塊油亮得令人流口水的東坡肉。肉形石和翠玉白菜、毛公鼎等三樣藏品，現在被認為是國立故宮博物院的三樣國寶級的藏品之一。雖然從藝術史的觀點來看，僅具一般的重要性，但是對訪客來說，肉形石是極受歡迎的故宮寶物。

　　這塊雕成東坡肉形狀的肉形石，是來自清朝的一塊瑪瑙。瑪瑙生成過程中受到雜質的影響，呈現一層一層不同顏色的層次，加上工匠將頂部的石材表面加工鑽孔和染色，做成了這件層次分明、毛孔和肌理都逼真展現的作品，外觀看過去就像一塊肥嫩的東坡肉。

陶瓷

　　陶瓷，是文明的象徵。從採石製泥、拉坯成形、施釉敷彩，至入窯燒成，軟泥轉變成了堅硬的陶瓷。中國陶瓷主要分成兩大類。低溫約 950~1200°C 燒製的叫陶器，高溫約 1250~1400°C 燒製的叫瓷器。每件作品背後的文化及社會因素，讓造形、釉色和裝飾紋樣呈現出豐富多元的面貌。帝王、官員、工匠和使用者，共同形塑出時代的風格。

　　國立故宮博物院典藏的陶瓷器，多數承接自清代皇室典藏，再輾轉播遷來臺。這些來自北京、熱河和瀋陽三處皇宮的陶瓷器，皆有清楚的典藏號可以追溯出它們原來陳設之所在，形成與其他公私立博物館截然不同的

附錄

特色。例如：宋以前的陶瓷器，在臺北故宮收藏不多，然而卻擁有傲視全世界的宋代名窯、成化鬥彩、清朝的瓷胎畫琺瑯，以及明清各朝的官窯瓷器。

宋金元時期則探索各個窯口瓷器的裝飾與美感。明朝部分旨在陳述景德鎮御器廠的成立，燒造瓷器成為國家大事，而地方民窯亦與之競爭市場。清朝部分，呈現康雍乾三朝皇帝親自指揮御窯廠，官樣影響發揮至極致的現象；隨著國勢式微，終導致晚清的官樣作品混合著民間趣味。

汝窯

汝窯燒瓷時間很短，也被認定是宋代五大名窯之一。但傳世珍品所存可能不足七十件，十分罕見名貴。窯址位於河南省寶豐縣，宋代隸屬汝州，因此稱為汝窯；其釉色近於雨過天青色，與不透明的綠色釉混合，就像玉。

景德鎮

景德鎮是現在中國江西省非常著名的陶瓷生產的中心。景德鎮的窯自從五代 (907~960) 時期開始就已經存在迄今。在南北宋 (960~1279) 時期他們主要的產品是青花瓷，是一種使用藍色與白色釉料的瓷器。在元朝時景德鎮生產青花瓷與釉裡紅的瓷器。元朝 (1279~1368) 末年景德鎮已經成為陶瓷的主要生產中心。明朝 (1368~1644) 及清朝 (1644~1911) 時官窯在此設立。他們為皇室宮廷生產最高品質的瓷器，此後景德鎮已經成為中國文化中、陶瓷之都的同義詞。

琺瑯彩

當琺瑯彩這項技藝在 17 世紀末從西方傳來中國之後，琺瑯彩很快成為清朝皇帝的最愛。而且逐漸發展成一種新的形式，是將東西方的裝飾藝術整合成不同的技術。琺瑯彩是一種在瓷器上畫琺瑯的技術，包括在容器的表面用琺瑯的釉料作畫，之後放入窯內，以低溫燒製。

成化鬥彩雞缸杯

這件明代成化時期約 1460 年代的瓷器鬥彩酒杯，瓷胎輕薄小巧、色彩鮮明豔麗，融合了宣德時期創始的鬥彩技法及當時官窯新創的杯型。這件雞缸酒盃所採用的鬥彩技法，是在素坯上，先用鈷料勾繪紋飾的輪廓，塗上透明釉料，以高溫燒成灰藍色調的青花紋飾；然後在青花輪廓紋飾內填入各種顏色釉料，再放入爐內以低溫燒製而成。這種技法巧妙的將高溫燒製的白釉青花與低溫處理的多種顏色釉料彩繪完美的拼鬥在一起。因此稱為鬥彩。杯身外壁精細彩繪了兩組子母雞圖，並以牡丹、蘭花與石頭巧妙的將兩組圖案分隔。圖中公雞與母雞率領著小雞一同到野地覓食，讓我們也能感受到牠們的溫馨喜樂。從這件作品中，我們可以發現釉上彩繪有紅、黃、褐、綠等多種色調，配色鮮明，描繪生動，架構了一幅活潑生動的天倫圖。這件珍品深受帝王與文人雅士的喜愛，據明朝晚期文獻記載，明神宗萬曆皇帝時，這類細薄的小杯子一對就已價值十萬兩。在當時已如此貴重的瑰寶，今日的價值更是無與倫比了！

汝窯青瓷蓮花式溫碗

此碗呈十瓣蓮花式，碗腹壁稍呈圓弧，口緣花瓣流暢貫連，圈足稍高。整件器物由底至口厚度均勻，釉薄不透明，釉色呈青藍，有細開片。全器滿釉，圈足內底以五支釘墊燒，支釘點極細，也是全器中唯一未施以釉料的地方。

灰陶加彩仕女俑

唐代強調隆重的葬禮儀式，經常以豐厚的物品陪葬。所以唐代的墓葬裡常常看到大量的、以陶土製作的人形俑作為陪葬品，這件仕女俑就是其中之一。這位仕女的身材豐腴，有著細細長長的眉毛和雙眼，櫻桃小口，臉部圓潤而神情安祥。她梳著高高而蓬鬆的髮髻，兩邊的頭髮環抱著臉部，正是唐代晚期流行的樣式。她穿著寬大的長袍，右手抬舉到胸前，左手微微下垂，兩隻尖頭的小靴子隨意伸出衣服下襬之外。

附
錄

定窯－白瓷嬰兒枕

定窯是宋代北方著名窯場，窯址以現今河北曲陽縣為中心，因其地古名定州，故稱定窯。

中國人會以嬰兒的形式，作成嬰兒枕嗎？類似的嬰兒枕全世界所知僅有三件，那是因為中國人強烈延續男性家族血脈的渴望。中國人總習慣說如果睡在小嬰兒枕之上，就比較有機會生男孩，小嬰兒枕實際上是代表了生男孩的價值觀。本件嬰兒枕的釉色牙白溫潤，頭部與身體分別左右模接後，並將身、首接合，再雕刻面容。特別的是，若舉而持之，可以發現器內有一泥塊，在移動時，會輕擊內壁叮叮作響。枕底並刻有在 1773 年春天，清代乾隆皇帝御題一首詩。

汝窯－青瓷無紋水仙盆

橢圓形狀的盆，深而且有些反光的內壁，平底，四個雲頭形的足；周壁胎薄，底足略厚。通體滿布天青釉，極勻潤；底邊釉積處略含淡碧色；口緣與稜角釉薄處呈淺粉色。裹足支燒，底部有六個細支釘痕，略見米黃胎色。全器釉面純潔無紋片，此種傳世稀少，溫潤素雅的色澤，正是宋人所欲追求如雨過天青的寧靜開朗的美感。

整件布滿釉品質完美沒有任何開片，在現存中是極罕見的案例。人們稱讚有蟹爪痕為佳，但是如果全部沒有開片的作品，更是極品！汝窯以高貴的天青色而聞名，同時也有優美典雅的造型。

這件青瓷無紋水仙盆可以說是精品中的精品。

霽青描金游魚轉心瓶

轉心瓶作套瓶造型，但外觀仍形塑如同一件完整的瓶子。器腹部分成內外兩層，內層飾淺青色釉，上繪落花、水藻和游魚，因係套瓶故握頸旋轉，可帶動內瓶轉動，透過外瓶開光望過去，型態各異的金魚便如同走馬燈般，悠游戲耍於觀者眼前。它的創意發想，無論來自中國傳統的走馬燈，或受到西方使用發條製造旋轉機巧的影響，因燒造過程須經零件燒成，再進行黏組的步驟。從完成後渾然如同一件單獨整器中，可感受成器的功力所在。

寶石紅釉僧帽壺

　　這件明代宣德時期的寶石紅僧帽壺，器形特別。這類紅釉壺很受清代皇家的喜愛，有一幅皇家畫作中顯示，雍正皇帝妃子房間的櫃子上，曾放置寶石紅僧帽壺作為陳列裝飾。明代永樂年間，約 15 世紀早期，成功燒製出呈色鮮豔的紅釉，到了宣德時期，紅釉的色澤更加濃密厚重，有如紅寶石般璀璨，因此獲得了「寶石紅」的美名。不過紅釉瓷器燒製成功的機率很低，留傳下來的作品也就很稀少。這件作品的紅釉在壺口、把柄和底部邊緣透出淡淡的白邊，是明代宣德時期紅釉瓷器的特色。

導遊篇 Unit 4

▶ 臺南孔廟

　　孔子被所有中國人所熟知。孔子是 2,500 年前居住在現在中國的東北部。臺灣的首座孔廟，位於臺南。並於每年 9 月 28 日，清晨 5 點就開始秋祭大典，慶祝這位中國教育家與哲學家的生日，也是臺灣的教師節。臺南孔廟是唯一仍實行供奉牛羊豬三牲祭祀孔子，其他孔廟則是以動物造型的三牲取代牛羊豬。而來到孔廟當然別忘了向偉大的孔老夫子求智慧，每年祭典結束後，滿滿的人潮爭相上主殿拔取智慧毛，據說智慧毛能為來年帶來智慧。不過拔智慧毛時請注意，最好自備透明塑膠袋或紅紙袋來裝牛毛，回家後得日曬乾燥過，才不會因為過於潮濕而無法保存。

　　臺南孔廟已經經過許多不同時期的轉變。而且因為臺灣歷史混亂的政治與殖民的本質，臺南孔廟也有改建數次。即使今天我們看到的建築物，未必都有超過 350 年的歷史，臺南孔廟在臺灣歷史中扮演重要的角色。臺南孔廟早在明鄭時期的 1665 年便已創立，在清朝時期一度是全臺童生（在明清兩朝代未進入官學的剛入門層級的考生），無論年紀大小，都稱「童生」，亦被稱為儒童，也是孔子的學生之意。東寧王國的統治者鄭經是國姓爺的長子，在他的參謀陳永華的建議下，興建臺南孔廟。東寧王國是國姓爺所建立，存在於 1661 到 1683 年之間，宗旨是重新建立明朝。開啟了臺灣儒學先鋒，成為培育知識分子的搖籃。在 1997 年，臺南孔子廟被指定為國定古蹟。

　　門口下馬碑為全臺僅存 4 塊下馬碑中年代最早、保存最完整的一塊，1687 年奉旨設立花崗石碑有滿、漢文字陰刻凹入，填紅色油漆，相當醒目。滿文在左，漢文在右。內文是：「文武官員軍民人等至此下馬」以示對孔子的尊崇，是全臺孔廟中保存得最為完整、毫髮無損的下馬碑。

　　三百多年來，臺南孔子廟歷經數次重大整修，在臺灣傳統建築中占有無可取代的地位，為臺南最完整的傳統閩南建築群，採標準的「左學右廟」

格局。前中後總共有三進，兩邊搭配從頭到尾相連接的廂房，形成兩個內部庭院區域。孔廟第一進為大成門，分別設立名宦祠、鄉賢祠、孝子祠、節孝祠。大成門是以 6 根柱子支撐的木構架，不像大部分的廟，每組門扇上面不繪門神，而是總共設有 108 根門釘，也不書寫任何楹聯，以示對孔子的敬重。中間是第二進大成殿，兩側有東、西兩廡奉祀 81 位先賢 77 位先儒。禮器庫、樂器庫，分別位在東、西廡的北邊，是收藏禮樂器之處。最後是第三進崇聖祠。

大成殿現在的樣貌，在 1977 年所整建，是孔子廟建築群中層級最高者。位居合院中間，被其他建築環繞，顯見其重要性，位於高起的臺基上，呈現一種崇高的意涵。大成殿裡面有一極簡單的神龕供奉孔子神位在紅色的桌上。有一種所有孔廟的特色是不供奉孔子的雕像。這個規定是在 500 年前的明朝皇帝宣布孔廟一致只能有神位，而不能有雕像。殿內則高懸自清朝康熙皇帝以來到臺灣，除了末代皇帝溥儀以外所有的元首頌揚孔子的匾額，也是全臺灣孔廟中擁有最完整匾額的地方。

在大成殿前的平臺稱月臺，也稱為丹墀。所有的孔廟均有月臺，每逢教師節清晨祭孔時大成殿前方的露臺，為祭孔典禮表演佾舞的場所。大成殿月臺前方嵌有御路，刻以棋琴書畫與龍頭。古時平常人不准行走，只有新科狀元與皇帝祭孔時才得以經過此御路步上大成殿祭孔，其實皇帝老爺和狀元是坐轎子上去的，而抬轎的人是走旁邊的階梯上去。屋脊中央至九級寶塔，民間傳說有震邪作用。

大成殿屋脊兩端各立一根筒狀物，謂之通天柱或藏經筒，上有蟠龍，下有鰲魚。據說為感念孔子德配天地，道貫古今故在修建孔廟時，便在廟頂裝上兩個陶製筒子稱為通天柱，表示對孔子的尊崇。又有傳說認為在秦始皇焚書坑儒時，讀書人為保護經書就在自家的屋頂上裝上看起來像煙囪的筒子，把經書藏在裡面以免被官兵搜去焚毀，後來人們便在大成殿屋頂上也裝上這種筒子來紀念這種珍惜書籍的精神而立謂之藏經筒。

　　大成殿之斜脊以水龍及卷草裝飾，據說水龍可以壓火神祝融，因而可避免火災。屋頂上另一種雕飾則為成排位垂脊之鴟鴞。本是最乖戾殘暴的一種鳥，俗名「貓頭鷹」，會啄殺母鳥吞食，實為一種不孝不祥之物。但卻流傳著另一個發人深省的故事，相傳梟鳥飛過當年孔子傳道授業之處，竟受孔子感化而馴良，佇足慕道。正象徵孔子無所不包的人格和有教無類的精神。

　　崇聖祠是祭祀孔子的五代祖先的地方。是木結構的無窗戶的開放空間，並以 18 根柱子支撐燕尾脊的尾頂。崇聖祠在 1723 年雍正皇帝時建造。這種安排，實與中國幾千年來宗族倫理制度有關，孔廟之布局，也與家廟或宗祠有相通之處。崇聖祠面寬五開間，崇聖祠室內的梁架與儀門一樣，採露明方式，可以看到屋梁及瓜柱之雕飾。它的屋架使用「三通五瓜式」，即有三支通梁與五支短柱。瓜柱作成金瓜形與木瓜形，造型圓融渾厚，頗能表現力道之美。尤其最上面的獅座，雕出馱負大脊桁重量之架勢，栩栩如生。

　　座落在孔廟的另一邊，明倫堂是儒學講堂最常用的名稱，包括大門以及庭院，主建物是開放空間，有良好的空氣流通。也是清代府學中的教室。以「明倫」堂為名，即以教授學生明白倫常，瞭解宗法制度概念下的人際關係和儒學對社會的認知，明倫是儒學的基礎，故以此為名。堂內有一塊「臥碑」刻著當時明倫堂的校規條文。

▶ 鹽水蜂炮

　　「南鹽水蜂炮，北平溪天燈，東炸寒單」是每年臺灣慶祝元宵節的三大主要節慶活動。鹽水蜂炮的起源有許多的傳說。有人說是要向當時訪問臺灣的嘉慶皇帝致敬，其他人說是鞭炮比賽。然而最普遍的說法是和 1885 年發生在臺南鹽水的霍亂疫情有關聯，當時臺南鹽水地區的關帝廟信眾，決定將關聖帝君的雕像置放在神轎上，在農曆元月 13 日至 15 日 3 天出巡繞境遶境鹽水地區。信徒隨神轎沿路燃放爆竹驅趕瘟神，也開啟了長達130 年的傳統。

　　人們不僅變化出「炮城」和多面向的發射模式，信眾還以炮城的創意設計及巧思造型表達對神明敬意。在早期鹽水蜂炮節慶的時候，以傳統鞭炮炸神轎酬神，鞭炮種類是「連珠炮」。到二戰結束（1945 年）後開始出現「蜂炮」。1984 年以後出現「炮城」，在傳統觀念認為，燃放越多蜂炮就越多繁榮與財富的觀念的鼓勵之下，規模日漸龐大。且因深具聲光娛樂效果，蜂炮也造就臺南鹽水區深具觀光魅力。近年來透過國際媒體報導後，更有了「世界三大民俗慶典之一」、「全球十大最危險祭典之一」、「全球十大最佳慶典」等頭銜。

　　炮城製作方式從早期簡單的幾排木條釘製，單向或雙向前後發射，逐漸演變成以角鐵做成基座的大型炮城，內部分成數層，上面鋪以鐵網讓蜂炮插在網上固定射向，並有多角度的發射設計，每支蜂炮以炮心相連，數量從數千到數萬，甚至達十幾萬支之譜，正中央放置火心，外觀再以紙糊上各種造型，從 1984 年開始，炮城設計開始造型化，此時紙質蜂炮也進化成塑膠彈頭，不僅鳴叫聲音更響亮，當炮城安放屋內等待神轎遶境時推出，燃放酬謝神恩。

　　活動原本只有元宵節當天，因耗時過長，後來改為分兩區輪流進行，活動最早的遶境從農曆正月 14 日上午開始，一直延續到最後 15 日深夜結束，為期兩天。每年蜂炮施放路線會依事前會議決定，在遶境活動當中，要燃放炮臺的各家都已先登記，神轎抵達門前後，就推出炮臺，由主人拉開紅布，撕下貼在炮臺上的紅紙，在神明面前與金紙共同焚燒祝禱後，引燃炮臺，讓神明點收，神轎則以三進三退方式接收。

　　但是為什麼讓鹽水蜂炮如此獨特？事實是炮城直接直射參與者。沒錯，只要夠勇敢及不怕被炮火攻擊都歡迎參加。建議參加活動的民眾應準備完整的保護裝備以免受傷。包括頭戴全罩式安全帽、脖子圍圍巾或毛巾以防備亂跑的蜂炮鑽入衣服內、棉質或牛仔外套、長褲、手套及平底鞋或運動鞋，切忌穿雨衣等可能融化或起火之衣物。

附錄

> 炸寒單

農曆正月 15 日是元宵節，同時也是臺灣舉辦許多獨特的宗教活動慶祝新年的時候。與鹽水的爆炸場面並駕其驅的是位於臺東市的炸寒單活動。這可能是每年臺灣東部最重要的民俗宗教活動，也必定是臺東市最重要的活動。

相傳寒單爺為商朝（約西元前 1562 到西元前 1066 年）的武將趙公明，死後在天界專司財庫，是道教的五路財神之一，坊間稱他武財神。據說，寒單爺怕冷，因此，當他出巡時，民眾便投擲鞭炮為祂驅寒。早期寒單爺金身由信徒輪流供奉，直至 1989 年輪值爐主請回家，建廟完成並命名為玄武堂，寒單爺才有了固定安奉的場所。炮炸寒單爺始於 1951 年，因炮炸形式太過震撼，曾被警察機關禁止，後來在信眾奔走下，讓炮炸寒單爺重現臺東街頭，1998 年開始與官方合作，提升為元宵佳節的重頭戲。近幾年，在臺東縣政府的重視與推動下規模逐漸擴大，已成了代表臺東的民俗活動之一，2007 年公告為臺東縣民俗文化資產。

近幾年臺東炮炸寒單爺逐漸受到大眾的歡迎。每年舉辦天數皆不同，大多都在 5 至 6 天之間，最熱鬧的重點，以農曆正月 15 日、16 日寒單爺隊伍在街上巡行，接受沿途商家民眾炮炸，農曆正月 12 日至 13 日由炮炸寒單爺的主辦單位舉辦研習營，介紹臺東炮炸寒單爺歷史由來，及舉辦小型的「炮炸寒單爺」活動，讓一般民眾獲得第一手的體驗。農曆正月 12 日至 14 日由臺東玄武堂開始準備出巡遶境事宜，包括在海濱公園廣場搭設臨時行館、請神、整轎、請兵將，並擲筊進行「安座」及神明在遶境進行的順序，完畢後以三牲、素果祭祀。

農曆正月 15 日至 16 日，炮炸寒單爺重頭戲「出巡炮炸」，分為出巡遶境與接受邀約炮炸兩種，出巡遶境為寒單爺跟隨「臺東元宵神明遶境活動　隊伍行進，僅接受沿途商家、民眾自備零星炮火炮炸。而接受邀約炮炸為商家事先向臺東玄武堂登記，邀約至商店前接受炮炸，寒單爺會依行程安排前往。國際交換學生體驗營：農曆正月 15 日下午由來自世界各地在臺東求學的交換學生扮演寒單爺接受炮火洗禮，體驗炮炸寒單爺的民俗文化。

因相傳扮演寒單爺者可獲得神明的庇佑，因此都為自願者，每年擔任寒單爺人數不定，會依照裝扮者的忍耐程度調整，通常扮演寒單爺者多為年輕人，其中也視情況，穿插老經驗的戰將。而寒單爺的外表裝扮依循傳統，早期肉身寒單爺需「開臉」（在臉上彩妝神明的面容，開臉之後就是神明的化身，具有神格之意），頸上掛元帥印，頭綁黃頭巾並打赤膊、紅短褲，以濕毛巾搗住口鼻，並用棉花塞住耳朵，後來因濕毛巾將臉包住，所以也取消開臉習俗，手上則持榕樹枝葉（道教相傳榕樹枝葉可擋煞）把鞭炮擋下，或擋住嗆鼻煙灰。

在竹椅武轎上放置寒單爺的神像，在敲銅鑼者的前導下，神轎一邊搖晃，一邊在街上巡行。等到達定點後，帶轎者會依據風向，選擇上風處作為椅轎準備與人員替換的場所，待領隊一聲令下，準備上轎的肉身寒單爺先向安座於椅轎上的寒單爺祈求平安後站上椅轎，轎夫起轎向商家行「三進三退」禮，並繞行一圈。

要如何炮炸寒單？以「排炮」以 3 至 5 排為一綑，並將引信纏繞並用橡皮筋固定，炮手會分散成一圈，手拿數綑排炮團，將鞭炮引燃後擲向寒單爺，肉身寒單爺則站於轎上在圓圈內繞圈子接受炮炸。肉身寒單爺則依照可忍耐程度換人。有些特殊地點，輪班的寒單爺們還會一起站在神轎上接受炮炸，並表現得毫無畏懼的樣子。排炮式（攻炮型）為最常見的炮炸方式。炮炸寒單爺的每年路線、時程均有些微調整，事先會在網路公布，報名體驗或前往觀賞的遊客，最好身著長袖長褲，佩戴帽子、護目眼鏡、口罩甚至耳塞，以確保安全。

附
錄

導遊篇 Unit 5

> 艋舺龍山寺

　　座落在臺北的萬華區，艋舺龍山寺在 1738 年建造，也歷經多次的重修，廟宇主神是觀世音菩薩及其他道教神明，包括海神媽祖以及武聖關公，在臺灣有一諺語說「一府、二鹿、三艋舺。」這個諺語說明了清朝三個主要城市。艋舺（現在叫萬華）是臺北市最古老的區域。艋舺在臺灣原住民的平埔族語是獨木舟的意思，也清楚地說明艋舺位處方便的船運之地，也鄰近當時的淡水河。艋舺龍山寺曾經數次被地震及暴雨而全部或局部被摧毀，但是臺北人持續重建與重修。

　　在日治時期，部分的廟被當作學校、軍營和辦公室。在 1919 年，因為嚴重的白蟻破壞木造結構，住持福智法師和地方的知識分子組織募款要重建破壞的龍山寺。他們找了來自福建南部的建廟大師王益順擔任建築師。龍山寺成為王益順在臺灣的主要作品，也奠定現在龍山寺外觀的基礎。1945 年二次世界大戰時龍山寺被美國轟炸機轟炸破壞，但是因為戰爭所導致的經濟蕭條而無法進行修復，一直到 1955 年才有經費進行重修。2018 年龍山寺被指定為臺北市的國定古蹟。

　　在 18 世紀初期的時候，福建的三邑人晉江、惠安、南安的移民來到艋舺。因為是家鄉古老龍山寺忠誠的信徒，所以他們在艋舺建立新的定居地，建立原先龍山寺祖廟的分香廟在艋舺。現在的龍山寺的建築包括三個部分：前殿、正殿、後殿。前殿被當作入口及祭祀的地方。正殿位居廟的正中間，祭拜的是主神觀世音菩薩。後殿主要是奉祀道教神明，又分成三個部分，中間的是海神媽祖，左邊（神明的方向）的是文學或考試之神的文昌帝君，右邊（神明的方向）的是戰爭之神—武聖關公。龍山寺總共奉祀數百尊佛教、道教、儒教的神明。

　　前殿的結構主要是分成三川殿、龍門廳、虎門廳，三川殿美麗的藝術雕刻以及牆上的綠色及白色的石頭形成賞心悅目的對稱美感。因為是在二十世紀初完成的建築，王益順已經知道西式的建築形式。他將混凝土山牆放在前殿牆上當作裝飾，增加希臘科林斯柱頭在某些龍柱上當作裝飾，將各種特色加總起來，使龍山寺成為臺灣傳統中式建築的地標。

在前殿位於三川殿正面入口處，是全臺灣僅有的一對青銅鑄造的龍柱，為 1920 年代由廈門匠師洪坤福所塑泥胚，並由臺北鐵工廠李祿星以翻砂技術鑄造而成。龍身線條分明，柱身以明朝小說「封神榜」人物雕刻陪襯，柱底則有海浪、鯉魚與柱珠，顯見當年匠師手藝之精巧。

在中式傳統中藻井的使用通常是獨一無二的尊貴建築才使用。前殿的八卦藻井以 32 組斗栱集中向中心組合而成，其間還穿插斜向的交叉拱，並分成內外兩圈，結構十分奇巧美觀，是出自泉州名匠王益順之手。所有牆與屋頂的連結完全沒有使用釘子。屋頂使用重疊的磁磚，並且用龍鳳及吉祥的生物作裝飾。

一般來說鐘鼓樓在傳統廟宇是獨立結構。鐘樓在廟宇東邊，鼓樓在廟宇的西邊。鐘鼓樓設計採轎頂式屋頂或像六角型的帽子，也是臺灣廟宇中首次出現的鐘鼓樓建築形式，並影響後來各地廟宇的建築風格。現貌也是泉州名師王益順所修。

在龍山寺的金爐及牆角，有憨番的影像出現。至於為什麼要將憨番放在厝角或爐頂，則有以下四種說法：1. 憨番是荷人據臺時，所引進的黑人奴隸。2. 以前漢人常稱呼力大無窮的平埔族為番仔。3. 相傳民間因不滿荷蘭人（紅毛番）的高壓統治，所以在廟宇中，匠師為表達不滿，處罰紅毛番去扛廟宇厝角或金爐。4. 相傳有個很喜歡批評別人作品的人，常常讓師傅很不高興，後來如果有人喜歡沒來由的亂批評蓋廟匠師的作品，匠師就照著那位喜歡亂批評的人的面貌去雕刻憨番，所以我們千萬不要隨便得罪匠師。龍山寺的金爐（金爐是用來插供神的香）數目將會在 2015 年中從七個降為三個，以降低廟中空氣中有害的 PM2.5 物質。龍山寺決定參與政府的綠色政策，而將廟中金爐從 2017 年使用的的金爐三個降為一個，在 2020 年 3 月降為零。

位於龍山寺正殿四根金柱之間正上方的屋頂有螺旋藻井，目前由 32 組斗栱組合而成。最初也是出自泉州名師王益順之手，原先設計以 16 組斗栱組合而成，逆時針方向散開，然而，戰後（1945 年）重建時改成以順時針方式組合。位於正殿有一尊釋迦立像，為日治時期出身艋舺的臺灣第一位雕塑家黃土水於 1925 年所作，立像以南宋梁楷水墨畫「釋迦出山圖」為藍本，二次大戰時遭戰火燒毀，後來由行政院文建會（現已改制為文化部）以原模翻製。

　　龍山寺總是以維持佛教為本質的寺廟，但是很多道教的神明也被奉祀在後殿之中，充分顯示地方民眾對宗教生活的包容心態。在旁邊也有人們同時在尋找對愛情、婚姻與小孩的祝福。雖然廟中有許多神明可以祭祀，但是只有月老吸引最多人的興趣。在地單身的人會來到龍山寺拜月老，祈求真愛，期待結婚之後能永遠在一起，他們也能向月老求一條紅線，將紅線綁在他們心愛的人的手腕上，理論上會將他們永遠綁在一起。

　　筊杯（擲筊）在臺語中被稱為ㄅㄨㄚˋ ㄅㄨㄟ，為一對新月狀的紅色塊狀物，音譯為「杯」。擲筊就像丟銅板。筊杯被道教人士當作占卜的形式或與神明的對話。不僅可以在廟裡擲筊，也可以在家裡做。如果沒有筊杯，也可以用銅板取代。站在神明前面，同時簡單地介紹自己。人們通常告知神明，自己的姓名、生日與住址。之後就可以往上擲筊，讓筊杯落在地上，然後去看最後的結果.。

　　筊杯有正反兩面，圓的部分及平面的部分，如果是兩個圓的部分都朝上，代表神明否定、生氣的意思，表示神明不答應請求。如果是兩平面都朝上，表示神明笑了，但不是神明回答「是」，而是代表解釋並不夠清楚，或那不是正確的時間去問問題。一正一反的筊杯，又稱「聖杯」，代表神明同意信徒所請示的事項。有一種很罕見的情況，就是筊杯直接站立在地板上。這種情形代表神明不瞭解信徒的問題。一般人擲筊，多半對神明有所求，但是如果是無所求，較容易出現「立杯」，會被信徒視為神蹟。

> 大龍峒保安宮

　　大龍峒保安宮也以臺北保安宮而知名。座落在臺北市大同區的臺灣民間宗教的廟宇。大龍峒是在臺北市區最古老的區域，接近基隆河與淡水河交界的地方。現在的廟是由來自福建的同安人所建，這些人在 19 世紀早期移民到此。並將此廟取名保安宮，也就是「保護同安人」之意。保安宮也就成為居住在大龍峒的同安人的精神中心。

　　1709 年清廷在臺北核准了第一張開墾的執照叫陳賴章墾號。大龍峒已經是在臺北陳賴章墾號的北方的邊界。44 坎是大龍峒早期的商業區，也就是現在的哈密街。據說當初建保安宮時所剩下的未用完的建築材料被當地的富商王、鄭、高、陳等姓氏的家族以低價取得之後，在保安宮的左邊蓋了兩排共 44 間的商店，每一間店又叫一坎。臺北孔廟就在保安宮的隔壁。

　　保安宮的歷史可以追溯自 1742 年的「大隆同」，也就是現在的大龍峒，當年來到臺灣的新移民在大龍峒保安宮的現址，興建一座小廟奉祀保生大帝，當人口逐漸成長，木造小廟已經不夠容納，所以就計畫募款改建一座更大的廟，1805 年開始重建，一直到 1830 年才興建完工。

　　保安宮的主神是身為醫神的保生大帝。保生大帝是眾生為自己及家人祈求健康，因此形塑保生大帝成為道教中的重要神明，在臺灣就有超過 300 間寺廟是供奉保生大帝。保生大帝也被稱為大道公或吳真人，是在中國閩南地區被奉祀的醫神。原本保生大帝又名吳夲（音同濤，非本）是執業的醫生和道士，他曾被稱讚展現了一些醫療奇蹟，而且在死後被封為神明。在 1150 年，在福建省白礁村以他為名建立一座廟。宋朝高宗皇帝賞賜並命名為慈濟宮。

　　保生大帝一生當中曾經展現了一些醫療奇蹟。例如他曾經對龍點眼藥水，而且替老虎移除喉嚨裡的異物。根據傳說在宋朝時有隻老虎吃了一位婦人，但是被婦人的髮簪劃破喉嚨，所以非常痛苦。老虎請求保生大帝的協助，保生大帝卻斥責老虎吃人，是天庭給的處罰，所以無法救牠。但是老虎沒有離開，很後悔牠所做的事，後來因為被老虎感動，保生大帝救了

老虎。為了感謝保生大帝，待在保生大帝身邊保護祂，成為祂的座騎，最後保生大帝將凶猛的老虎轉化成神。每年的 4 月 16 都有儀式紀念「黑虎將軍」。當宋高宗還是太子時被送到金朝當人質，保生大帝的神聖力量幫助宋高宗回到中國。在宋高宗繼位之後，他命令建廟及賜與保生大帝的頭銜。明成祖的文皇后罹患胸部疾病，朝廷的醫生束手無策，保生大帝以道士身分現身醫治，他以絲線去感受脈動，而治好皇后的病，明成祖要用黃金感謝祂，保生大帝婉拒之後乘鶴而去，明成祖為了感謝保生大帝而加封祂。

在日治時期的 20 世紀，保安宮曾經歷許多次的改建與增建，才造就現在的樣子。2018 年保安宮被指定為臺北市的國定古蹟。因為自然的破壞以及白蟻所導致的嚴重損害，1995 年在當時的副董事長廖武智先生領導之下，自己募款找老匠師用傳統的方法來修復廟宇。由於嚴格遵守文化資產保護法的規定以及修舊如舊的方法，和現代科技的協助。此次重修受到聯合國教科文組織的認可，獲得 2003 年的亞洲資產保存獎，保安宮是唯一獲得此亞洲資產保存獎獎項的臺灣寺廟。

3,000 坪的保安宮是全臺最大的奉祀保生大帝的廟。保安宮的方位是朝南，主要的結構在中間是包括三川殿（前殿）、主殿、後殿，兩邊是東西廂房及鐘鼓樓。所有組合在一起形成「回」字形的造型。主殿是最高的，其次是後殿、前殿及東西廂房，如此的尊卑順序是和儒教的禮儀與道教的結構一致。

在保安宮的東西兩邊門的牆上有書捲形狀的竹節窗。石頭窗框是書捲形狀的，在窗框內是石雕的竹節窗。奇數的竹節代表「陽」，偶數的竹節代「陰」，如此代表陰與陽的調和。

在保安宮的前殿入口的兩邊有兩隻石獅，一隻公，一隻母。經常母獅嘴巴是關閉的，公獅嘴巴是打開的。據說工匠因為搞錯了，而將母獅嘴巴雕成是打開的，而被因為違約而減薪。東西兩邊門前的兩隻石獅與傳統的不太一樣，擁有大的眼球，大尾巴，捲毛，大嘴巴，崩角平頭，在古時後被稱為「仁獸」或「麒麟」，相傳「仁獸」或「麒麟」是一種儀式性動物。

　　保安宮三川殿的八角龍柱，為嘉慶九年（1804 年）所作，是保安宮最早的石雕作品，臺灣廟宇的龍柱，又被稱為「蟠龍柱」，指的是還未升天的龍。三川殿的龍柱，為嘉慶年間（清朝中期）完成，所以造型相對簡單，龍是四獸之一。也有傳說，龍有九似，像駱駝的頭、鹿的角、獅鬃、牛嘴、狗鼻、蛇身、魚鱗、鷹爪及蝦眼。

　　在 1983 年，保安宮重新彩繪三川殿的門神秦叔寶、尉遲恭二門神時，是由劉家正執筆，他對門神眼睛的繪畫技巧，吸引很多人的注意。「四顧眼」的技巧，觀者能從任何角度看門神，而且都有被看的感覺。

　　鐘鼓樓建於東西護室的頂上，為歇山重簷式建築，其四角形樓閣，與臺灣常見的六角形有所不同，造型甚為特殊。兩邊的鐘樓與鼓樓，就有對場作的操作。東邊的鐘樓與西邊的鼓樓，分別由陳應彬和郭塔兩位匠師主持工事，在木雕設計與彩繪圖案的風格上不盡相同，在鐘鼓樓正面分別題有「鯨發」、「鼉逢ㄊㄨㄛˊ　ㄆㄥˊ」匾額，從鐘鼓樓的命名來看，保安宮是臺灣最具文學氣質的廟宇，是當之無愧的註解。鯨發，據說龍生九子中之三子叫做「蒲牢」，形似龍而小，性好叫吼，極為害怕鯨魚，一見到鯨魚，便害怕大叫，古人因此在鐘上刻上蒲牢的獸紐，再用形似鯨魚的木槌去撞它，就會發出響亮的鐘聲。鼉逢，鼉又稱鼉龍，因生長於長江下游、太湖一帶，又稱為揚子鱷，是鱷魚的一種。相傳以鼉皮縫製而成的鼓皮，鼓聲最為優美動聽。另有一種解釋是無論是鯨發或是鼉逢，皆是狀聲之詞。兩字連讀，即能模擬出鐘聲及鼓聲。

　　保安宮正殿四周走廊牆面上有彩繪壁畫。壁畫是來自臺南的國寶級大師潘麗水的作品，完成於 1973 年。潘麗水自兒童時期就跟隨他的父親學習水墨畫，尤其是人物畫。他的父親潘春源也是一位很有名的畫家，在 1993 年獲得教育部的民族藝師薪傳獎的殊榮，是首位民俗畫家獲獎。這些壁畫的主題主要是受到中國民間與歷史故事所啟發，七件壁畫主題分別為：「韓信胯下受辱」、「朱仙鎮八槌大戰陸文龍」、「鍾馗迎妹回娘家」、「八仙大鬧東海」、「花木蘭代父從軍」、「虎牢關三戰呂布」、「賢哉徐母」等七幅。

　　日治時期的 1917 年左右的重修是由漳洲的大木匠師陳應彬及郭塔一起施工，每人負責一半的廟宇工程，兩位大師在高度精緻的木工展現他們獨特的技巧，這也是稱為對場作（兩位大師的競爭）的建築工法。然而不管工作是如何分配的，工匠仍必須遵守基本的尺寸規定，例如長與寬的尺寸，所以並不會影響寺廟的完整性。對場作的原因為什麼非常重要，因為最大的目標是贏得口碑去獲得其他廟宇的合作機會，尤其是在社會環境相對封閉的年代，經濟動機是扮演最重要的角色，最後的結果看起來是藝術且有價值的，例如三川殿的木雕員光（垂梁），以及主殿重簷下的「八仙大鬧東海」木雕都是很好的例子。

　　自 1994 年開始保生大帝的生日慶典，保生文化祭從每年 3 月初到 5 月初，已經從傳統廟宇活動轉換成熱鬧的文化慶典。每年都會有一系列的活動包括三天的祈福儀式，慶祝保生大帝生日才表演的藝陣，以及由傳統家族表演的家姓戲等等。

Good morning, my name is Ming-Der Liu（劉明德）. I teach as a part-time lecturer in the Center for General Education at both National United University and Hung-Kuang University. I have a great passion for working in the tourism field and I think it has a lot of potential.

I graduated from National Taiwan University with a Master's degree in Microbiology and Bachelor's degree in Public Health. I worked in private companies and taught in senior high school. It is these experiences that made me a person with communicative competency. I always devoted myself to my jobs, and I'm adaptable to any new challenge.

In my leisure time, I enjoy reading novels and some science magazines, especially news of medicine, tourism and environmental protection. I am interested in traveling and making friends. I consider that tourism is not only an important industry in Taiwan but also the best way to learn how to know the histories and cultures of our island and country, even marketing to others.

A few years ago, I went to Beijing, Tokyo and Shanghai several times for self-guided travels. I visited the Great Wall, Forbidden City, Beijing University, Temple of Heaven and Summer Palace. I tried to learn the local customs and world cultures during the trips and upgraded my humanistic qualities from history.

In the short term, I'd like to enrich myself to be a competent tour guide and do my best to solve any guest's problem. It is my honor to present/talk about myself to you. Thank you again for this opportunity.

附
錄

❯ 必備

PNR / e-ticket 旅客訂位紀錄或電子機票	tour guide / manager's contact number 領隊或導遊的電話
credit card 信用卡	traveler's check 旅行支票
shopping list 購物清單	emergency phone number 緊急聯絡人電話
journal 日記	flashlight 手電筒
itinerary 行程表	luggage lock and key 行李箱鑰匙
passport & visa 護照及簽證	digital camera 數位相機
travel insurance policy 旅遊險保單	rooming list 分房表
waiver 切結書	mobile phone & charger 行動電話（手機）及充電器
powerbank 行動電源	laptop & charger 筆記型電腦及充電器
App of the Travel Emergency Guidance 旅外救助指南 APP	

❯ 用品

compass 指南針	coat 外套
jacket 夾克	belt 腰帶
earplugs 耳塞	gloves 手套
raincoat 雨衣	slippers 拖鞋
tooth brush 牙刷	tooth paste 牙膏
dental floss 牙線	travel pillow 靠枕
hat 帽子	cap 棒球帽
scarf 圍巾	whistle 哨子

shorts 短褲	blindfold 眼罩
slacks 便褲	sweater 毛衣
backpack 背包	pen and paper 紙筆
purse, wallet 錢包	handbag 手提袋
swimsuit 泳衣（女）	trunks 四角泳褲（男）
speedo 三角泳褲（男）	resealable plastic bag 可封口塑膠袋
razor and shaving supplies 刮鬍工具	sunglasses 太陽眼鏡
cosmetics 化妝品	skin care product 保養品
umbrella 雨傘	lip balm 護唇膏
facial mask 面膜	

❭ 藥物

insect repellent 防蚊液	bug spray 防蟲液
sunscreen / sunblock 防曬乳液	medicine 藥品
prescription 處方箋	thermometer 溫度計
face mask 口罩	

附
錄

Terminal 航廈	Departure Hall 出境大廳
Arrival Hall 入境大廳	Domestic Flights 國內航班
International Flights 國際航班	Self-Service Check-In Counter 自助報到櫃檯
Check-In Counter 報到櫃臺	Carry-On Baggage Guide 隨身攜帶行李須知
Baggage Storage & Packing 行李寄存及打包	Insurance Service 保險服務
Souvenir Avenue 伴手禮大街	Lavatory 盥洗室
Convenience Store 便利商店	Tax Refund 退稅服務臺
Customs Duty Payment 海關課稅處	Immigration 證照查驗
Quarantine 檢疫	Boarding Gate 登機門
Transfer Desk 轉機櫃臺	Baggage Claim 行李提領
Customs 海關	Currency Exchange 外幣兌換
Lost & Found 遺失招領處	Smart Luggage Lockers 智慧置物櫃
Mobile Network Service 行動通訊網路服務	Airport MRT 機場捷運
MRT to High Speed Rail (HSR) 捷運轉乘高鐵	Terminal Shuttle Bus 航廈巡迴巴士
Pick Up Area 小客車接送處	Bus to City 客運巴士
Car Rental 租車	Airport Shuttle 機場接駁
Taxi Stand 計程車招呼站	Meeting Point 會面點
Ground Staff 地勤人員	

MEMO

MEMO

國家圖書館出版品預行編目資料

領隊導遊英文/劉明德, 王清煌, 張誠仁, 林溢祥編著.
-- 初版. -- 新北市 : 新文京開發出版股份有限公司,
2021.02
　　面；　公分

ISBN　978-986-430-690-9（平裝）

1.英語　2.導遊　3.讀本

805.18　　　　　　　　　　　　　　　110000404

領隊導遊英文　　　　　　　　　　（書號：HT33）

編　著　者	王清煌　張誠仁　林溢祥　劉明德
出　版　者	新文京開發出版股份有限公司
地　　　址	新北市中和區中山路二段 362 號 9 樓
電　　　話	(02) 2244-8188（代表號）
F　A　X	(02) 2244-8189
郵　　　撥	1958730-2
初　　　版	西元 2021 年 05 月 20 日

法律顧問：蕭雄淋律師
ISBN　978-986-430-690-9

New Wun Ching Developmental Publishing Co., Ltd.

New Age · New Choice · The Best Selected Educational Publications — NEW WCDP

新文京開發出版股份有限公司

NEW
WCDP

新世紀・新視野・新文京 — 精選教科書・考試用書・專業參考書